**Praise for *New York Times*
bestselling author Lynn Kurland**

"One of romance's finest writers." —*The Oakland Press*

"Both powerful and sensitive . . . A wonderfully rich and
rewarding book."
—Susan Wiggs, #1 *New York Times* bestselling author

"Kurland weaves another fabulous read with just the right
amounts of laughter, romance, and fantasy."
—*Affaire de Coeur*

"A story on an epic scale . . . Kurland has written another
time travel marvel . . . Perfect for those looking for a happily ever after." —*RT Book Reviews*

"[A] triumphant romance." —Fresh Fiction

"Woven with magic, handsome heroes, lovely heroines, oodles
of fun, and plenty of romance . . . Just plain wonderful."
—Romance Reviews Today

"Spellbinding and lovely, this is one story readers won't
want to miss." —Romance Reader at Heart

"Kurland infuses her polished writing with a deliciously
dry wit . . . Sweetly romantic and thoroughly satisfying."
—*Booklist*

"A pure delight." —Huntress Book Reviews

continued . . .

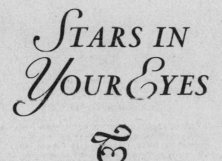

STARS IN YOUR EYES

LYNN KURLAND

JOVE BOOKS, NEW YORK

JOVE

An imprint of Penguin Random House LLC
375 Hudson Street, New York, New York 10014

STARS IN YOUR EYES

A Jove Book / published by arrangement with Kurland Book Productions, Inc.

Copyright © 2015 by Kurland Book Productions, Inc.
Penguin supports copyright. Copyright fuels creativity, encourages diverse voices,
promotes free speech, and creates a vibrant culture. Thank you for buying an authorized
edition of this book and for complying with copyright laws by not reproducing, scanning, or
distributing any part of it in any form without permission. You are supporting writers and
allowing Penguin to continue to publish books for every reader.

JOVE® is a registered trademark of Penguin Random House LLC.
The "J" design is a trademark of Penguin Random House LLC.
For more information, visit penguin.com.

ISBN: 978-0-515-15615-7

PUBLISHING HISTORY
Jove mass-market edition / December 2015

PRINTED IN THE UNITED STATES OF AMERICA

10 9 8 7 6 5 4 3 2 1

Cover art by Jim Griffin.
Cover design by George Long.

Penguin
Random
House

Prologue

Berengaria of Artane stood at the doorway of her small house and stared at the keep rising up in front of her. She had a place inside those walls, of course, a healer's house she had lived in as a child and been offered again as an old woman. She used it, on occasion, when she felt the need of secure walls wrapped around her. It was comforting and safe, that place inside the castle.

But today, she needed to breathe.

She looked to her left. The view was glorious, for her small stone house overlooked the sea. The sea air was good for her lungs and her house sturdy enough to withstand almost any gale. The lord of the keep up the way tended to insist that she come inside the keep when the storms became too fierce, but he was that sort of lad. She would know, having been acquainted with him since he'd been a wee thing. His children were just as solicitous, especially the eldest and heir. Then again, chivalry was particularly important to that one—

"Ah, by all the saints Magda, there is no hope for you!"

Berengaria smiled to herself. The sea breezes also provided her house with a steady flow of cleansing air. Given her companions' business, that seemed positively providential, though she supposed that the sighing that was going on behind her might have seen to that with enough time. Obviously there was trouble afoot. She turned and looked at the two white-haired, very seasoned women who were peering into a blackened cooking pot hanging over a robust fire.

"And I was so close this time," Magda said, looking wistfully at the tar-like substance that clung to her spoon with a tenacity better suited to an alewife clinging to a coin.

Nemain, her companion and chief haranguer, scooped up her own bit of blackened ruination and scowled at it. "*Close* is optimistic," she said briskly. "I despair of you making anything that isn't better used for daub."

Berengaria refrained from comment, for that same conversation had been going on for as long as she could remember. There was no sense in interrupting its course now. She turned back to her contemplation of the castle in front of her. A banner fluttered against one of the walls, black, with a lion rampant. It belonged to the father, but would eventually belong to the eldest son. It snapped in the wind, so fiercely that Berengaria almost stepped forward to stop it from being ripped away and sent flying places she wouldn't be able to go.

That was ridiculous, of course. The banner was flying high on the battlements, and she was well outside the walls. That and she knew she couldn't control the fate of either men or their cloth.

Well, perhaps she could, but she knew she shouldn't.

She leaned back against her doorway and pulled her cloak more closely around her. There was a change in the wind, something that felt long overdue. She considered for whom that change might have come calling, though in truth she didn't have to think about it overlong.

Phillip of Artane had best be steeling himself for what the wind would blow his way.

He was in residence at his father's keep. She knew this because she'd seen him not a pair of days earlier. He never returned from his attempts to find marital bliss in the north without stopping by her hearth for something strengthening. He was a good lad, that one: sober, well aware of his duties to his family, possessing endless amounts of patience. He was going to need a great deal of that last bit given the path he'd put his foot to.

He had been betrothed to a lass from over the border for several years. Berengaria had wondered at the match, though she had acknowledged the practicality of it. The girl brought a rich holding and the promise of a bit of peace between warring neighbors. She was a Scot, which was troubling, but what could be done? Phillip was driven by duty. If peace needed to be made, he would do what was needful to assure it.

"My thumb bone is gone!"

"I only used a pinch, Nemain."

"A pinch was all I had left!"

"The potion called for it, so what else was I to do? I'm intending to make something special for Lord Phillip to use on his bride."

"'Twill take something far stronger than anything *you* might put in a pot," Nemain said with a heavy sigh. "I'll need to be manning the spoon, obviously."

"Perhaps so," Magda said hesitantly. "But what about your thumb bone?"

"I'll need to be off to look for another one. My goodly work is never done, or so it seems. Berengaria, you'll come, of course."

Berengaria looked up at the banner fluttering black against the gray walls. She didn't like to meddle, for in the end she couldn't control the fate of either men or their cloth. But perhaps she could offer something tasty along with a bit of advice should anyone come to her cooking fire looking for either. She glanced over her shoulder.

"Aye, of course I'll come. In a day or two."

"I'll go pack," Nemain said briskly. "Never too early to have your gear gathered."

Berengaria had already gathered what she needed and was ready to leave when the time was right. But before she did, she had business to see to, a conversation or two to have, and patience to exercise as she watched events unfold. She glanced one more time at the keep, then turned to watch the sea and its endless waves.

Aye, she would wait. She could do nothing else.

Chapter 1

PRESENT DAY
ENGLAND

The next time she traveled halfway across the world, she was going to pack all her belongings in a bag with a functional zipper.

Imogen Honoria Maxwell looked at what her too-full suitcase had just belched out in untidy piles around her and wished she had the energy to be embarrassed. As it was, all she could do was imagine how blissful it might feel to lie down on those piles and nap.

She looked up what seemed an endless number of stairs at King's Cross station, then wondered if she would draw undue attention to herself if she simply sat down in the midst of the unmentionables and cried. She didn't cry as a general rule, preferring to sort of slide past Fate's notice whenever possible with a cheerful smile and a stiff upper lip, but she was in unusual and dire circumstances. She'd just finished a hellish trip she'd been sure would last the better part of eternity, she was in a foreign country where they drove on the wrong side of the road, and she had one shot at being brilliant at a job that could potentially bring her one step closer to her dream career. It was best not to add any more drama to what she already had going.

At least there didn't seem to be a crowd of Londoners scooping up her stuff and running off with it. That was the last thing she needed, to be in the wilds of England with no clean underwear.

"Here, miss, let me help you."

Imogen looked blearily at the people pushing past her and realized that someone had actually stopped to help her. She would have blushed at the sight of a very masculine hand gathering up her underclothes and stuffing them back into her suitcase, but she was too jet-lagged to do anything but stand there and yawn. She made a halfhearted effort to feel bad about not helping—no, that was too much trouble, too. She would have made a mental note to remind herself to get more sleep next time before a big trip, but she didn't have a pen and her mind was a blank. Maybe she would remember it later.

The man straightened and picked up her suitcase, broken zipper and all. "Is the rest of your gear manageable, think you?"

She would have laughed a little at the turn of phrase, but before she could, she got a good look at her rescuer.

All right, so she wasn't one to go for blonds. That guy there was definitely gorgeous enough to leave her wondering if she'd made that decision precipitously. He smiled, and the sight of his dimple left her smiling as well.

"Well," she began.

"I'll fetch your other case along as well, shall I?"

"Um—"

He didn't seem to require more than that, which was good because she didn't have any more than that to offer. He moved her second suitcase away from where she'd been standing guard over it, then fumbled very briefly with the extended handle before pushing it back inside its hiding place and simply hefting it as he had its misbehaving companion. He started up the stairs, then paused and looked over his shoulder.

"Can you manage your wee rucksack?"

"Rucksack?" she echoed.

He smiled and Imogen reconsidered again her hesitation about men with fair hair. Maybe it was the personality that mattered, not hair color, but she really didn't have a chance to give that too much thought. She was too busy trying to haul herself and her wee rucksack up the stairs after a guy who should have had the decency to look as if he were lugging two heavy suitcases up those same endless stairs.

Maybe he was a hallucination. She paused on the landing to catch her breath and examine that idea. After all, what were the odds that a very handsome stranger would simply up and help her in the middle of a big city? She couldn't even begin to face that math. All she knew for sure was that she wasn't currently wrestling two suitcases all by herself and that was the sort of thing that didn't happen outside hallucinations. It was probably best to just play along until she snapped back to reality.

She gathered her strength and started off after a guy who seemed to know where he was going, which she couldn't argue with. At least he didn't seem to be having nefarious designs on her underwear.

"Headed north, are you?" he asked pleasantly, dropping back to walk beside her.

She looked up into gray eyes—so that was their color— that perhaps should have seemed at odds with such blond hair but didn't. "Ah . . ."

"Beautiful country up north," he said, "and look you, here's your train right there. Have your ticket, aye?"

She was fairly sure she did, but that would have necessitated looking in her rucksack—er, her purse—for it. She supposed the best she could hope for was a seat where she could rummage through her stuff and hope it was still there. She could hardly believe they'd come so far through the station without her having noticed it, but maybe delusions were just like that.

"Imogen!"

She looked around blearily for the originator of that shout and finally saw a petite, dark-haired woman waving at her, obviously trying to get her attention. Imogen sighed in relief, realizing then just how nervous she'd been about her UK guide managing to find her. She waved back, then remembered her rescuer. She looked up at him.

"Thank you . . ." She waited for him to supply a name, but he only smiled.

"Of course," he said with a little bow. "Chivalry is *always* convenient."

Chivalry. What an interesting way to put it. She stared after the man thoughtfully, watching him walk away, then melt into the crowd.

"Who was that?"

Imogen struggled for one last view of him. "No idea. I've never seen him before in my life."

"Next time, Imogen, get a name and number."

Imogen looked at Tilly Jones, the woman who had promised to be her lifeline for the next four months, and sighed. "I would have, but he just spent five minutes rifling through my underwear. I was too off-balance to do anything but hope he wasn't making value judgments."

"Rifling through your knickers?" Tilly asked, looking as if she very much wanted to laugh. "Not that."

"Well, I suppose there was less of that and more just stuffing them back into my suitcase, but honestly I was just too sleepy to really identify which it was. Getting his name and number was beyond me." She yawned. "I think I need a nap."

"And to think you could have been napping on that shoulder if you'd worked a little bit harder just now."

"That kind of luxury would have been wasted on me, I'm afraid." She rubbed her eyes, wondering how it was possible that so much grit could have found its way into them. "I think I left my ability to recognize a good-looking guy somewhere back on my endless trip here."

It wasn't the only thing of the male persuasion she'd left behind, but she supposed that was something she didn't really need to discuss at the moment. The truth was, her love life wasn't complicated; it was a disaster. If her life had been her suitcase, the contents wouldn't have been strewn hopelessly all over King's Cross, they would have been piled in a gutter where the only thing to do would have been to stand on the curb and admire the wreckage.

No, better not to even begin to think about it.

"I think I'd make the effort for someone who looked like that," Tilly said.

"Oh, please just don't make that effort now," Imogen said. "I have no idea where I'm going. I don't even think I could find the train, much less figure out when to get off it."

"The train's right here, Imogen," Tilly said, sounding faintly alarmed. "And we're going to Edinburgh. Don't you have the itinerary I sent you?"

"Of course I do," Imogen lied. She'd meant to download it to her phone on her way, but she'd been too busy trying to keep up with all the plane changes to think about anything past London. She'd been planning on enjoying a nice cappuccino in a café with Wi-Fi before looking for the right train, but then her suitcase had exploded and she'd been distracted by a blond demigod, and . . . She took a deep breath and smiled at Tilly. "I'm just grateful you found me before I wandered off somewhere I shouldn't have. You know, until I'm more awake and can be captain of my own ship again, as it were."

"Of course," Tilly said with a smile. "You did it for me last year. Turnabout's fair play."

Imogen wasn't going to argue with her, especially now that she was at her mercy, but the fact was Tilly was very over-qualified for her current job as Imogen's assistant. Tilly had a pair of degrees from prestigious film schools while she herself had two degrees in subjects she was too tired to name at the moment. She had leaped at the chance a year earlier to be an assistant to Tilly, who had been one of the minor assistants to the set designer of a major period film. That the roles were now reversed was a gift. It also could have been that the son of the executive producer was trying to bribe her into dating him, but maybe that was something she could think about later, after she'd had a good night's sleep and could face it.

All she knew with certainty was that Tilly couldn't have been thrilled about the reversal of roles, but she was an expert at placating cranky people and Tilly was, from what she could tell, a pragmatist. They would manage. Besides, she might find herself in the middle of nowhere without anyone to rescue her. Tilly might be her only link to civilization, so it was a good idea to keep her as happy as possible.

"Long journey so far?" Tilly asked politely.

"Endless," Imogen said, with feeling. "I think I've seen half a dozen airports."

"Your sister the travel agent was having one over on you?"

"Yes, and she'll pay, believe me," Imogen said grimly, try-ing to forget the recent memory of landing on grass thanks to what had been billed as a *luxury flight with scenic bonuses galore*. The only scenic bonus she'd been interested in had been getting off that puddle jumper and onto something with more than four seats. Pristine Maxwell had started and sold an alarming number of businesses in her short corporate career, but her current interest was travel. Imogen wasn't sure she hadn't decided on that just so she could send her siblings on horrible trips.

"What did you do to her this time?"

"Who knows?" Imogen asked carelessly. "And if I knew, which I'm not saying I do, I don't want to think about it. I'd rather think about my revenge for the fifty-three-hour trip I've just enjoyed. I'm planning on repaying her by posting on all possible social media platforms unflattering pictures of her wearing braces. Then I'll unfriend her. She'll be crushed, I'm sure."

"And you'll be out of the country where she can't kill you."

Imogen smiled. "See? Things are looking up already."

Tilly laughed. "Absolutely. Now, what can I get you to enjoy with your revenge?"

"I need coffee," Imogen said. "And chocolate. Preferably together, but at this point, I'd take either in any form I can get them, thank you."

"I'll see what I can come up with on the train."

Imogen paused and looked at her seriously. "This trading places thing is very strange. If I weren't so tired, I'd feel worse about it, I promise."

"Life changes," Tilly said, shrugging.

Imogen wasn't sure how to even begin to respond to that, so she put it off for later. Tilly was right, of course, but that didn't make it any less uncomfortable. But what could she do? She hadn't considered for a nanosecond turning down her current job opportunity. If Tilly was committed to being a part of the moviemaking process, Imogen was past obsessed.

She had wanted to live in the world of filmmaking for as long as she could remember. She'd tried to distract herself with university and grad school degrees that had gotten her parents' notice mostly off her, but her true calling had been singing a Siren's song to her the entire time. When the chance to be a grunt on a real, live movie set had come along thanks to a roommate breaking her leg—such a shame and fortunately something she'd had nothing to do with—she had ditched her PhD program without a backward glance and jumped without hesitation onto the dream train. Her parents had been appalled and her siblings speechless. She'd been thrilled.

That job had turned into other jobs as grunts on other shoots, opportunities to cement a reputation as a dependable, creative sort of gal to have around. All part of her master plan to eventually nudge some good old boy out of the director's chair and plant her own backside there.

She couldn't blow her current gig, no matter how jet-lagged she might have been.

"Let's get ourselves seats, then I'll find us something to drink."

Imogen nodded, then let Tilly take one of her suitcases, leaving her with the one that hadn't vomited its contents all over unsuspecting Londoners. She followed Tilly onto the train, trusting it was the right one.

She paused at one point only because there was no possible way to get past the foot that was extended into the aisle. The stiletto adorning that foot was something even her functioning suitcase would have suffered from an encounter with. She frowned. That hadn't come out right in her head and she half feared she'd said it aloud. She was going to post braces pictures *and* anything else she could dig up on her phone when she had a decent connection and the mental wherewithal to make use of it. Prissy would pay dearly.

"Excuse me," she said, trying not to slur her words.

The owner of that foot pulled it back into her own space. "Not to worry."

Well, she wasn't worrying, though maybe she should have been. She wasn't entirely sure she wasn't looking—blearily, of course—at some species of nobility. She didn't suppose royalty traveled in regular train cars, but what did she know? If ever there had been a passenger out of place on a regular old train, it was that woman there who simply dripped class and elegance. Imogen suppressed the urge to try to resurrect her own appearance. She couldn't remember when she'd last brushed her teeth or combed her hair. Probably better not to think about it.

She managed to shuffle past the stunning Audrey Hepburn lookalike, shove her suitcase where Tilly told her to, then collapse into a seat. She was thrilled to leave the rest of the details to someone far more awake than she.

She leaned her head back against the seat and considered whether or not she deserved to be as wasted as she felt. She had, at her father's insistence, trusted her sister to get her a good deal on her flight. That had been her first and last mistake. She had taken off from Denver and landed at Heathrow. That she'd visited a dozen different airports and enjoyed little hops in planes better suited to dusting crops than carrying passengers and their luggage was perhaps beside the point. Her older sister had known exactly what this job meant to her and how badly she needed not to look like an idiot at any time during its execution. It was payback, pure and simple.

She had hoped one of her other three siblings would have been the target of Prissy's ire over that recent summer barbeque incident where they hadn't intended to leave Prissy behind with the folks and half a dozen children under the age of four. Without a car. Or a wallet.

It hadn't even been her own idea. She might have been the one to enjoy it the most, but who could blame her? She and Prissy were a mere eleven months apart and she had her own list of insults to be irritated over. Quietly, of course, but she was beginning to think that maybe she was past the quiet stage.

The truth was, she had been so surprised to be included on the instigating side of familial shenanigans instead of being the target of them, she'd gone along without pausing to think what Prissy might do to her after the fact. She should have known travel would be involved somehow.

Well, that was behind her for the moment, behind her with half a dozen other things she didn't want to think about. Her immediate future was mapped out very clearly, her job description was unambiguous, and she had a once-in-a-lifetime chance to make a name for herself. If that weren't enough, she had four months in Scotland and England to look forward to. What wasn't to love about that?

She yawned and decided she would give staying awake one more try. The sooner she got past the time change, the better. She would have made small talk, but Tilly wasn't back yet.

Perhaps that was for the best. There was something about being on a train pulling out of an historic station in London that called for something more than idle conversation.

She stared out the window at the endless number of flats and houses and tiny backyards and let herself wonder about who lived there, what they did to feed their families, if they wished they lived somewhere else. It was something she did wherever she traveled, mostly because imagining herself in someone else's life had been a great escape from her own. It was the reason she'd first fallen in love with movies. And once she'd realized that movies were a great escape to simply watch, she'd wondered what it would be like to actually make one. She'd saved her allowance, cleverly hiding it behind cleaning supplies her siblings wouldn't have lowered themselves to use even if death had loomed, then bought herself the cheapest video camera she'd been able to afford.

Her world had changed the moment she'd first pushed the *on* button.

The rest of the story was probably no more interesting than the flights of fancy any other teenager with a crazy family took, but it had been *her* life and she'd discovered for herself not just a way to make it bearable, but make it wonderful. With any luck, all the exercising of her imagination she had done over the years would come in handy when she was a famous filmmaker.

In time, the sway of the train and the charm of the British countryside was so comforting and peaceful, she found herself closing her eyes to better enjoy the first. And once her eyes were closed, it seemed a shame to waste all that rocking without using it as a reason to nap. She leaned her head against the wall and felt reality slipping away.

She woke an indeterminate amount of time later. She realized her face was adhered to the glass of the window only because it hurt to pull it away. She managed to unstick her eyes long enough to look at Tilly and mumble a few coherent words.

"Where are we?"

"An hour or so out of Edinburgh," Tilly said. "Close enough for another nap if you like."

"I'll never sleep tonight if I don't pull it together now,"

Imogen said, rubbing her eyes. She wished she had something else pithy to say, but she was too tired for pithy.

"Your coffee's cold," Tilly said. "Sorry about that."

Imogen didn't care. She was simply grateful for something that resembled food, no matter its temperature. She drank, waited for some of her brain fog to recede, then propped her chin on her fist and tried to concentrate on the scenery. She watched the coast, wondering if there might be a spot of sand there for a good stroll. There looked to be a decent amount of sand. There also looked to be an enormous castle out there. She suspected she was either still dreaming or she had wandered into a dream. She was fairly sure she was seeing things that couldn't possibly exist in real life.

She rubbed her eyes and looked again out the window. The castle was still there, though it was going to be out of frame soon. She looked at Tilly.

"What is that?" she asked, pointing with what she realized was a shaking hand.

Tilly frowned. "What is what?"

She waved her hand toward what she was seeing and only succeeded in rapping her knuckles smartly against the window. She sucked on them. "That out there."

"Farmland."

"No, over there," Imogen said. "By the ocean."

"Oh," Tilly said, peering thoughtfully into the distance. "That's Artane." She looked at Imogen and smiled. "It's a castle, Imogen. You might want to get used to them if you're going to be crawling over them for the next couple of months, looking for the good stuff."

"But it's enormous." Imogen had another look. "At least it looks enormous from here."

"It looks enormous from there as well," Tilly said dryly. "We could rent a car and go, if you like."

"It's probably just a shell, isn't it?" Imogen asked, hardly daring to hope for anything different.

"Oh, definitely not," Tilly said. "It's been owned by the same family for the past eight hundred years. From what I've seen, they've managed to hold on to quite a bit of history over the years, which is a polite way of saying I don't think they've thrown anything out."

"You've been inside?" Imogen asked in surprise.

"Years ago. I guess you can take that to mean they do let the public in now and then. Stephen de Piaget is the current lord, I'm fairly sure. I had a class from him at Cambridge. I'm not sure I can parlay that into a personal tour, but I could try if you like. Who knows what you might find inside the walls?"

"I've been sent on a mission for the unusual and quirky," Imogen said, "not just the regular old medieval stuff." She tried to ignore the regret she felt over that. To her mind, medieval was medieval and it was all amazing. To actually be in the same room with things that had been used by others centuries in the past . . . well, how could she not get excited about that? Quirky was great, but so was an original sword forged hundreds of years ago. When she had her own projects and wasn't beholden to the whims of a director who wasn't her, she would look for authentic over odd.

Unfortunately, she wasn't in charge, and her director was, she had to admit, one of the worst in the business. He was in charge of not just a medieval period piece, but a medieval period piece with music. Dancing knights, singing swords— she had no idea what else he wanted, but she knew it had to be quirky. And given that she'd been given a big, fat promotion on this project, she was going to deliver quirky if it killed her. Which it just might.

"I should have just googled *quirky medieval stuff*," she said, wondering how much of what had been going on in her head she'd said aloud. Tilly didn't looked shocked, so perhaps she'd managed to hold on to her complaints more successfully than she'd thought.

"At least you're not having to look for locations."

"Oh, I'm supposed to keep my eyes open for that as well," Imogen assured her. "And provide lots of unusual stuff that looks medieval but doesn't cost medieval."

"Well, that's what happens when Max Davis is writing the checks," Tilly said with a sigh. "He likes to be really hands-on about it all. At least he's safely tucked away in Manhattan until after New Year's."

"He is, but Marcus is coming over in a month to see how things are going."

Tilly swore. Imogen understood. Marcus Davis was a royal

pain in the backside, the son of a producer with unlimited funds, a man who thought he should be in front of any camera at all times. The guy lived his life worried about presenting his best side for whomever might be looking his way. With a camera in their hands, of course. Or a phone. Or just an admiring audience comprised of souls who had no sense of pitch. The thought of that was almost enough to make her wonder if her sister could put her on another puddle jumper and send her off into Podunkville where she could lose herself in a field of something tall and not have to deal with giving Marcus Davis the tour of future locations.

Never mind facing the moment where she would have to tell him that no, she really didn't want to date him. It wasn't going to go well.

She yawned. When that didn't help, she yawned again. Artane had gotten itself too far behind them for her to gape at it any longer, so she supposed it would be all right to close her eyes. And once she did, she realized she was going to miss the rest of the scenery. She would have to catch it with Tilly in the car when they traveled south.

She realized there was something that was bothering her, and it wasn't just the raw spot she now had on her forehead thanks to too much contact with the window. It took her far longer to figure it out than it should have, but when she did, it was almost enough to wake her up.

How had that blond guy known which train she was supposed to be taking?

She tried desperately to attach enough importance to that to keep herself awake, but it was hopeless. Sleep beckoned. She was fairly sure it had a comfy, overstuffed chair and a plaid blanket right there, calling to her in a way she couldn't resist. She fought the urge valiantly for a few more minutes, then decided that if there was one thing she knew, it was when to throw in the towel. A little nap, then on to being brilliant at finding all sorts of odd and quirky medieval items.

She could hardly wait to see what she might find.

Chapter 2

Y*ou're* going to have to choose one of them, you know."
Phillip of Artane, heir to the vast estates of his father, swordsman of decent mettle, and avoider of all things matrimonial, looked at his uncle and couldn't muster up the energy to scowl at him, much less curse him.

"Grandmère's ghost will haunt you otherwise," Nicholas of Wyckham added, nodding sagely. "She would no doubt be doing it herself, were she here to do so."

"Your uncle knows of what he speaks," Phillip's father said from where he sat on Nicholas's far side. "Having had the lady Joanna present him with his own large and unruly selection of eligible misses over the years."

"Over the years?" Nicholas said with a snort. "You mean, *over a shortened, painful period of time*, one I would prefer never to think on again. Though I find watching the same happening to my oldest nephew from the safety of my own matrimonial perch to be more entertaining than I thought it would be."

Robin de Piaget, lord of Artane and chief instigator of the evening's sport, only smirked. "I will admit to being rather relieved myself that I'm not the one looking down the length of the sword, if you know what I mean." He shivered delicately. "What an unpleasant business."

"Don't remind your lad of it," Nicholas said with a laugh, "lest he think falling on his sword is preferable to the entertainments you've provided for the evening."

"Now, why would he be that stupid?" Robin said, blinking innocently. "A hall full of finely dressed lassies all come to present themselves to him in hopes of winning his hand? I'd say Phillip should just put his feet up on the table, sip his wine, and let them show off their wares. I did the like in my youth."

"Robin," Nicholas said with a sigh, "you know you did nothing of the sort. I'm not sure I would proceed much further down this path if I were you."

Phillip agreed. His father's exploits during his youth were the stuff of legends, though the retelling of those tales by enthusiastic siblings generally left the lord of Artane squirming uncomfortably.

But that had been his father. Now he was the one in their sights, and he didn't find that a comfortable place to be in the least. Besides, none of it was necessary given that he was already betrothed. If one looked at it in a certain light. Perhaps from a distance where one couldn't see the disaster he had created for himself.

He leaned back in his chair and sighed. Much as he would have liked to have credited someone else for his current muddle—his father or one of his uncles came immediately to mind—he knew he had only himself to blame. He'd seen to the contract himself, sure that it would benefit him politically as time carried on. It hadn't occurred to him, arrogant fool that he was, that the gel in question might not feel the same way or be quite so impressed with the name of de Piaget as he might have hoped for. He'd also not considered overmuch that her sire might be willing to sign a contract but not be willing to enforce it. Robert of Haemesburgh had thrown him out of the keep the first time he'd returned to present himself to his future bride, then Heather had subjected him to several more humiliations over the past several years. Lord Robert had comported himself in an increasingly erratic manner until he'd simply stopped appearing at the gates, leaving Phillip to try to shout pleasantries at the younger brother, who had answered them with arrows and curses. The situation had become so untenable that his sire had begun to invite women with suitable pedigrees to come have a meal or two at Artane. Not formally, but in an offhanded, *are you certain* sort of way that was so unlike Robin of Artane, Phillip had hardly recognized his father.

Tonight was something else entirely, though.

The lassies in front of him were, he knew, very serious indeed about landing a husband. He'd been watching their mamas at court for years, doing his damndest to hide behind some uncle or other in an effort to remain undetected and undecided upon as a fitting marital prospect. That he should currently be seeing the most difficult-to-please of those mothers in his father's hall should have frightened the hell straight from him

Which it did, actually, for it bespoke quite clearly exactly how dire his father considered his straits to be.

He looked around for a place to bolt but there didn't seem to be a useful exit in sight. Robin cleared his throat pointedly, but damn him if he wasn't grinning as he did so, Phillip glared at his father, glared at a pair of equally irreverent uncles, then excused himself from the table. He put on a pleasant if not slightly impatient expression he hoped would suggest to any watching him that he had pressing business somewhere else. He greeted those he knew he had to and slid past the rest where possible.

He managed to get himself out of the front door without being assaulted, then paused on the top step and looked up at the sky to judge the usefulness of the moon. A day or two away from full, but very bright nonetheless. At least he wouldn't break a leg if he engaged in his usual exercise in the lists.

He nodded to his father's guardsmen and his, then loped down the stairs and started toward the lists. The men followed him across the courtyard, which felt quite suddenly very strange. He had had guardsmen of one sort or another from his earliest memory, either men hired to protect him or men retained by some uncle or another who had been given especial charge of him. But to have them there at the moment felt as if he were somehow the one out of place. What would it be like to walk into a crowded hall and blend into the background where no one would know who he was, no one would have expectations of him, no mother would look at him and start calculating just how many silk gowns her daughter might possess as his wife?

He almost stopped to try to determine where those useless thoughts had come from, but decided it would make him look daft. He was very grateful to reach the lists, where he might outrun such useless speculations. He was who he was, his responsibilities were what they were, and he was damned grateful he had a hall to lay siege to in order to increase his own bloody holdings until he could push his sire off his lordly chair and take over his duties as master of Artane.

It was, he decided an indeterminate number of laps about the lists later, rather remarkable how far irritation over one's current situation could carry a body when it came to physical distance crossed. It was also remarkable how soon a body simply attempting to outrun his life could acquire an audience. He spared the effort to glare at a group of cousins and such loitering uselessly near a bench. The lazy whelps seemed inclined only to watch and not join him, which perhaps shouldn't have surprised him. It was possible that his expression wasn't particularly welcoming.

His expression apparently wasn't forbidding enough to intimidate his younger brother, who had joined him at some point. That he couldn't remember exactly when was slightly alarming, but in his defense, he'd had much to think on. Kendrick was in very fine condition for someone who spent so much time flirting with any available—or unavailable, as it happened—female and so little time in the lists. Phillip finally had to stop and lean over to catch his breath. He ignored the fact that Kendrick wasn't doing the same thing. He closed his eyes and concentrated on drawing chilly air into his burning chest.

"Father does this," Kendrick remarked idly.

"Where do you think I learned it, dolt?"

"Just making an observation."

"What would you rather I do?" Phillip said, heaving himself upright. "Train with you?"

Kendrick only regarded him, silently and far too astutely. "Not now, I don't think. I'm not interested in your sword in my gut."

"Then why do you care how I think?"

"How, or what?"

"Either," Phillip said impatiently. "Both. Take your pick."

Kendrick frowned thoughtfully. "You're suffering from ill humors, obviously."

"I'm suffering from a lack of strong drink."

"I wouldn't suggest taking it up now. You're too old for such assaults on your delicate form."

Phillip dragged his sleeve across his forehead and scowled at the man a pair of years his junior. "Did you come out here simply to tell me not to be a drunkard or did you have a loftier purpose?"

"I came out to avoid the stampede that will ensue inside once the ladies realize you didn't simply step outside briefly to take a breath of healthful air. Thought I'd save you the insults to your clothing such a frenzy would cause." He smiled. "Altruistic, as always."

"Self-serving, rather," Phillip said, "as always." He looked over Kendrick's shoulder, realizing with a start that he'd been doing the like for the whole of his life, always checking to make certain his brother was safe—

"Phillip?"

Phillip looked at his brother and felt a little as if he weren't exactly seeing him. Kendrick looked at him in surprise and clapped a hand on his shoulder.

"Perhaps you should imbibe," he said seriously. "Or at least sit. You don't look well."

"I just need to walk off all that running away from my future I've been doing."

Kendrick smiled faintly. "You don't run away from anything."

"I thought I might try it and see how it feels."

"Idiot," Kendrick said, taking Phillip's arm and pulling it over his own shoulders. "Lean on me, old woman, and let's discuss this frailty you're experiencing."

Phillip refused to notice that his brother was indeed supporting him more than he should have been. The saints be praised they were still of a similar height. If Kendrick had surpassed him in that, he might have truly had to lie down to recover.

"Well?" Kendrick prompted after a turn about the lists.

Phillip continued to walk with his brother for another lengthy stretch before he stopped and pulled away. "I need to go secure my keep."

Kendrick clasped his hands behind his back. "And your bride?"

"Her as well."

"No one's been inside for quite some time, you know," Kendrick remarked carefully.

"And what do you mean by that?" Phillip asked.

"I wonder what lies within the walls these days," Kendrick said with a shrug, "if anything."

"Think you everyone inside is dead?" Phillip asked in surprise.

"The saints forbid," Kendrick said. "It was just an observation." He stared up at the moon for a moment or two, then looked at Phillip. "I wonder what sort of mischief the lady Heather is combining these days."

"She's limiting herself to making a fool out of me," Phillip said grimly. "She might be a woman, but 'tis past time I put my foot down with her."

"That will end well, I'm sure."

Phillip would have smiled, but he was too damned tired to. "She'll come around."

"Well, you are pretty," Kendrick offered, "and clean. What else could a woman possibly want in a lad?"

"You would think that would be enough, wouldn't you?"

Kendrick laughed. "I would, but I'm also a hopeless optimist who believes fully in the power of love."

What Kendrick believed in, Phillip was quite sure, was acquiring as much property as possible, then spending the rest of his days with his feet up, watching the gold spill into his coffers. The lad would have an easy, comfortable life, of that Phillip was certain.

"Tell me again how things have gone before," Kendrick suggested. "I vow I've forgotten."

Phillip sighed, because he couldn't bring himself to simply plant his fist in his brother's mouth as he should have done. He also didn't have the strength to recount any of the truly embarrassing details. Besides, Kendrick had been with him on every visit thus far. There was no need to enlighten him.

"Very well, let us walk for a bit longer and I'll see if I can reconstruct your dealings to this point," Kendrick said thoughtfully, as if he were truly having to dredge the pond deeply to bring up any memories. "Or her dealings with you, which might be more interesting. I believe you've only seen her twice and you've never seen her dressed as a woman."

"She's inventive," Phillip said, stomping alongside his brother. "She obviously wants to encounter life on her own terms."

"As a man," Kendrick repeated, "which I suppose I can understand given the alternative, which would be enduring marriage to you. You've also never seen her not covered in filth."

Phillip refrained from comment.

"You've also only exchanged the most banal of pleasantries with her and that was several years ago."

"We've exchanged things more recently than several years ago."

"The contents of her cesspit flung at you over her walls don't qualify as things."

"She hasn't _only_ flung the contents of her cesspit at me," Phillip protested.

"Nay, she's flung sheep entrails, rotten beer mash, _and_ cesspit delights over her walls at you."

That was unfortunately all too true. The amount of speech he'd had with the gel paled in comparison with the interactions he'd had with the various and sundry nasty things she'd found inside her keep. "'Tis possible," he conceded, "that I might need to convince her of a thing or two before we continue on to the chapel."

Kendrick laughed. "What, to behave like a proper noblewoman? She's a damned shrew, brother. What are you thinking?"

"I'm thinking that I'm a score and eight and still standing behind my sire's table, flattering his sorry self, and keeping a close eye on the amount of wine in his cup lest it need to be filled again. I'm thinking that I'm seeing several more years of the same stretching out in front of me before he relinquishes his place at that table so I might sit there myself."

"And you think that keep at Haemesburgh will provide you a clearer path to that place?"

Phillip turned to face his brother. "How many times has the border moved during the course of your lifetime?"

Kendrick frowned. "What has that to do with anything?"

"Just count. Use your fingers if you need to."

Kendrick considered, then shrugged. "I suppose I hadn't thought to keep track."

"Well, I have and I don't fancy having that border dip so far south that Artane becomes part of Scotland."

"Uncle Jake is farther north than we are," Kendrick said slowly, "and he doesn't seem to be worried."

"He's uncommonly complacent about things he shouldn't be," Phillip said. "I don't sleep as easily as he and I'll not have my lands overrun in a score of years when I can stop the creeping now."

"All for your empire, eh?"

"Aye," Phillip said simply. "For my children and their children for as long as they manage to hold on to this damned pile of stones."

Kendrick looked at Phillip thoughtfully. "Care for aid in the venture?"

Phillip considered it very briefly, then shook his head. "I appreciate that more than you'll know, but you've your own life to see to."

"Ah, but think on what joy it would bring me to see you happily settled."

"I imagine I won't get that far."

"I would enjoy that as well," Kendrick said solemnly.

Phillip fought a smile. "Which is why I'll deny you that sport, thank you just the same. Nay, I'll manage well enough on my own."

"But you'll send word if you need me," Kendrick said carefully. "The reason doesn't have to be as dire as you might think it need be."

"Thank you." Phillip would have added a list of reasons why he was grateful for Kendrick's offer, but he imagined he didn't need to. His brother knew his mind almost as well as he knew it himself.

"Then off you go, lad, and lay the foundations for future

glory and riches. I'll come rescue you if you need it. For now, I'm going back inside to sample the goods—er, the food left at the table."

Phillip snorted, then watched his brother trot purposefully back to the hall. He almost pitied the offerings still left inside. Kendrick was, he could admit in a fairly detached way, difficult to resist when he'd set his mind to something. The gels inside hardly stood a chance of escape, not that any of them would have wished to, no doubt.

He collected his sword from his squire, then rounded up his cousins who had come to watch the sport. He didn't want to admit Kendrick might have things aright, but he couldn't deny that he'd had little success at either securing his bride or his hall. One might suspect she wanted nothing to do with him, though he couldn't imagine why not.

Apart from the fact, of course, that he'd given her no choice in the matter.

Damnation, what else could the woman want? He was Robin of Artane's son and possessed not only wealth but sword skill. He wasn't as ugly as his brothers and was a damned sight less difficult to look at than many of his cousins. There had been many women over the years who had seemed not opposed to either his gold or his person. That one irascible Scottish wench should spurn his advances, and that in spite of her father's wishes for her . . . well, it was almost past what he could believe. He would rectify the situation as soon as possible.

He paused on the way back to the hall. It wasn't unthinkable, he supposed, when venturing forth on a quest of that seriousness, to seek out some sort of aid prior to embarking on said quest. Spiritual aid. Supernatural aid, even. Fortunately for him, he knew just where to go, having seen that sort of thing be sought before by others.

If worse came to worst, he would simply visit his father's cellars for something strengthening, something of an earthier nature.

Perhaps a visit to the first ale keg he encountered might be best seen to sooner rather than later before he thought on his present business overlong. He had a bride to acquire, a keep to conquer, and death to avoid in the bargain if at all possible.

It would keep him sober, no doubt of that.

Chapter 3

Imogen stood on the sidewalk of the Royal Mile and was grateful for the awning above her head. She was less grateful for the rather expensive raincoat she'd bought before she left that had obviously spent time with someone familiar with puffy fabric paint.

She took a moment to attempt to identify the culprit. She had been recently staying with her sister the shrink, crashing on her couch because she had only needed a place for a couple of weeks. Given that those two weeks had turned into a couple of months, maybe it was Barbara behind the assault as retaliation for that extended stay. Then again, it could have been Pristine, she who had sent Imogen on that endless series of visits to remote and terrifying airports. Prissy was well versed in both retaliation and all things crafty and had had both the motive and time to get creative with Imogen's outerwear.

Maybe in the end it didn't matter because regardless of who was responsible, she was still the one walking around with *I'm available* and her cell phone number written in florescent pink on the back of her coat. It had only taken three overly friendly gentlemen patting her on her phone number and asking her, *do*

I really need to ring you when you're right there, ducks, for her to realize what had happened.

She'd retreated to a bathroom to try to scrape off the offending advertisement, but succeeded only in putting a hole in the fabric. The upside was, she had felt absolutely guilt-free about buying a cashmere scarf to wrap around her derriere. The downside was that when the rain had started up with enthusiasm, she hadn't been able to bring herself to wrap her scarf around anything but her neck. In the end she was, as she had discovered just a moment ago, still available.

She could only wish all her reasoning faculties were likewise at the ready because then she would have had the good sense to stay at her hotel, watch some television, and survive the day. That's what Tilly had planned for her. She'd considered, then realized that for a girl who'd never seen anything older than a few Old West ghost towns, the chance to see a real, live Scottish castle was too good to put off. Even the simple pleasure of walking on slick cobblestones in a medieval city was worth the effort of venturing out into the rain.

She pulled a damp piece of paper out of her coat pocket and squinted at it. It was a map Tilly had left for her with the location of her hotel marked in red. Tilly had also included a handful of red Xs marking the locations of interesting shops. It was tempting to check them off the list one by one, but maybe that could wait for another day or two. As long as she could eventually find her way back to her room, she thought she could allow herself to simply take the day and see where her feet led her.

She folded the paper back up and stuffed it back in her pocket, tucked her cashmere plaid scarf more securely into the neck of her raincoat, then left the security of the shop's awning. She'd been starting to get cranky looks from the proprietor anyway. She supposed she couldn't blame him given that her scarf had come from across the street.

Maybe the castle was the best place to start. At least she could hike up there and get all the work of walking uphill out of her way before she decided on anything else.

She tried not to think about that being a metaphor for her life, but it was hard to avoid. Being the youngest of five children born to overachieving parents had been alternately exhausting and terrifying. She had to admit that one of the things that had been appealing about crossing that big blue ocean had been the chance to get some distance from her family. It was hard to be the ordinary brown bunny in a gaggle of white, impressive bunnies with big job descriptions and even larger bank accounts. Her dream career definitely didn't fit in with what her parents wished for her. It was a wonder they let her in the house for Thanksgiving, really.

After all, what use were degrees in history and eighteenth-century French poetry? Worse still, how could she sleep at night knowing she had abandoned her PhD before she'd really nailed down exactly what Further Studies in Humanities might mean? That hadn't been her fault—well, it had been her fault. The truth was, she didn't want to be a mogul, she didn't want to be a professional, and she didn't want to toss and turn at night until she'd obtained tenure at a university up to her parents' snuff.

She'd wanted to make movies. While her siblings had been pretending to argue cases before the Supreme Court and make gazillions taking over companies and selling off the pieces, she'd been scribbling out screenplays and working on story-boards. Everything she'd done, all the classes she'd taken, even her degrees had been either to potentially further her yet-to-be-obtained career or to throw her parents off the scent of what she really wanted to do with her life.

And then, that miracle of getting to take over her room-mate's job as an assistant's assistant to the set designer on an obscure indie film shoot.

She hadn't dared tell anyone in her family about either the leaving of school or the taking of a job with pay so low she could have made twice as much working fast food. The family had discovered her deviation from the plan eventually, but by then, she'd been on her second shoot and she had gained enough courage to at least ditch her apartment and sublet something else under a fake name so they couldn't find her.

Her family was complicated.

That had been four years ago. Since then, she'd been repeat-edly told it was time to break free of the dastardly clutches of bringing stories to life on film and get on with her father's plans that she at least put her foot to the tenure path. As appealing as that might have sounded to someone else, she couldn't bring herself to even consider it. The film bug had bitten her and the infection had taken up permanent residence.

She owned nothing that couldn't fit into her two suitcases and wee rucksack that were now parked safely back in her hotel room. One day she would acquire stuff. For the moment, all she wanted was to be able to pack for travel to potentially exotic shooting locales in less than half an hour.

She made it almost all the way to the castle before she finally had to give up trying to go uphill any longer. That and she was getting really tired of the comments her coat was eliciting. She backed herself up against a soggy wall and looked for the closest shop. It was past time she solved her coat problem. If it meant shelling out money for something new, so be it.

She looked around her, but apparently she had left the numerous stores selling all kinds of tartan products behind. All that seemed to be left were places that were pricier and less touristy. She pushed away from the wall and started back down to where she thought she might be able to afford something, then felt her feet come to a stop. She frowned, then looked at the shops she was standing in front of. Lovely, but nothing that called to her.

Apparently she was looking in the wrong direction.

She knew that as surely as if someone had spoken the words to her. She turned slowly and looked across the street. *Curiosities in Plaid.*

She shivered in spite of herself, then gave herself a good shake. It was just a store. She looked both ways, realizing she was looking to the left first when she should have been looking to the right, then realizing there was no car traffic where she was so it was all moot anyway. She took a deep breath to calm the babbling in her head, then walked across the street and stopped in front of the shop. The hair on the back of her neck stood up, but maybe that was from the contact with rather lovely cashmere. It couldn't be from anything more, well, *odd*. She didn't believe in ghosts or spooky things, never mind that it was what she'd come to the UK to look for. That was film; this was reality.

Unfortunately touching the door was another experience in weird. She knew she hadn't been there before, but she felt as though she'd made that motion an endless number of times.

Maybe she was going to need that nap sooner rather than later.

She pushed the door open and walked into controlled chaos. There wasn't an inch of floor, wall, or ceiling that hadn't been used to either prop up or hang something. Curiosities, indeed.

Imogen wandered around, having assured the saleswoman that she would ask if she needed aid, until she realized she wasn't the only shopper in the store. Stranger still, she recognized the other person there, who definitely wasn't Tilly come to check on her.

It was that woman from the train. The one with the dangerous shoes.

She did a double take, but her eyes were definitely not deceiving her. The woman was intently studying a collection of vintage-looking bottles, so Imogen took the opportunity to slink off somewhere else and avoid an encounter with potential nobility.

"Coffee?"

She looked at the shop's owner holding out a cup and saucer. Imogen accepted it without thinking and had downed an enormous mouthful before she thought to ask if it contained anything poisonous. After all, she was in a strange store in a foreign country where she was having all sorts of bizarre experiences. Who knew what sorts of things she might find in the bottom of her cup? Given the events of the last ten minutes, she wouldn't have been surprised by anything.

She felt instantly better, which she appreciated. She took the spoon and stirred, only then realizing that stirring wasn't exactly possible with whatever was occupying the bottom half of the cup. She pulled the spoon out and looked at the sludge clinging to it with the tenacity of sentient goo that didn't want to go back into the drink, as it were.

"Here, let me take that for you."

She looked at the woman standing next to her. That wasn't a witch, was it? She looked a little unconventional, but that could have been simply her own faulty judgment being affected by really lousy coffee and jet lag. Then again, maybe it was something else. She was tempted to go back outside the shop and make sure she hadn't misread the sign. She was beginning to think she'd walked into a store full of hexes and potions.

"Thank you," she managed, handing the little woman her cup.

"My Great-Gran taught me how to make that," the proprietress said with a smile. "She wasn't a very good maker of brews, but that's a tale better left for a different time."

Imogen agreed that was wise. Her quota of weird was already starting to feel pretty full. She thanked the woman for the drink, then wandered around the shop because that seemed like a reasonable thing to do. The goods on the shelves were unusual, to be sure, but nothing that leaped out at her. She browsed for a bit longer, then thanked the proprietress for the cup of coffee and escaped before the woman offered her anything else undrinkable—

Only to run bodily into someone standing right outside the door.

It was the woman from the train.

Imogen held out her hands to steady her. "I'm so sorry," she managed.

The woman waved aside her words. "Nothing to apologize for, of course," she said. "Looking for something inside?"

"Actually, I'm looking for medieval—" Imogen stopped herself once she realized there was really no good reason to be telling a complete stranger what she was up to. "Why do you ask?"

The woman drew her coat up around her chin. "I have a keep full of treasures."

"A keep?"

"A castle," the woman said impatiently, then took a deep breath. "A castle."

"Wow," Imogen said. "That must be amazing."

"Well, 'tis less amazing than it might otherwise be when the tax lads come visiting, but those are the perils of living in any age, I suppose."

Imogen smiled before she thought better of it. "I imagine that's the case."

"I'm Heather," the woman said, extending her hand. "Mistress of Haemesburgh."

Mistress? Imogen had to believe that at some point she would get used to the way people were talking to her, but she didn't hold out any hope for it any time soon.

"I couldn't help but overhear your conversation with your friend yesterday," Heather continued. "I don't usually put myself forward this way, but if you're decorating a movie set, I have a few things you might be interested in."

Imogen could hardly believe her ears. She could also almost not believe that the woman in front of her was for real. She was elegant, true, and stunning, but what if she was just pretending to be nobility? Imogen was fairly confident in her ability to spot a nut from across the room, but she was in a foreign country and she was seriously sleep deprived. Her radar might be malfunctioning and who knew where that might lead?

"I have a car and a driver, if that eases you any," the woman continued, as if she'd read Imogen's mind. "I'm the chief of a tiny little clan, you see, and one must keep up appearances. 'Tis more of a courtesy title than anything else, but I wear it with pride."

"Ah—"

"Or, if you prefer, you can take the train." Heather, the reputed mistress of Haemesburgh, pulled out a business card and held it out. "We have a website, of course, with directions. I have a very fine chef and a small tea shop, if you want to come for an early luncheon. Aye, take the train and come in the morning. I'll have a tour planned out for you when you arrive."

Imogen looked at the card in her hand. It looked legit and Heather of Haemesburgh certainly looked the part of a castle owner. Maybe Fate had decided she'd suffered through enough crappy jobs and deserved a metaphysical raise of sorts. She might be holding the ticket to that in her hand. It would be ridiculous to pass up an opportunity for a private tour of a castle full of history.

"Thank you," she said, putting her shoulders back and attempting what she hoped was a professional, confident smile. "This is very kind."

The woman nodded slightly. "Happy to be of use, of course. Tomorrow, then?"

Imogen managed to nod, then watched the woman walk away. Heather was wearing very sensible boots, though they were obviously very expensive. Maybe she managed to avoid filling the tax man's pockets more successfully than she let on.

Perhaps it was time to call it a morning. Imogen checked her map and headed back to her hotel, deciding she would stop for some sort of takeout on the way. She had things to digest, things that would be better considered after a serious nap.

There was something about that woman that bothered her, though she didn't know where to even begin to identify it. Maybe it was that of all the people she could have tripped over on the train north, she'd tripped over a real, live specimen of nobility. More amazing still that the woman had a castle, stuff inside that castle, and a willingness to have both be examined. It was almost too good to be true, but Imogen had made a commitment while landing on a grassy farmer's field, sure she would die in the process, that she was going to become an optimist. It was time to put up or shut up.

She pulled her coat more closely around herself and continued on her way.

Chapter 4

Phillip stood on the steps of his ancestral home and stared off into the distance, his hand on his sword, his eyes scanning the countryside visible over the walls for bad weather and enemies. He saw neither, which he considered to be an auspicious start to the day. A pity his proximity to the front door made it all but impossible to ignore the less-than-enthusiastic conversings going on there.

"Think he'll make it inside Haemesburgh's gates this time?"

"Not bloody likely."

Phillip attempted with renewed vigor to ignore the discussion, if discussion it could be called. His cousins had gathered to see him off, no doubt eager to vomit out all the stupidity lodged between their ears before they reached anything useful they might want to offer. The tenderhearted ladies of the keep had been content to send him forth with encouraging words given next to the warmth of the fire inside. Unfortunately, outside he was left with his sire, an uncle, and a gaggle of cousins who would have been wiser to have kept their bloody mouths shut.

"I'm surprised she hasn't covered him in arrows instead of, well, you know," a young voice piped up.

"Mayhap that is her plan this time," offered a second lad who had scarce learned to feed himself. "But no doubt Phillip has already considered that."

Phillip glanced over his shoulder at Samuel and Theopholis de Piaget, both with barely ten years to their credit, and gave them a brief, approving nod. They might have been young, but they were wily. He always slept better when he knew they had been contained somewhere. He had the feeling his father—and theirs—did not sleep at all with them near.

The rest of the family who stood gathered around him were perhaps less unnerving, but far more irritating.

Or perhaps that was unfair. There were a few who were irritating, a handful of others he wouldn't have wanted to meet behind the stables on a dark night, and one or two whom he would have trusted to guard his back no matter the cost.

And perhaps that was more unfair still. He knew, hard-hearted lout that he was, that any member of his family would have stepped between him and danger without hesitation. They would have mocked him endlessly afterward about having spared him the mussing of his clothing, but at least he could say they would have been there for him.

"Are you sure you want to send him off alone?"

Phillip turned to look at his uncle, Nicholas, who was watching him whilst barely suppressing a grin.

"Lest the venture prove dangerous, of course," Nicholas added. "Might be good to send along a lad or two for company."

"He's off to subdue a woman," Robin said with a snort. "If the lad can't manage that on his own, well . . ." He threw up his hands. "It's a *woman*, Nick, not an army."

"And women are weak-kneed, delicate creatures," Nicholas agreed.

Robin looked over his shoulder quickly, no doubt to make certain his own delicate bride wasn't standing behind him, then made a few blustering noises. "Of course. He should be able to manage this with a few stern words."

"Can he dredge up any of those, do you think," Nicholas asked, stroking his chin thoughtfully, "or has he spent too much time at the lute?"

"I wouldn't recognize the effects of such foolishness, having spent my time more usefully in the lists," Robin said archly. "You, however, did spend an unholy amount of your youth plucking at strings and causing the rest of us to run very far away, generally to the lists, in order to escape your efforts."

"So you benefit yet again from my altruism."

"And your lack of ability to keep your instrument in tune."

Phillip was just sure they would come to blows soon, but unfortunately they seemed to remember just in time that they had joined forces to vex *him*. He listened to them speculate on his chances of success—and his own labors with out-of-tune strings—for only a moment or two before he had to descend to the courtyard where he might have a hope of not listening to them any longer.

Unfortunately, he didn't go far enough. The good-natured jesting at his expense continued, though with more enthusiasm than he might have otherwise expected. That, he supposed, should have unnerved him. It was something the dotards in his family did when they were truly worried about the outcome of any given skirmish. He didn't imagine his father would send an army along after him to aid him, but with Robin of Artane, one just never knew.

He turned to something he could control, which was who he intended to take along with him. He looked at the lads who had gathered around him, just to make certain he wasn't going to wake up on the morrow and find that one of them had tucked himself into a saddlebag.

His brother Kendrick was there, of course, though he wasn't dressed for travel. That was a good thing, for Phillip would have sent him back inside the hall otherwise. His youngest brother, Jason, was standing next to Kendrick, looking sober with his new spurs clinking at his heels. He was also, very wisely, merely dressed for a chilly morning. But that was where the good sense of his relations seemed to end.

There were two of his aunt Amanda's children standing there, Rose and her younger brother Jackson. They had been at Artane for reasons he honestly hadn't taken the trouble to discover. They tended to come and go so often that he never questioned why they did anything. At the moment 'twas possible they were simply intending to turn for their father's keep, but there was something about the way they were watching him that made him uneasy. He frowned at them, had very bland looks in return, then decided he would put his foot down with them later.

He looked at the handful of others standing there. The group was finished—and he meant that in very deed—by a selection of his uncle Nicholas's children including Connor and the twin evils of Theopholis and Samuel de Piaget.

Phillip considered them all, looked at their gear, then pointed at his eldest female cousin, Rose.

"Absolutely not," he said firmly.

"I don't know what you're talking about," she said.

"You're dressed in hose and you've cut your hair again," Phillip said sternly. "I know what that means."

"You might need a woman's touch—" She turned on her brother Jackson before he could speak. "Don't add anything."

Jackson held up his hands. "I wouldn't dare, though Phillip has it aright. This could be a dodgy business. Not women's work, surely."

"Aye," Rose said, "avoiding whatever disgusting missiles she intends to fling at him will be a heavy labor indeed. Nay, what you louts need is a woman with you to keep you from making complete arses of yourselves. I will come along to make certain Lady Heather understands the magnitude of my cousin's desirability as a husband."

Phillip had to concede there was something to that, but the thought of being responsible for a woman of Rose's beauty and deviousness . . . well, that was enough to give him pause. He looked at her and shook his head slightly.

"I can't," he said quietly. "I don't dare."

"I could stand behind you," she said quietly. "With a bow."

"Your father would kill me."

"He wouldn't know."

Jackson snorted. "Our father *always* knows."

Phillip looked at Rose and gave thought to what her sire would do did she run afoul of trouble. Jackson of Ravensthorpe wouldn't kill him, he would murder him slowly, painfully, and, if he could have managed it, repeatedly. Then again, it wasn't as if they were headed into battle. It was simply a peaceful journey to a castle that was his by agreement, peopled with men and one particular woman who had sworn loyalty to him. What could possibly go wrong?

He glanced at his sire, who was only regarding him
steadily, as if he were stepping back from the fray. Phillip
looked at Rose, sighed, then ignored her own sigh of relief
coupled with triumph. 'Twas little wonder her father could
deny her so few things. Her brother would come along to
guard her, if nothing else. Besides, she had her own collection
of lads following her, lads who tended to remain in the shadows and only appear at night when they could inspire the most
terror, like bogles from the forest. She would be safe enough.

That left him with his uncle Nicholas's children to sort.
The eldest, James, had other things to be seeing to, Phillip
knew, which complicated and simplified things at the same
time. James would have been extremely useful in a fight, but
he was too pretty by half and might have been distracting for
the lady of Haemesburgh.

That left him with Connor and, as he had noted with no
small bit of apprehension, Connor's younger brothers, Theo
and Sam. The three were dressed for a long journey and their
father was looking very relaxed. Obviously that trio of trouble-
makers was intending to come along. Phillip didn't bother to
try to discourage them. Connor would have ignored him and
the little ones . . . well, they would have come along anyway
and popped up unexpectedly and left him squeaking like a gel.
He knew that because they'd done it before, repeatedly, damn
to hell for it.

"I can see the party is shaping up nicely," Kendrick said,
stepping forward and putting his hand on Phillip's shoulder,
"but I feel there are things that still need my attention."

Phillip shrugged off his brother's hand and suppressed the
urge to acquaint him with the feeling of a fist in his mouth. "I—"

"Am too tenderhearted to lay out what must be done," Kendrick finished, "we know, Phillip. So allow me to inform your
company about the near-impossible task before them." He
cleared his throat importantly. "A siege is in the offing."

Phillip would have interrupted, but there was no use. Once
Kendrick had marched into the fray, there was no stopping
him. The cousins were accustomed to treating everything
spewing forth from his mouth as holy edict, so all Phillip
could do was stand to the side and watch, wishing he had such
a spellbinding gift. The perils of missiles flung over the wall

were described, the importance of presenting Phillip in the best light possible touched upon briefly, and the promise of spoils to be enjoyed dangled before the lads until they were fair stamping with impatience to be off and doing. Above all, Kendrick stressed the importance of comporting themselves in a manner that would invite lays to be sung over their deeds. Phillip listened until he simply couldn't bear it anymore.

"Chivalry is always convenient," he began, "and—"

"And it can ofttimes be fatal," Kendrick interrupted. "Which in this case is quite possible."

Robin and Nicholas seemed to find that terribly amusing, which set the bolder of the cousins to feeling comfortable enough to add their own opinions to the discussion. Phillip swept them all with a look, which they ignored. He found himself flanked suddenly by his uncle Nicholas's identical spawn.

"Why don't you kill them?" they asked, in unison.

Phillip shivered in spite of himself. Even though he knew they couldn't possibly be demons, there were times . . .

"They're not taking this adventure very seriously," Sam added.

"I don't think they're taking *anything* very seriously," Theo corrected. "Listen to them."

Phillip could hardly avoid that. He glared at his father and uncle, then looked at his young cousins.

"I love my mother and my auntie Jen," he said grimly, "and I hesitate to rob them of their husbands, else I would do them in. But one thing I will do is absolutely not take them with me."

"But you'll take those two," Nicholas said, gesturing to his sons.

"Aye, *please*," Robin added. "Before they drive me mad."

Phillip wondered what his sire thought the lads would do for him save a similar service, but he had a soft spot for his wee cousins and imagined giving them a bit of an adventure couldn't be a bad thing.

He made note of three other souls heading toward the stables—two lads and the heiress of Ravensthorpe pretending to be a lad—and sighed. A handful of not only his own men but a few of his father's fiercer lads were already waiting by the gates, so he supposed he would manage to return sons and daughter to their respective parents safely enough. He paused, then looked at his father leaning negligently against his front door.

"Thank you for the loan of your men."

"My pleasure," Robin said with a grave smile. "Best of luck with your quest. Send word if you need an audience. I don't imagine you'll need any aid."

Phillip shifted, more annoyed by his unease than he should have been. "She's a woman," he said with a shrug. "How much trouble can she possibly be?"

He turned and strode off before he had to listen to any chuckles sounding from the vicinity of two seasoned men who had certainly had their own share of adventures with their wives and daughters. Phillip had no intention of beginning his own brush with marital bliss on anything but the right foot, which meant he would instruct his bride on how she should comport herself and things would proceed exactly as he intended.

Chuckle was such a terrible word. It didn't quite describe the gasping guffaws that Robin and his brother were currently engaging in. Obviously they'd had too much ale for breakfast. Phillip promised himself a good chat with the pair about their consumption of the like upon his triumphant return.

For the moment, he supposed it was best to trot out the front gates before he killed them both.

He had one brief stop to make before carrying on for the day and it was made without fanfare and without company. He knew the garrison knights were uncomfortable with the halt, but he left them on the road and struck out on his own. He had a task ahead of him that would require, he feared, all the aid he could muster.

He knocked on the door of a small stone house. It opened and less smoke than usual poured out, leaving him only with watering eyes, not doubled over with coughing. He left his squire and his two youngest cousins standing outside—realizing only then that they had followed him without asking leave—and entered when bid.

He made himself as comfortable as possible on a stool by the fire and couldn't help but remember all the times he'd done the same thing as a lad, sitting by Berengaria of Artane's hearth wherever it had found itself. She'd spent her share of time in other keeps, true, but he suspected the little stone house in the woods was where she had felt most at home. His grandfather, Rhys, had built it for her as a place of refuge when the castle walls had become too confining, and he'd made certain no villager dared entertain any idea that she was anything but a purveyor of herbs.

That had been made substantially more difficult, as it happened, by the two bickering companions who had sought refuge with Berengaria as time had worn on. It was perhaps fortunate that the three of them lived so close to the shadow of Artane's walls and wore the favor of the castle's master as a shield. Phillip didn't like to think about what might have become of them otherwise. Peasants were a suspicious lot, which he supposed he could understand. There were things in the world that were truly inexplicable.

He didn't like to think on why he knew that, truth be told.

Nemain sat down across from him with a heavy sigh. "I don't know why I press on."

Phillip smiled. "Magda burns fewer things than she used to."

Nemain snorted heartily. "You're trying to spare her feelings, there's no doubt about it, and it does you credit, lad, but you know the truth."

Phillip conceded the point with a reluctant nod. "The char adds flavor, at least."

"Ha," Nemain said. "It adds nothing but char, but there you have it. I've grown accustomed to the taste, but I try not to taste too often, if you understand me."

"My father sent wine." He smiled. "Uncharred."

"I was hoping you'd say as much," Nemain said. "Ah, and look at those two little imps who've come inside to bring it to us."

Phillip sighed in spite of himself, but supposed if the lads were to have a proper adventure, they might as well begin it at the hearth of a trio of healers who most considered full-fledged witches. He left the twins manfully agreeing to taste several new concoctions and rose to speak with the mistress of the house. Berengaria stood with him at the door, watching Artane in the not-so-far distance, just as he did.

"It is magnificent," she said.

"Aye," he agreed.

She smiled up at him. "I believe your father sees to it so well in great part for you."

"My father sees to it mostly for himself," Phillip said dryly, "but I can't blame him. I will likely do the same." He paused, then leaned back against her doorframe. "Any tidings?"

"About your sword?" Berengaria asked. "None but what we've already heard. Rumor has it that it has rested in the hall at Haemesburgh for the past five winters, driven into the floor behind the lord's chair there so firmly that none can pull it free."

Aye, the five winters since someone—he didn't like to think on who that someone was—had removed his sword from his unconscious hand and scampered off with it. As for its resting place, he honestly wouldn't have been surprised by anything. He looked at Berengaria and smiled dryly. "That bit about the sword in the stone floor sounds like a jongleur's tale I seem to remember having heard elsewhere."

"There's a reason those tales circulate so thoroughly."

"Not very original, are they?"

"The lads from Haemesburgh?" Berengaria asked, clearly amused. "I daresay not. They don't seem to be very strong either, or perhaps that is due to something else." She paused. "Perhaps the blade is rumored to be unremovable from its resting place because 'tis enspelled."

Phillip knew his mouth had fallen open and it took a bit to retrieve his jaw. "You can't believe that."

"I believe many things, my lord, though that surely sounds like something that belongs in a bard's tale, doesn't it?"

"The only sounds I hear are the ones that haunt my dreams," he said darkly, "and those would be the sounds of the blacksmith taking that damned blade and driving it into the lord's cracked and ruined floor by means of his hammer against the hilt. I shudder to think of what will be required to liberate it."

"Your grandfather's sword," Berengaria said, unnecessarily.

"Given to me at my knighting," Phillip said, also unnecessarily. "And taken from me whilst I was napping."

"I believe the tale is a bit more involved than that."

Phillip shrugged. "It might be, but I forget the particulars."

"I believe, my lord Phillip, that you have forgotten nothing, which will serve you well in the future. You sword would serve you equally well. Indeed, I'm not sure you will see yourself on the lord's chair there without it."

Phillip suspected the same thing, but it wasn't something he allowed himself to think on very often.

"Now, how may I serve you? I'm assuming you didn't come here for my blessing on your journey."

"Unless you've a small bag of herbs useful in giving me the stomach to wed a woman I can't seem to have, aye, that is all I've come for."

Berengaria smiled. "I think, my lord, that you'll find what you need along the way."

He almost didn't dare hope for that. He nodded, then paused before he pushed away from the door. "Enspelled?"

"Is that the word I used?"

He smiled. "Utter rubbish."

"Most likely."

He laughed, because she had cured his bumps and bruises and set at least two broken bones that he could remember and she had never sent him off into the fray without a cup of something tasty. He accepted the same, indulged in enjoying a long tradition of imbibing something neither Nemain nor Magda had brewed up, then bid all three farewell. He gathered up his cousins and his men, then started off toward the north.

His sword enspelled?

He snorted and continued on his way.

Chapter 5

I mogen stood in front of the station where she'd just arrived
by way of a very nice train ride, looked at the backseat of
the taxi she was about to get into, and hesitated. It was only
her imagination that left it looking like the gaping maw of
something otherworldly.

Wasn't it?

She had been in Scotland for two days and that had obviously been two days too many. The place was simply saturated
with what she could only call magic, and she would have told
anyone willing to listen just how ridiculous that sounded in
her own head. If she could just have a few pedestrian encounters with the local flora, fauna, and noblepersons instead of
encountering all manner of odd things, she might have been
able to revise her opinion. As it was, she suspected that if she
spent too much time there, she would become just as slathered
in otherworldliness as everything and everyone around her.

She rolled her eyes at herself, took hold of her rampaging
imagination, then climbed into the back of the taxi and pulled
the door shut behind her.

"Haemesburgh," she said to the driver confidently, suppressing the urge to add, *and step on it*.

He shifted in his seat and looked at her in surprise. "Really, miss? There?"

"Yes," she said confidently, "I'd like to go to Haemesburgh. I've been invited, actually, by the owner of the castle."

The man looked at her as if she had asked him to drive her to the gates of Hell. "Och, miss—"

"It's just a castle," she pointed out. She had to stop herself from repeating that three times like some sort of charm. Obviously her brief trip inside a shop with plaid curiosities had done something to her common sense. Haemesburgh was just a castle, Lady Heather pulled on her pantyhose one leg at a time, and she would eventually stop having chills run down her spine every moment of every day she spent in a place so slathered with history that she could almost touch it.

The cabbie looked as if the money just might not be worth it to him. "As you say, miss."

Imogen shivered and gave in to the hair standing on the back of her neck. "What's wrong with the place?" she asked grimly. "Ghosts? Too many tourists? A bloody history spilling over into the current day?"

"Och, nae, miss," the cab driver said quickly. "Ghosts and unwholesome happenings limit themselves to the square keep on the border—can't bring myself to say its name, you see—not Haemesburgh. With Haemesburgh, though, weel, there're oddities enough there to suit most." He turned back to his wheel. "Oddities enough, to be sure."

Well, that was just what she wanted to hear, wasn't it? She was on the hunt for unique stuff. She could make do with odd in a pinch. And it could be worse, couldn't it? She could have been heading toward that unnamed square castle where there were unwholesome happenings to be found. She was obviously going somewhere much safer.

Besides, as she'd said before, she knew the owner of the castle. She had a card with the address written on the back in a medievalish looking script. The whole project was coming together for her, yessir. All she had to do was get in and out of a castle that might or might not have been haunted but was definitely being run by a woman who gave her the willies. It was morning, the sun was shining, and she had a cell phone. What could possibly go wrong?

The cabbie seemed perfectly happy to simply drive and leave her to her own thoughts. She stared out the window and was happy to think them.

The countryside she had traveled through on the train had been beautiful, but this was absolutely spectacular. She loved the ocean, true, but there was something about the rolling hills and tidy fields divided by charming stone fences that made her feel as if she'd just been wrapped up in a warm blanket and set down in front of a cheery fire. Maybe if that had been the view she'd been looking at every day, she might have ceased to be delighted by it, but somehow she suspected not.

The rolling hills continued only briefly before she saw not only a village up ahead, but a castle that dominated the sky-line. She gasped in spite of herself.

The cabbie only nodded knowingly without turning around to look at her.

She fished out unfamiliar money to have ready to pay the driver. He stopped the car near the front gates, put it in park, then shifted and looked at her over his shoulder.

"You're certain, miss?"

"I am," she said, trying to sound more confident than she felt. "If you have a card, perhaps I can use that to call your company after I'm finished here and get you to come pick me up."

"I could wait," the man offered. "I'd do it without pay."

"She'll be safe with me."

Imogen almost jumped out of her skin. She looked out the driver's window to find none other than the lady of Haemes-burgh standing there, regal and not to be argued with. Imogen looked at the driver.

"I'll be safe with her," she said, because saying anything else seemed out of the question. "I'll call you when I need a ride back to the station."

The man looked completely rattled, but maybe he didn't usually have encounters with castle owners. Heaven knew she could sympathize.

She paid the driver and got out of the cab, making sure she didn't leave her backpack behind. The cabbie drove off slowly, the driver looking back several times as if he just couldn't come to grips with the thought of leaving her behind. She had to admit there was a moment when she wished she could chase him down and have him take her back to the station, but she wasn't a coward and she had a job to do. After all, what could possibly happen to her? It was a public place. The dungeons were probably boarded up. Lady Heather would have been in jail if she'd been in the habit of kidnapping tourists.

"I'll give you the tour I promised you, if you like."

"That would be great," Imogen said, trying not to fall at the woman's feet and kiss her ring, if she even owned such a thing. She followed her guide on heeled boots she had definitely not put in her suitcase. In fact, none of the sensible shoes she'd packed had apparently made the journey with her, which was less a disaster than an inconvenience. An evil sibling at work again, no doubt.

"You may call me Heather, if you like," the woman said casually. "No need to genuflect."

Imogen smiled. "That's good to know. I'm not sure of the protocol, actually."

"You're American?"

"Yes."

"And you're here in the UK looking for items for a movie," Heather stated.

"Medieval things," Imogen said. She was actually supposed to be looking for English medieval things, but Tilly had suggested they start in Scotland. She had been happy not to argue. Besides, who knew what sorts of antiques were tucked away north of the border? "It's why I was so surprised by your offer, actually." She smiled. "It felt a little like Fate."

"Ah, well, I'm very familiar with Fate," Heather said. "Scotland's saturated with it, you know." She nodded toward the front gates. "Shall we?"

She nodded, then looked up at the gatehouse as she walked through it, feeling rather relieved she wasn't going to be dealing with trying to escape that anytime soon. She followed Heather across the courtyard, wishing she dared stop her and ask how many of the inner structures were original, though she suspected the only things that had lasted over the centuries had been made of stone. The tea shop had to be new, and seeing it made her realize she couldn't remember the last time she'd eaten. Maybe she could talk the lady of the house into breakfast sooner rather than later.

She paused at the steps to the great hall and looked back over the courtyard. It was ridiculous, of course, but she couldn't help but feel like she had just walked over her own grave. She'd rarely been back to the places where she'd grown up—her father had never wanted to stay in places where he'd left scorched business earth—but even when she had been, she'd never had the feeling as strongly as she did at the moment.

"We'll start upstairs, if you like."

Imogen pulled herself back to the present and blinked at her hostess. "Sure," she managed. "Whatever you like."

And that was, she was certain, the last coherent thing she said for at least an hour. In fact, she wasn't sure she managed to speak at all, though she thought she might have made a few babbling noises.

The keep was spectacular. She wasn't sure how anyone had managed to preserve so many fragile things without an army of preservationists with stern words at the ready, but it was obvious someone had done it. She stood in what had been the lady of the keep's private solar, turned around a time or two, then looked at Heather in surprise.

"I'm speechless."

Heather was leaning back against a priceless table as if it were something that had come from the local thrift store. She was dressed impeccably, with an effortless chicness that Imogen knew not even her most stylish and annoying sister ever could have matched. How she had managed to keep the place up and running was something Imogen didn't want to begin to speculate on. Then again, maybe it wasn't so unthinkable. If anything, the woman in front of her had a toughness about her that not even expensive clothing could mask.

Heather shrugged. "'Tis a castle, to be sure."

Obviously familiarity bred contempt, which in this case Imogen could hardly believe. "Were you born here?"

Heather looked at her coolly. "Aye."

Well, so much for chitchat. Even with all her skills at reading people so she could avoid confrontations she didn't want, she had to admit she had no idea what the deal was with that one. She'd been pleasant enough up to that point.

Or perhaps she hadn't been. Imogen honestly had no idea. She'd been too busy gaping at an amazing medieval castle and wondering how it was she was going to beg Lady Heather to let her recommend it as a set location to really pay attention to her hostess's mood. Did she hate her current car? Was it tax season? Did she have a business deal currently going south?

Having exhausted her checklist of things she would have considered with her father, Imogen gave up trying to psycho-analyze the owner of the keep and simply smiled pleasantly.

"Thank you for the tour."

"I have one more thing you might like to see."

"Oh," Imogen said, faintly surprised, "of course. I'd love to." Anything to move things along.

She followed Heather from the room and out into the hall-way, marveling again at the period details. Even the lights looked authentic. Getting the rights to use the castle she was in would have been a career-altering coup. She took several steadying breaths to keep herself from blurting out an annoy-ingly long list of reasons why Heather should let her produc-tion use Hacmesburgh as a set, then simply followed Heather down the hallway. Maybe she would give it a try when they landed in the great hall again. Only, when she put her foot on that stone floor, she forgot everything she'd been thinking to that point. She was stunned she hadn't noticed it before.

It being that enormous broadsword with the aqua stone in the crossbar of the hilt jammed into the floor behind that gigantic table at the lordly end of the great hall.

Heather was saying something, but she couldn't hear her. She didn't want to be rude, but the truth was, she couldn't have cared less what Heather was babbling about. It seemed sud-denly that she had no choice but to get herself across the room toward that sword. She went with the impulse and hoped she wouldn't land in the dungeon as a result.

The sword wasn't even in glass. It was just stuck in the floor there behind the table, unprotected and un-tourist-proofed. She stood next to it for several minutes in silence, then looked at Heather.

"Aren't you afraid someone will steal this?"

Heather shrugged. "How? It's lodged in the stone of the floor behind the lord's chair. Makes it difficult to clean around, but there you have it."

Imogen could see that Heather was right. That sword was

forced so thoroughly into a crack between two paving stones, she didn't imagine anything was going to get it out. She curled her fingers into the palms of her hands to keep herself from reaching out and touching the blade.

"Why am I thinking Arthurian legends here?" She looked at the lady of the keep. "Perhaps the original inhabitants did this as flattery. You know, imitation and all that."

"I daresay the original inhabitants of this keep couldn't be bothered to look up from their trenchers long enough to consider such a thing, but you can believe what you want." Heather leaned back against the wall and gestured at the sword. "You can touch it, if you like."

"How old is it?"

"I believe it was driven into that stone circa 1250. Perhaps sooner, depending on whom you ask. Some sort of disagreement between a suitor and his unfortunate choice of bride, or so the tale goes."

Imogen smiled in spite of herself. "Are you telling me that a girl swiped some knight's sword and shoved it in this stone herself? I didn't realize women in the Middle Ages were so empowered."

"They weren't," Heather said, her smile gone, her eyes shuttered. "But you and I are in this blessed age where things are very different from what went on the in the past." She nodded toward the sword. "Go ahead and see if you can pull it free."

Imogen reached out, then hesitated. There was something about that sword . . . maybe it was just the thought of touching something so old. It didn't look fragile, but medieval weapons were not her specialty. She looked at Heather.

"Do you let the tourists do this?"

"The great hall is generally roped off and the high table is never open to visitors. You're the first to be allowed here in quite some time, as it happens."

"Lucky me."

"Lucky you," she agreed. "Perhaps you would like to take advantage of your privileged status and put your hand on that bloody blade."

Imogen supposed it was a good thing she'd become somewhat accustomed to Heather's mercurial changes of mood or she might have been a little unnerved by the woman's tone. If the lady of the keep wanted her to finger priceless treasures, she wasn't about to say no. She took a deep breath, then faced off with an almost-eight-hundred-year-old sword.

It was amazingly well preserved, if Heather was right about its age. The stone was an amazing shade of blue, obviously cut centuries earlier yet stunning nonetheless. She couldn't begin to imagine the cost or even where such a stone had been found. She knew next to nothing about the forging of medieval weapons—something she thought she might want to remedy fairly soon—but the dangerous part looked very lethal. The hilt was inscribed with something—

"Just touch it, would you?" Heather demanded impatiently.

Imogen refrained from pulling the sword free and beaning her hostess with it only because she'd spent a lifetime scooting past irascible family members. She took a deep breath, reached out, and touched the hilt of the sword.

And the world exploded.

She stumbled backward into the lord's table, very hard, then felt herself go rolling right over it. She landed, winded, on the stone floor. It was so shocking, all she could do was lie there and try to catch her breath. She closed her eyes because she thought she might recover faster from the way her head was spinning as if it wanted to spin right off her shoulders. She couldn't believe that Heather had punched her, but she wasn't sure she was equal to determining that. All she knew was that she felt as if she'd just been blindsided by a freight train.

Just what in the hell had happened to her?

She put her hand over her eyes and concentrated on carefully breathing in and out. That was made substantially more difficult by the horrendous smell she was suddenly enjoying. Had the sewer just exploded around her? She supposed that was possible. At the moment, she supposed anything was possible. She gathered her courage, took her hand away, took a deep breath—an unfortunate decision, really—then opened her eyes.

Bigfoot was leaning over her.

She shrieked. He shrieked. He might have made some sort of sign to ward off something unwholesome, or he might have just been scratching his very unkempt beard. She wasn't sure and she really didn't want to know.

"Her eyes!" he bellowed. "The color of her eyes! A demon has taken over our lady!"

Or words to that effect. Imogen wasn't quite sure what that garbled bellowing was, but that's what it sounded like, so she was going to go with it. She patted herself, though she wasn't sure how that was going to potentially improve the condition of her eyes that were apparently doing something her new friend didn't like.

"Blue," he wailed. "Then brown!"

Well, hers were actually sort of brownish-green, but who was she to quibble? Heather really needed to make sure the crazies in her castle were a little more careful about their observations, something Imogen decided she would share with her hostess as soon as possible. Perhaps over that brunch she'd been promised but hadn't had yet. It had been an interesting morning, but she thought she might have had enough of weird for the day. She scrambled unsteadily to her feet, rubbed her eyes, and looked for Heather.

She was gone.

Unfortunately, Heather had been replaced by several other less elegant things. Imogen turned in a circle, gaping at what she was faced with. So she'd thought to herself just how authentic and well-preserved Haemesburgh had seemed. She hadn't intended that to be any sort of signal to Fate that she wanted to see the place with a layer of medieval grime on it. Apparently while she'd been passed out, someone had come in and thrown the contents of the local sewer all over the floor. With some hay. She wasn't sure she wanted to see what else she was standing on. She was also surrounded by a dozen extras from an ultra-realistic medieval movie set, extras who were really giving it their all. Obviously there was a casting director hiding somewhere in the wings, taking notes.

It had to be a joke. She attempted a weak laugh.

"All right," she said, "who's the kidder?"

The unkempt guys didn't look like they were in on the joke. They were simply gaping at her in astonishment. Obviously there were things going on that she hadn't been told about, and honestly she just wasn't enjoying being the target of someone's lousy sense of humor. She frowned and looked around for the lady of the keep. It was time someone called that cranky noblewoman on her lack of courtly manners. The sooner that happened probably the better. She put her hands on her hips and turned around in a circle, taking in the whole of the great hall until she was again facing the lord's table. Heather was gone.

And so, unfortunately, was the sword.

She could hardly believe her eyes. She rubbed them for good measure, then staggered a pair of steps closer to get a better look. Nope, there was nothing there but that heavy table, a selection of decently built chairs in desperate need of a good cleaning, and a hay-strewn floor. No sword. No lady of the keep in expensive trousers and a cashmere sweater. Nothing but raw and, it had to be said, not-very-nice-smelling surroundings.

Where was that sword that Heather had thought important enough to protect by roping off the entire great hall? And why were the people around her babbling in a language she could hardly understand? Why were they dressed in period costumes that took authentic to an entirely new level? Why were there ratty tapestries on the walls?

She had obviously stumbled onto a set. It was the only thing that made sense. Whether she had been clunked over the head and went temporarily into oblivion as a sick joke while the whole thing had been set up was something she would have to determine later. The one thing she could say with certainty was whoever had thought the whole thing up would pay.

The head extra was obviously looking to further his career with his absolute unwillingness to break character. He made a production of scratching his head—no doubt to reconcile himself to the color of her eyes—before he put on a scowl and stepped forward toward her. The rest of them would have given the Buckingham Palace guards a run for their money with their inscrutable expressions.

Damned method actors.

She decided abruptly that maybe a bit of fresh air would be the best thing for everyone, especially herself. A joke was a joke, but she was done. She would find the craft table, go for the most caffeinated, sugar-filled thing she could find, then get down to business. The culprit would then be identified, she would get her brother the lawyer on the phone, and whoever was responsible would seriously regret having messed with her. She glared at the extras, then turned and walked quickly from the great hall.

All right, she might have run as if all the hordes of Hell were after her, but what difference did that make? Whoever was playing that rather tasteless joke on her was going to make fun of her anyway. She might as well give them something to truly laugh about.

She managed to get the front doors wrenched open and herself down the stairs without landing on her face. She skidded to a halt in what wasn't a nicely tended bed of gravel but a marshy soup of mud and other things she didn't want to identify. It wasn't raining currently, but it had obviously rained enough to turn the courtyard into mud.

That was bad enough, she supposed, but worse was the utter lack of movie paraphernalia. No cameras, no crew, no assistants, and definitely no craft table with things she could use to stave off a losing battle with low blood sugar.

Obviously, there were things going on she couldn't quite wrap her mind around. It was entirely possible that she was hallucinating for real this time. She considered, then shook her head. Impossible. The joke was just extending to the courtyard. If she could just get beyond the castle walls, everything would return to normal. She was probably just overcome by the sheer magnificence and potential paranormal possibilities of the castle behind her. Hadn't that cab driver warned her that strange things went on in Haemesburgh? She would have to give him a call and let him know he'd been right.

She took her good sense in hand and bolted toward the front gates.

The drawbridge—and damn that thing if it didn't look like it was actually working for a change—seemed to be thinking about creaking to life. She ran under the gate and started down it. It was a good thing she'd spent so much time in the gym running on a treadmill pushed up to a fifteen percent incline, because that's about where that long slice of wood was heading. The difference between then and now was she'd never before had the opportunity to fling herself off the end of a treadmill and cling to its edge as it continued its slow but inexorable climb skyward.

She only realized as she made a grab for the end and swung herself over it into thin air that she had perhaps made a serious tactical error.

Chapter 6

Phillip stood fifty paces away from his future home and wondered if he had imbibed one too many charred brews at Mistress Berengaria's fire, because he could have sworn there was something hanging from the end of his drawbridge.

"Well, that's new," Connor of Wyckham drawled. "Flinging herself over the gates instead of handfuls of refuse."

He shot his cousin Connor a glare. "Thank you."

"Just making an observation."

"I imagine you can make them silently from now on."

Connor only smiled slightly and turned back to his study of the madness going on in front of him. Phillip didn't bother to look at any of the others in his company. His men—and his father's, for that matter—were too discreet to say anything, much less poke at him about his current straits. His cousins were unfortunately not so circumspect. They were lined up next to him, obviously torn between gaping at the spectacle of the shrieking woman dangling from the end of the drawbridge and the no doubt quite fascinating view of his own visage. He sighed, then strode forward. The silly wench was going to kill herself, which he supposed he shouldn't have been overly devastated by, but she was the means to an end and she was a woman.

Chivalry was *always* convenient.

He had to repeat that several times before he could even mutter the words without gritting his teeth. He had a great respect for women. He simply found them to be a bit trying when they felt compelled to fling cesspit contents at him. No doubt he and Heather could come to an understanding about that on their way to the altar.

He stopped far enough away from the end of the draw-bridge that he could exchange a pointed look with someone leaning over the parapet, looking officious.

The man made a rude gesture.

Phillip made a ruder one.

Tittering ensued. He wasn't sure from which direction but he was sure it wouldn't go unrewarded the first chance he had. He walked back and politely invited Rose to hand him her longbow—a very new and useful weapon. She rolled her eyes at him, fixed an arrow to the string, and sent it through the lead guardsmen's hood.

All laughter ceased, along with the raising of the draw-bridge. A bolt from a crossbow sped past his ear and went to ground several feet behind him. Fortunately that seemed to be the extent of the attempt to defend the keep, which was per-haps understandable considering the lady of the keep was still dangling from the end of the drawbridge. At least her lads had sense enough not to sacrifice her for a pile of stones.

He was momentarily tempted to hand his sword off to his squire, pull himself up onto the end of the bridge, and then trot down it to go disable any future attempts at defenses. Unfor-tunately, that would do naught but leave him defenseless him-self once the keep was his. Kendrick would have had the drawbridge disabled without delay, and perhaps even restored shortly thereafter, but that was Kendrick. Phillip had been content to watch his brother taking things apart, but the truth was he hadn't wanted to get his own hands dirty. He supposed that might say more about him than he cared it to.

He drew his hand over his eyes. He never should have sam-pled Berengaria's herbs. Perhaps she had confused *manly vic-tory* with *maudlin self-pity*. He didn't give a damn about his motives or his character. He just wanted the bloody draw-bridge down and the key to the castle in his greedy hands.

However that had to be accomplished was simply all part of the bargain. He supposed removing the lady of the keep still clinging to the end of that drawbridge might be wise, before someone released the winch and crushed her against the rocky bed where the wood would rest when down.

He walked over and put his hand on her foot. He hardly had any idea what to call those pointed bits of business she was wearing there, but they looked as if they might be shoes and they might double as weapons. He jiggled her foot.

"Drop," he commanded.

She squeaked out something he didn't understand. It sounded something like a curse, though, which he supposed he could appreciate. He took a deep breath and reminded himself he was a gentleman.

"I'll catch you," he assured her as politely as possible. "Drop."

More incoherent babbling ensued.

Phillip suppressed the urge to indulge in a very unchivalrous sigh and continued to tug on his errant betrothed. "Let go, woman, before they drop the bridge and kill you."

She stopped babbling. "Kill me?"

It was no wonder those barbarous Scots had such trouble holding on to their border. 'Twas obvious they couldn't even manage to hold on to the Mother Tongue in any sort of fashion, though he supposed he shouldn't have expected anything else. He was likely fortunate she could string two words together without kicking him in the head to remind him just how much she loathed him.

Perhaps he should have listened to his sire and chosen a well-groomed, well-gilded English bride.

He stopped himself before he ventured down that dangerous path and tugged again on Heather's foot. It was possible that he tugged with more enthusiasm than necessary, but damnation, what else was he to do? Scrape her off the spot where, likely without too much encouragement, the drawbridge would pin her between itself and its rocky resting place?

She let go of the wood with another screech of what might have been mistaken for genuine terror. He was too jaded for that and identified it for what it was: the cry of a woman who had realized that she could no longer avoid her doom.

He caught her, fully prepared to have a great whiff of someone who likely smelled as if she had just finished rolling in a duck pond. But she didn't smell of pond; she smelled of something sweet from the garden. Roses, perhaps.

That was something new.

He looked into pond-colored eyes and frowned. What untoward magic was this? Had he caught her so unawares that she'd actually bathed? He found himself almost powerless against the urge to simply stand there and sniff. And then he realized something else.

He wasn't entirely sure he was holding Heather of Haemesburgh in his arms.

He was so surprised by that thought that when she suddenly pushed out of his arms, he almost dropped her. She landed rather unhappily on one foot that buckled underneath her. She hopped about for a minute or two on her good foot, then regained her balance by pulling his squire over to stand next to her where she could use his shoulder as a place to lean.

Phillip could do nothing but stand there and stare stupidly at her. She was, he had to admit, extremely lovely. And she smelled very good. He was tempted to surreptitiously pinch himself lest he have slipped into a dream without having realized it, but he didn't think he was asleep.

Heather, who he still wasn't sure was Heather, pulled a little flat box out of her pocket and waved it at him. Speaking, however, seemed to still be beyond her. He couldn't decide if she was incoherent with rage or frustration, but whichever it was had rendered her almost mad. She eventually found her tongue, which wasn't an improvement.

"I am going to send off a strongly worded text, buster, and tell your boss exactly what you're doing—"

Phillip glanced at his squire. The poor lad was watching the wench with a look of terror that might have been better reserved for a robust collection of demons from Hell, which Phillip had to admit he couldn't argue with. Bartholomew was the son of a former monk—a tale worthy of retelling if ever there were one—and had seemingly had implanted in his scrawny breast the desire to endlessly scribble down anything he found noteworthy. His fingers were already twitching, no doubt longing for quill and ink with which to note the odd happenings going on before him.

Phillip was quite sure he never wanted to read any of that collection.

He looked at the men hanging over the parapet, watching the spectacle with less respect than outright amusement. He didn't think he could blame them. He was facing a madwoman.

A madwoman he was fairly sure he didn't know.

He was a practical man. Too practical, his brothers might say. Too focused on what he wanted and prepared to damn anyone who got in his way. He didn't like mess, and he particularly didn't like the unexpected. He had laid a siege of sorts to Haemesburgh for seven years, seven long years spent ignoring every single obstacle that was put in his path. He knew his father wouldn't force him to wed where he didn't wish to, but that Robin was feeling the need to import women for him to look over . . .

Well, that was tantamount to a voicing of doubt that Phillip would manage what he'd set out to do. A fond, concerned doubt, but doubt nonetheless, and that was something he couldn't bear. He was going to turn his current situation to his advantage and he was going to do it immediately. And if that meant demanding to know who exactly that delicious-smelling woman thought she was, then so be it. He wasn't one to shy away from the difficult.

What in the hell was a *text*?

"Hey," she said in annoyance, "I'm talking to *you*."

Her accent was, as he'd noted before, atrocious. He considered the possible reasons for that. If the rumors were true and she'd been without her father for a handful of years now, who knew what sort of talk she'd learned from the garrison lads? Hard on the heels of that came another thought. What if before he'd died, her sire had imported a lady-in-waiting of sorts to teach Heather a few decent manners? For all he knew, Heather had learned to bathe, comb her hair, and comport herself with some small bit of decorum. He hadn't seen her in several years. Perhaps she had, with that same bit of help, grown into herself, learned to guard her tongue, and relinquished her desire to see him dead.

Or perhaps not. He listened to the words she continued to spew at him and wondered not for the first time why in the hell he'd pursued her for so long. He was a knight of the realm, for pity's sake. He had cut his teeth on chivalric tales of duty and all manner of other knightly virtues. There were scores—well, perhaps not scores, but at least half a dozen—very eligible women who would have been happy to call him husband. Instead, he was trying to convince the irascible wench in front of him to wed where she obviously didn't want to.

Perhaps what she needed was to sit and rest before a hot fire. Mayhap then she would stop wagging her finger at him and calling him things he was sure he didn't want to know the meaning of.

He looked over her head and identified the garrison captain, a man who at least had the good sense not to let his tongue hang out as he leaned over the parapet and grinned. Phillip pointed at the man, then pointed at the drawbridge.

"Down," he mouthed.

The man mouthed back a suggestion for what Phillip could do with himself. Another arrow went flying over the moat and tore through the hood of the man's cloak as it lay behind his head. Phillip didn't give any indication of his thoughts, but he had to admit he was very glad that Rose was not the one he was going to be facing over an altar. She frightened him.

The drawbridge came down with a bang. The lady of Haemesburgh released his squire at almost the same time she flung herself into his arms. He supposed that was progress. Or it would have been if she hadn't come close to knocking him senseless with that damned box of hers that clipped him on the side of his jaw as she'd been about her flinging. He didn't feel the need to spit out any teeth, so he supposed he was safe there. He put his arm around her and patted her as his men carefully forged a path into the keep. His father's men were seasoned; his were proud of their ability to inspire fear in any foe. All in all, he didn't think he would want to belong to Lady Heather's garrison at the moment.

He imagined he would put off supper until he'd come to an understanding with her captain.

He listened to the shouting coming from inside the gates, then watched as his own men took over posts that had very recently been held by Haemesburgh's men. Once he was certain things were as they should have been and his own men were in command of the front gates, he turned his attentions to his betrothed. Before he could invite her to take her ease in front of her own fire, she glared at him, then stomped back across the drawbridge. Or, rather, she would have stomped if she hadn't been limping so badly. Bartholomew shot him a pleading look, but Phillip shook his head slowly. His squire sighed, then went to offer the lady of the keep his arm. She looked startled, which left Phillip something else to chew on.

Perhaps she hadn't had the luxury of chivalry in her youth.

The twins and Rose followed her across the drawbridge. Phillip found himself standing with Connor and Jackson. At least they had the good sense not to smirk.

"Interesting," Connor said.

"Didn't you say that before?" Phillip asked politely.

"Nay, I said, *well, that's new.* This is a different observation."

"Why did I bring you?"

Connor smiled. "Because you love me so well. I wonder if there is anything edible inside?"

Phillip watched him walk off, no doubt to investigate the larder, then looked at Jackson. Rose's younger brother looked as if he'd seen a ghost.

"What is it?" Phillip asked, tempted to indulge in a brush with genuine alarm.

"Nothing," Jackson said faintly. "Nothing at all. I'm surprised she bathed, 'tis all."

"Perhaps she knew her doom was arriving today," Phillip said confidently, "and wanted to be prepared to meet it."

Jackson continued to stare at the keep for a moment or two, looking very unsettled. Then he shook his head sharply, which seemed to help him set aside whatever troubled him. He clapped a hand on Phillip's shoulder. "Let's go see your keep. I shudder to think what she's left of it."

Phillip did, too, but he wasn't going to say as much. He watched his cousin cross the drawbridge, then paused to simply take in the sight in front of him. There was work to do to make the place secure and definitely some tidying that needed to be seen to. But all in all it was a decently sized keep, the walls were sturdy, and with any luck it would be his before the fortnight was out. The marriage banns had been read years ago, so he could only assume they were still in force. He would perhaps ask Bartholomew his opinion on the matter.

He wasn't sure Haemesburgh still had a priest, which might present a bit of a problem, though at the moment he suspected that was the least of his worries. He wasn't going to need a priest if he didn't have a bride, and he wasn't going to have a bride if he didn't get himself inside the walls before she managed to hobble up the barbican stairs and drop the portcullis on him.

All things considered, it had been a successful morning.

Or it would be, if he could discover why Heather of Haemesburgh seemed so different from how he remembered her. Granted, he hadn't had speech with her over the years past having her shout at him before she threw things over the walls at him, but still . . .

He took a deep breath and started across the drawbridge. He would solve it all and his life would be as tidy as he expected it to be.

He would accept nothing else.

Chapter 7

Imogen stood on the edge of a castle courtyard that should have looked familiar—and unfortunately did in a sort of disgustingly filthy way—held on to her phone for security, and tried to make sense of what was happening to her.

Her choices were limited. While it would have been nice to have believed she was caught in an exceptionally realistic dream or a fantastically vivid hallucination, she had to rule both those things out. She was awake and she was in full control of her faculties. What she *could* believe, however, was that she had been drugged. She wasn't sure when it had happened, but obviously she should have known better than to trust an impeccably dressed noblewoman she'd met inside a shop selling witches' paraphernalia. Maybe it had been a delayed reaction to that sludge she'd drunk in Curiosities in Plaid the day before.

Or perhaps it was just one of her siblings behind her current misery. Her family was different, there was no getting around it. Her father was brilliant, always sitting on piles of money made by taking over and destroying whatever company had caught his roving eye. Her mother was brilliant in an entirely different way, having an encyclopedic knowledge of every political happening over the past hundred years in any country one cared to quiz her about, but possessing absolutely no social skills at all.

How her parents had managed to produce five children was a mystery, but four of them were overachievers to an embarrassing level with devious minds bent on tormenting the weakest of the pack, who of course happened to be her. She was the youngest child, possessing absolutely no desire to put on panty hose and swim with corporate sharks, with only her wits and an uncanny ability to smell trouble to keep her from being completely at her siblings' mercy. She wondered how it was she'd managed to emerge from that group with any part of her soul left intact.

Her current situation was one they definitely could have planned.

She would have called any one of those siblings to tell them exactly what she thought of them, but she'd already discovered that she had no signal. That in itself was odd because she'd specifically made sure she could be reached anywhere.

She leaned against stone that looked about how it had looked the day before and stared glumly at her surroundings. She had to believe she was trapped on a movie set because it was the only thing that made sense. That also made her situation slightly easier to accept than trying to come up with some otherworldly reason as to why she seemed to be losing her mind. She took a deep breath and forced herself to admire her surroundings.

Whoever had decorated the set had done an amazing job of it. The whole place looked as if it had been dumped back in time. Someone had put up some sort of blacksmith's shop where the tea shop had been. The chapel was in the same place, which made sense given how hard it would have been to move all that stone. There were some useful additions by way of stables and a small, overrun garden, and what was perhaps a training field of sorts for the very fragrant extras she'd already encountered inside the gates.

She considered the actors she'd encountered outside the gates. They were a different story, though she would admit she hadn't paid very much attention to them short of threatening to have them fired for participating in such a terrible practical joke.

She nodded to herself. It was a joke of course, unless . . .

Unless she'd been dumped into some sort of reality show. She was tempted to consider that seriously, though she couldn't imagine why anyone would have chosen her for that sort of thing. She was a nobody in the film world and not really anybody anywhere else.

Well, except for the fact that the tone-deaf son of the executive producer of her current gig had been trying to hit on her for the past year. She had honestly hoped that escaping into the wilds of Scotland might be what saved her from having to listen to any more of his suggestions for ever-more-serious commitments. She hadn't even gone for coffee with the guy; she wasn't at all ready to be talking about picket fences and the number of children he wanted.

She glanced to her left. The teenager she'd been using as a crutch was still hovering about twenty feet away from her, watching her nervously. She couldn't bring herself to be rude to him—he had let her lean on him to get back inside the castle after all. She smiled at him. He looked at her warily in return.

"I won't have you fired," she promised.

That didn't seem to leave an impression, but then again he looked fairly stressed. Maybe his dream was to be a leading man and he was trying not to blow any sort of impression he could be making. She couldn't blame him.

Her ankle finally stopped throbbing enough that she could think straight, which unfortunately left her little choice but to take a good hard look at her surroundings. She eased around the corner to the front of the castle and perched on the edge of the stairs. It left her feeling a little more exposed than she was comfortable with, but she had to get off her foot for at least a minute or two.

She almost couldn't believe what she was seeing. Whoever had been hired to transform the castle into a medieval abode had done an amazing job. She wasn't sure if her director would have been pleased with the serious lack of hygiene—a period piece notwithstanding—but there was no denying it looked damned authentic. It smelled damned authentic as well.

As she sat there, she realized she was looking at the wrong things. Walls and manure spread around were great, but the courtyard was filled with all kinds of people who were really doing a bang-up job of living the medieval dream. In fact, there were a couple of groups of them right there in front of her, just ready for her to observe them at close range.

It didn't take her long to realize what she was seeing was a thrown-together production of *West Side Story*, with two groups of guys facing off about twenty feet in front of her. She knew which group belonged to inside-the-castle versus outside-the-castle mostly because of the way they were dressed. The inside guys were definitely less well-groomed. Their leader was standing in front of the ragtag group having himself a really good scratch. She shuddered and turned her gaze elsewhere.

The other guys looked like extras from a high-budget medieval set. Their clothing was very nice, their faces washed, and their posture ramrod straight. Their leader . . .

Oh.

Him.

She realized with a bit of a shiver that it had been that guy there to catch her. She wondered how she could have been so distracted that she'd missed *that* view.

The teenager stalking her had his hand on her shoulder suddenly, which made her realize she had almost fallen off the steps. Well, in her defense, the leader of the cleaner group of extras was exceptionally . . . well, exceptional.

She had dated her share of toads, really. She wasn't sure why she attracted such jerks, but there you had it. Her dating life was, in a word, awful. That said, she certainly hadn't come to the UK to date. She was there to do a job brilliantly so she could climb to ever higher heights of filmmaking happiness. Still, it probably wouldn't hurt to have a look at that guy standing over there, just as sort of an academic exercise. She settled more comfortably on her step and looked at him from a casting director's perspective. If she had been looking for a leading man for a major movie, she would have stopped her search and considered her star found.

He was standing in front of his little group of extras, looking rather lordly and in charge. He had well-fitting clothes, nice boots, and a sword that she supposed he at least knew how to pretend to use. He was tall and filled his costume out in a way that was muscular without being indicative of too much time spent at the gym.

She studied his face. Now, that was a face the camera would have loved. Not pretty, but instead absolutely stunning with just the right amount of cheekbone definition to provide angles for the lighting guys to get excited over. When she escaped the set and sued whoever was responsible for her current trauma, she would definitely keep that guy out of the carnage.

She wondered if he might be interested in going out for a coffee.

Just looking at him made her feel a little breathless, which wasn't at all useful at present, so she left him taking care of his medieval-looking business and concentrated on her own problems. She wondered why no one seemed willing to at least give her the odd, conspiratorial wink to let her know that it was all just an elaborate prank, but maybe there was a casting director hiding in the ranks, looking for the next big star. She couldn't imagine she was being considered for that role, which meant that she had probably just been in the wrong place at the wrong time. That realization was enough to leave her breathing a bit easier. She might have been trapped on a movie set, but she had a step to sit on and it wasn't raining. It could have been much worse.

She looked at the kid standing close by. Maybe he was there to keep an eye on her and keep her from wandering off where she wasn't supposed to be. She considered the possibilities of that for quite a while before she decided that whatever he was, he might be bribable. All the more reason to make friends with him.

She scooted over on the step and patted the place next to her. The kid eyed her warily, then perched next to her with the enthusiasm of a bird sitting next to a chops-licking feline. She smiled reassuringly.

"I'm Imogen. Who are you?"

He looked momentarily perplexed, then seemed to get what she was saying. "Bartholomew."

Of course he was. "Thank you, Bartholomew. What's your job here?"

He frowned, as if he simply couldn't fathom what she might possibly be saying. She gave him time to think about it, giving him the occasional encouraging nod.

"Do," she repeated finally. "Here. On set."

He was still looking at her as if she were the one who was absolutely crazy, which she supposed might have been part of the story arc. *Woman out of her depth being driven crazy by the people around her as they treated her like she was the one who was nuts.* Genius. Maybe the best thing she could do was try to frustrate that plan.

"I think I'll go have a look around," she announced, glancing at him to see how he was taking the news.

He was, unsurprisingly, still looking at her as if he couldn't understand a thing she was saying. He also looked a little nervous. Maybe he was afraid if he did the wrong thing, he would get canned after all.

Imogen tested her ankle and decided that it could definitely be walked on presently and iced later. She used Bartholomew to get fully to her feet, patted him on the shoulder, then eased past him to head inside the great hall. It seemed like the best place to start an investigation. She would walk around casually and keep a weather eye out for extension cords leading to hidden cameras.

The occupants of the inside seemed to have decamped for more interesting locales outside, because she had the whole place to herself. The floor was just as disgusting as she remembered it being and the place smelled just as bad. Obviously there was a terrific set designer at the helm, someone Imogen decided she would show mercy to when she was suing the whole crew for pain and suffering.

She paused in the middle of the floor and turned in a circle, looking for things that might give some indication that there were practical jokers in the area. Maybe that wouldn't be as straightforward as she had hoped. It was a castle, after all, and she supposed it hadn't been originally plumbed for running water or built with electrical conduits in mind. But she didn't even see anything on the walls except a few rather ugly tapestries and a few sconces holding torches. There was a large fire pit in the middle of the hall. Not even a fireplace set into the wall to possibly conceal a sibling or two.

She looked at the high table for a minute or two, then frowned. There was still no sword there. She walked over to the table, then peered over it to see if she might have knocked it over in her enthusiasm. No, there was definitely no sword hiding there, or under the table, or behind the tapestry that hung in tatters behind the high table. There was, however, a bit of a hole in the floor where she could easily imagine a sword once residing.

That was definitely weird.

She forced herself to remain calm and think about where the sword might have gone. There had certainly been no lack of them outside with those extras. She supposed it might have been far-fetched to think that the sword might have opened some trapdoor that she'd fallen through and clunked her head on long enough for some set decorating to go on, but she realized she was starting to get a little desperate for answers. Or maybe she was getting desperate for something to eat.

All she knew was that she was never going to enter another reputedly haunted castle ever again.

She decided abruptly that the sword had to be the key. Obviously someone had scampered off with it leaving no one but her own sweet self to go after it and get it back. She hadn't survived a fifty-three-hour trip to the UK only to get side-tracked by a few bad apples with rotten senses of humor. The only thing that made sense to her was the trapdoor idea and obviously the trapdoor was only going to be activated when the sword was jammed into the floor.

There, that seemed reasonable. She nodded to herself as she walked back across the floor. The door to the hall was still open, so she stepped out into the grayness of a day that looked like it was about to threaten more rain, wished she'd bought a different coat the day before so she didn't have to keep wearing the one she was wearing with her personal advertisement on the seat, and took a hard look at what was going on.

Well, there were swords aplenty and no lack of stunt guys who seemed to know how to at least wear them. The leaders of those two groups seemed to be thinking about actually drawing their swords and putting them to use, if the tone of their conversation was any indication. She was half tempted to point out that they were putting on a really good show for people who were so well hidden as to possibly be off at lunch, but given how serious they looked, she supposed they wouldn't listen to her.

She supposed they also wouldn't listen to her if she told them that maybe drawing their swords and hacking at each other was a potentially very dangerous activity. She analyzed their technique based on the best of the stuntmen she had seen over the course of her rather long career as a movie-set grunt and decided that in this, at least, those two knew what they were doing.

She watched dispassionately for quite some time, deciding at one point that there might be a correlation between how nicely a character was dressed and how well he could wield his sword. The guy with smudges on his cheeks wasn't bad, but he wasn't even close to his lordly opponent's standards.

The languages they were speaking were also odd. Although her graduate degree had involved enormous amounts of French, it had been mostly a reading sort of French, not a speaking sort of the same. The nicely dressed guys were speaking French among themselves, though with an accent that made her head hurt. The other guys . . . well, she had no idea what they were speaking. It could have been Anglo-Saxon for all she could make of it. All she knew was that the next time she found herself trapped in some sort of horrible reality show, she was going to demand a translator.

The fight continued, if a fight it could be called. Without warning, a sword went flying up into the air. She watched it flip end over end on the way up, then continue the spinning at a much slower pace on the way down. It was odd how the closer a sword came to one's face, the bigger it looked. She realized it was going to hit her approximately three seconds before she felt as if her head had just split open.

And that was, she suspected as she felt herself fall into blackness, the end of her brush with reality TV.

Chapter 8

P*hillip* caught her as she fell.

He had seen the sword coming toward her, shouted for her to move, then bolted across the courtyard to try to jerk her out of the way. He'd managed to spare her dashing her head against the stone of the stairs, but perhaps that was cold comfort when she was going to have a knot on her forehead the size of an apple.

She looked at him blearily, then her eyes rolled back in her head and she fainted.

He turned to find the captain of Haemesburgh's guard standing behind him. He stared at Sir Neill until the man put up the sword he'd retrieved from where it had fallen from the sky by way of a woman's forehead. Neill shifted uncomfortably.

"That wasn't intentional," he said defensively.

"No doubt," Phillip said. "Where is her bedchamber?"

Neill blinked at him as if Phillip had asked him a question he simply couldn't fathom. "Ah, milord—"

"The lady of the hall's bedchamber," Phillip said crisply. "Surely you can at least tell me where to find it."

Neill looked at him with an expression that could only have been properly termed consternation, but he seemingly chose to bite back anything he might have planned to say. He shrugged, then nodded for Phillip to follow him into the great hall.

Phillip entered the hall, but warily. If a pair of his own lads followed hard on his heels, who could blame him? He would have been mad to walk into a tight space with the unconscious lady of the hall in his arms and not expect someone to protest.

He followed Neill across a disgustingly filthy great hall and up a set of truly perilous steps to the upper floor. Neill paused before a door, then turned and made Phillip a slight bow.

"Here ye are," he said, as if he'd just paused in front of a cell designed to house him for the rest of his life. "As ye requested."

Phillip looked at the man pointedly. Neill looked no less enthusiastic than before, but he did open the door. He stepped back quickly, as if he expected something untoward to happen to him. Phillip wasn't surprised to find one of his own men joining Neill on the far side of the door, though he suspected it wasn't to keep Neill company.

He looked inside the chamber, then stopped himself just before he allowed his jaw to slide south. He had expected to see many things in Heather's bedchamber: bedbugs, weapons, perhaps even a pile of things she had collected to throw over the walls at him should he dare show his face anywhere near her home. What he hadn't expected was to find a lad standing in front of a smokey peat fire in a brazier, a lad wearing skirts.

"What are you doing in my bedchamber?" the boy demanded.

Phillip struggled to find a response to that, but couldn't latch on to a damned thing.

"And *who* are you to think to do such a thing?"

"Phillip de Piaget," Phillip managed, "and I daresay I think quite a few things you wouldn't care for. Who are *you*?"

"The lady Heather," the young man said, brushing at a filthy wimple, "as you can plainly see."

Had he stumbled into a foul dream? He reaffirmed his vow to be more careful at a witch's fire in the future, then studied the lad standing there in front of him, patting the hair under his veil into place. By the saints, how long had that one been at the current ruse? Was it possible *that* was the soul who had been flinging chamber pot contents over the walls at him all this time?

He could scarce bring himself to consider such a possibility, but he knew he had to. For all he knew, he had never actually seen Lady Heather herself. 'Twas possible she was nothing more than a figment of her father's imagination and he had gotten himself betrothed to a woman who never existed. After all, it wasn't as if he'd actually stood in front of a priest with her. When he'd come to put his hand to the letter of promise her sire had demanded, she had been indisposed.

Had she been of an indisposition that was closer to death than pains in her head?

The thought of *that* left him wanting to find either a seat or an ale keg, neither of which would serve him at the moment. He glanced at the bed and decided abruptly that he wouldn't have put an ancient steed to rest on that nasty bit of business. He would have to find another place to lay the woman in his arms.

The woman who apparently wasn't Heather of Haemesburgh.

But if she wasn't Heather, who was she?

The circles his poor mind was going in were dizzying. He would have to sort them all at some point, but he would see to the woman he was carrying first. He looked at Neill.

"How are the stables?" Phillip asked.

"As ye might expect, milord. I wouldn't put a woman there."

"Yet you've allowed the lady Heather to sleep here," Phillip said in disgust. "Or whoever that is there."

"She's made of stern stuff."

No doubt. Phillip had wanted to avoid killing any of Haemesburgh's men-at-arms, but he had the sinking feeling things were not going to go well with the man standing in front of him.

"The stables," Phillip said. He glanced at the lad still standing there fiddling with his wimple and decided he would see to that one later. One mystery at a time.

He could scarce believe what he'd just seen. Even if Lord Robert were dead, surely he would have made it clear how things were to proceed. They had initially signed the betrothal agreement seven years earlier. That seen to, Phillip had turned his mind to other things. That wasn't to say that he hadn't

arrived now and again at the gates in the style of a dedicated
suitor, bearing gifts and delicacies designed to curry his future
bride's favor.

The parleys had never gone very well, but Lord Robert had
always been too busy to engage in anything but the most banal
of speech about the weather, generally held out in front of his
gates *in* the weather. Phillip had been determined not to be as
rude as his own sire would have been in similar straits—Robin
would have stormed the keep and made himself at home in the
lord's chair with his feet up on the table at the first sign of
reticence—but perhaps he had been more patient than he
should have been.

Patient or stupid; he wasn't sure which.

If he hadn't wanted the hall so badly, at the moment he
might have been tempted to label the whole thing a horrible
failure, gather up his family and guardsmen, and simply walk
away. But there were the politics of the place's location to be
considered, as well as the land attached to the keep. He wasn't
one to grow misty-eyed over the sight of rolling hills of heather
and flocks of sheep trotting happily over bucolic greenswards,
but he had to admit the surroundings were spectacular.

For something that wasn't Artane, of course.

The hair on the back of his neck stood up suddenly. He
didn't look, but felt one of his men step up more closely behind
him and the one in front of him pause briefly to close the distance between them. It was something those two had done
countless times for as long as he could remember. His men
were not cast-offs from his father's garrison, but men he had
acquired on his own and only accepted after having watched
them over an extended period of time. These two were truly
the most ruthless of the lot. If he'd been entirely honest with
himself, he would have said they made him nervous.

They definitely made his captain nervous, but that situation
was complicated. Sir Cederic was one of his father's men who
had become head of Phillip's own garrison by virtue of his
experience and character. He was a good, solid soldier and
properly cautious, but in a fight, Phillip had to admit he preferred the pair paving his way and bringing up the rear.

Sir Myles glanced over his shoulder briefly, met Phillip's
eyes, then looked past him at the knight behind him, Sir

Wiscard. Phillip didn't like the feel of the hall and he knew they didn't either. He sincerely hoped he wouldn't be fighting his way out of it with an unconscious woman in his arms.

He glanced over at the high table and swore, just on principle. The sword was gone. *His* sword was gone. Robert's eldest son, also named Robert, had taken great pleasure at sending word several years ago that Phillip's sword was residing behind the lord's chair in the great hall. He had intimated it was occasionally used to hang cloaks upon when the hall grew uncomfortably close, but Phillip had supposed he had said that merely to be an arse. The only satisfaction now came from realizing there was no sword there to use as a pole, though that was cold comfort indeed and left him with another unpleasant mystery to solve.

Where the hell was his grandfather's sword?

He left the great hall, cursing under his breath. He had anticipated trouble, but assumed it would come at him in a straightforward manner and be easily managed with steel. He was in a courtyard full of men who were not his and whose loyalty was to the saints only knew whom. Robert the elder was obviously dead, Heather was nothing more than a lad hiding upstairs in skirts, and her brother Robert the younger was nowhere to be found.

And he was holding on to a woman he had never seen before.

He gained the stables and was relieved to see that at least the horseflesh was being well cared for. Given the things he'd found inside the walls already, he was perhaps more relieved about that than he should have been. He left Myles and Wiscard to securing the area and looked for a likely place to put his burden.

Theo and Sam popped up from behind a half wall, making him jump a little in surprise. He cursed them briefly before putting them to use spreading clean straw on the floor of a stall, then covering it with a horse blanket. He lay the woman who couldn't possibly be Heather on that blanket, then jerked his head toward the stall door to send his young cousins scampering. They went willingly, which left him perfectly confident that they wouldn't go far enough to give him any hope of privacy.

He took off his cloak and covered the woman in front of

him with it. That seen to, he sat back on his heels and looked at a woman who couldn't possibly be his betrothed.

Who the hell was she?

He took a deep breath, then pulled her cloak aside as discreetly as possible, just to see if her gear might give him any clues to her identity. Her clothing was such as he'd never seen before in his life. Scandalous, truly, those hose with that long tunic made of stuff he began to think he shouldn't be looking at. He recovered her and supposed he had gotten what he deserved. Perhaps she was a noblewoman from the north who had been waylaid at Haemesburgh. She could have been trying to escape as the drawbridge had been going up.

He stared at her thoughtfully. That was possible, he supposed, and he wondered why he hadn't considered it before. After all, why else would a woman be in such a place without a guard about her? And it certainly wasn't as if she'd been trying to impersonate the lady of the keep. That silly lad inside had been proof enough of that.

Her eyelids twitched, then she opened her eyes and looked at him. Phillip leaned forward to talk to her.

"My lady—"

"I'm going to be sick."

He wasn't surprised. One didn't take a blow to the head such as she had without feeling the effects of it. A bucket was shoved into his hands before she vomited all over the both of them. He felt a little queasy himself, but ignored it. The bucket was taken away, water was provided—he could only hope it hadn't been drawn from the horse trough—and he suddenly found himself with a stall full of help. Lads fell all over themselves to offer aid, cool damp cloths, and advice on how best to tend a woman who had just heaved the rest of her guts all over one of the little twins. Sam bore the insult manfully and excused himself to go have a wash. Phillip spared a kind thought for his aunts' efforts to teach their children manners, then pointedly invited the rest of his cousins to leave. They did so, though reluctantly. He suspected they wouldn't go far.

Once they had gone, he turned his attentions back to the woman in question. He had just decided that perhaps he would begin with proper introductions when she seemed to recover somewhat. Before he could trot out his best manners, she had found her tongue.

"Listen, buster, if you don't get me back to Edinburgh right now and cut out this reality crap, I am going to kick your—" She stopped speaking briefly, then seemed to regroup for another go. "I'll kick something all the way to Sunday, damn it anyway."

He thought it might be impolite to gape at her, so he kept his mouth shut and tried to make sense of her words. He groped for the memory of where he'd heard that accent before, but he supposed that might take more time than he had at present.

"Ah, your name, lady?" he asked, because it was the first thing that came to mind.

"Imogen Maxwell," she said, waving a shaking finger at him.

And then she was off, babbling things he simply couldn't understand. Or, rather, things that he didn't want to understand.

The unfortunate truth was, he had a very long memory. He would admit that there were several things over the course of his years that he chose not to remember. His sire called them *paranormal oddities*. As a child, Phillip had decided never to ask what those might be.

That resolve had been tested sorely during his time spent squiring for his uncle Montgomery, for there were strange and unusual happenings associated with his uncle's wooing and winning of his bride, Persephone. But he'd eventually left them to their bliss and gone on to pass the rest of his youth either at Artane or spending the occasional stretch of time with this uncle or that aunt. He hadn't noticed anything untoward.

Though that might have been because he'd made a concentrated effort to keep his head down and his thoughts to himself.

It was true that he'd watched his aunts and uncles do peculiar things from time to time, but he'd supposed that was how all families in England conducted themselves. It had only been as he'd begun to travel about more and watched others come and go in various keeps that he began to see that what he'd considered normal might not be quite so normal.

Damn it anyway.

He'd heard words pronounced in just that way, though he most definitely didn't want to think about where. He had to take a bracing breath, which he rarely needed to do. He tried muttering a few of the words that woman there had babbled. They were strange upon the tongue—

He flinched in spite of himself when he realized Imogen Maxwell was groping for his hand. He took hers in both his own, surprised at how hard she was trembling. If he hadn't known better, he would have suspected she was afraid.

"Who are you?" she whispered.

"Phillip," he said. "Phillip de Piaget."

She let out a deep, shuddering breath. "I want to go home."

Aye, that was definitely fear in her voice. He opened his mouth to tell her that she had no reason to be afraid, not when he was there to aid her, but he realized the words would be lost on her. She had taken a deep, shuddering breath, then fainted. He sat there, holding her hand, and found himself without a single useful thing to think, he who always knew what to do and how to do it.

I want to go home.

He understood her words. He didn't want to think about why or how. He could only hope that he was the only one to have heard them—

He realized quite suddenly that he wasn't alone. He looked to his left to find his cousin Jackson leaning on the stall door, watching him. He forced himself to remain still and give no indication that he was at all affected by the sight of someone who came from a family where paranormal happenings were not exactly unusual.

"Been there long?" he asked in as offhanded a manner as possible.

"For a bit," Jackson answered.

Phillip nodded toward the woman lying in the hay. "She took a blow to the head."

"Aye, Phillip, I was there and saw the whole thing."

"She's babbling."

"So she is."

Phillip would have shifted, but he never shifted. It was something he'd learned from his sire. Robin de Piaget could stare at a miscreant, unmoving and unblinking, until the poor whoreson dropped to his knees and blurted out anything to end the torment.

He had to admit that he admired his sire to the depths of his soul, damn the immortal rogue.

"What's her name?" Jackson asked very quietly.

Phillip supposed there was no reason not to be honest. There were several people in his life he trusted completely. His mother and father, of course. Kendrick, surprisingly enough. He trusted Rose with the matters of his heart and his schemes both.

He also trusted Jackson Alexander Kilchurn, the Fifth.

He had wondered, as he'd watched his younger cousin grow to manhood, why the hell they'd saddled him with a name better fit for a king. He'd never found a good reason for it, but he'd also discovered that he hadn't needed a reason. Jackson was a vault, truly, a repository of all manner of things he held in absolute silence and never revealed. Phillip knew this because he'd watched Jackson be pressed past the point where he himself might have been able to bear the strain. Jackson never budged even a hair's breadth.

Phillip looked at his cousin. "Her name isn't Heather."

Jackson lifted his eyebrows briefly, then contemplated the woman lying there senseless. "Any thoughts on what it might be instead?"

Phillip looked at him evenly. "She said her name was Imogen Maxwell and if I didn't get her back to Edinburgh right away, she was going to kick my arse seven ways to Sunday." He paused. "Or words to that effect."

Jackson let out his breath slowly. "Interesting."

"Do you think so?"

Jackson shrugged. "I think many things. Whether or not they're useful for anything but keeping me distracted from other things, I wouldn't presume to say."

Phillip studied his cousin for a moment or two, then looked back at Imogen, who was obviously not the lady of Haemesburgh. Why was she dressed so strangely and why did she think threatening him with text was something he would take seriously? Why did he find her words so familiar?

Why was she still clutching his hands even whilst senseless?

He would have asked Jackson, but something made him hesitate. Good sense, hopefully. The truth was, he had spent possibly more time with Jackson and Rose than he had the rest of his cousins combined. Jackson was every bit as driven as he himself was, and Rose had her own demons that she was continually outrunning. He had never been quite sure that his parents and theirs hadn't spent their evenings closeted in Artane's solar discussing ways to keep the three of them in check. He supposed he could safely say the only soul who knew him better than Rose and her younger brother was Kendrick. But even so, there were things they'd all seen that they simply didn't discuss.

He looked at his cousin. "I loathe mysteries."

"And you think I love them?"

"I think you're surrounded by them, and that makes me uneasy."

Jackson rolled his eyes. "You're daft. Come find me when you've regained some semblance of good sense."

Phillip hoped that would be sooner rather than later, but with the way his day had proceeded so far, he didn't hold out any hope for it.

Before he could contemplate that for any length of time he found Jackson's post taken up by a different cousin. Connor of Wyckham stood there, looking far too at ease for Phillip's peace of mind. Then again, Connor was one of ten terrifying spawn. Perhaps if someone wasn't trying to light his tunic on fire, he considered life to be just too dull to get worked up over.

Connor leaned on the stall door. "Lovely place you have here."

"The keep or the stables?"

Connor smiled. "I have no complaints about the stables."

"And the rest should likely be razed," Phillip finished for him. "'Tis tempting."

"Oh, I imagine you'll tidy it up soon enough." He gestured to the woman lying senseless there in the hay. "What are you going to do with her?"

Phillip looked at him sharply. "What do you mean?"

"Exactly what you think I mean, cousin," Connor said seriously. "I've been making this pilgrimage with you for seven years now, since that notable occasional when I first put my wee hands in yours and pledged you my squirely fealty. Did you think I've been napping the entire time? I don't have a clue who that wench there is, but I can hazard a fairly good guess as to who she isn't. I was wondering, given who she *isn't*, what you were going to do with her."

"Hell."

"Well, you could use that to describe the state of your future home, but perhaps not much else." He nodded toward Imogen. "Who is she?"

"I've no idea."

"I don't think the lads in the keep know either, which makes them very nervous. You'll want to see to that sooner rather than later, I suspect."

Phillip sighed. "What are they saying?"

"The usual rubbish any suspicious lot would say. It doesn't help that you've arrived at about the same time. They're connecting you with her, but the thread they're using is very knotty."

"Thank you for that." He looked at his cousin. "I don't believe in witches. Or odd happenings that can't be explained away easily."

Connor smiled. "Did I claim you did? Now, what do you need?"

Phillip supposed there would come a time when he would have to take himself off in private and bawl like a babe over the generosity of those who never hesitated to surround him. He wondered, given the expression on Imogen Maxwell's face when she'd talked about going home, if she had never enjoyed that luxury.

"And it grows dark, in case you hadn't looked," Connor said seriously. "I'm not sure the lads here are organized enough to do anything then, but I suppose I wouldn't put it past them. Do you want to remain inside the walls or take our chances in the forest?"

"Where is Cederic?" Phillip asked. His captain generally spent his time instilling fear and loathing into whatever collection of ruffians they intended to fight, but with the way things had gone so far that day, Phillip didn't dare hope for anything useful from him.

"He's terrorizing the keep's garrison, as you might expect. I didn't suggest we not accept any offers of supper because I thought that should come from you, but I don't think any of our lads would be interested in that. If what you truly want to know is if we'll survive till dawn, I think our chances are good. Better inside than out, at least."

Phillip nodded. "Then we'll stay and see what the morning brings."

"I'll take my turn here, if you want to see things for yourself."

Phillip nodded, disentangled his hands from Imogen's, then traded places with his cousin. He paused at the stall door and looked back at her. He supposed if he'd had any sense at all, he would have rummaged through the rucksack she'd been wearing on her back, but perhaps later, after he'd seen to the safety of his company. She might be awake then and able to answer his questions. Or perhaps he would do the chivalrous thing, refrain from vexing her, and simply see her back to wherever she'd come from. Surely it couldn't be that far nor that difficult to escort her back to her home, then be about his own business.

And to think he had endlessly boasted that chivalry was always convenient.

He hoped he wouldn't come to regret having said as much.

Chapter 9

Imogen squinted into a castle courtyard that seemed lit with an unusual brightness and experienced a moment of elation that finally someone had turned on the floodlights. Now she was going to have siblings pop out from behind pillars and yell *surprise!* She would kill them all slowly and then her life would return to normal because no one could possibly hold her accountable for her actions after the night she'd just been through. Horses, hay, and a trip to a bathroom that had been more disgusting than anything she'd ever seen at Girl Scout camp. Those were definitely grounds for some serious retribution.

She sighed. The problem was those weren't floodlights—that was the sun—and she was still trapped in wherever the hell she was. Hell itself, maybe. Somewhere not boasting running water and a cell signal, definitely.

Something was up. She could sense it in the air, like a thunderstorm before it let loose on the hapless inhabitants underneath it. She steadied, then leaned against a wooden pillar at the entrance to the stables, wishing she had somewhere comfortable to sit down, preferably in a trendy coffee shop with free Wi-Fi.

The scruffy guys—locals, she supposed—were milling

around the courtyard with studied aimlessness. For some reason, they made her extremely nervous. She looked around and found herself relieved to see so many of the clean extras doing less milling and more standing around purposefully. If a battle erupted—something she honestly couldn't imagine even using her formidable powers of the same—she thought she might duck behind the better dressed extras to be on the safe side.

Then again, maybe the best way to avoid any sort of unpleasantness was to be on her way back to Edinburgh. Tilly was probably frantic over her not having checked in the night before, so the sooner she got back, the better. She pulled her phone out of her coat pocket, checked for a signal, then sighed and put it back. She wasn't sure how she was going to get a cab without a phone, but the last thing she was going to do was go back inside that great hall and hope for a landline that worked.

Obviously the only thing to do was to get away from the castle and out of the clutches of whatever crazy was going on. She would run to the village, seek refuge in the first likely shop she found, then make a call and get herself back to where she belonged.

She eased along the wall toward the front gates. The locals didn't seem too interested in what she was doing, which she appreciated. She watched a couple of the good guys take notice of her and begin to frown. Skedaddling before they did more than frown seemed like a fabulous idea, so she did.

She made a measured dash for the front gates, grateful that her ankle was limiting itself to twinging and her head had stopped pounding enough for her to see where she was going. She didn't dare look over her shoulder to see if she was being followed; she simply ran across the drawbridge and was grateful it was back down where it belonged. She hopped off the end of it, looked up, then stumbled to an ungainly halt.

She stood with the castle behind her and gaped at the sight in front of her.

So there hadn't been all that much civilization before, but there had been a charming little village at least, full of cottages and cute little shops that she had considered wandering through. Now, there was nothing but a rutted road and a few huts.

It occurred to her, as she stood there staring in horror at her surroundings, that she probably wasn't going to find a phone in the village square.

She would have scratched her head, but just brushing the bump on her forehead made her wince. Obviously physical displays of her distress were out. She would have preferred a pen and paper or even her phone with more battery than she had left, but she would do as others had done in equally primitive circumstances. She would make a mental list.

Her situation was simple: she was in deep crap. She didn't like to put it so bluntly at the top of her list, but the truth was hard to deny. She was standing heaven only knew where looking at heaven only knew where else, with lots of dedicated extras in the castle behind her who had obviously decided—either singly or collectively—that she must have some sort of pull with a big-time director and their job was to make her medieval experience as authentic as possible. She hadn't seen a single one of them break character yet.

Someone had also taken away the village in front of her. Either she'd been unconscious far longer than she'd suspected or . . . well, she frowned as a new thought occurred to her. What if she had passed out in Heather of Haemesburgh's castle and someone had taken her to some remote location where they intended her to be a participant in some sort of twisted experiment? There was a crazy sort of logic to that because there was just no possible way that anyone could have altered the keep behind her so thoroughly in such a short time, even if she had been unconscious for hours.

But it *was* possible that someone had spent months reproducing Haemesburgh in a different location. Set designers did it all the time.

The only problem was, she couldn't come up with a good reason why anyone would have bothered to build a keep that looked so much like Haemesburgh just for her. She was nobody. She was close to broke, she had no connections, and she didn't even own a couch. As tough as it was to accept, not even her siblings would have made that kind of effort for her.

Where in the hell was she?

She wrapped her arms around herself, looked out over the countryside, and scraped the bottom of the villain barrel in a search for suspects. The only one really with the money and time to do anything as extravagant and over-the-top as what was going on around her was Marcus Davis. She was, as it happened, undating him—or doing her best not to date him. He'd been growing increasingly tired of her pleading the inadvisability of getting involved with a coworker as a means of getting out of everything from coffee to an all-expenses-paid trip to the Bahamas. Maybe Marcus was behind it all. He had the cash and he was just about that crazy. The only problem with that theory was the undeniable fact that he never would have let something of this magnitude go on without somehow hogging center stage. If he'd been behind it, he would have taken the starring role as leader of the good guys for himself. No, there was something else going on.

She considered other items for her mental list. She wasn't hallucinating, though she supposed maybe that should go a bit lower on her list. She had a raging headache, but that could have been from that sword prop clunking her in the forehead as she stared stupidly up at it on its way down. She was a little light-headed, but that could have come from her lack of coffee that morning and food for the past who knew how long.

She closed her eyes briefly and concentrated on the things that felt familiar. That helped a little. The breeze was brisk, there were a few things chirping, and she could hear noises in the castle behind her that sounded like noises that belonged in that environment. A rooster or two, a horse, a few guys shouting things she couldn't understand. If she was in a delusion, it was at least a well-rounded one. If someone had orchestrated it, that someone had hired a very imaginative set designer. If her siblings were behind it, they were on their game to a level they'd never been before. It was almost like they'd transported her to another planet.

She froze. Even the pounding in her head paused as if it wanted her to have quiet to better appreciate the moment.

Another planet? She wasn't going to go there exactly, but she thought she could maybe consider some strange, Dr. Who-ish sort of transportation to another . . .

Another time?

She laughed lightly, because the thought—now that she'd allowed herself to think it—was so ridiculous. Time travel was the realm of fiction and TV. Besides, there weren't any of those cute British telephone boxes anywhere she could see and she would certainly know if she'd stepped into one and had it carry her off—

Well, there had been that sword.

She felt her world stop. She had touched a sword, passed out, then woken up in something that looked like it was straight from some a medieval period piece. What if the sword had been some sort of conduit to something straight out of a sci-fi TV show? The cabbie had warned her Haemesburgh was an odd place, hadn't he? He couldn't have known just how odd, surely.

But the lady Heather certainly could have.

Damn that woman. She had issued a specific invitation to touch something she'd known was slathered in paranormal, um . . . slatherings. Imogen hardly knew what to call what had coated that sword, never mind the utter preposterousness of even entertaining the possibility that she might have gotten sucked back in time simply because she'd touched a sword crammed into the cracks of the floor between two medieval stones.

She really needed something strong to toss back with abandon. It was too bad she didn't drink. She thought she might have ordered a double of anything at the moment.

Well, there was no time like the present to investigate the depth of her straits. If she had somehow traveled through time thanks to a sword in the floor, the best way to get back to where she had come from was to stick another sword in the floor. All she had to do was find a sword she could borrow. Problem solved.

She took a deep breath of surprisingly pleasant air, then turned around and looked at the place that couldn't possibly be a medieval castle sitting in the middle of a medieval field surrounded by medieval times.

A man was standing by the barbican gate, leaning against it with his arms folded over his chest, watching her. It was him, that good-looking one who was in charge . . . Phillip, she thought his name was. She had no idea why there was something about him that seemed familiar, but she'd slept through quite a bit of trivia while traveling north on the train with Tilly. Who knew what she'd missed? The one thing she did know was that she had grossly mischaracterized his looks. He wasn't handsome.

He was breathtaking.

She could bring to mind half a dozen current leading men who would have probably killed for a face like that. That didn't address the rest of him, but she supposed lusting after a guy she'd just met was a bad idea. She could lust later, when she knew a bit more about him, such as when he'd been born and whether he thought it was more likely that she'd traveled through time or lost her mind. Her dating experience wasn't all that vast, but she figured those were pretty important things to get out of the way right off.

He had pushed off the wall with an effortless sort of grace that said he'd done that kind of thing before. He walked across the drawbridge toward her as if he didn't give the slightest thought to the absolutely disgusting water in that moat. Then again, she was too overwhelmed by the sight of him to give it much thought either, so maybe she wasn't one to criticize.

He stopped directly in front of her and simply looked at her. She wasn't sure how to begin a conversation with a guy she couldn't guarantee spoke English, text, or anything approximating her very rusty eighteenth-century French, but she supposed she could try.

"Hi," she said.

He looked up briefly, looked baffled, then looked back at her. He seemed to be searching for something useful to say, which she appreciated. He finally simply inclined his head in a formal, Mr.-Darcy-ish sort of way and smiled gravely.

"'Tisn't safe to be outside the gates with the mischief going on inside the walls."

Or words to that effect. The man had to be an actor. No regular guy could possess such a lovely accent and sound like a prince. Never mind that his English sounded likely something she might or might not have heard during a very long two weeks spent working at a Renaissance Faire thanks to one of her siblings signing her up without asking her first, bodice and uncomfortable shoes included for her convenience.

Really, she was just too nice. One day in the future, she was going to put her foot down and tell her siblings where to go.

"Thank you," she managed. "I'm Imogen," she said. "Imogen Maxwell."

"So you said yestereve," he said carefully.

She didn't want to remember yestereve. She wasn't entirely sure she hadn't barfed on the guy standing in front of her. It was all a bit of an unhappy blur, compounded by a headache, hunger, and an intense desire to find a quiet place to have a nap.

"I am Phillip de Piaget," he said slowly, "but I believe I mentioned that yestereve as well."

She nodded absently, not because she wasn't interested, but because he was just so damned distracting. Medievalish-sounding accent, flawless face, a shoulder that was just the right height to lay her head on and have a wee snuggle. If she'd felt comfortable enough with him for that sort of thing.

Wee. She shook her head. Now she was starting to sound like all the crazies around her. It was obviously past time she got herself back to where she belonged.

"Might I offer you aid?"

Chivalry on display as well. She certainly was running into a lot of those rescuing types of guys in England

She frowned. It was odd, wasn't it, how her first encounter with the natives had been with that guy who had hauled her suitcase for her. He'd certainly been into the chivalry thing, and his accent had been . . . well, now that she thought about it, it had had a little of the same medieval twang to it that her current knight in shining armor possessed. In fact—and it was entirely possible she was imagining it because she wasn't entirely compos mentis—they even looked a bit alike.

Very strange.

But so was her whole experience and probably the sooner she had it all figured out, the better. She took a deep breath and looked at her potential rescuer. She mustered up her best Renaissance-faire accent and hoped for the best. "I think I'm lost."

"I wondered if that might be so—"

He looked over her head and swore suddenly.

Imogen looked over her shoulder and saw other guys in the distance, riding on horses. That didn't seem so unusual, though her new friend didn't seem to care for it. She understood why when she realized that an arrow had just come so close to her ear that it made a noise. A noise that sounded a bit like *you're dead.*

Phillip took her hand—she saved the shiver that went through her at his touch for examination later—and pulled her toward the drawbridge. She went, because it seemed like a damned fine idea to get out of the open. What seemed like a less stellar idea was pulling up the drawbridge. She skidded to a halt in front of it, unsure if she should jump onto the end or not. That decision was made when Phillip lifted her as if she were a feather and set her on the end of it without asking first. She stumbled a bit before she caught her balance, but that was probably thanks to the incline increasing so rapidly.

She turned to try to help Phillip only to land on her knees. Apparently he had some experience with drawbridges going up when they shouldn't have, because he simply caught the end of it, hooked a leg over it, then pulled himself up. He rolled past her, almost taking her with him in the process. She would have told him to be more careful, but she was too busy suddenly rolling after him down the last few feet of wood.

The portcullis dropped.

The unfortunate thing was, it dropped in front of them, leaving them outside. It was amazing how easily curses translated across time and language barriers. She wouldn't have messed with Phillip currently, but the guys in charge of the front gate didn't seem to be intimidated.

A man came shrieking over the walls and fell to the ground next to her, an arrow sticking out of his chest. He lay there, completely still.

"Let us in, you imbeciles!" Phillip bellowed.

Another trio of men fell off the walls. Imogen looked up and realized they weren't doing so of their own volition. She clapped her hand over her mouth before she started throwing up. It would have been nothing but dry heaves accompanied by tears, she was sure of that. Suddenly things were starting to feel much less like a set and quite a bit more like reality.

Phillip took her by the arm and quickly pulled her toward a very small gap between spikes and ground. "Under," he said shortly.

"Are you crazy?" she wheezed. "What if they drop it?"

He wasn't listening to her; he was too busy snarling at the men standing above them on the wall. She decided abruptly that when a person was between the devil and the deep blue sea, maybe inaction was the wrong choice. She dropped and rolled under those spikes, then found herself hauled to her feet by someone holding a bow. She turned around and watched Phillip roll under the spikes a split second before the portcullis dropped completely. He crawled to his feet, swearing and looking as if he would have cheerfully murdered someone. She left him to it, then turned to thank the guy who had helped her. She blinked in surprise.

"You're a girl."

"A woman, actually," the woman said with a faint smile. "Rose Kilchurn."

Imogen could hardly believe her ears. That was a posh British accent if she'd ever heard one, and that was definitely modern English that gal was using. Before she could ask Rose Kilchurn what the hell was really going on, she found herself in the middle of absolute chaos. She listened to swords clanging against swords, then watched in astonishment and no small bit of horror as those swords began to inflict wounds that just couldn't possibly be fake.

And Phillip de Piaget was right in the middle of it all.

Her first instinct was to try to at least warn him that he was getting involved in things that she could see were fairly dangerous, but that inclination was swiftly replaced by deciding that while it had been nice to inhabit a delusion or visit another time or be an unwitting part of a reality show, she was done. If she didn't get herself out of the fray immediately, she wasn't going to be *able* to get herself out of the fray.

She suffered a small twinge of regret that she wasn't going to get to know Phillip a bit better, her dismal dating record aside, but maybe some things just weren't meant to be. Besides, he looked to be awfully involved in a battle that didn't look all that choreographed to her. What she knew for certain was that he definitely didn't need either her opinions or her help. She made sure her daypack was still residing on her back, patted her coat pocket for her phone, then indulged fully in her well-developed sense of self-preservation and looked for a way to make a break for freedom.

It didn't take long to find an opening in the chaos. She bolted across the courtyard and up the stairs to the great hall without being hit by any stray swords, arrows, or insults. That she was relieved by any of that was almost bizarre enough to have her stopping to make sure she hadn't lost her mind. She shook her head and continued to run. She would examine her sanity later.

She shoved the doors open and pushed her way past the men standing there. They looked as uneasy as she felt, but she figured they could look however they wanted to as long as they got out of her way and left her free to either find that damned sword or jam another one into its slot.

No one stopped her as she ran for the back of the hall. She realized on her way by that the well-preserved stone floors weren't quite as uneven as she remembered them being but they still made up for that with their covering of straw and other things she didn't want to identify. She slipped and slid until she skidded to a halt in front of the lord's high table. A young woman stood there, guarding the way.

"Move," Imogen commanded.

"Nay."

She realized two things immediately. First, with enough practice, she might get that medievalish British accent down. Second, she wasn't looking at a woman, she was looking at a teenage boy dressed in skirts. She looked at him narrowly.

"Don't make me hurt you."

He drew himself up. "I am the lady Heather—" he began in crisp French.

Yes, he was Heather of Haemesburgh, she was the queen of England, and there was no damned sword behind that table. She pushed past him to examine the place where the sword should have been. There was a slit there where something had obviously resided previously. Something would again if she had anything to say about it. She turned abruptly and looked at the teenager standing there in skirts. Funny thing, he had just the thing she needed belted around his waist. She pointed at it and looked at him sternly.

"Give me that."

He drew back as if he'd been bitten, then his hand went protectively to his sword hilt. "Nay."

Well, the last thing she was going to do was be bossed around by a skinny sixteen-year-old pretending to be the lady of the house. She needed to get back home and the only way she could see that happening was to use the same method to go home as she'd used to get to her current locale.

She was going to have a sword to stick in that stone if it was the last thing she did.

Chapter 10

Phillip suppressed the urge to take his sword and run Neill of Haemesburgh through.

He was surrounded by his own men and his family, all of whom he imagined shared his feelings. Sir Neill was flanked by the castle's garrison, men who should have at least had some sense of their peril. Yet none of them seemed to. It didn't bode well for the future.

"Of course we raised the bridge," Neill said, jutting his chin out. "We saw the lads making for ye and knew ye'd want the keep to remain safe."

"I believe I would have preferred to be inside it," Phillip said coolly, "whilst you were about your safekeeping."

"Ye're well enough now, aren't ye?"

And it had taken four dead garrison knights to accomplish that feat. Phillip forced himself to unclench his jaw and keep his hand away from the hilt of his sword. He'd anticipated resistance when he arrived at the keep, but this was something else entirely. Anyone with two wits to rub together would have taken a look at Phillip's entourage and realized how any battle would end. That Neill stood there, bold and defiant, said that he was either far too stupid to have his current position or he was counting on aid—

Aid from another direction.

Phillip craved time to think as badly as he currently craved a decent amount of sleep. He couldn't believe Neill was a complete fool, which left him with the truth possibly being that those lads riding in from nowhere hadn't been simply out for a lark.

"You're going to want to come to the great hall."

By the saints, what next? Lads springing up from the rushes to vex him? Phillip continued to look at Neill lest the man think he had the advantage, but gave an ear to his cousin. "Why do I, when you say it thus, want to do anything *but* come to the great hall?" he murmured.

"Because my ability to convey the nuance of any situation with few words is limitless," Connor said, sounding slightly amused. "And you'll want to hurry."

Phillip glanced at him. "Is it worse than what lies out here?"

"I wouldn't presume to determine that."

Phillip was beginning to suspect the entire bloody venture had been doomed from the start. Enemies outside the gates, an unfriendly garrison inside the gates, and heaven only knew what now inside the hall itself. And that didn't begin to address his other mystery—

He looked at Connor quickly. "Where is Imogen?"

"Inside the hall."

"Still breathing?"

Connor smiled very faintly. "Words can't describe the scene. Why don't you go have a look and Jack and I will keep things from going completely south here. Look you, here is Sir Cedric as well, his sword hoisted in your defense."

Phillip thought it might be best to leave that alone. There was no love lost between his captain and both Connor and Jackson, something he had wondered about from time to time but never found unpleasant enough to merit his attention. He considered, then nodded. How anything going on inside could be worse than standing outside facing off with the captain of the keep's garrison who obviously wasn't interested in much besides seeing him dead, he didn't know. Obviously he wasn't going to manage a peaceful takeover without digging deep for powers of persuasion he didn't often need to use. He already had four dead at the gates because of Neill's actions. He had no intention of seeing that number increase.

Phillip exchanged a glance with his own captain, Cederic, knew he didn't need to do the like with his cousins, then walked away. He could only hope he didn't return to find his lads in a pitched battle, though at the moment, he wouldn't have been surprised by anything. He reminded himself that his current straits were his own doing, searched for those increasingly elusive reasons as to why he'd thought Haemesburgh was necessary to his future, and comforted himself with how continuing on his current course would save him from having to watch his father come rescue him. Cold comfort, indeed.

He walked into the great hall, bracing himself for the worst. He only made it halfway across the rather decently laid stone before he came to an ungainly halt. Heather—er, Imogen, rather—and the lad styling himself as the lady of the keep were fighting over a sword.

"Look there, cousin," Rose said suddenly. "I believe 'tis a battle over a sword."

Phillip shot Rose a dark look. "Aye, I can see that. Do you have any idea *why* they're fighting over that sword?"

"I think your lady wants it and the lad posing as Haemesburgh's lady doesn't want to give it up."

Phillip supposed he should have been surprised by what he was seeing, but he just wasn't. Imogen was indeed there and so was the lady—er, the lad of the keep, whoever he was. The boy was still dressed in skirts, but apparently the events of the day had been dire enough that he'd foregone the wimple. Phillip wondered who he was and what had left him with the cheek to attempt such a ruse.

Where in the bloody hell was Heather?

He walked across the floor and stopped just short of the high table. Imogen was babbling things in that tongue he still had trouble deciphering even though it still sounded and felt familiar, like the echo of a foul dream he'd all but forgotten. The lad who wasn't Heather seemed to have no trouble understanding her intent, at least, for he was clutching his sword to him as if it were a precious child about to be snatched by ruffians.

Unfortunately for that lad, he was no match for her, especially after she reached out and poked him in the eye. She seemed to regret that, but that didn't stop her from tossing the sword's sheath away and rushing over to the lord's chair. She shoved the blade into the floor with a sigh of great relief. Instead of hanging her cloak upon that sword, though, she put her hands on it as if she expected it to do something magical.

There was that word again. He suppressed a curse. He could never hear it again in his lifetime and it would be too soon.

He put his hands on the table and looked at her. "What are you doing, lady?"

She didn't look at him. "I'm going home."

She said it in French, but her French was as atrocious as was her English. He would have given some thought as to why that might be, but he was distracted by the ridiculousness of what he was seeing. Rose seemed less troubled by it, but she had a strong stomach for that sort of thing. She leaned her hip against the table and looked at Imogen.

"Won't work," she said cheerfully.

Imogen turned and pointed a finger at Rose. "Hey, you spoke English before."

"Well, aye, I do," Rose said. "After a fashion. I prefer Gaelic. Or French."

Which seemed to be the case given that she launched into a fair bit of both. Phillip suspected his head would only stop pounding when he wasn't listening to at least three different languages being tossed about with abandon.

"That's not Phillip's sword," Rose offered finally in a slow, careful French she might have used with a foreign lord who didn't speak the language past wanting to know where the wine might find itself. "Perhaps you need Phillip's sword." She pointed at him in an exaggerated fashion. "That sword there."

Phillip would have cursed his cousin, but he couldn't bring himself to. She was one of his favorite people, after all. He realized quite suddenly that Imogen was looking at his sword with the same sort of calculation that he feared he used whilst looking at Haemesburgh. He watched in astonishment as she rounded the table and stopped in front of him.

She only pointed at his sword. "Let me have that."

"Absolutely not," he said, feeling faintly horrified. She might have been very lovely and in sore need of a rescue, but there were things he just didn't do. Giving up his sword was first on that list.

"Oh, be a love, Phillip," Rose said with a smirk. "Let her have your sword for a minute or two."

"How do I know she won't put it in the floor and it will never come free again?"

"Because neither you nor I see your knighting sword there at the moment," Rose said. "Obviously that spot in the floor isn't a permanent residence for anything."

Phillip promised himself a lengthy speculation on that later, after he was certain he would see dusk. Where his sword was at the moment, though, the saints only knew. It wouldn't have surprised him to have dredged the moat and found it there on the bottom, rusting past any usefulness.

"Sword," Imogen insisted.

He drew himself up, fully prepared to lecture her on why he, Phillip de Piaget, did not ever hand over his weapon—

Her hand shook.

He closed his eyes briefly. Damnation, the woman's hands were going to be the death of him. Trembling the night before, shaking now. If there was one thing he simply couldn't bear, it was a woman in distress. He had no idea who Imogen Maxwell was or what she was about, but it was obvious she was in trouble. How could he not do what he needed to in order to aid her?

He sighed and drew his sword, then looked at the lad in skirts. "Your name, lad?"

"Hamish, my lord."

"Pull your blade free of the floor, Hamish."

"But—"

"Now."

Hamish had obviously been too much at his ease in the keep, for he not only hesitated, but grumbled as he then did as he was bidden. That would be changing quite soon. Phillip looked at Imogen and nodded toward the back of the table. She seemed slightly unsure, so he led the way. He waited until she had joined him behind the lord's chair before he sighed.

Very well, so the sword he'd been given by his father at his knighting was, according to Berengaria of Artane, enspelled. Losing it had been a blow he had found painful for perhaps longer than he should have, sentimental fool that he was.

The sword he was holding in his hands, however, was an entirely different matter. It might not have had magical properties but it was, in a word, perfect. He had come close to making the smithy his home during its fashioning. The balance was perfect, the steel flawless, and the hilt suited to his hand alone. If ever a sword could have been called magical, 'twas the one he held in his hands. His knighting sword was equally spectacular, true, but the one he held currently was . . . well, it wasn't anything he particularly cared to leave behind. But Imogen looked so desperate—

He took his sword and drove it into the crack between the stones.

Imogen put her hands on the hilt, stilled it, then closed her eyes, as if she expected something to happen. Again.

Nothing did, of course. Phillip wasn't surprised, but what else was there to be done? He could have tried to warn her, but to what end? The woman was obviously determined. He glanced about himself to gauge others' reactions to the madness. The twins were standing on the other side of the table, looking far too interested for their father's peace of mind. Phillip could only imagine what sorts of mischief Theo and Sam would now attempt to combine in the great halls of anyone who would let them through the doors. Floors would be assaulted, he was certain.

Rose was simply staring at Imogen thoughtfully, as if she hadn't expected anything else.

He put his hand over Imogen's. "Perhaps a rest, aye?"

She looked absolutely stricken. He started to reassure her that the world had not ended when he heard a commotion outside that made him wonder if he might need to rethink that. He pulled his sword free of the floor.

"I'll bring it back later," he promised, wondering if that was perhaps the most daft thing he'd said all day. He left Rose with the little lads, then walked out of the great hall, half expecting to see a pitched battle.

Instead what he saw was the remains of a failed mutiny. Heather's men had been herded into a little group with his own men surrounding them. He loped down the stairs and walked over to where his captain stood, looking impossibly grim.

"They're unhappy with the change of command," Cederic stated.

"Are they?" Phillip asked politely. "And do they have a suggestion on how that might be resolved?"

"I believe," Cederic said, "that they would like to see your head on a pike, my lord. Preferably outside the front gates. They're a tidy lot, apparently."

"Aye, who are ye to march in here and take over?" Neill spat, all pretense at friendliness gone. "You, the least of the spawn of that heartless whoreson from Artane—"

Neill stopped speaking. Phillip supposed that might have been because his fist was currently residing in Neill's mouth. He took a deep breath, examined the back of his hand for embedded teeth, then looked at Heather's captain to see if he'd had a change of heart. Apparently not.

"I am someone whose right it is to manage this keep," Phillip said evenly, "my father's parentage aside, though you will pay for that insult to my honored grandmère. Do you dare dispute my claim?"

"I do," Neill shouted. "Prove it!"

"The banns were read," Phillip said, "and not recently, if memory serves. I've heard nothing of anyone claiming I have no right to this cesspit of a holding. Your lady is missing, your lord is dead, and his son doesn't seem to be manning the high table."

"But—"

"Show me to your priest," Phillip said shortly. "We'll see what he has to say on the matter."

Neill hesitated only briefly before dragging his sleeve across his mouth, then turning and walking away. Phillip followed him with a pair of cousins and his two fiercest guardsmen at his heels.

He held out hope that the chapel would be at least as clean as the stables, but once he reached it, he wondered why he'd wasted any energy wishing for the same. He paused and looked at a dark substance that seemed to have flowed from beneath the front doors, dripped down the stairs, and pooled on the courtyard. Blood?

Ah, nay. Ale. He realized that as soon as the doors were opened for him and he had the opportunity to look inside.

The priest was indeed in the chapel, which seemed fitting, with what looked to be the entire collection of the keep's libations, which seemed less fitting. How no one had noticed their lack of drink he couldn't have said, but perhaps those at Haemesburgh were of a less pious bent than others and had never set foot in the chapel.

It only took a moment or two before he thought he might understand the hesitation. The priest was not only beyond drunken, he was angry. Phillip hadn't but walked into the chapel before the man was spewing out slurs against Scots, Englishmen, and the makers of the ale he'd obviously had far too much of.

"Bartholomew," Phillip bellowed.

His squire was, as always, there by his elbow, uneasy but dependable. "Aye, my lord Phillip?"

"I seem to sense this one is babbling in the priests' language."

Bartholomew's eyes were very wide, but that was nothing noteworthy. He was perhaps better suited to the peace and tranquility of a monastery than he was the rigors of more earthy pursuits, but that was not his lot at present. He gulped, then nodded.

"He is, my lord," Bartholomew agreed.

"Translate for me, would you?" Phillip didn't need that aid, to be sure, but there was no sense in anyone in the keep knowing as much. It was always wise to have a secret or two in reserve. He'd learned that from his sire, whom others underestimated at their peril.

He had to admit that Robin of Artane was a damned fine chess player.

Bartholomew hesitated. "Would you prefer me to leave out all the vile bits?"

"Oh, nay," Phillip said, "just give me the unvarnished whole."

Bartholomew took a deep breath, then faithfully relayed all that was said. It consisted of little more than the same disparaging of anyone the priest seemed capable of bringing to mind. Phillip had to admit even he was having difficulty understanding the man, but Bartholomew was doing his manful best to give a faithful recounting of what he was hearing.

There was a great deal about secrets and shadows and undiscovered plots, which Phillip credited to the man being very possessive of his drink.

It took another quarter hour, but the priest finally seemed to run out of dire things to talk about. He gasped out a final curse or two, then his eyes rolled back in his head and he slumped over a sack of what Phillip was sure would turn out to be hops. Once he began to snore, Phillip set a guard over him, then turned back to his most pressing problem.

"Do you have a dungeon?" he asked Neill. "You'll need proper accommodations, wouldn't you agree?"

The man's eyes fair bulged from his head. "As if ye'd have the—"

He grunted, his eyelids closed, and he slid to the ground in a very untidy heap. Myles stood behind him, resheathing his sword. He looked at Phillip.

"They have a rather austere garrison hall, my lord," he said easily. "The others have been invited to take their ease there. Shall this one join them?"

"I don't like the look of him," Cederic said with a frown. "I think we should make an example of him, if you'll have my opinion, Lord Phillip. A final example, if you understand me."

His captain was generally not wrong in his opinions, but Phillip couldn't bring himself to consider Sir Neill anything but ambitious and irritated to find his ambitions thwarted. There was no sense in not simply confining him until he had better reasons to look for another solution.

"I'll meet him in the morning in the lists instead," Phillip said. "Perhaps we'll come to a better understanding there."

"If you wish, my lord," Cederic said slowly. "I'll simply say that I've seen his kind before. He won't rest until he's had what he feels he's due."

"Perhaps I'll manage to convince him to take a different course," Phillip said firmly. "Tomorrow, in the lists. I appreciate your aid, Sir Cederic. If you can see to a guard for the lads locked up in the garrison hall, I'll see to our defenses."

And what lay outside the walls as well, though he supposed that would keep for another few moments. He watched his captain direct a pair of lads to heave Neill up and over their shoulders. He was carried off without delay. After exchanging a glance with Sir Wiscard, which he knew would result in the keep being secured by their own men, Phillip paced along the edge of the courtyard and examined the most pressing mystery of all: what had happened to the lord of Haemesburgh's family.

Heather was most definitely missing, perhaps either dead or escaped. Her squire had been masquerading as chatelaine for the saints only knew how long. The keep's captain had been acting as the keep's lord for a likewise indeterminate amount of time and didn't seem particularly inclined to give up the opportunity to take his turn in the lord's chair. For all Phillip knew, Neill had been the one to insist that Hamish don gel's clothes and pass himself off as the lady of the keep.

Obviously things were not as he'd assumed they would be. Granted, he hadn't visited but a time or two in the past five years, but he'd accepted being rebuffed by a woman leaning over the walls and telling him to go to hell, a woman he'd been fairly sure had been Heather of Haemesburgh but now suspected might have been her squire. He'd sent missives, true, and Heather had deigned to reply, telling him in no uncertain terms that he wasn't welcome in the keep. He wondered now if that hadn't been Heather, but rather someone writing in her stead? Perhaps it was time to have a look at the priest's hand and see if it looked familiar.

And perhaps whilst he was about that goodly work, he could look at himself in a water trough and learn to recognize a complete idiot when he saw one.

'Twas nothing more than he deserved for having allowed events to proceed along without him for so long. His father would have agreed.

He stopped thirty paces from the great hall when he realized that Imogen was standing at the hall door, looking as if she had no idea what to do with herself. There was another mystery there. She was obviously not Heather of Haemesburgh, but that left him with no clue to who she was in truth. He would have simply asked her who she was and why she found herself in his betrothed's keep, but he had trouble understanding her.

He paused. That was perhaps not as true as he would have liked. Her accent was very odd, but she wasn't completely beyond understanding. There were other things about her that he found much more disturbing, but he wasn't quite ready to face those as yet.

At least she'd given up trying to filch a sword. He had aunts and cousins of the feminine persuasion who thought nothing amiss with a woman hoisting a blade. He hadn't wanted to offend them, but secretly he'd been appalled. A woman with a sword? What next? Nay, 'twas a man's duty and privilege to protect those weaker than he and in his case, that included every woman he knew.

He paused, looked at his cousin Rose standing next to Imogen, and wondered if he might be wise to revisit that opinion. 'Twas possible, he had to concede, that he might be wrong.

"My lord?"

He turned to see Sir Myles standing there, looking fierce. Ah, a distraction. He welcomed it gladly.

"Aye?"

"I wondered if you cared to send a scouting party outside the gates?"

"Of course," Phillip said with a nod. Damnation, he was in trouble. He was going to be dead if he didn't solve a few of the tangles in front of him. A daft, terrified wench inside his walls, a garrison he couldn't trust also inside those walls, and unknown foes waiting for him outside.

He didn't want to think about what else he might discover at the most inconvenient time possible.

Chapter 11

I mogen sat on the steps leading up to the great hall, reflected on the crazy that had become her life, and tried to pinpoint just where she'd gone wrong.

She had been a dutiful daughter. She had tried to keep the peace with her siblings. She had stayed out of trouble, bitten her tongue, avoided conflict like the plague. It was possible that she'd been a little too agreeable to whatever plan her most determined sibling had hatched, plans that always seemed to put her in the hot seat, taking the blame for not only instigating but carrying out whatever nastiness had taken place, but surely that shouldn't count against her when Karma was tallying things up, should it?

All right, so she'd escaped to college as quickly as possible without obtaining the obligatory validictorial pole position, but she had attended a pair of exclusive institutions for both her undergrad and graduate degrees. She'd even paid for it all herself thanks to the jump start of a small inheritance from her late grandmother.

She paused. So she'd almost run over one of her older brothers when he'd tried to appropriate her college money, but he'd had the reflexes to get out of her way—something she'd been sure would serve him well in the future with angry clients—so that was all good. But the truth was, it had been one more in a very long series of things she shouldn't have put up with.

She wondered if the universe was now trying to tell her to stop lying down and letting people walk all over her.

She stared out over the courtyard of a castle she never should have come to and wondered where in the world she was. Or, more to the point, when in the world she was. It looked like Haemesburgh, but then again not. Gone were the modern trappings, the floodlights, the bare walls where wooden outbuildings had no doubt stood in the past but suffered the ravages of time. Now, the place looked so damned medieval, she thought she might never want to see anything medieval again.

She had resigned herself to the possibility of being in a time not her own, though it still seemed so far-fetched as to be impossible. People didn't travel to other time zones unless they were on board a nice 747 with complimentary meals and drinks. She didn't believe in paranormal happenings and she had most definitely not wasted any time watching all the shows Marcus had recommended. That guy was just short of crazy with his enormous collection of super-duper paranormal spying stuff that he was sure would camouflage him enough that ghosts wouldn't notice him, leaving him free to get said specters on tape and thereby cement his reputation as a first-class ghost hunter.

It had done nothing but cement his reputation in her mind as a first-rate crazy person, but now she was beginning to wish she had at least listened occasionally to what he'd been saying. She almost had the urge to give him a call and find out what he thought of her current straits.

She didn't bother to pull out her phone. She was out of range and out of explanations for what had happened to her. She'd hoped for power chords, mischievous siblings, big-name directors putting her to the test to see how she operated under pressure. She had clung to the possibility of a hallucination, a barely adverted insulin coma, the fallout from not enough coffee before getting on the train.

She had even hoped for something more . . . well, something more paranormal, like Heather being a witch, the cabbie being a kindly though unsettled guide to another dimension, or time travel without a phone booth. She'd gotten a sword away from a teenager and jammed it into the floor to see if it would transport her back to where she'd come from. Nothing had changed her situation. She was trapped in a place full of things she didn't understand, people she didn't know, and languages she didn't speak.

She needed to get home. She just had no idea how she was going to manage it.

The shadow of someone sitting down next to her left her jumping a little in surprise. She saw she had been joined on her step by that woman who she was just sure had spoken English but now seemed incapable of speaking anything but French. Well, to be entirely accurate, she spoke a bizarrely accented French and that equally weird English that everyone seemed to be speaking, as if they'd minored in Anglo-Saxon and needed to keep up their language on the off chance they might run into Geoffrey Chaucer. The woman sitting next to her claimed she also spoke Gaelic, though Imogen couldn't be sure about that, not being a Scot herself yet having a deep fondness for plaid in all its varieties.

She looked at her new friend and had to admit she was drop-dead gorgeous. Aqua eyes that would have been the envy of any print model, perfect skin, perfect teeth . . . and a mouth like a sailor. Imogen listened to her chew out a lad who seemed not to be doing what he was supposed to and had to laugh a little at words that seemed to cross language barriers.

"Understand that, did you?" the woman said.

"Yes," Imogen managed.

"I'm Rose," she said. "Still. And you're Imogen."

Well, she could understand that much French, especially when it was liberally sprinkled with names she recognized. "Yes," Imogen managed. "I am."

"But you're not the lady of Haemesburgh."

"No," Imogen said slowly. "Why would I be that?"

Rose shrugged. "You're here and Heather is gone. I was just curious if you knew her or had decided to trade places with her for some reason."

"Heather," Imogen echoed, feeling quite suddenly as if she were having an out-of-body experience. "You know Heather?"

"Of her," Rose corrected. "I've never met her myself."

Imogen started to say that she certainly had met the woman—and she was very tempted to list a few of her more unsettling qualities—but good sense stopped her just in time. Whatever current Heather Rose thought she might know couldn't possibly be the same person as the Heather in twenty-first-century Scotland. The names were the same, but that happened a lot in families. It was a coincidence.

Surely.

"That was an interesting scene inside with the swords."

Imogen followed that, eventually, but the effort was starting to give her a headache. "Yes, it was."

"You seem to be interested in swords," Rose continued relentlessly. "I prefer arrows, but that's just me. If you need Phillip's sword, I'm sure he'll bring it back eventually. Did you have a particular reason for wanting it?"

Imogen wasn't sure where to even begin with that, so she made a few inarticulate sounds and willingly relinquished the floor when Rose carried on as if she'd already answered.

"You could borrow a sword from one of my cousins instead, perhaps. Let me point the lads out to you, that you might recognize them at a later time if you need them."

Imogen nodded because she didn't have the strength to protest. If Rose wanted to identify potential victims so Imogen could indulge in sword-stealing activities later, there was no point in stopping her.

"That lad over there is my brother, Jackson," Rose said. "Those are my cousins Connor, Theopholis, and Sam standing next to them. And that is Phillip there. See him?"

Imogen did indeed. She had the feeling that no one could look at anyone else anytime he walked into a room.

"'Tis his squire, Bartholomew, standing behind him. Heather of Haemesburgh's men are currently being held in the garrison hall."

At least that's what Imogen hoped she was saying. All that time in grad school spent studying Renaissance and eighteenth-century French poetry just wasn't helping all that much. Rose wasn't speaking in iambic pentameter, which hampered Imogen's ability to understand her, and there was that truly wacky accent she seemed to be using, but the upside was that Rose was speaking to her as if she'd been approximately six years old. Maybe if she spent the rest of the day listening to that, she might actually begin to understand a little of what was being said around her.

"Let's go find something unpoisoned to eat."

That translated fairly well. Imogen pushed herself to her feet, swayed, then decided that everything would look better if she just had a clear head. She couldn't make a plan to get where she needed to go unless she knew where she was starting from and had had a good breakfast. Her father the corporate raider said as much and while he might have been perennially in the race for worst father of the year, he was very good at cleaning up messes. He would have had a robust culinary start to the day, then looked at her situation with a pitiless eye and a stack of pink slips at his elbow.

She couldn't fire the people in front of her, but she could certainly do her best to figure out whom to trust. Phillip seemed actually like the safest bet—

She froze. He had said his name was de Piaget, hadn't he?

Stephen de Piaget is the current lord of Artane . . .

Tilly had said that on the train north. At the time, she had pushed the conversation aside because it hadn't seemed critical to what she'd needed to do. Now she wished she had let Tilly go on about it for a bit longer. Actually, she wished she had let Tilly rent a car and take her to that enormous castle on the edge of the sea. Who knew what might have happened? She might have had an encounter with a real live nobleman and gotten a private tour of his castle.

She didn't want to think about what she'd gotten instead. The truth was, she was in deep trouble and sinking fast. There were no jets traveling overhead. Her cell phone wouldn't stay charged forever and there wasn't a plug in sight. People were speaking languages she struggled to understand and wasn't sure she wanted to become more familiar with. Guys were carrying swords, and those didn't look to be swords from the prop trailer. She didn't see any running water, and there was definitely no catering service pulling up with sandwiches she would have turned her nose up at twenty-four hours ago but was now thinking would look pretty damn five-star.

She watched Phillip de Piaget give a teenager an encouraging shove in her direction, then take himself off to do heaven only knew what. Imogen recognized the kid. He'd been the one she'd used as a crutch that first day after she'd dropped off the drawbridge into Phillip de Piaget's arms—what a pity she hadn't enjoyed that nearly as much as she should have.

"What is it, Bartholomew?" Rose asked.

"My lord Phillip asked me to come and help the lady Imogen with her tongues."

Imogen sized up the trembling, skinny teenager in front of her, then looked at Rose. "My tongues?"

"Bartholomew is the son of a monk," Rose said with a shrug, "and knows all sorts of useful things about several languages. Phillip obviously thought it might amuse you to have a lesson or two."

"Very kind of him."

"He is that."

Imogen wasn't sure she should ask what sort of lessons they were beginning, so she didn't. She also decided it was best not to ask why little Bart had a board, quill, ink, and parchment. There was obviously someone who was truly into reenactment.

She took the opportunity while he was making himself comfortable on a stool in front of her to indulge in a minor, silent freak-out. She was tired, hungry, and out of her depth. She didn't like that feeling of not knowing exactly what the lay of the land was so she could get out of the heat of battle, so to speak, at a moment's notice. Worse still was to have seen what the landscape looked like and know it wasn't going to be of any use to her.

She'd already tried the front gates, but that way lay dead knights and other bad guys lurking out in what should have been the village. She'd tried the great hall, but that way had proved equally unresponsive. She supposed she could go around the keep and borrow swords from every single guy there, but she suspected none of them would behave any differently than what she'd already tried.

What she needed was to find that sword with the big blue stone in the crossbar.

But even beginning that search was going to be impossible unless she could ask the right questions of the right people and she wasn't going to be able to do that until she could understand everyone around her better.

She couldn't say she was good at very many things outside of avoiding familial drama, but she was good at organizing things. Language first, then she would consider her next step. She could only hope it would include a sword, a trapdoor back to where she was supposed to be, and something with chocolate at the end of the road.

Chapter 12

Phillip paced along the edge of the lists, grateful he was still alive to do so. It had been a very long day that didn't look as if it intended to end any time soon, no matter what the sky might be telling him.

He knew he shouldn't have felt so uneasy with so many of his own men around him and all of Haemesburgh's men safely tucked away in the garrison hall, but he was. He supposed his unease came less from the men inside the keep and more from who was outside the keep wanting in. He had walked the walls that afternoon, scanning the countryside and wondering who on his list of enemies he could credit for the annoyance of the day before. He wasn't sure he was enough of a pain in the arse to have earned all that many enemies, but perhaps he was. His father and uncles would have been proud of him.

He stopped, sighed, then leaned back against the stone and stared unseeing at the muddy ground in front of him. His list of problems was quite short and the solutions to them simple enough. He needed to determine what to do with Imogen, find his grandfather's sword that seemed to have gone missing, and reassure Heather's squire, Hamish, that he never need put on skirts again.

He wasn't sure any of that constituted an auspicious start to his days of being lord of Haemesburgh.

At least he'd had the good sense to bring his own stores with him, though the little twins had volunteered to take on the dangerous task of investigating the priest's larder on the off chance they would need something else to eat. He suspected their constitutions would survive just about anything they might find, but he didn't like to think about having to tell his uncle Nicholas that he'd had to bury his youngest lads. He had sent Connor off after his brothers, happy to give at least three of his company something constructive to do.

He looked toward the garrison hall to make certain there was no untoward activity there, but apparently Cederic had secured the lads without trouble. Haemesburgh's defenders were not numerous and thankfully not very well trained. That would need to be remedied at his earliest convenience, though he was half tempted to simply send them all back to their homes and start over. He also had to admit there was a part of him that wondered just what in the hell he was thinking to come inside a keep that wasn't his and simply take it over. He supposed others had done worse. At least he could claim his betrothal to Heather as right to the lord's chair. Not even Sir Neill could claim that.

Or at least he *hoped* Neill couldn't claim that. The saints preserve him if Heather had decided to exchange him for the captain of her father's garrison.

He glanced again at the garrison hall, then walked away thoughtfully. The truth was, he couldn't keep the entire garrison locked up there forever. He was going to have to have answers and hopefully have them before the sun set. He had the feeling waiting any longer would lead to things he didn't care for, such as a battle within walls he very much wanted to call his own.

The first thing, he supposed, was to start from the most pressing problem and work his way on from there. He had to find out why neither Heather of Haemesburgh nor Imogen Maxwell were where they were supposed to be.

He wandered around the courtyard as carelessly as possible lest anyone think him as troubled as he felt. He didn't hear any shrieking coming from the chapel, so perhaps the twins had left the priest's ale alone for the moment. He started toward the stables only to find himself stopping in front of the smithy. He was surprised by two things: one, that there didn't seem to be a blacksmith inside the hut doing any pounding; and two, that the place seemed to be occupied by the study of language. He paused just outside the doorway where he could listen to what was going on inside without being seen.

He would have to give Bartholomew a day of liberty more often, for the lad was certainly earning it presently. He leaned against the wall and listened for a bit longer, just to make sure he was hearing things aright. It was hard to believe that a gel who had been babbling nonsense for two days could have made such improvements already in her speech, but perhaps she was extraordinarily clever.

It only took half an hour before he was sorry he hadn't confined himself to the garrison. Her French had improved, true, but she still occasionally muttered in a language that unsettled him. The targets of her ire seemed to be her siblings and something called *damned method actors*. If she occasionally gave vent to ruminations about shows of reality, well, who was he to blame her? The reality of his own straits was sobering. The saints only knew what hers entailed.

He eventually followed her as she left the smithy and made her way to the stables. He found himself a decent place to lean and watched her dig about in a stall, looking behind piles of hay and under saddles and tack. *Trying this one last time* was what she said as she did so. She muttered about other things as well, occasionally giving vent to what he could only assume was a curse in her language.

It was an unusual language indeed.

He was left considering things he hadn't wanted to before. He had spent his share of time at other keeps during his youth, squiring for a pair of his uncles in turn, spending a year with his aunt Isabelle in France. He had seen and heard strange things from time to time, but ignored them. He'd been a serious lad with dreams of swords and glory with no time for things that didn't fit into his plans. The oddities of his family had been brushed aside easily enough.

That had changed a little when he'd grown older and acquired what he'd thought to be a sufficient number of years to be admitted to the parleys of men. He had been included in most discussions of the happenings of the day. But there had been other meetings between his uncle Jackson, his uncles Montgomery and Nicholas, and his father, meetings he'd never been privy to. He'd rarely doubted his own worth, but he had to admit there had been times—

Well, that was foolishness. His father had been fair enough with him, and who was to say what his elder relatives discussed? They were welcome to their secrets.

He came back to himself to find that Imogen had given up her searching of the stall and was simply standing there in the straw. She looked impossibly tired. She had even ceased giving voice to what she'd been saying in that tongue he didn't recognize.

He cursed silently. Very well, so he shouldn't have recognized anything she'd been saying. But he did. He could have sworn she had blurted out a word or two that in his youth he'd heard his own auntie Persephone use now and again when she had thought no one was listening.

Who the bloody hell was that woman and why was she babbling things that made him uneasy?

He didn't like where his thoughts were taking him. He didn't like being forced to face all sorts of things he hadn't wanted to look at, things he'd buried in his past, things he'd ignored for years but were now floating to the surface of what was left of his mind.

The first thing that presented itself to him in all its uncomfortable glory was the courtship of his aunt Amanda and her husband, Jackson Kilchurn IV. It had been, from all accounts, a tumultuous affair, fraught with difficulties and adventures. His uncle had gone to London to gather gold to buy Amanda's hand, which might not have been anything noteworthy except that Amanda had believed he was gone forever and entered a nunnery. Only Jake's quick tongue and bags of gold had soothed not only the king but Phillip's grandfather Rhys enough to purchase time with his love in front of a priest.

Phillip was beginning to wonder if there was more to that tale than he'd been led to believe. He had spent his share of time at Ravensthorpe, after all, haunting the keep and the surrounding environs with Rose and Jackson. He had stumbled upon his uncle Jake about his labors of being the keep's lord with its attendant necessity of indulging in the heartfelt curse now and again.

Curses that sounded remarkably like the curses Imogen had been using.

Imogen left the stall suddenly, startling him. He stepped back into the shadows only to almost give vent to a less-than-manly squeak when he realized he wasn't alone. He didn't feel any steel against his throat, though, so he felt safe waiting until Imogen and her small entourage of Rose and Bartholomew had left the stables before he turned to see whom he had backed into.

It was, somewhat unsurprisingly, Jackson Kilchurn V.

Phillip shifted. He didn't do that sort of thing as a rule, but he was presently uncomfortable past what he could reasonably be expected to endure. He looked at Jackson and simply couldn't bring himself to give voice to his thoughts. It occurred to him—and he had to spare a brief wish that those sorts of things would stop occurring to him—that not only had he heard his uncle Montgomery's wife, Persephone, use those curses Imogen had been using, he'd heard Jackson's sire do the same.

By the saints, was he surrounded by lunatics?

He took a bracing breath. "How long have you been there?"

Jackson didn't shift. "Long enough."

Phillip didn't like the look in his cousin's eye. "She seems distraught. Imogen, I mean."

"I knew who you meant."

Phillip imagined Jackson did, damn him for never looking as if anything could unsettle him. He cleared his throat. "Imogen's tongue is strange."

"Her French is almost unintelligible," Jackson corrected. "As is her English. If that's what it can be called."

Phillip looked at him. "And yet she seems to know what she's saying in that strange tongue of hers."

"She could be mad."

"She could be," Phillip agreed. "But the thing is, I've heard the words she's saying in other places, spoken by other souls. Persephone, for one." He paused. "Uncle Montgomery's wife, Persephone."

"Thank you, Phillip, for making the connection for me."

Phillip would have glared at him, but he was too damned unnerved to. "What do you think?"

Jackson looked at him in disbelief. Phillip would have smiled, but, again, he could barely breathe normally.

"What do I think?" Jackson asked in a furious whisper. "What in the hell do you *think* I think?"

Phillip had thought himself jaded past the point of being surprised, but surprisingly enough, he wasn't. "Well, I honestly wouldn't presume to guess."

"Wouldn't you?"

Phillip would have thrown up his hands but he feared they might tremble overmuch. "I don't like where my thoughts are taking me."

"And where would that be?"

Phillip looked at his cousin evenly. "To Ravensthorpe, Jackson, to have a pointed conversation with your sire about a few of things he mutters under *his* breath."

"I'll come along."

Phillip imagined he would. He hardly dared voice his thoughts, but he supposed he didn't need to. Jackson had, after all, grown to manhood as Jake Kilchurn's son. He stared off into the shadows of the stables and wondered where Imogen had learned to speak as she did. He wondered how it was she had come to be in Haemesburgh where no one knew her. He wondered about those odd numbers on the back of her cloak that was like no cloak he had ever seen.

He wondered why Jackson had so many things he refused to speak of.

He looked at his cousin. "Do you think thoughts you shouldn't?"

"Every day," Jackson said grimly, "though the price for doing so is steep. Most of the time, cousin, I simply try not to. My life is too full of irony and it tends to have sharp teeth when it rears its ugly head." He pushed away from the door. "I'll go see how the madness is progressing. I'm not sure the keep is entirely safe."

Phillip was beginning to suspect that the keep was the least of his worries.

There was a mystery before him named Imogen, a mystery

he knew he was going to have to solve sooner rather than later, a mystery he honestly didn't want to investigate. It would have been so much easier to have had Heather back on the walls, flinging disgusting things at him. Only it hadn't been Heather doing it, it had been her squire, Hamish. Hamish, who likely knew many things he wouldn't want to divulge.

And all the while there was a woman who was currently standing in the middle of the courtyard, looking so lost that Phillip hardly knew what to do to offer her comfort, and he was far more skilled in the chivalric arts than either of his brothers.

He considered all the things he could do over the next fortnight and held them up against what he *should* do over the same span of days. It would have been so simple to wish Imogen good fortune and send her on her way whilst he continued on with his plan to build an empire in the north.

Simple, but not exactly the chivalrous thing to do.

He sighed and dragged his hand through his hair. His honor demanded that he aid her however he could. If that meant helping her home before he attended to his own affairs, so be it. He watched her for another moment or two before he walked out into the courtyard and stopped next to her.

She looked at him bleakly, but said nothing.

"Let's find supper," he said quietly. "We'll sort getting you home on the morrow, if that suits."

She closed her eyes briefly, then looked at him. "Thank you."

"My pleasure." He offered her his arm, then escorted her to the great hall where it seemed someone from his ranks had been busy preparing a meal. He saw Imogen seated, started to leave her there, then decided that something to eat would serve him as well. And he did his damndest to ignore her hands that trembled just a bit as she took a cup from one of the twins.

He would help her get home, because it was what he needed to do. Unfortunately, he had the feeling that if he wanted help with that, he was definitely going to have to have a pointed talk with one of the elder statesmen in his family.

He just didn't want to know what that talk would reveal.

Chapter 13

Imogen wandered around the castle courtyard, resigned to the fact that while she was acquiring lots of quirky ideas, she wasn't going to be able to use them anytime soon because she was hopelessly trapped in the past. She wasn't sure how far in the past because she hadn't dared ask anyone the current date.

There were two things that made life seem a little more bearable. First, she'd had a decent dinner and a safe night's sleep the night before. Of course, her dreams had been troubled by an endless hunt for power cords and perturbing siblings, but maybe she couldn't have expected anything less. Her search for either the evening before had proved fruitless. All she'd gotten herself was handwringing from Bartholomew and a never-ending string of alarmed looks from everyone else.

Second, Phillip de Piaget had promised to get her home.

She'd been clinging to that offer as if it were all that stood between her and a life without modern sanitation and a decent Internet connection, which she supposed it was. Phillip hadn't said when he would help her, or even how, but since she was fresh out of ideas, she was more than willing to let him see what he could come up with. It was very strange to think of turning her future over to someone she didn't know, but maybe dire circumstances called for unusual solutions. Until then, maybe the best thing she could do was soak up the local culture and stay out of the way.

She was currently being accompanied by Rose and those blond boys, Theo and Sam. Imogen paused, then turned to look at them. Twins were unusual, but identical twins carrying swords and stirring up mischief in a medieval castle—

She felt her mouth fall open. Maybe jet lag had been more debilitating at the time than she'd feared, but she could have sworn one of those boys had to be related to that gorgeous guy who had stuffed her underwear back into her suitcase in King's Cross station. Talk about a family resemblance. And that guy had used some interesting language, hadn't he?

She shut her mouth with a snap. If she didn't pull back on those reins, her rampaging imagination was going to run so far away with her that she would never get back to where she needed to be.

Rose touched her arm. "Let's go to the lists, shall we?"

"Sure," Imogen managed, grateful for the interruption. She chalked her speculations up to not enough sleep and an intense desire to try to fit puzzle pieces where they surely weren't meant to go, then followed Rose to what looked to be an all-out battle.

All right, so she'd worked mostly on movies where romance abounded and sappy scripts were the order of the day. That didn't mean she hadn't seen prop rooms. She'd brought coffee to casting people interviewing stuntmen who were boasting about their fighting skills. She'd even gone so far as to watch the bonus features on several DVDs where the details of fight-scene choreography had been revealed. But she'd never seen two guys really look like they wanted to kill each other.

She declined an invitation to venture farther into the lists. She was more than happy to stay on the outskirts where she could make a break for it if the show got too intense. That and she'd already been clunked on the forehead with a sword. It was something she really didn't want to repeat.

She realized one of the twins had brought her a stool only because she almost backed over it and went sprawling. The tweenager apologized profusely and with such genuine regret, she couldn't hold it against him. She also couldn't hold herself up on her feet once she realized that one of the combatants was none other than Phillip de Piaget, the guy who couldn't possibly have anything to do with anyone from that gigantic castle she'd seen on her way north to Edinburgh.

Rose sat down next to her stool on a bench that the boys subsequently produced. It had also seen much better days, but she supposed that shouldn't have surprised her. The whole castle needed some serious remodeling. Maybe that was why Heather of Haemesburgh had orchestrated her being trapped in it with no hope of escape—

She almost fell off her stool. Had Heather orchestrated her whole nightmare for something that ridiculous?

Imogen stared at her surroundings with an entirely new eye. If the Heather of the future was—and she could hardly believe she was allowing herself to even consider it—the Heather of the past, then surely she would know all about the condition of the castle. She might have been looking for someone to fix up the place while she was masquerading as a very rich, very well-dressed modern noblewoman. She was probably just tapping her foot, waiting for Imogen to take care of staging the place so she could rush back in time and . . . what? Return to no running water and no Internet?

"He's very good."

Imogen realized one of the boys was speaking to her. The second thing that occurred to her was that she understood him more easily than she would have the day before. Maybe all that time with Bartholomew the scribbler had done her some good. He'd been fairly enthusiastic about tidying up her French, but when he realized she could understand rudimentary Latin, his joy had been visible. That had given her a headache for more than one reason, actually, because where the hell in the world was she that Latin was a happy experience for a teenager?

"Well, of course he's very good," said the other one. "He's Uncle Robin's son after all."

She listened to the twins discuss Phillip, critiquing him as ruthlessly as any modern kid would have pulled apart an action hero. Only Phillip de Piaget looked a bit like he was about ready to kill someone, so she wondered why they dared say anything at all.

"You are unaccustomed to this."

Imogen looked at Rose sitting next to her and wondered just what *that* gal was accustomed to. "Um, no," she managed. "We don't do this every day at home." That was an understatement, but there was no point in trying to explain it. "Do you?"

"I don't," Rose said, "but that is only because I'm a woman. I do exercise with the bow, though even that was a hard-fought battle with my sire."

Imogen could sense that there was a topic that was going to get her somewhere pretty fast. She left off watching Phillip try to kill the guy who was trying to kill him, then shifted to look at Rose.

"Your father was all right with a bow," she repeated, "but not a sword?"

"Aye, but he's fairly forward-thinking." She smiled. "That, and my mother is very strong-willed. She insisted that I be allowed this boon. My sire generally lets her have her way in things."

"Sounds like a great guy."

"Oh, he is," Rose agreed. "I daresay that has much to do with why I'm not already wed, though my years weigh heavily on me now. 'Tis difficult to find a man as reasonable as my sire."

"But you're so young," Imogen protested.

"A score and four," Rose said. "Very old indeed."

Imogen supposed it was probably best not to mention she was twenty—er, a score and six herself. But since they were talking numbers, maybe there was no reason not to get a few details. She could hardly believe she was even willing to consider her current situation anything but an elaborate hoax created by her evil siblings—she realized she was still clinging to that hope—but she'd spent two nights sleeping on hay, and she was looking at a guy in chain mail who was using a medieval-looking broadsword like it was a fencing foil. She took a deep breath to stop any lustful thoughts in their tracks and turned back to her new friend.

"And what does the current monarch think the appropriate age is for women to marry?" she asked casually, hoping she wasn't accidentally inquiring about the location of the local witch tribunal. It wouldn't have surprised her to have had her second eldest brother arrange that kind of thing for her, being the dastardly lawyer he was.

"Henry?" Rose shrugged. "He's too busy fretting over the loyalty of his barons to worry about that."

"Loyalty of his barons," Imogen repeated, wanting to make sure she was getting that right as well.

"Aye," Rose said. "There are stirrings amongst the nobles for more rights for themselves and less for the king." She smiled. "But such is life in the Year of Our Lord's Grace 1254, wouldn't you agree?"

Imogen felt herself begin to shake. She looked at Rose and realized that the edges of her vision were beginning to blur. It was the oddest thing she'd ever had happen to her.

1254. That just couldn't mean what it sounded like it meant because that would mean she was eight hundred years out of her comfort zone . . .

She woke, only then realizing that she'd been asleep. Or maybe she'd fainted. She wasn't sure which it was, only that Phillip de Piaget was leaning over her, looking at her with alarm.

"Don't stab me," she croaked.

He looked at the sword in his hand, then handed it off to someone. "Are you ill?" he asked, sounding genuinely concerned.

"Oh, no," she said, though she supposed she wasn't going to be sitting up for another few minutes. She wasn't ill. She was absolutely, positively, unarguably crazy.

It was a comforting realization, really. She'd been worried that she wasn't being a good sport about the whole reality show thing. She'd deliberately pasted on smiles when she felt like screaming, on the off chance that some director or other was hiding in a back room, watching her remotely to see how she did under pressure. She had held it together long past when she would have liked to have freaked out, simply to deny any potential brother or sister the pleasure of having a really great story to tell about that time they'd put their baby sister in a castle full of horse manure and watched her go bonkers.

1254.

It wasn't possible, but unless everyone was in on the joke, it was the truth.

She accepted help up from the twins and did her best to perch back on her stool without tipping it over. She looked at the boys, mirrors of each other, and guessed they were pushing ten. A guy stood behind them, probably about eighteen, who had to have been their older brother. He wasn't the guy who had helped her in King's Cross, though he certainly could have been related to that knight in shining armor.

She laughed. A knight in shining armor. She was certainly going to be surrounded by those in 1254, wasn't she?

"Phillip, should we bring her something to drink?" one of the twins said nervously.

"Aye, she looks unhinged," said the other one.

"If you can pry wine away from the priest, do so," Phillip said, looking unsettled himself. "She's had a shock. Rose, what did you say to her?"

"Nothing at all," Rose said. "I just waxed poetic about the desirable qualities of my sire. Perhaps her sire is not so perfect."

"My sire is an ass," Imogen said before she thought better of it. She looked at Rose. "I think I said that right."

"I think you did," Rose agreed with a smile. She looked at her cousin. "Phillip, we'll take care of her. Go back to your labors, if you like."

Imogen concentrated on breathing in and out. It occurred to her that she was breathing in and out some pretty medieval air and for some reason that made it more difficult to tolerate. That could have been because of the pervasive scent of horse manure, but then again, maybe not. Maybe it was the smell of panic—

She found herself with her head between her knees and from there it seemed like a pretty easy thing to just take a little roll into the muck. That was a mixed blessing to be sure. She now had mud—she hoped it was mud—in her hair, but the upside was she also had mud—she still hoped it was mud—covering up the personal ad on her backside. Her father, Mr. Motivation himself, would have approved of her positive outlook.

She again had help getting back up on her stool. She pushed her mud-slathered hair out of her face, then decided that was probably about as good as it was going to get for her with any attempts at grooming. Phillip watched her for a moment or two before he exchanged a pointed look with Rose and walked back out into the middle of the yard. Imogen knew that look. It was the sort of look one person sent to another that warned the one receiving the look to keep an eye on the crazy person in the vicinity. She sat up a little straighter and tucked a lock of hair behind her ear. She wasn't crazy, she was overwhelmed and slightly out of her depth.

And Phillip de Piaget was out of his mind. She watched him go at the guy in front of him again with his sword and was tempted to warn him that it might not be a good idea, but she supposed he knew what he was doing. The twins, however, seemed to have a slightly different opinion.

"He would be better with his own sword."

"Sam, that *is* his own sword."

"Nay, Theo, I speak of his knighting sword," one of the twins insisted. "It has magical properties."

"Don't be daft. 'Tis just a sword. Steel does not have magical properties."

"But that was Great-Grandfather's sword. There is much history and other things attached to it."

Imogen leaned back against the stone of the wall, hoped her hair would dry and flake soon enough, and let her mind wander. She listened to Sam and Theo discuss the magical properties of Phillip's sword and wondered if she could possibly be understanding them correctly.

A magical sword?

She looked at Rose. "What are they talking about?"

"Phillip's sword," Rose said. "'Tis rumored to have properties beyond the norm. I daresay those rumors were too tempting for those here at Haemesburgh to ignore."

Imogen uncrossed her eyes long enough to look at Rose in surprise. "What do you mean?"

"The lads stole Phillip's sword. It seems to have gone missing recently, which I'm sure irritates him greatly."

"What does it look like?"

Rose shrugged. "Much like a sword, I suppose. There is a stone in the hilt, though." She smiled. "'Tis the color of my eyes, which happen to be the color of my grandmère's eyes. Romantic, isn't it?"

Imogen would have put her head between her knees again, but she knew where that led. She concentrated on breathing in and out carefully so she didn't suck in anything that was dripping from her hair. She had the feeling she might have an idea what Phillip's sword looked like because she'd seen it resting in the spot behind the lord's chair in the great hall behind her.

Damn that Lady Heather. And speaking of Heather, she supposed that was something she could clear up right then. She looked at Rose. "What does Heather look like?"

"The lady Heather?" Rose asked with a frown. "Again, I've never seen her. I'm not even sure Phillip has seen her. We could ask her men, I suppose."

Imogen almost told Rose not to bother. She could almost not wrap her mind around it, but she was beginning to suspect that she might be the best one to ask about the missing lady of Haemesburgh.

"She has never appeared at the gates where she wasn't covered with manure and other off-putting things," Rose continued, "which didn't add to the inducement to wed with her."

"Did someone want to wed with her?" Imogen asked.

Rose looked at her as if she'd lost her mind. "Phillip did, of course. That's why we're here."

"He was going to *marry* her?" Imogen asked in surprise.

"That was the plan," Rose agreed. "He offered for her several years ago. Actually, he signed a betrothal with her father several years ago."

Imogen could hardly believe her ears. Phillip de Piaget had wanted Heather to marry him and she'd ditched him? What was she, nuts? She looked at Rose in disbelief. "Why aren't they married already?"

"She hasn't seemed to care for the idea, hence the flinging of things over the wall at him. Cesspit offerings, for the most part."

Imogen looked at Phillip. The only thing she thought she would ever fling at that guy there was herself. She shook her head. "He's gorgeous and she's an idiot."

"He can be a bit of a prig now and then." Rose smiled. "Too tidy, you know, and focused on things that might be tedious to a maiden, such as building an empire, training more intensely than his sire, making appearances at court."

"Sounds awful," Imogen said, suppressing the urge to roll her eyes. "And you said appearances at court. In London?"

"Or wherever Henry finds himself, but aye, most there." Rose looked thoughtfully at Phillip. "Heather was young, though not overly, and I think the thought of being wed to an Englishman might have troubled her." Rose shrugged. "She isn't here, her father isn't here, and her brother isn't here. Her father is reputedly dead, and we haven't found her brother's remains anywhere. Heather's whereabouts are a mystery."

Imogen stopped just short of snorting. Again, she had the feeling she knew exactly where that runaway bride was. Worse still, she had an even clearer feeling that Heather was not about to give up the luxury of a driver and French press coffee for a one way ticket back to the Middle Ages, all of which left her in a bit of a bind. It occurred to her abruptly that Heather hadn't sent her back to the past on a whim; she had sent her back as a substitute. It was tempting to indulge in a lengthy contemplation of what it might be like to be Phillip de Piaget's bride—

Nope, she couldn't even begin to go there. He might have been good looking and chivalrous, but he was also out there hacking at a scruffy-looking knight—one of Haemesburgh's natives, she guessed—and looking as if he meant business with that hacking. Life and death in medieval mud was just not for her.

Well, there was obviously going to have to be a switch, but that wasn't without its problems. First, she was going to have to find Heather and convince her to come back. Second, she was going to have to convince Heather to cough up Phillip's sword so she could go back. Third . . .

Well, third, she was going to have to figure out a way to get back to the future so she could try to see to numbers one and two. And she had the feeling getting home wasn't going to be the easiest of the three tasks.

She had no idea even where to start. It wasn't as if she could simply look at Rose and say, *hey, I need to get back to the twenty-first century; don't suppose you'd have any one-way tickets lying around in that quiver of yours, would ya?* She supposed she could ask around for a list of spooky British sites and go investigate those. But she wasn't sure she dared go on her own, and just how was she to get Phillip to come with her, never mind his having promised to help her? *Hey, stud-muffin, how about you leave off your empire building long enough to help me get home?*

She paused. That actually sounded less crazy than it might have otherwise. She could tell him that she knew where his sword might be hiding—

And then he would want to know why she knew and where she thought it was and that would likely end badly for her. She couldn't say she was up on the current level of tolerance for paranormal happenings, but if seasoned cab drivers were still freaking out about it eight hundred years in the future, that didn't bode all that well for it presently.

No, she would bide her time. Maybe she could talk someone into helping her get back to Edinburgh. Lots of spooky stuff happening there. She would get back to civilization, wander around until she felt the hair on the back of her neck stand up, then she would somehow get herself from one century to another. The exact mechanics of that were still in question, but she would work on that.

One thing was for sure: Heather of Haemesburgh had quite a few things to answer for.

Chapter 14

Failure was a bitter draught to swallow.

Phillip leaned on his sword and dragged his sleeve across his face. He had gone through the garrison knights one by one, besting each with more ease than he should have, all to no avail. The men had all been rotated in over the past three years and seemingly not a bloody one of them had ever had anything to do with anyone save Neill. The only thing they knew of the lady Heather was rumor that she was permanently unwell from the terror of having to wed with an English demon from Artane.

He suppressed the urge to roll his eyes. How Neill had managed to acquire the most superstitious and simpleminded of men in the area, he didn't know, but he had the feeling it had been deliberate. It was difficult to convince lads that he meant them no harm when they were continually looking at him as if he'd just sprung like a demon out of the forest, but there it was. As far as having any answers from them, there was little hope of it.

Neill was refusing to talk and Phillip couldn't bring himself to beat the tale out of him. He supposed his father would have simply stared the man down until Neill gave up and babbled his secrets in a bid for relief. Phillip didn't have his father's charm or his stamina. At the moment all he wanted to do was join that damned incoherent priest for a hefty tankard of ale and drink himself into oblivion.

The only hope left him was the lad standing against the wall, finally no longer dressed in skirts. Phillip caught his eye, then nodded pointedly toward the field. Hamish trotted out with a bit more enthusiasm than he'd displayed to that point, which boded well. Hamish also seemingly possessed a sword but didn't seem particularly inclined to use it, which boded less well. Phillip frowned at him.

"Let me see your skills."

"I'd rather talk," Hamish said, as easily as if he'd been speaking to a mate, "if it's all the same to you."

"'Tis not all the same to me," Phillip said sternly. He couldn't deny that before him likely stood a veritable font of information, though what he suspected he would have to go through to liberate it from that lad gave him pause. "I don't need someone to converse with at table," he continued, "I need men to stand with me and fight."

"I prefer to keep my boots unbloodied."

Phillip could have said the same thing himself, but his life was what it was and he needed men he could rely on. He looked at Hamish coolly.

"I could kill you as easily as to talk to you."

"But you wouldn't," Hamish said promptly. "I know about your code of chivalry."

"I could, within the limits of that code, make your life so miserable you wished for death."

"You could, my lord, yet I suspect you won't," Hamish said without hesitation. "I know ruthless, and you aren't it."

Phillip thought he might find a goodly amount of the same if he were forced to carry on much more conversation with the cheeky lad before him. "I should beat you senseless for your lack of respect."

"Oh, I respect you well enough," Hamish said. "But you need frankness and that's what I'm here to provide. I also might have the answers you need, if you were willing to take me with you when you go."

Phillip looked at him sharply. "Am I going somewhere?"

"I think you might want to, my lord."

"And why is that?"

"Because Haemesburgh is a hellhole, my lord."

There was no point in denying the truth of that. Haemesburgh would likely benefit from being unbuilt, then redone. If he'd had the stomach for it, he would have done it himself.

Phillip considered. "And what's to stop me from torturing the answers out of you and leaving you behind here just the same?"

"You need answers, my lord," Hamish said frankly. "I have them, as you might imagine. That, and you're too full of chivalry to leave an innocent child to fend for himself in a nest of vipers such as we have here."

"Innocent," Phillip echoed with a snort, wishing he could dredge up more irritation than amusement. "You?"

"Forced into skirts," Hamish said, innocently. "Threatened with death if the wimple and veil weren't donned. How can you not wish to see me rewarded for all these years of trauma by welcoming me into your service?"

"I think a good whipping would serve you better," Phillip muttered, though he certainly didn't have that in him either.

He couldn't avoid a sigh that felt as it if came from the soles of his boots. Haemesburgh *could* be a lovely place—for not being Artane, of course—but at the moment, as Hamish had unfortunately pointed out, it was an utter hellhole. Filthy, smelly, untended. He wasn't sure how it was that a place that had obviously been built in the past decade could look so derelict so quickly, but perhaps it took a determined effort by those inside the walls. In the end, he might do better to simply raze the place.

One thing was certain and that was, regardless of the state of the keep, the location was ideal. Nay, it was critical. The truth was, he would eventually be the lord of Artane—should his father ever decide to finally take the necessary step into the next world—and his duty and privilege would be to pass on to his children a collection of holdings as free from strife as he could make it. The political situation at present was one he didn't dare ignore. The time would come when the king's hold over his barons would diminish and Phillip had no intention of being on the wrong side of that fight.

Add to that the unpredictability of the Scots to the north

and he would need an outpost in enemy territory, at the very least. Haemesburgh was perfect, damn its crumbling walls and cesspit that had obviously never been visited except perhaps by Hamish, who had mined its depths for things to fling over those crumbling walls.

The choice that lay before him was stark and unpleasant. He could either stay and fight an uphill battle against his own future garrison, or go and let the place go to ruin for another pair of months. If he left, he might find Heather and then things would look different, or he might find her brother and things would look different still. The truth was, the situation at present was untenable and unraveling quickly. There was a part of him that wished for his father's advice.

Actually, he couldn't help but wish he had taken his father's advice in the first place and settled for a well-connected London lass who came with a collection of guardsmen who had never had to don skirts and pretend to be who they weren't.

But then he wouldn't have met Imogen—or, rather, been available to aid her, which was surely all he intended to do with her.

He glanced at the small collection of souls huddled on stools and benches pushed up against the walls of the keep proper. Imogen was there, looking muddy and exhausted. Rose was sitting next to her, stunning and lethal as always. Jackson was leaning back against the wall, lethal and ill-humored, as ever. The twins and Connor were golden spots in the gloom, though he had the feeling that if he turned his back the little ones would be gone immediately to go undermine his foundations and look for buried riches.

Well, his first task was laid out before him with undeniable clarity: he would need to see Imogen home. And who knew but that solving the mystery that was Imogen Maxwell would lead him to other things?

He looked back at the lad who had seen so much at Haemesburgh but seemed so ready to bargain away his freedom for the chance to leave the keep.

"If I agree to take you with me," Phillip said slowly, "what guarantee do I have that you'll provide me with the answers I need?"

"When a squire swears fealty unto his lord, that fealty comes with answers."

Phillip felt one of his eyebrows go up of its own accord. "Am I acquiring a polisher of my mail?"

"A lad to guard your back in tight spots, rather," Hamish said seriously. "I've more experience with that than you might think."

Phillip had something wash over him, something he wasn't sure wasn't pity. If nothing else, perhaps he could see the lad before him fed until he didn't look as if he were fair starving to death. "I do have a squire already, you know," he pointed out.

"You have a *scribe*, my lord, not a squire. That little Bartholomew might be able to stab a ruffian in the eye with his quill, but defend you with steel?" Hamish shook his head. "I can't see it. I, on the other hand, couldn't scribble my name to save my soul but I don't need to count your ribs to know which ones have a large enough gap to welcome my dagger." He nodded wisely. "Handy, that."

Phillip smiled in spite of himself. "By the saints, lad, you have a mouth on you."

"Desperation leaves me no choice but to speak boldly."

Phillip had the feeling his life was about to take a radical turn to the left when he'd intended that it should go straight. He studied the lad before him. He couldn't have been more than ten-and-six, poorly fed, with a look of desperation in his eye that was covered likely as best he could with bluster.

"Where are your parents, Hamish?" he asked quietly.

"Dead, my lord."

"No siblings?"

"Slain, my lord." He shrugged. "'Tis just me, making my way in the world. Happy to be free of gowns, if I might say so."

"You might indeed, my lad," Phillip said with a sigh. He blew out his breath. "You'd best have tidings that will serve me."

Hamish dropped to his knees and held out his hands. Phillip suppressed a sigh, checked Hamish's spindly fingers again for hidden blades, then held out his own hands to accept the lad's fealty.

"They pressed me into pretending to be the lady Heather five years ago," Hamish said without hesitation.

"Who did and why?"

"Her brother and Sir Neill," Hamish said, "and the reason was to keep you coming to Haemesburgh regularly that they might be confident of your whereabouts and intentions."

"Was Heather here?"

"Nay, my lord. She's been missing these past five years. I was roused from my spot in the piggery one fine morn and simply told to don wench's gear. No one spoke of her any longer. It was as if she'd been spirited away by ghosties." He crossed himself fervently. "Unsettling, that."

Phillip somehow wasn't at all surprised. "Where is Robert the younger?"

"That I do not know, my lord, but I have thoughts on where we might go look."

That was perhaps good enough for the moment. Phillip hauled the boy to his feet and clapped a hand on his shoulder.

"Pack your gear, lad. I think we'll leave tonight."

"Already packed, my lord. Shall I leave Sir Neill with a token of our affection before we go?"

The saints preserve him, he suspected he might have just bound an assassin to him. "Nay, lad, I think we'll leave him with himself intact."

"Then shall I loosen his ropes only far enough for him to work himself free and that only after we're away?"

Phillip supposed Sam and Theo might be willing to aid Hamish in that goodly work. "Aye, take my youngest cousins with you to see to that." He paused. "Anyone else we need to carry with us?"

Hamish beamed. "I knew ye was a kindhearted master," he said, looking as if he were suddenly a lad of eight summers. "Kindhearted, indeed!"

"Ah—"

Hamish embraced him awkwardly, then dashed off to collect Sam and Theo. The three of them conferred for a moment or two, then continued on, presumably to gather up others who also needed a fresh start. Phillip resigned himself to leading something of a children's crusade, then turned and walked off the field. He noted that Imogen and Rose were deep in conversation, prayed he wasn't the subject of that conversation, then leaned against the wall next to Jackson.

"I've decided 'tis impossible to find the answers I need here," he said carefully.

Jackson only looked at him steadily. "I can understand that. What did the brat say?"

"He has things he thinks I'll want to know, but he'll only tell me those things when we're not here any longer."

"Clever him."

"Isn't he, though?" Phillip asked. "Given that Neill isn't going to talk without a turn on the rack and the rest of the men don't know anything, I thought he might be a decent hope."

"Agreed. What now?"

"I'm not overly fond of the idea of abandoning the post here," Phillip admitted, "but I must help Imogen find her way home and I need somewhere to think. And as we discussed last night, I have a question or two to pose to your sire."

"I'm sure he would gladly house us for a few days. When do you want to leave?"

"Now."

Jackson nodded. "I'll speak with Cederic and arrange things."

"Thank you." He hesitated, then reached out and clapped his cousin on the shoulder. "Thank you, Jack. For more than just this."

"You are a sentimental old woman," Jackson said with a faint smile. "Go fetch our lassies and we'll be away before you can wipe the tears from your eyes."

He watched his cousin saunter off, more grateful than he wanted to think about for such souls to call family, then walked over to where Rose and Imogen were sitting. He squatted down in front of them and attempted a pleasant look. "I thought we might make a journey."

Rose was having none of that. "Abandoning the battle here, are we?"

"For the moment," he agreed. "My plan is to travel to Ravensthorpe. 'Tis closer than Artane, of course."

Rose regarded him with eyes he knew always saw more than he was comfortable with. "My father will, of course, be happy to have you. What do you intend to do with your keep whilst we're away?"

"Nothing. I imagine it will still be standing upon my return, don't you?"

"Phillip, my lad, you may be the only soul in England who wants it," she said seriously, "so you know I'll agree with you on that. Perhaps the lads will rise up against Sir Neill in your absence and you'll find everything rearranged upon your return." She tilted her head toward Imogen. "Our lady has mentioned she might want to visit Edinburgh in the near future if you're interested in a journey there."

Phillip looked at Imogen in surprise. "You would?"

"Yes, but I can get there on my own—"

"Of course you won't," he said without hesitation. "I promised I would aid you however I may and so I shall. After we make a brief stop to see my uncle, we'll go."

Imogen looked at him. "You'll still help me?"

She looked so surprised, he wondered what her life had been like to that point. Hard on the heels of that thought came the one that told him he was acquiring more mysteries every day. Why would Imogen want to go north? What would Hamish reveal about Heather's whereabouts?

Would he have a damned keep to come back to if he left that afternoon?

"Is Edinburgh your home?" he asked, realizing she was waiting for him to respond.

"Close enough," she said.

"Then we'll make for it in a few days," he said.

And perhaps along the way he might manage to pry a few more details out of her such as how she'd come to be at a keep in the midst of nowhere at all without a guard or servants or anyone to care for her. His mother never would have endured the like, but then again, his father never would have sent his beloved wife off past the front gates without half a garrison to keep her safe.

Where the hell was Imogen's family?

He rose, nodded to the ladies, then took himself off to at least attempt to look as if he weren't distracted beyond what he should have allowed himself. First, his uncle's keep. And perhaps whilst he was in a place where he wasn't continually looking over his shoulder to make sure he wasn't going to die, he could find a few answers to those mysteries that troubled him.

He ignored the distinct impression he had that he wasn't going to like those answers at all.

Chapter 15

Imogen stood at the edge of a hastily made camp with a tree comfortingly at her back and tried not to shake.

She didn't like to be in situations where she had no control over the events swirling around her. Too many unpleasant hours spent at the mercy of her siblings, no doubt. This was exponentially worse. She was out in the wilds of England, completely at the mercy of people she had only met a couple of days earlier, and her only reasonable method of transportation was a horse she wasn't at all sure wouldn't bite her for being a lousy rider.

Well, that, and she was eight hundred years away from where she was supposed to be.

She took a deep breath and forced herself to look on the bright side. She was cold, but she had a decent coat. She was hungry, but it looked like someone was taking care of that over there by the fire. She was tired, but maybe *we'll stay here tonight* spoken in the local vernacular really meant a chance to close her eyes for a while. Her hair was full of mud and muck and she had never wanted a bath more in her entire life, but at least they were out in the open where she couldn't smell herself quite so accurately.

Camping was not her favorite activity, but she had to admit it was preferable to remaining behind in a castle that definitely didn't contain anything resembling a tea shop. There had been no way in hell she'd been willing to stay there by herself.

Not that Phillip would have left without her, she supposed. He had carefully rounded her up with his family and his men and herded them out the gates, all before noon. She had to admit, she'd never been happier to see the last of a place than she had been of Haemesburgh, even though seeing it from the back of a horse she hadn't known how to ride had been one of the more sobering moments of her life.

She was in trouble.

At least she was in trouble standing on her own two feet for the moment, though that wasn't doing much to help her tamp down the terror she was feeling. She was accustomed to practical jokes that weren't funny, jokes perpetrated by her brothers and sisters. She was used to parental craziness that she could see coming and avoid. She was even very familiar with looking at her bank account and angsting over how she was going to keep herself afloat long enough to make it big in the film industry.

She was not at all accustomed to facing the fact that, still, she was in the wrong place at definitely the wrong time.

She realized at that moment that although she had toyed with the idea of it, she had never fully bought into the idea of time traveling until earlier that day. Looking back on the castle from the perspective of a departing horse had helped her realize just how rustic the environs were. Having no choice but to be on a horse had helped her realize that there were no cute little cabs with the steering wheels on the wrong side waiting around to take her where she wanted to go. All she'd had was a company of men who seemed extremely familiar with traveling as a group of soldiers and looking to Phillip de Piaget for their marching—or, rather, their riding—orders.

Looking at him at the moment seemed like a good idea, so she did so. He was standing just outside the firelight, just as she was, but he wasn't by himself. He was talking to someone named Cederic who seemed to be in a position of some authority over the men at least. Behind Phillip were his two shadows, guys she wouldn't have wanted to meet after she'd inadvertently threatened him in any way. She'd been watching those two for most of the afternoon, not so much for their good looks but their general dangerousness. If they'd had antennae, they would have been constantly using them. She had absolutely no doubt that they knew where Phillip was at all times and were prepared to keep him safe at all costs.

Then there was the man himself. She'd spent the afternoon in the middle of the group with Rose, who seemed to find that somewhat annoying, because Phillip had insisted that they ride where he could keep them safe. Imogen hadn't cared because it had given her a bird's-eye view of a guy who just couldn't possibly be related to the current crop of de Piagets inhabiting Artane.

Surely.

To call him gorgeous just didn't do him justice. If she'd been creating costumes for him, she would have dressed him like a prince. If she'd been hiring leads for a big-budget shoot, she would have paid him whatever he wanted to star in her show. If she'd been looking for someone to cast in her own personal role of *unattainable boyfriend*, he would have been her first and only choice. He was stunning without being pretty, muscled without being obnoxious, in charge without being overbearing, and walking her way without her having noticed.

She really, really had to get home before she lost her mind.

"Mistress Imogen," he said, coming to a stop in front of her. "Supper will be ready soon."

"Is there anything I can do?" she asked. She supposed her teeth might have chattered as she said it. She knew she looked like the sort of dinner guest an upper-crust British family would have invited to clean up scraps in the kitchen with the downstairs maids. Again, she needed to get home before she made a complete fool of herself.

He looked faintly startled. "Nay, my cook will see to it."

Of course he would. She nodded, trying to look as if she hadn't expected anything else.

He gestured toward a fallen log. "Would you care to sit?"

She would, actually, and took him up on the invitation before she realized that maybe she shouldn't have. He looked like a man with things on his mind. She would have bolted right then, but she had nowhere to go. She was in the wilds of

England—she supposed—with all that stood between her and those wilds being guys dressed up as soldiers who were obviously beholden to the dangerous man sitting next to her.

Though he didn't seem all that dangerous at the moment. He looked tired in a way that almost left her patting his shoulder before she thought better of it.

"What can I do for you?" she asked.

He looked genuinely startled. "Why would you aid me?"

"Because I'm a nice person?"

He smiled. She almost fell backward off her perch into an indeterminate pile of what she could only hope might be leaves. It was just a small smile, but it left her wondering why it was he didn't have a hundred gals lined up just to see that. Maybe he did and he'd left them back wherever he'd come from. Maybe he ignored them all in favor of Heather of Haemesburgh who Imogen was definitely going to have a little chat with as soon as possible if for nothing more than the chance to ask her what in the world she'd been thinking to pass up a gorgeous guy like Phillip de Piaget.

Phillip looked at his hands, rubbing them together for a moment or two, then glanced at her. "Things at Haemesburgh were not what I expected them to be."

"It was the same for me." She supposed that was the understatement of the year, but maybe he wasn't quite ready for the sort of elaboration she could provide. After all, how did one go about telling a medieval knight that he was talking to a modern woman? For all she knew, he would decide she was a witch and burn her at the stake. Worse still, they were out in the boonies and she didn't want to get ditched there. She already knew how that felt.

He shifted to face her. "If you don't mind my asking," he said slowly, "how did you come to be at Haemesburgh? I didn't see a guard that belonged to you."

"I left, um, them in Edinburgh," Imogen said, figuring that was as close to the truth as she dared get.

"And you traveled to the keep by yourself?"

She scrambled for something believable to say. It wasn't as if she could tell him about the enjoyable train ride she'd had, or that cab driver who'd warned her she was heading into Paranormalville, or that his erstwhile fiancée really knew how to rock a pair of high heels. She supposed the simpler the dodge, the better, so she forced herself to shrug casually.

"I had help getting there," she said, "but then I found myself on my own." She smiled. "It's hard to get good help these days, isn't it?"

He looked as shocked as she'd expected him to. "Your guardsmen should be dismissed immediately, at the very least."

"I agree. I'll make sure that happens right after I get home. Absolutely." She rubbed her hands together purposefully. "What about you? I see you have a good supply of guardsmen."

He smiled. "So it would seem."

"Do you always take that many with you wherever you go?"

"Not usually," he said, "but my errand was perhaps a bit more perilous than the usual sort of jaunt to a neighboring keep. And my father, may he live only as long as he needs to, likes to watch after his children until we all want to scream for him to cease."

There were two things that struck her quite suddenly. First, she was sitting in medieval England talking to what could potentially be the most amazing source for period details that anyone could have wished for; and, second, Phillip de Piaget was without a doubt the most charming man she had ever met. She decided that maybe she needed to add a third thing and that was that maybe the weirdest thing about the whole situation was that she was sitting on a log with a drop-dead gorgeous guy and she wasn't nervous. Her siblings would have been speechless, though she suspected Barbara the shrink would have been making some serious mental notes for examination later.

Imogen left her family back in the future where they belonged and smiled at her new friend. "You're a daddy's boy, then?"

It took him a moment to apparently translate that in his head, then he smiled. "Perhaps less that than my father prefers me as his heir over my younger brother, Kendrick. I imagine he fears for the inner workings of his defenses."

"Heir?" she repeated.

To his credit, he didn't look down his nose at her. "To Artane. Do you know it?"

"That gigangic castle on the coast?"

Bless his heart, the man wasn't afraid to translate on the fly. "The very same."

She would have laughed or made him a curtsey or trotted off to fetch him his tea and slippers, but all she could do was sit there and wonder what Tilly would say when she found out Imogen had been rescued by the guy who was no doubt Stephen de Piaget's grandfather. Great-great-great a few times grandfather, actually.

"You seem so normal," she said, before she thought better of it.

"Daft, rather," he said with a self-deprecating smile. "I'm the one who endured having things flung at me over Haemesburgh's walls for all these years, after all." He looked at her with an expression of mild curiosity. "Do you know the lady Heather?"

"I've met her a time or two," Imogen said honestly. "But I don't know her very well." Well enough to recognize her in a crowd and know she was strangling the right person, but maybe it was better not to mention that. "Do you?"

"Not at all," he said frankly, "which likely contributes to my difficulties."

"But Rose said you are engaged to Heather."

"So the tale goes," he said with a sigh, "though at the moment I'm beginning to wonder if I imagined the entire affair. At the very least, I'm beginning to accept that she's not interested in facing me before a priest."

Imogen would have reassured him that Heather was nuts and maybe if Phillip asked her nicely she might reconsider, but the woman seemed to be having a fairly decent time in twenty-first-century Scotland, so maybe it was just best to leave her there where Imogen could find her.

"Why did you want it?" she asked. "Haemesburgh, I mean. And I guess you still want it, don't you?"

"Fool that I am, aye," he said, rubbing his hands over his face, then smiling at her. "It rests along the border, as I'm sure you already know, which makes it of great advantage to whomever possesses it. A foothold in Scotland strikes me as a sensible thing to have."

She couldn't say she knew all that much about the history between Scotland and England over the years, but she had the feeling he was going to have less a foothold than a continual battle, but maybe Artane was just too darned boring and he was looking for some excitement.

"And you were willing to marry Heather to get her keep?"

"Aye, though when you put it that way, it sounds rather on the mercenary side, doesn't it? But who marries for love? Well, save my sire and all his siblings." He paused. "The rest of my family as well, I suppose. I appear to be the only one desperate enough for land to wed a gel for a pile of stones." He sighed deeply. "I'm not sure what that says about me."

"You're a good businessman?"

He looked baffled, which she supposed he couldn't help. Her French was radically improved, but not perfect by any means. He seemed to file that away for future examination, then shrugged.

"There is a fair bit of mystery surrounding the lord of the keep and his daughter," he continued, "a mystery I must solve very soon or I will lose that keep." He looked at her seriously. "I am planning to see to you to Edinburgh, but I must make a slight detour to my uncle's keep. I have questions that I believe only he can answer."

"About Heather?" she asked.

He opened his mouth, then shut it. "Ah," he said, shifting uncomfortably, "aye. Other things as well."

Well, he wasn't a good liar, she could say that much for him. It was definitely a point in his favor. Her siblings were masters at the art of prevarication—they called it *putting little sprinkles on the truth*—so she always appreciated someone who wasn't.

The material point was he was willing to take her north eventually, so she wasn't going to argue about how long it took them to get there. And if she actually managed to get to a spot where she thought she could get back to her proper time, she would tell him what she really knew about Heather. She wasn't sure how that could possibly help him, but maybe he would figure out a way to have what he wanted without Heather needing to be involved.

One of his bodyguards stepped suddenly out of the shadows, almost sending her backward off the log. Phillip caught her by the arm, smiled briefly, then looked up.

"Aye, Sir Myles?"

"A word, my lord, if you will."

Phillip exchanged a look with the man and Imogen suddenly found herself with someone intimidating looking standing five feet away from her, watching her. Watching *over* her, rather.

Medieval times were unsettling, that was for sure.

Phillip put his hands on his knees and pushed himself to his feet. He smiled at her. "'Tis no doubt something dire about supper. Not to worry."

Well, that was putting more than a few little nonpareils on the truth. She looked at the guy watching over her but he wasn't looking at her, he was looking at their surroundings, bad-guy antenna fully operational.

She decided abruptly that she wouldn't give heading off to Edinburgh on her own another thought.

It also occurred to her that maybe if someone had decided that she was trouble they might want to be rid of sooner rather than later, but there didn't seem to be any discussions going on about the proper height of a fire in relation to her own self. That was somewhat comforting until she realized that their camp was not settling down for a spiffy dinner before bedtime, it was breaking up for a quick exit offstage. One of the little twins came over and stood in front of her.

"My lady, there are undesirables in the area."

"Undesirables?" she squeaked.

"Aye," he said, his eyes bright with what could only be called excitement. "With any luck at all we'll have a goodly skirmish." He paused. "I daresay luck will not be with us with Phillip in command, which is disappointing, but perhaps ruffians will catch us up before we reach Ravensthorpe."

She was absolutely positive she didn't share his enthusiasm for that possibility, but there was no point in raining on his parade. Her trip to the Middle Ages had been fairly uneventful as far as fearing for her life was concerned, but maybe that would be changing soon. Regardless of what was really out there in the dark, Phillip and his crew seemed to believe something was out there, and that was good enough for her. She had driven all night on road trips, so there was no reason not to try to ride all night as well.

She made haste with the rest of them and hoped, rather belatedly, that leaving Haemesburgh and her only verifiable doorway into the past hadn't been a mistake.

B_y the time the sun had risen and was starting to set again, she realized what she was seeing in the distance wasn't a mirage, it was the sea. It felt so much like her first day in the UK, she wasn't quite sure she wasn't still on that train, looking out toward the coast and wondering what that amazing castle was.

There was a castle in front of her, true, but it wasn't the one she'd gaped at from the train. Well, she wasn't entirely sure she hadn't also seen this one from the train, but she would be the first to admit that whole trip had seemed like a dream. Better a dream than the nightmare she was currently in, no matter how kind the people peopling it were. Riding all night was, from the reactions of those around her, not ideal. Riding all night when one was profoundly unskilled at staying in the saddle was a misery she wasn't sure words could adequately describe. If she ever managed to walk again, it would be a miracle.

She had to get back to her normal life. She just wasn't cut out for the features provided by the Merry Medieval Mayhem theme park. She needed coffee and cell service and a functioning Internet search engine. She wasn't sure how much more she could take of saddle sores, her finger as a toothbrush, and no nicely scented shampoo. She didn't have shampoo, much less anything scented nicely.

She had to get to Edinburgh. She wasn't sure why, but she was fairly sure if answers were to be found, they would be found there. It was a peculiar sort of place, saturated with paranormal vibes. For all she knew, she would find Heather haunting the same shop she'd obviously been haunting eight hundred years into the future. With any luck, she would find Heather holding on to Phillip's sword.

Which she would promptly take away and use to direct Heather into some sort of useful wagon, then further point at her all along the speediest trip possible south and a bit west toward that castle where there was obviously a certain patch of floor that was quite a bit more than just a patch of floor.

She suppressed yet another yawn. Civilization loomed and that was perhaps all she could hope for at the moment. She would hopefully be given even a clean scrap of floor to call her own. She might even manage to sleep off her time-travel lag.

Then she would get down to the business of getting herself back home.

Chapter 16

Phillip stood at the door of the great hall and wondered just how long Jackson Alexander Kilchurn IV thought he could hide in his own castle without being discovered.

He'd seen his uncle the morning before, of course, as he'd ridden with his company into Ravensthorpe's courtyard and heard the comforting clang of the portcullis slamming home behind them. Jake had seemingly been unsurprised to see them, but perhaps he'd been in communication with those two annoyances, Robin and Nicholas de Piaget, who had no doubt felt the need to warn him that Phillip was off on another attempt to get inside Haemesburgh's gates.

Phillip had given his uncle the briefest of details about his stay inside the keep, told him as much as he'd known about his suspicions that they were being stalked on their journey east, then listened to his uncle order scouts to be sent out to see what could be learned.

He'd watched Rose lead a blanket-swaddled Imogen off to points unknown and trusted that both of them would sleep safely. He'd seen to his men, thanked his uncle for his hospitality, then tossed himself down onto a pallet in front of a fire. He didn't remember falling asleep.

He did, however, have vague memories of waking a time or two, but the effort of rousing fully had been just too much. There was a terrible luxury about knowing he was in someone else's keep with their walls keeping his enemies at bay. He didn't dare accustom himself to the feeling, but he was glad of it on the rare occasions he was able to enjoy it.

Enemies. He honestly hadn't imagined that he would have acquired all that many over the course of his life, but perhaps someone from Haemesburgh was less pleased with the thought of him as lord than he would have suspected.

Dawn had broken again, he'd had a wash and dug clean clothes out of his gear, and then he had shouldered the burden of facing his own life. That had seemed quite a bit more palatable after a decent breakfast that his aunt hadn't had anything to do with cooking. Amanda of Ravensthorpe was beyond beautiful, but the woman couldn't place food within ten paces of a fire without burning it to a crisp. The first thing his uncle had done upon wedding her was find a decent cook for them. Gold very well spent, to be sure.

Phillip stepped out into Ravensthorpe's courtyard and took a moment to reconcile himself to sun instead of drizzling rain. It was chilly, though, which concerned him. He had intended to be inside Haemesburgh with his feet up in front of the fire well before any snow fell, which was obviously not going to be the case that year. He suspected that unless he solved several mysteries in rapid succession, the only place he would be putting his feet up was in his grave.

He realized that Aunt Amanda was coming his way, looking as lovely as she always did. She hesitated when she saw him, which led him to believe that she might be sharing her husband's aversion to robust conversation. A memory came to him through the fog that was the previous day of his life. He wasn't entirely certain he hadn't dreamed the like, but since it was possible he hadn't, he examined it carefully.

Amanda had seen Rose and Imogen settled, then come to have a quiet word with her husband. Phillip had been yawning too much to hear anything she'd said, but the look on Jake's face came back to him. Or, rather, the lack of expression. As if he'd heard tidings he absolutely hadn't expected to be faced with.

Interesting.

"My lady aunt," he said, making Amanda a low bow. "A pleasure, as always."

Amanda laughed and leaned up to kiss his cheek. "Now that you're no longer alternately drooling and snoring, I'll return the greeting. You look less shattered than you did yesterday. Long journey from Haemesburgh, I take it."

"Too long and made in great haste," Phillip admitted. "Any tidings from your scouts?"

"Nothing out of the ordinary," she said, shrugging, "but you know better than to attach any meaning to that. 'Tis a bit difficult to look for what you can't identify. Any ideas on who might be stalking you?"

"I couldn't begin to guess," Phillip said grimly.

"Too many suspects, or too few?" she asked with a smile.

"The latter, assuredly," he said. "Why would anyone want to do me harm?"

"That, my little lad, is the most puzzling thing of all," she said, her smile fading. "You are definitely not your father, which is something in your favor. The only thing I can think is that you do want a fairly strategically desirable keep, never mind that I can think of few who would want to live there."

He had to agree on all counts. And if none of the scouts had seen anything untoward, perhaps he and his men had been imagining things. For all he knew, someone of Imogen's ilk had been following them to make certain she remained unharmed. That seemed quite a bit more farfetched than thinking someone might want him dead, but the thought of making a list of souls who might want to slit his throat was not something he thought he wanted to face at the moment. There were other less perilous mysteries to be solved first. He smiled at his aunt.

"I'm sure 'tis nothing more than jealousy over that fine keep. You wouldn't know where your husband is, would you?"

She blinked. "Jake? Haven't seen him. Is he missing?"

"He's made an art of hiding so far this morning."

"Then best of luck with your hunt," she said. "I've things to do. Important things."

He wouldn't have been surprised if one of those things was to go and warn her husband he was being sought. Phillip shot her a dark look, which she only smiled at before she walked briskly back inside her hall. He resumed his perch atop the stairs to better keep an eye on the courtyard for reluctant relatives. And whilst he was about that goodly work, he made a list of all the places he'd already looked for Jake that morning.

He had sought the man out in his own bedchamber, his solar, and his kitchens only to be told each time that he had narrowly missed the lord of the hall and perhaps he might like to try the stables, the smithy, or the lists. Unfortunately, those locales only yielded suggestions from the masters of those domains that Phillip continue on his search. His patience was wearing very thin.

He was beginning to suspect Jake didn't want to talk to him.

He formulated a new plan. He would chase his uncle out to the lists and threaten to slay him unless he provided the answers Phillip wanted. It was his only hope, truly, given that Jake was a master at avoiding topics he didn't care to discuss. A hearing loss that ever seemed to conveniently come and go. Pains in his head that, now and again, rendered him incapable of speech. A blank look, as if all his wits had deserted him temporarily. Phillip knew what to expect and had no intentions of being put off by any of it.

What did *I'm available* mean and why was it scrawled in an almost indecipherable hand across the back of Imogen's cloak, followed by a series of numbers?

He felt certain Jake might know, though, again, he didn't like to think overlong on why that might be the case. It was, put simply, past ridiculous.

He had avoided the most likely possibility so far that morn, but he realized he would have to face the truth eventually and that truth was that he was daft. Indeed, the more fully he faced it, the more it seemed the only explanation. His sire and uncles had been closeted in the lord's solar at Artane because they wanted peace for drinking the finest of the keep's wine and indulging with equal abandon in the telling of ribald jests whilst not having to share any of the same with their sons. There was no conspiracy of secrets, no desperate effort to hide paranormal oddities, no continuous effort to present a façade of normalcy when the truth was far more complicated and dangerous.

He caught sight suddenly of his uncle Jake strolling across his courtyard. More interesting still, Jake caught sight of him, jumped a little, then trotted off in the opposite direction.

Phillip cursed. So, that's how it was. Phillip hurried after him, determined to have speech with him before Jake managed to bolt himself inside his solar. It turned into a full-on dash for the nearest bolt hole, which, unfortunately for Jackson Kilchurn, Phillip was intimately familiar with, having spent more than his share of time at Ravensthorpe in his youth.

He caught his uncle just outside a gate that led to a rather uncomfortable passage to the kitchens.

"Let me aid you," Phillip said, slapping his hand on the wood and blocking Jake's ability to flee. He glared at his uncle. "With whatever goodly work you're about."

"I don't need aid," Jake wheezed.

"You look to be needing a bit of exercise."

"I just had some," Jake said. "What I need is a strong drink."

"If only you indulged."

"I'm considering turning over a new leaf."

Phillip paused at the turn of phrase. That was something, wasn't it? His uncle did that often, that unusual turn of phrase. Phillip couldn't say he'd noticed it overmuch in his youth, but now it seemed strange indeed. Where had he learned it? He studied the man before him, considering things he hadn't wanted to pay heed to before, but found he couldn't ignore now.

His uncle was an excellent swordsman, true, but there was something about his ability to fight that Phillip had always found curious. It was likely something only he and his father would have noticed, but it was clear to him that Jake had learned swordplay later in life. He wasn't sure how to describe how he knew that, but he did.

There were other things about his uncle that had never exactly bothered him but had given him pause for some reason. Jake's uncanny calm in the face of wars and famine. His insistence on every soul in his kitchens washing their damned hands before they prepared meals. His truly unparalleled skill in drawing. But perhaps the most glaring thing was his name. Jackson Alexander Kilchurn IV.

What madman named his son that when that son was not in line to some throne or other?

He looked at his uncle purposefully. "Let's train."

"Oh, let's not," Jake said, looking about himself, no doubt for a rescue. "I'll find you someone more your speed."

"Only you have the skill to stand against me."

Jake started to speak, then shut his mouth and laughed. "Appeal to my vanity, why don't you?"

"I thought I would try."

Jake studied him for a handful of moments, then sighed heavily. "All right, I can see I won't win this one. You can tell me all about your sorry tale while you're trying to kill me."

"I don't want to kill you."

"I don't want to know what you want to do with me, but I have the feeling it's going to be very unpleasant."

"It needn't be," Phillip said smoothly. "Not if you tell me what I want to know."

Jake muttered something that sounded a bit like a prayer, but nodded just the same and walked out into the middle of his training field. Jake's squire took his swordbelt and scabbard, just as any squire would have done for his lord. Phillip wanted to find it reassuring, but for some reason it struck him as odd, which was odd in itself.

What was going on in his family that he had been oblivious to?

He drew his own sword, then set to. It only took a few moments before he revised his opinion of his uncle's swordplay. Jake might not have had a sword put into his hands as a wee thing, but he was a damned fine swordsman. Phillip found himself more challenged than he'd thought he would be, which led him to realize that perhaps he was being more arrogant than he should have been. Arrogant and daft. There was nothing odd in his family, nothing untoward going on where he hadn't been watching, nothing being said that wasn't said in every other castle in England. Obviously he wasn't sleeping well at night. Perhaps all he needed was a turn on a decently clean goosefeather mattress to put his poor wits to rights.

In time, he called peace to catch his breath. He dragged his sleeve across his face, then words came out of his mouth he hadn't intended.

"There's something odd about her."

"About whom?" Jake asked, without so much as a hitch in his breathing.

Phillip supposed now that he'd begun, there was no reason not to press on with his madness. "Imogen," he said. "There are things about her I find odd."

"Women can be peculiar," Jake offered sagely.

"Not womanly odd," Phillip said in exasperation. "A more substantial odd than that."

"And your mother wonders why you aren't wed."

Phillip glared at him. "I know how to behave properly."

"And keep your mouth shut?"

"Aye, that, too!"

Jake laughed as he propped his sword up against his shoulder. "Is this what you dragged me out here to talk about—no, wait. I think it might be very enlightening. Tell me how it is that when you went to fetch your bride from her pile of rags, you managed to come away from your keep with another woman entirely. We'll peer at the details and see where you ran afoul of trouble." He smiled pleasantly. "I think I'm going to be able to offer you quite a few suggestions."

Phillip was beginning to regret not having let his uncle escape earlier. He rolled his eyes and resheathed his sword. "Very well, but I'll need to walk as we speak."

"Run, you mean," Jake said, putting away his sword as well, "but I'm full of energy, so don't worry you'll outrun me."

"I wasn't worried," Phillip muttered, though he supposed he should have been. Whatever else his flaws, Jackson Kilchurn had not gone to fat.

He handed off his sword to a cousin he didn't bother to identify, then walked with his uncle around the perimeter of his training field. Now that he had a ready ear, he hardly knew where to begin. Perhaps stating the most obvious would be easiest.

"Heather wasn't at Haemesburgh," he said with a sigh. "I don't think she's been there for quite some time."

"Indeed," Jake said slowly. "Then whom have you been treating with each time, if treating it can be called?"

Phillip steeled himself for the laughter he knew would be coming his way. "Her squire."

Jake looked at him in surprise and, it had to be said, a fair amount of amusement. "You can't be serious."

"Oh, I am," Phillip said. "Apparently young Hamish is the one who has been holding court on the parapet, wearing her skirts, and flinging things my way."

"Don't you have a Hamish in your company?"

"Indeed I do."

Jake laughed. "I have to admit I'm surprised by the twists and turns your life is currently taking, but I suppose they're good for you. I can hardly wait to hear what the lad has told you, but why don't you start at the beginning. I'm old and have trouble following these troublesome details."

Phillip ignored his uncle's grin. "I arrived at the keep to find Imogen hanging from the drawbridge," he said grimly. "I had thought her to be Heather, but soon realized my mistake. After rescuing her and forcing my way inside the keep, I found Heather gone, Hamish taking her place as lady of the keep, and the garrison captain eyeing the lord's chair with undisguised fondness."

"Where is Lord Robert?"

"The elder or the younger?"

"Either."

Phillip shrugged. "I've no idea. The garrison is relatively new, which I'm imagining wasn't a happy accident, the priest was senseless with drink, and Sir Neill particularly unwilling to divulge any tidings. Hamish the squire has promised me all manner of answers did I liberate him from Heather's gear, so at the moment he is my only hope for the truth." He paused. "I haven't seen him yet this morning. I'm assuming he hasn't fled."

"He's chatting with the ladies in Amanda's solar."

"I'm unsurprised."

Jake laughed a little. "He's already done what he considers his duty in the lists, assured me of his unwavering devotion to your own poor self, then trotted off to see if he could pour wine for my wife. I thought it was probably best to keep him contained."

"Likely so," Phillip said. He sighed. "So, there is the whole of it. My betrothed is missing, her father likely dead, her brother nowhere to be found, and her garrison captain fully prepared to send me speedily into the next life. I'm counting on answers from a lad who's too clever by half, and I now have a woman who can barely speak intelligible French to look after."

"Your life is complicated."

"'Tis untidy."

"Worse still."

Phillip wanted to ask Jake if he had misunderstood him at various times during his youth when he'd heard him curse in a tongue that had sounded a bit like the peasant's English Imogen also seemed to know. He wanted to ask his uncle if he'd really been born in London, where he'd learned to put ink to parchment and draw such fantastical things, why Rose especially seemed to always be carrying secrets she seemed reluctant to share. Jackson was another matter entirely, endlessly gnawing on a burden he absolutely wouldn't talk about.

He wanted to ask him what he thought of Imogen.

"I think there's the call for lunch," Jake said brightly. "Let's go eat something, shall we? I'm sure things will look better on a full stomach."

"But—"

Jake had already gathered up his squire and was trotting back toward the house.

"I haven't asked my questions of you," Phillip shouted.

Jake only waved over his head and bolted for the house. It would have taken a dead run to have reached him before he gained the front doors. Phillip suspected arguing with Jake's belly over the timing of any conversation wouldn't go well.

He supposed he wasn't adverse to another meal so quickly after the first, so he followed his uncle from the lists and back to the house. But that was the last delay he would tolerate. He had questions to put to the man scampering around the corner of his keep and have answers to them he would.

Chapter 17

Imogen stood in a tower room in a medieval castle, dressed in medieval clothing, and felt just a little like Rapunzel.

She didn't have yards of really great hair, but hers would do in a pinch and the genuine medieval clothing was making up for lots of things. Besides, with enough perseverance maybe she would learn how to put her hair up in a bun. Who was going to be looking at her hair anyway? Her dress was amazing, the bodice covered with all kinds of embroidery she would have to examine later, and she had medieval shoes that fit. What else could she ask for?

Well, a cup of coffee and working Wi-Fi would have been nice, but she wasn't going to complain.

She put her hand to her head. Complain? No, she wasn't going to complain, she was going to have a complete nervous breakdown. She was standing in a castle's tower room, wearing clothing made eight hundred years before she was born, and she had no idea how she was ever going to get back to where she was supposed to be.

She walked over to the window, such as it was, and looked out over the sea. It was truly one of the oddest sensations she'd ever had, that of looking at a sea that didn't really change and realizing she was looking at it centuries away from when she should have been.

If she'd had any sense, she might have been tempted to just hang around for a few weeks and soak up the local culture. What a dissertation she could have written after that. She could take notes with Bartholomew's gear, reapply to that exclusive little university in that sleepy little East Coast town she'd ditched without remorse, and knock the socks off her advisor and his committee. They would probably award her a degree on the spot.

And then what?

That was the question, wasn't it? It was a question she'd never had a good answer for. She'd only known that in her house, it was always about the next big thing. There had never been any time to simply have an accomplishment be good enough. *Upward and onward* was her father's motto, something his investment broker could readily attest to. Never rest, never be content, never enjoy what he'd worked for.

Maybe there was something to be said for a little sabbatical in the Middle Ages where savoring the current meal was a good idea just in case there wasn't another one around the corner. And that right there was probably reason enough to want to go home. The question was how to get there.

Her location on the map was undeniable. Her spot in time was equally hard to deny. The only thing that was even remotely in question was the exact mechanics of how she'd come to be so out of her time and place. The only thing she could figure was that it had to do with Phillip's sword. His grandfather's missing sword with the blue gem in the hilt.

She would have to find it.

The problem was, she had no idea where to begin to look for it and very few of her usual resources at her fingertips. Her phone was useless, the local library hundreds of years out of reach, and her options for transportation limited to hooves belonging to an animal she really couldn't control. The impossible nature of what she needed to attempt was almost enough to leave her hyperventilating.

She forced herself to focus on what she had going for her because that helped her feel like things weren't hopeless. She'd had a wonderful sleep in a bed that had felt like a featherbed and woken to find her phone still under her pillow. She'd had a bath. She'd been dressed in the aforementioned amazing clothes.

Realizing she had no idea what had happened to her clothes or her backpack was terrifying, but she was almost sure the girl who had helped her had said something about her gear having been put in Rose's trunk, which was good. The alternative was that her knickers had been put on display in the great hall below. They'd already been on display in London; why not Ravensthorpe? Well, that was something to gnaw on later. What she needed was a plan to find Phillip's sword and she wasn't going to find that in her current location. Maybe she could ask Rose a few pointed questions and see where that led.

She walked over to the door and opened it, then jumped in spite of herself. The blond twins were loitering out on the landing, obviously waiting for her. They immediately turned to her and made her low bows.

"We're here to watch over you," one of them said.

"And not lose you," the other added.

Imogen looked from one to the other and decided those two were a good place to start with her questions. But first things first.

"How do I tell you apart?" she asked.

"Sam's the stupider one," one of them said. "I'm Theo, the clever one."

The other one, Sam, if his brother was to be believed, snorted heartily. "Theo is an idiot and not at all clever. I'm Sam, the clever *and* smart one."

She decided immediately there was no possible way to tell the two apart. They were obviously exacerbating the problem with identical haircuts and clothes. She looked at the one on the right.

"You do this on purpose, don't you?" she asked.

"What?" he asked.

"Dress alike," she said, "right down to the boots."

He looked at her approvingly. "Of course."

"So you can blame each other for whatever trouble you get into?"

One of them looked at the other. "She's canny."

"I like her."

"Let's keep her."

"You can't just keep a person, Sam, you lackwit," Theo said with a snort. "We'll have to woo her with tales of our vast accomplishments and convince her to stay."

"Have you been alive long enough for vast accomplishments?" she asked politely.

"Ten summers," Sam said proudly. "Barely."

"Meaning we've barely survived this long," added Theo with a heavy sigh. "We have found ourselves in various pieces of dire peril from which we scarce escaped with our lives." He looked at her seriously. "I don't anticipate that ending anytime soon."

"Not with the work we've set ourselves," Sam agreed thoughtfully.

"And what would that be?" she asked, trying not to smile. What a couple of charmers.

"We investigate," Sam said.

"Mysteries," Theo added.

"Of all sorts and varieties," Sam finished. "We intend to go down in history for it."

Charming and extremely dangerous. She wasn't sure if she should ask them for help or run away before they figured out just what sort of mystery she was in the middle of. For all she knew, they would think *she* was a mystery to be solved and then she would definitely be finding herself standing in a pile of kindling.

"We came to fetch you for an afternoon of leisure," Sam said.

"Outside the keep walls," Theo added. "Uncle Jake thought we might like room to stretch our legs."

"Tell the truth," said a voice from the turn of the stairs.

Imogen saw the twins' older brother, Connor, standing there under the torch. He smiled at her, then turned a stern look on his brothers.

"The truth," he insisted.

Sam sighed first. "Very well, we're being tossed out the front gates."

"Because Uncle Jake is overprotective of his wine cellar," Theo added. "We weren't drinking anything."

"Just looking behind things."

Connor straightened from where he'd been leaning against the wall. "Don't believe them. They were likely pawing at the foundations of the keep in an effort to find hidden gold. They do it all the time. I shudder to think what they'll stumble upon eventually. Outside, lads, before Jake realizes you're still within his walls." He let his brothers scamper past him, then smiled at her. "We have been invited to take our ease for a bit just the same, if you care for it."

"It would be wonderful," she said honestly. It beat the hell out of the week she'd had so far.

She followed the boys through the hall, collected a few more people she didn't know and a couple she did, then walked with them out the front gates and around the corner to a bluff overlooking the beach. She was horribly tempted by the water, but she didn't see an easy way down that wasn't a bit of a hike and she wasn't sure how safe it was to go that far without out a guard.

Without a guard. That she was even thinking like that was probably reason enough to believe she'd been in the Middle Ages just a bit too long.

She sat down on a blanket of some sort and found herself in the middle of lots of kids. She guessed most of them belonged to her hosts given that the boys looked a lot like Jackson and the youngest girl, who had to have been about Sam and Theo's age, looked just like a younger version of Rose.

It was utter chaos.

But there was food and drink and she felt safe. The twins were looking at her with far more curiosity than she was comfortable with, but she supposed there wasn't much she could do about that. At least she wasn't wearing her decorated raincoat any longer. Her French was apparently passable enough that she didn't earn any strange looks, she understood most of what was going on, and she was getting an up-close-and-personal look at medieval life.

If she'd been able to draw, she would have been sketching madly. She would have been tempted to take a picture with her phone—

She froze and her blood ran cold. She had left her phone in the tower room, on the window ledge.

"Imogen?"

Phillip had dropped down to sit next to her and he was looking at her with alarm.

"Nothing," she croaked. "Nothing."

"You don't look well."

"I'm fine," she said. She pasted a smile onto her face because what else was there to do? Run back to the castle like a madwoman? The tower room had been empty and didn't look as if it were used very often. All she had to do was get back to the castle as quickly as she could and find a reason to get back upstairs. If she didn't look like a lunatic, no one would get suspicious, and life would go on. She couldn't imagine that anyone would find her phone, much less examine that little box made of materials they would have never encountered in their worst nightmares, then immediately run to the local witch-burner and blurt out all kinds of details she would have rather kept private.

Would they?

Phillip handed her a cup. "Drink."

"Poison?"

He smiled briefly. "Wine. I think I can personally guarantee that 'tis drinkable. My uncle keeps a very fine cellar, which I understand"—he shot the twins a pointed look—"two of our company have discovered personally this morning."

"We didn't taste," Theo said promptly. "Well, nothing that wasn't already opened."

"Your poor father," Phillip said. "My poor father. Poor anyone who must needs host you two terrors for more than a day or two."

"Oh, we hardly need that long to begin our investigations," Sam said cheerfully. "Wouldn't you agree, Theo?"

"We don't dawdle," Theo agreed. "Our father always said timeliness was a virtue."

"That's not all our father says," Connor said with a gusty sigh, sitting down on Imogen's other side. "But because there are ladies present, I'll refrain from repeating any of it."

Imogen sipped at wine that was supposedly drinkable, but she never had dared learn to appreciate anything past a good cup of coffee so she supposed she wasn't one to offer an educated opinion. She felt immediately better, but that could have been because no one was looking at her as if she'd suddenly grown horns. She forced herself not to think about how much worse someone finding her phone could make things.

She watched the cousins alternately sparring with swords and wrestling, laughing and teasing each other, and realized at one point that she was experiencing some serious envy that she had never had relationships with her siblings that even remotely resembled what the people in front of her had.

"Do you have brothers and sisters?"

She realized Phillip had stretched out on his side next to her and was leaning on his elbow, watching her. She wondered how long he'd been doing that and what had shown on her face.

"Several," she admitted. "Two brothers and two sisters. All older than I am. You?"

"Two younger brothers and a younger sister," he said. He continued to study her. "Were they unkind to you?"

"Aren't all siblings?"

"Nay."

She took a deep breath. "My family is . . ." She groped for the right word in English and couldn't find it, never mind looking for it in French. "Different," she managed finally.

And just how did she go about describing her very driven family to a medieval guy who probably wasn't going to understand what lawyers and doctors and psychiatrists and entrepreneurs were, even if she could manage to describe them properly? Well, Prissy might have translated across time, but the rest? Probably not. The only thing she could say was that they were painfully driven, dutifully following their parents into careers where stress was not only acceptable, it was sought after. They were all drama junkies.

And all she wanted to do was make movies. Barring that, she wanted to be trapped in a Jane Austen novel, but maybe that was something to examine later when she didn't have a gorgeous man approximately twelve inches from her, looking at her as if he expected her to say something intelligent.

He had the most amazing colored eyes she had ever seen.

"You have gray eyes," she said, before she thought better of it.

He smiled. "And yours are a happy combination of green and brown."

"Ordinary."

"Rather lovely, actually," he said. "I've looked into my father's for perhaps too much of my life to find mine anything interesting." He sighed. "He'll have much less to say about my eyes than my actions, I fear."

"Why is that?"

"Aye, Phillip, why is that?" Connor asked brightly. "Do tell."

"Wait, don't start without me," Jackson said, kicking Connor's feet aside and collapsing onto a corner of the blanket. "I can scarce wait to enjoy these tidings."

"Are you being helpful?" Phillip asked shortly.

"Oh, we never promised that," Rose said, sitting down next to her brother and turning to lean her back against his. "But we'd best have a discussion of it all sooner rather than later, don't you think? The last of the scouts is back in."

Imogen watched Phillip go still. It was something she'd seen actors try to portray on screen, but she'd never seen it in real life. She could hardly believe she was even thinking it, but there was a guy who probably kept himself alive thanks to gut feelings.

"And what did he find?" he asked casually.

"Nothing," Rose said with a shrug, dislodging her brother, who cursed her, then resettled himself. "But I daresay that doesn't surprise you." She shook her head. "I could have sworn we were being followed, but perhaps I was imagining things. All the lads say they've seen nothing unusual."

"Well, Phillip does tend to overestimate his importance in the world," Connor drawled. "I have serious doubts that anyone would want his head on a pike outside their gates. Perhaps there was someone who had a look at either you or Imogen and decided 'twas past time he took a wife."

"The saints preserve me," Rose said with a shudder. "Imogen can do as she pleases, but please, not me."

"Oh, no thank you," Imogen said, wishing her hands didn't feel so cold. That was the last thing she needed, to get stuck in medieval times with a guy who had no clue what indoor plumbing was.

"Are you wed, then?" Connor asked.

"No," Imogen said firmly. "I haven't found the right guy." And the guy who wanted to marry her was absolutely the wrong one, though she had to admit he would have been absolutely beside himself with excitement over her current straits if they had been his straits. She could only imagine what kind of craziness he would have been causing. She doubted he would have lasted more than ten minutes without becoming very familiar with the inside of the nearest dungeon.

"Phillip's available," Jackson said with a smirk. "Apparently."

"Imogen should aim much higher than him," Rose said, elbowing her brother in the ribs. "Phillip snores."

"So do you," Phillip said, throwing a handful of weeds at her.

"I do not," Rose said archly. "I breathe enthusiastically from time to time, especially when trying to keep my temper in check thanks to the louts who vex me from morn till night." She threw the weeds back at her cousin. "Tell Imogen why you're not wed, unless you want me to do it for you."

"She already knows," Phillip said, lying back on the grass and putting his arm over his eyes. "She was with us at Haemesburgh, remember?"

"Aye, trying to get out whilst you were trying to get in," Rose said dryly. "For a moment there, I half suspected Imogen was actually Heather trying to escape her fate."

Imogen felt things go very still. She would have thought that was just in her head, but she felt that stillness settle over the rest of the group. Well, that wasn't entirely true. The younger kids were still going at it as if nothing had happened. Phillip was unmoving, though he could have been asleep. Rose and Jackson were seemingly studying various parts of the beach where interesting things were perhaps to be found. Connor, though, was looking at her thoughtfully. He smiled, then kicked Phillip's foot.

"We should go find supper," he said.

"In a bit," Phillip said. "I want another quarter hour of sun on my face before I must needs face the reality of my life."

Imogen thought she might understand the sentiment. The reality of her current life was definitely not what she'd bargained for, though now that she had a bit of time to think about it, she couldn't deny that as she'd traveled to Haemesburgh, she had been thinking it would have been amazing to have seen the castle in all its medieval glory. How coincidental that she should get that wish. Even more fantastical was that Heather had been right there to watch her put her hand on Phillip's sword—no, Heather hadn't watched her do it, Heather had *insisted* that she do it.

Had Heather been looking for someone to take her place in the past?

"If you ask my opinion," Connor said quietly, "Phillip was fortunate to find Imogen there instead of Heather. 'Tis odd, though, isn't it, how alike they look?"

"As if you would know," Jackson said with a snort.

"Phillip and I both heard a detailed description of her," Connor insisted. "There is a resemblance."

"Nay," Phillip said, not taking his arm from his eyes, "Imogen is much prettier."

Imogen was terribly tempted to blush, but if there was one thing she had, it was iron control over her own reactions. Phillip was making conversation, not complimenting her. No point in getting all worked up over it.

"I think he's well rid of Heather," Rose said, "but 'tis a pity he couldn't have found Grandfather Rhys's sword."

Imogen suspected that Phillip would never find his grandfather's sword as long as Heather of Haemesburgh had anything to say about it. What she couldn't force herself to entertain seriously was the thought that Heather had used Phillip's sword as a means for a time-travel sort of switcheroo. No one could be that devious. Well, with the possible exception of her siblings, but that was a different story. This was a medieval noblewoman trying to escape an unwanted marriage to a truly gorgeous, chivalrous man, not a crazy Maxwell spawn trying to inflinct pain and misery on other Maxwell spawn.

"I think we need a hot fire," Phillip said. "Imogen's shivering."

She was, but it wasn't from the sea breezes, which were glorious, or the fact that Phillip had taken one of her hands in his and was rubbing her fingers to perhaps bring some circulation back into them. She was shivering because she thought she just might have discovered the reason Heather of Haemesburgh had been insistent on getting her to her castle.

Now all she had to do was find Phillip's sword, convince a woman who apparently really didn't want to be hanging around the Middle Ages that that was where—or *when*, rather—she belonged, and further convince that same woman that that gorgeous man there was worth the trouble of coming back for.

When that was what was on the agenda, getting to the future in order to do any of the three seemed like the easy part.

Chapter 18

Phillip couldn't remember the last time he'd enjoyed so much comfort and ease. The afternoon had been pleasant, the weather unusually fine, and the victuals provided by his aunt's cook some of the best he'd ingested in quite some time. He'd happily watched the antics of his younger cousins, engaged in interesting conversation with cousins closer to his age, and had the privilege of looking at a very lovely woman. If he hadn't known better, he would have sworn someone was trying to make a match between him and a woman he'd just met.

He wasn't certain his sire would have approved, but then again, he wouldn't have been the first one in his family to give his heart where no title lay.

A terribly premature thought, no doubt, so he contented himself with watching Imogen playing at alquerques with his cousins and allowing himself the luxury of wondering about her. The list was unfortunately not terribly different than it had been the first time he'd made it.

How had she come to be at Haemesburgh without a guard, proper gear, or any idea—or so it had seemed at first— of how to make herself understood? How had she managed to get herself inside gates that had been so readily barred to him whilst not having any idea at all who the garrison captain was? Why had she been trying to poach swords from anyone willing to relinquish theirs so she could shove them into the hole in the floor behind the lord's chair?

Why did she have to be so terribly lovely in a way he couldn't quite lay his finger on?

The final thought that baffled him was why she had bolted for Ravensthorpe's tower chamber the very moment they had walked into the hall. He'd assumed she had left something behind earlier, but she had dodged his question about it and simply fled. He'd nodded to Theo and Sam to follow her lest she find herself lost, but he'd wondered what she had been so desperate to find and why she had looked so unnerved when she'd returned empty-handed.

She was a mystery, and, as he'd made clear to anyone who would listen, he didn't care for mysteries. He liked his problems to come at him with swords. That was the sort of thing he understood. But women with odd clothing who were loitering in keeps where they shouldn't have been? Nay, those were things he knew spelled trouble for his peace of mind should he pursue them any further.

Yet her laugh was like a bubbling brook.

Actually, it was closer to hiccoughs, but it was charming nonetheless. She still looked slightly ill at ease, but less than before. It was hard to resist the mischief of his cousins. If he hadn't been such a hard-hearted bastard, he might have smiled as well.

He was beginning to wonder what it was he'd ever seen in Heather of Haemesburgh—not that he'd ever had a good look at her. Even her castle wasn't as attractive a place as he'd remembered it being.

By the saints, was he losing his wits?

He continued to watch Imogen whilst at the same time trying to ignore the things he found strange about her. Her clothing, her manner of speech, the expression of utter confusion and terror she'd allowed to surface when she'd thought no one was watching her.

But the question he simply couldn't move past was how she had come to be at Haemesburgh by herself. He would have preferred to have ignored it altogether, but he couldn't. There were

things a woman simply didn't do, and travel without some sort
of escort was one of them. His father never would have sent his
mother off without an enormous guard. Even Rose, as fiercely
and perhaps dangerously independent as she was, didn't leave
the keep without her collection of lads that made even him
nervous.

How had Imogen managed to travel so far without someone
to at least guard her back?

He wondered if he was the only one who found any of it
odd. If his cousins found anything strange about her, they
hadn't said as much. Then again, Theo and Sam were too busy
competing for her attention to even pay any heed to their sup-
pers after they had inhaled most of what had been set before
them. Rose seemed content to have someone of her age to pass
time with. The rest of her siblings were used to visitors and
paid no especial heed to Imogen short of testing the waters to
see if she would pay them any heed. Connor was obviously
affected by the fairness of her face, which he understood. He
wondered if his cousin understood that she was not for him.

He realized abruptly that Jackson was watching not Imogen but him. He mouthed an obscenity at his cousin, but Jackson only lifted an eyebrow. A tame reaction for that sort of
vulgarity, but the sad truth was, he had passed so much of his
life with Jackson, Rose, and Kendrick, they had all likely
become immune to one another's slurs.

Phillip turned his attentions to less vexing souls and examined the diners still left at table. His uncle Jake was still there,
of course, presiding over the hall with a comforting, steady
presence that Phillip knew could disappear in a moment if a
threat were sensed. He studied his uncle to see if there might
be unease simmering below the surface of his smile and was
faintly surprised to find that Jake seemed to be less at ease
than he might normally have been. He looked like a man who
knew his doom was approaching and knew with equal certainty that there wasn't a damned thing he could do about it.

Interesting.

Amanda was watching her husband watch the souls gathered in front of the fire, playing at their game. Phillip blinked
in surprise as Amanda slipped her husband something that
Phillip recognized. Indeed, he wasn't sure how, having seen

that little box, anyone could forget it. It was the most assaulting shade of pale red—nay, it couldn't even be called that. He didn't have a name for that color, but it wasn't something he'd ever seen before. He had, however, certainly felt it clout him on the jaw.

Why did Amanda have it and why had she given it to her husband?

Jake froze, then looked at his wife with wide eyes. Phillip immediately looked at the cup of wine he was holding in his hand so he wasn't caught looking at his aunt and uncle. He saw out of the corner of his eye that Amanda had leaned closer and was whispering quite intently with her husband. He didn't care to eavesdrop, but there was something about their aspects that bothered him. He smiled and nodded as they excused themselves from the hall and headed toward the kitchens. He counted to a score before he rose as well, simply to keep from arousing suspicion.

He almost clapped his hand to his forehead. If he didn't watch himself, he would soon be acting like the little twins, forever looking over his shoulders for anyone who might be following him. At least those two had good reason to fear a scowling adult. He had nothing to fear but his own stupidity.

Which he was apparently going to be courting like a lover that evening. He surrendered to his curiousity and had a final sip of his wine, as if he had planned it that way. He yawned as if he might be thinking of seeking his rest, then made a point of tromping out of the great hall and down the passageway toward the kitchens. Fortunately for his untried-at-spying-on-others self, there was a turn in the passageway and he didn't run bodily into his aunt and uncle before he realized how close he was to them. He flattened himself against the wall, refrained from rolling his eyes in disgust at himself, then leaned forward and eavesdropped shamelessly.

"She must be terrified."

"Absolutely."

"You weren't, though. Not when it happened to you."

"I had you to protect me."

Amanda laughed uneasily. "I suppose so."

"I thought you were a princess."

"Well, you paid enough for a princess," Amanda said, "so

your purse at least agrees with you." She paused. "You need to help her."

He sighed. "I guess I don't have a choice, do I? It's not like I can let her wander around aimlessly. We could pawn her off on Nick and Jenner—"

"Jake!"

"All right, but we'll have to do it privately. In my solar, where she can freak out behind a locked door."

Freak out. Phillip felt as though his ears belonged to someone else. He knew Imogen had said those same words, in just that way, in just that accent, followed generally by *damn method actors.*

Why would Jake know those words?

Things began to occur to him that hadn't before, things he absolutely didn't want to look at but realized now he had no choice but to face.

He started with the most obvious oddity: his uncle, Jackson Alexander Kilchurn IV.

Jake claimed to be from London, but it occurred to Phillip that in all the times he himself had been to London, he had never once encountered any of Jake's relatives by chance nor been invited to dine with them. Indeed, it was as if Jake didn't have any relations. He said that his father and siblings were lost to him, but what of his cousins? His uncle Montgomery had once hinted that Jake had simply sprung up from the grass, but Phillip had discounted that as the ramblings of a man who was too fond of the tales his jongleurs told.

But now that he thought about it, that was another thing he had no explanation for, namely his uncle Montgomery and his wife, Persephone. They lived in the south, in a keep that was part of his grandfather Rhys's holdings, a keep that Phillip had spent a pair of years in whilst squiring for his uncle. To say he had seen odd things was to understate it badly. Montgomery was a reliable, jaded sort, but his wife, Pippa . . . well, she was wont to mutter the occasional epitaph under her breath that he'd grown accustomed to but never understood the origins of.

Things that sounded far too much like Imogen's mutterings, truth be told.

Then there were the trunks that simply appeared for Pippa now and again, trunks that she had shared with no one but

Montgomery. He supposed Kendrick would have had them open an hour after they'd arrived, but he himself had been a more circumspect lad and he'd allowed his aunt her privacy.

But what was he to think about that unusual spot at the end of their drawbridge, a spot that carried dire warnings and a flat stone placed atop it? It was almost as if there were some sort of untoward something attached to that particular spot.

It made him wonder just what that something might be.

He was beginning to suspect he'd had an enormous mystery sitting there right under his nose and he'd neglected to pay it any heed.

He was still trying to reconcile himself to what he hadn't been willing to look at when he realized what he was looking at was his aunt and uncle, who had come around the corner and were looking terribly guilty about something.

"Oh," Amanda said.

Phillip looked at her sternly. "Aye, oh."

Jake sighed deeply. "He should come along as well. Damn it anyway."

Phillip folded his arms over his chest, realizing as he did so that he was using his father's exact pose of intimidation. He thought he might just understand why his father did it. A pity it didn't aid him past hopefully concealing that his hands were trembling just the slightest bit.

"Come along for what?" he asked sternly. "Have you things to confess?"

Jake pursed his lips. "I can still kick your arse in the lists, my little friend. Don't forget that."

"Shall we test it?"

Amanda only smiled faintly. "Why don't you two leave that as something to be tested on the morrow? I believe we have more important business tonight."

"What sort of business?" Phillip asked. He asked it politely, because he was speaking to his aunt. He turned a much more forbidding look on his uncle. "Do you care to tell me here what you're about or shall we seek out the privacy of your solar and I cut it from you?"

"My solar," Jake said, "after you've left your weapons outside my door."

Amanda smiled and slipped her hand under her husband's

elbow. "I'll keep you safe. Come along, Phillip love, and let's have speech together."

"I like to know beforehand what a parley will include," he said, not moving. "Lest I feel the need to keep my sword with me."

Jake rolled his eyes. "This is me you're speaking to, nephew, and I'm the one you drooled on more times than you'll remember, when you were barely two. You'll be perfectly safe with me." He paused, and his eyes were serious. "There are things you need to know, Phillip," he said very quietly. "They require privacy."

Phillip didn't put his shoulders back, but he was tempted. "As you will."

"You'll want to fetch your lady."

"She's not my lady," Phillip said without hesitation. "She's just a woman in the wrong place at the wrong time."

"Just in time for you to rescue her?" Jake asked with a grave smile. "Of course. If you wouldn't mind bringing her just the same, this will interest her."

Phillip nodded as if he prepared to learn nothing more interesting than what Amanda planned for the next day's meals. He turned and walked back toward the great hall, unable to decide if he was looking forward to the next hour or dreading it.

The one thing he thought he could say was that he suspected a few of the bigger mysteries of his life were about to be cleared up.

Chapter 19

S o, this was how the other medieval half lived.

Imogen paused just inside the doorway of Jackson of Raventhorpe's private den and realized how it was someone during the Middle Ages might actually survive without the yet-to-be-conceived comforts of modern life, like cheesecake and limeades made with crushed ice.

The room was sumptuous. The walls might have been stone, but they were covered with gorgeous tapestries that had to have cost a fortune. There were rugs on the floor, a roaring fire in the fireplace, and ample places to sit that definitely had a medieval flair but left her suspecting that she wouldn't feel as if she'd spent the evening sitting on a plank.

The lord of Ravensthorpe was standing next to the fire, looking lordly. His wife, Amanda, was sitting down in a chair next to where he was standing, looking stunning. Imogen had grown used to looking at Rose, so she wasn't as startled by Amanda as she might have been otherwise, but there was no denying that somewhere along the line, someone had been absolutely beyond gorgeous and passed down all those good looks. Amanda was both beautiful and serene.

Or, maybe not so serene. She was wearing a calm expression that Imogen might have believed if she hadn't been tapping the toes of her feet inside her shoes. Maybe no one else would have realized that, but Imogen had made it a habit to notice that kind of thing. Occupational hazard, maybe, from always having to know what her siblings were thinking and what that might mean for her. She'd had an interesting life so far, that was for sure.

Phillip touched her elbow. "Let me see you seated by the fire," he said quietly.

Imogen looked up at him quickly. There was something in his voice that was definitely reflected in his face. He looked like someone who had suddenly allowed himself to entertain the possibility that unicorns were real and that he might see them the next time he went outside. He didn't look good.

"Yes, please come in, Imogen."

Imogen looked at Lord Jake . . . and that was an odd name for a medieval lord, but they pronounced it with a soft J so maybe it was less weird than she thought. She nodded and took the seat Phillip indicated for her to take, across from Amanda and close to the fire. It was a relatively comfortable chair, she had to admit. Furniture store level while still managing to retain some medieval character. She wasn't sure that kind of thing would fly on a medieval movie set, but what did she know? It wasn't so much about what people would believe as it was that things looked like what people already believed.

She hoped that wasn't a metaphor for her life.

Phillip sat down in a chair next to her—or perched in the chair next to her. Really, the man looked as if the slightest twinkle of fairy dust would send him bolting. Jake looked profoundly uncomfortable. Amanda continued to wiggle her toes in her shoes. Imogen wondered briefly if they were trying to come up with a way to tell her they had decided once and for all that she needed to be dealt with so they could get back to their medieval lives, but she didn't see any sharp things in anyone's hands. Phillip had left his sword by the door, which she supposed boded well.

She almost put her hand to her head. She was noticing where weapons were. Her life had become very weird.

Jake cleared his throat. "I'm not sure where to begin."

"You should begin at the beginning, husband."

"Difficult to decide where the beginning is, don't you think?"

Imogen wasn't about to help them. All she could do was wonder why they had asked her come talk with them. Maybe they were gearing up to tell her that they'd found her phone and someone was warming up the fire pit outside . . .

And then she realized what was so strange.

They were speaking in English.

She looked at Phillip and realized why he looked so uncomfortable. He was watching his aunt and uncle as if he expected them to do something truly unpredictable, as if perhaps speaking modern English in a medieval solar wasn't enough. She looked back at the pair across from her. Well, *look* wasn't the right word, she supposed. She gaped at them. It was all she could do to keep breathing normally.

"You're speaking English," she wheezed.

Amanda glanced at Jake, then looked at her. "That's true."

Imogen found herself on her feet. The only reason she hadn't tipped her chair over backward was because Phillip had caught it. She groped for something to hold on to and saw a hand come into her field of vision. But that was Phillip de Piaget's hand, Phillip de Piaget, medieval knight. No help from that quarter. She wrapped her arms around herself, then thought better of it and pointed an accusing finger at both Amanda and Jake.

"You're speaking modern English."

Jake nodded slowly. "We are."

"But . . . but this is 1254." Imogen found herself sitting down and realized that was far preferable to swaying right into the fire, which she'd been on the verge of doing. She didn't dare look at the man who had pulled her down into her chair because regardless of what anyone else believed, she was fairly sure he thought he was in 1254. "How in the world would you know modern English—unless this isn't 1254 and you all have been running a really method-actingish reality show that I never want to be on again."

Jake smiled. "No, this is the real thing." He looked at Amanda. "And we should speak in the current tongue, in deference to Phillip."

Imogen didn't want to look at Phillip, but he'd saved her

from singeing herself without an accusation of witchcraft to keep her company, so maybe she owed him at least a look.

He was still wearing that same look of horrified anticipation, as if he had finally come to grips with the reality of mythical creatures but now fully expected to see a few tromp through his uncle's private den. She wished she could have said something to help him, but she was too busy trying to figure out something intelligent to say to his uncle.

She looked at Amanda. "You spoke English."

"That's what happens when you're wed to a man from the Future," Amanda said calmly.

Imogen shook her head. She shook it again when the first try didn't help her make sense of what she was hearing.

"The future?"

"The Future."

She supposed she might be able to appreciate the difference with enough time, but at the moment, all she knew was that she had heard someone speak words she could understand without trouble, never mind the posh British accent tinged with something that sounded a little like Brooklyn.

It was bliss.

She looked at Jake. "You're from the Future? Really?"

He nodded. "Guilty as charged."

"Wait," Phillip said, holding up his hand. He was speaking in Norman French. "Wait. I don't understand."

"Do your kids know?" Imogen asked, because she couldn't help herself. "Well, of course they know. Rose spoke English—"

She stopped at the look on their faces. Amanda's and Jake's, rather. Phillip still looked as if someone had definitely confirmed the unicorn thing for him.

"Would someone," he managed in a garbled tone, "please tell me what is happening here."

Jake pulled up a stool and sat down, looking at his nephew. "I have an interesting tale to tell you. I don't share this with very many people," he said carefully, "but I will trust you with it."

"And my father?" Phillip said hoarsely. "Have you trusted him with it?"

Jake looked as if he wished he weren't sitting where he was. Maybe he wished he were back wherever he'd learned that posh English accent he'd been using. "Robin was the first one I told."

"Before your wife?" Phillip asked incredulously.

"Before my wife—a sore point with her still, thank you for reminding her."

Phillip didn't look as if he appreciated the humor Jake was obviously trying to inject into the situation. Imogen appreciated it only because she'd been watching Amanda's face and had seen that while it might have been a sore spot initially, it had obviously become a cherished private joke between them. She also could plainly see that there was a deep, lasting affection between the two sitting there.

She envied them.

"Did you tell anyone else?" Phillip demanded. "Are there others you entrusted with these important tidings?"

"Nick," Jake admitted, "but there are special reasons for that. Perhaps a few others."

"But not me." Phillip looked less stricken than the beginning of very angry. "You couldn't bring yourself to trust me yet you could trust . . ." He spluttered for several moments. "My father? My giddy uncle Nicholas? By the saints—"

"If you can be patient, Phillip, I will tell you what I know and answer any questions you have," Jake said patiently, "and I do trust you. That was never the issue."

"Then what, pray tell, is the issue?" Phillip asked angrily.

"The perilous nature of what I'm about to tell you," Jake said. "This truth isn't so much secret as it is deadly. And there was no reason for you to know. Well, no reason before, that is. Now? Now, I think you have a very good reason to know quite a few things you haven't before."

Imogen didn't want to speculate on what that reason might be and she was definitely not about to interrupt what was going on. She zipped her lips, mentally tossed away the key, and waited for the details to come out. She had the feeling that Phillip wasn't nearly as excited about the thought of it as she was.

A man from the future. She could hardly believe it.

"I am not from our current day," Jake said carefully, "but where I am from requires a bit of a tale."

"What do you mean," Phillip said, "*I'm not from our current day?*"

"I was born in the Year of Our Lord's Grace 1973," Jake said carefully. "Seven hundred years from now. Well, seven hundred and a bit."

"Impossible," Phillip said, but he didn't sound as if he thought it were all that impossible.

Imogen realized what Jake had said and gaped at him. "What?"

"Child of the seventies," Jake admitted. "And everything tacky that entails."

"1973," Imogen repeated. "You were born then."

"Yes."

"But now you're here."

"In 1254," Jake agreed. "Yes to that, too."

Imogen looked at Phillip. He was watching his uncle with now absolutely no expression on his face. She thought that might have been a bit more worrying than having him look shell-shocked.

"It's an interesting story," Jake continued, "but obviously fairly unbelievable unless you've lived through it. Which apparently, Imogen, you have."

Imogen thought she might have babbled something. She was torn between wanting to agree with Jake and wanting to tell him to shut up so Phillip didn't turn that expressionless look on her.

Jake looked briefly at Amanda before turning back to addressing . . . well, she was unsure whom he was addressing. Either her or Phillip, or maybe both. He looked like he would have rather been talking to a less-invested-in-the-story-type audience, but hell, the guy was living hundreds of years out of his time. Maybe he was used to it.

"The details of my trip here are not really all that important, I suppose," Jake said, "though I'll give them to you anyway for the sake of being thorough. I was driving along in a perfectly restored 1967 Jag, it flipped, and I woke up here. Well, not here. I woke up near Artane."

"I found him in the grass," Amanda said. "I was running away from a marriage and ran into him."

Imogen was torn between watching Jake and Amanda squirm and watching Phillip grow stiller and stiller. Rose's parents were interesting. Phillip was frightening.

"I thought she was a princess," Jake said. He smiled at his wife. "Still do."

"You paid enough to the king for that to be the case," Amanda said, "as I continue to remind you."

"You were well worth it," Jake said. He sighed and looked at Imogen. "I managed to talk a king out of this hall and Amanda's father out of his oldest daughter and here we are several years later, living our lives in bliss."

"In the past."

"In the present," Jake corrected. He shrugged. "It depends on how you look at it."

"You said you were from London," Phillip said in a low voice. "You've said that to me scores of times."

"I did say that," Jake agreed slowly, "and there is truth to it, in a manner of speaking. I had a business—a trade, if you will—in London, of importing very expensive gems and selling them to those with money to purchase them."

"You're a merchant," Phillip accused.

"In a former lifetime," Jake said, "aye. And to be perfectly honest, I wasn't born in London. I was born in a different country."

"Which one?" Phillip asked curtly. "One that hasn't been discovered yet?"

Jake looked at him solemnly. "Exactly that."

Phillip snorted, then looked at his aunt. "And you knew. You know. You've known this all along!"

"Aye, Phillip," she said gently, "I've known."

"And you didn't tell me!"

"If it eases you any," Amanda said seriously, "we haven't told our own children."

Phillip pushed himself back in his chair. "This is too fantastical to be believed—" He stood up. "That language you spoke."

"English," Jake said. "It is spoken in my former time."

"Your *future* time," Phillip snarled.

"Well, that, too."

"But Jennifer," Phillip spluttered, "and Persephone . . ." His mouth worked for a moment or two as if he searched for words direct enough to express what was going on in his head. "Are you all from that accursed place?"

Jake only looked at him steadily.

Imogen watched Phillip consider, then simply turn and leave the solar. He pulled the door shut behind him and it closed with a bang. Imogen sat there with Jake and Amanda and listened to silence descend, a silence broken only by the crack and pop of the wood in the hearth as it was consumed by the very lovely fire. She realized it was the first time she'd been warm in days. If she had to live in the past, she would have built that kind of fireplace as well. No wonder Jake had.

She looked at the man who had been born in her time and tried to smile. She didn't imagine she'd done a very good job.

"I'm not hallucinating," she said.

He shook his head. "Nope, you're not."

He was speaking in modern English. That she was starting to qualify what version of the language being spoken based on its position on a timeline was a little alarming. She wanted to start shaking her head, but she was afraid if she started, she would never stop.

"And you're stuck here," she said.

"Oh, no, not stuck," Jake said.

She felt her heart stop. "You aren't?"

"Not at all. I'm here because I choose to be here."

"But he could go back to the Future at any time," Amanda said. "If he wanted to."

Imogen felt her heart start beating again, which she supposed was a handy thing. "Then I could, too. Go home, that is."

"In theory, yes," Jake said. He rubbed his hands together. "There are spots here in the UK—England and Scotland both—that seem to act as gates of a sort."

"Gates," Imogen repeated.

"Through time."

"I didn't go through a gate."

Jake tilted his head. "How did you get here, then?"

"I put my hand on a sword and passed out. I woke up in Haemesburgh. Not the Haemesburgh in the twenty-first century, if you know what I mean."

"I do," Jake assured her. He looked at his wife. "That's interesting."

"How do I get home?" Imogen asked.

"Do you want to go home?"

"Of course I want to go home!" She looked at him in shock. "Why wouldn't I?"

Jake shrugged. "No Wi-Fi signal keeping you up at night. Lots of peace and quiet."

"Lots of lack of coffee," she said pointedly. "You're also missing several other critical inventions like refrigeration, indoor plumbing, and random Internet searches."

"But we have silence," Jake said with a smile. "A slower pace. Good food, good wine, endless stars when the skies are clear." He reached for his wife's hand. "Someone to love."

"Well, I'm fresh out of the last," Imogen said, though she had to admit her prospects back home weren't very good, either. "How do I get home, do you think?"

"What'd you do with the sword when you woke up?" he asked.

"It was gone."

His eyebrows went up. "That's a bit of a problem."

"Apparently it's Phillip's sword from his grandfather," she added. "Or so I've been told. Heather of Haemesburgh stole it, I think."

"How do you know?" Amanda asked. "Though I'm not doubting you."

"Because Heather is the one who brought me to Haemesburgh in the future and had me put my hand on Phillip's sword. In the Future." Good grief, she was starting to capitalize it as well.

"We'll have to give this some thought," Jake said.

"Please think fast." She started to get up, then looked at Jake. "I've lost my phone."

He pulled something out of a pocket. "This one?"

She felt relief wash over her. "That's it."

"Amanda found it upstairs," he said, "and I understand that your things are in Rose's trunk. She doesn't know what they are, I'm sure."

"Oh, I'm sure about that, too," Imogen said, because she held out as much hope for that as she supposed Jake did. She smiled grimly. "I'll go talk to Phillip."

"He doesn't like secrets or mysteries."

"And this was both," Imogen said. "I'll see if he'll talk to me."

Jake looked at his hands for a moment or two, then up at her. "Be careful."

"Do you think he'll stab me?" she asked, trying to muster up a laugh and only succeeding in making a sound that sounded a bit like a bleat instead.

"I'm afraid he'll be rude."

"I don't know him very well," she said, "but I think he's less likely to punch me than he would be you."

Jake smiled. "There is that."

"And he left his sword there in the corner. I'll take it to him. Maybe that will make him feel better."

"Punching me is the only thing that's going to make him feel better," Jake said with a bit of a laugh, "but I'll leave that for later. Good luck. See if you can get him to come back inside. He'll run himself into the ground if we leave him out there."

Amanda nodded. "My brother—his father—does that. It drives his wife mad, but there you have it. Men of energy and purpose, those lads."

"And what does that make me?" Jake asked, sounding as if he were trying to muster up an offended tone.

"The love of my life, when you sit still long enough for me to tell you the same," Amanda said, leaning over and kissing her husband.

"I'm outta here," Imogen said, but she realized she wasn't being heard. It was just as well, she supposed. She needed to find Phillip and talk him down off the wall before he did something stupid.

She understood, really. There was nothing like having one's worldview shattered to leave a person feeling a little unhinged.

She left the solar to find Sam and Theo waiting for her. She started to tell them to get lost, then decided she would find out from them where Phillip had gone and *then* tell them to get lost.

Chapter 20

Phillip ran about the perimeter of the lists, knowing it was what his sire did when he was thinking but unable to stop himself from doing the same thing. It wasn't as if he didn't love his sire or admire the man to the depths of his soul. He did. Robin of Artane was the stuff of legends, a knight of unmatched prowess, a deep thinker, fiercely protective of his wife and children, a champion of those who needed someone to stand in front of them and keep them safe.

And a damned liar, apparently.

He tried to comfort himself with a string of vile profanities that would have earned him a month on his knees in the chapel if his mother had heard him. He kept at that for quite some time because it took his mind off other things, namely what in the hell was going on in the world that he hadn't noticed.

He didn't like being oblivious.

He also didn't like feeling like a child. Why hadn't they trusted him with this? It wasn't as if he had a loose tongue or was prone to babbling things to anyone who would listen. He was a vault, a catacomb of silence, a repository of tidings about anything perilous and dire—

He realized he wasn't alone. Jackson had joined him. He

couldn't say his cousin looked any better than he felt. He glanced at him.

"Need a run, too?"

"Nay, simply coming along to try to keep you from killing yourself."

Phillip stopped. He wished he weren't breathing so raggedly, but in his defense, he'd spent the breath he should have been reserving for his run cursing. That sort of thing took a toll on a man.

He looked at Jackson. "I've learned things I cannot tell you."

Jackson rolled his eyes. "I have grown to manhood in this keep, Phillip. I doubt you've learned anything I didn't already know." He paused. "Plus, I eavesdrop a great deal."

"Were you just eavesdropping at your father's door?"

"Didn't need to."

Phillip considered. There were few people he trusted—nay, he couldn't say that. There were quite a few souls he trusted. He realized that it perhaps should have bothered him that he felt the need to continually make a list of those souls, but that was definitely something he could think about later.

He continued with his accounting, because it made him feel secure. He trusted his parents. He trusted his siblings, particularly Kendrick, who knew every last damned one of his few secrets. He trusted Rose, obviously; Connor, assuredly; Jackson, without reservation. His cousin was five years younger than he was, but sturdy and unwavering and silent as the tomb. And, as Jackson had said, he'd grown to manhood in the keep behind them. If anyone would know Jackson Kilchurn IV's secrets, it would be his son.

He dragged his sleeve across his face. "I'm having thoughts about Imogen."

"I can see why," Jackson said grimly. "She's terribly beautiful."

"Not those kinds of thoughts—very well, I've been having those kinds of thoughts as well, but these are different thoughts."

"Oh, please enlighten me."

Phillip would have smiled, but he was too damned unnerved to. "'Tis odd that she simply appeared at Haemesburgh, don't you think?"

"Perhaps she and Heather played a game of chance with you as the prize and Imogen lost."

Phillip snorted. "And to think I was prepared to confide in you."

Jackson almost smiled. He rarely did, which Phillip supposed, knowing what he now knew, he could understand. "Confide away."

Phillip took a deep breath. "I think Imogen might be from a different place." He had to gather his courage to spew out the rest of what he knew he now needed to say. "A different time, actually." He looked at his cousin. "Your father's time."

Jackson only regarded him steadily. "I suppose that's possible."

"Possible?" Phillip said, choking on the word. "By all the bloody saints, Jack, do you realize what we're discussing here?"

"I think I might have a fair idea."

Phillip supposed 'twas only good breeding on his cousin's part that left him not enjoying the feeling of Jackson's fist in his mouth. "Forgive me. Of course you do." He dragged his hands through his hair, realizing only then that he'd left his sword behind in Jake's solar, damn it anyway. "I have always hoped that perhaps Pippa and your sire were distant, unwitting cousins, having learned things in separate locales without knowing each other . . ."

Jackson looked as if he might have wished the same thing. "But you know better."

"Now. And I didn't have to eavesdrop to learn it."

Jackson only closed his eyes and let out his breath carefully.

"It seems fanciful," Phillip added.

"That's one way to put it."

Phillip looked up at the sky. It was all too fantastical to be believed. A man moving from one year to the next without having to live through the moments that made the up the days spanning the distance? A man traveling over hundreds of years without seeing any of them? He could honestly say he would sooner believe a man being a specter for centuries and watching the time unravel before him before he could believe that.

But Jake wasn't a liar.

He looked around him, trying to make certain he was still

in his proper time and place. Aye, he was still in 1254, in the lists at Ravensthorpe, standing next to his cousin who had also grown to manhood in the current century. He was currently looking at—

Looking at a woman from the Future.

She was standing against the wall, wrapped in a cloak, the last of twilight leaving her looking more like a ghost than a corporeal being. He stared at her and let the truth of her origins give him a bracing slap across the face.

She wasn't from Edinburgh.

She was from the Future.

"It is hard to deny," Jackson said quietly.

He looked at his cousin. "Do you think so?"

"Most of the time, cousin, I try not to think."

"But the . . . the . . ." Phillip couldn't bring himself to even voice the word.

"The Future?" Jackson supplied. "Is that what you're trying so unsuccessfully to say?"

Phillip looked at his cousin and felt a wave of sympathy wash over him. "You poor bastard."

"Which I'm not, as you well know, but the sentiment is appreciated."

Phillip shook his head. It provided him with no relief, but he shook it again because he simply couldn't believe what he'd learned. "Your father could be daft, you know."

"If it eases you to think that, feel free. I know I've considered the like more times than is polite." He sighed deeply. "She must be terrified."

"I should see to her."

"Altruistic to the last."

Phillip shot his cousin a brief smile before he clapped him on the shoulder in passing. "We'll talk later."

"I'm sure we will."

Phillip crossed the lists to come to a stop before Imogen. She was watching him warily, as if she fully expected him to do something dire. He supposed the list of what those things could have been was rather long, but he was nothing if not measured in his reactions to things that bothered him. It was also true that what bothered him at present was slightly out of the scope of everyday vexations, but that wasn't her fault.

He offered his arm. "Care for a stroll about the lists?"

"Your cousin Rose loaned me boots for just that possibility."

"She is nothing if not prepared."

She held out his sword. Either it was heavier than she was accustomed to, or she was uneasy, for her hand shook badly. He took the blade from her, belted it about his hips as he'd done countless times over the course of his life and never found it strange until that moment, then extended his elbow her way.

"Shall we?"

She nodded but said nothing. She did, however, take his elbow. He wasn't sure he'd ever had a woman touch him in such a simple way yet leave him scarce able to keep his feet.

His life was definitely not proceeding as planned.

He walked with her for quite some time, more relieved than he'd anticipated not to be required to say anything at all. Torches were lit, something that made him smile a bit in spite of himself.

"What is it?" Imogen asked.

He nodded toward a lad who was hurrying around the perimeter of the field and lighting fires. "They're doing that for us."

"Are they? Why is that funny?"

Funny was a word he didn't know, but he supposed that wouldn't be the first time he heard something he had to scratch his head over. He decided he would ask her its meaning later and instead simply forge ahead with what had amused him.

"My father is famous for running about the lists at all hours to clear his head. He has a cadre of lads whose sole task it is to make certain he doesn't stub his delicate toes against a rock in the dark. I'm not sure my lord uncle engages in the same madness, but they have definitely taken a care for us."

He looked at her briefly, just to see if she was catching what he was saying. She didn't look baffled. She looked like she was fair to shattering, though. He covered her hand with his and stopped in the circle of torchlight.

"Imogen—"

"I'm not a witch," she blurted.

He blinked in surprise. "Of course you're not."

"If you try to go collect kindling, I'll . . . I'll . . ."

He smiled. "You'll what?"

She pulled her hand away and glared at him. "I'll take your sword and stab you with it."

"You're very fierce," he said, "but definitely not a witch. You need have no fear of anyone accusing you of that."

"I think lots of people could accuse me."

"Not in front of me," he said seriously, "which is perhaps why you should remain near me."

She blinked at him. He wasn't sure if that was because the thought was horrifying or distasteful, but he wasn't going to ask her which it was. She looked a little bemused, actually, as if she just wasn't sure how to take him, if taking him was something she was interested in doing.

He promised himself a good rest very soon. He was starting not to make sense inside his own head and that worried him.

And then she smiled.

"Thank you," she said, looking genuinely touched.

"Chivalry is always in fashion," he managed. "And always convenient."

"Is that what this is?"

He laughed a little in spite of himself. "Nay, just good breeding thanks to my mother, as well as a bit of selfishness on my part. If I keep you near me, you stay protected, and I'm able to be dazzled by your lovely green eyes."

"They're brown," she said with a smile, then her smile faded. "I appreciate it, but it wouldn't be for very long. I need to go home."

He'd known she would want to go, of course, but he hadn't expected the hearing of it to be so unpleasant. "Of course. The offer stands for as long as you're here."

"I'm getting in the way of your empire building, I think."

To hell with my empire was almost out of his mouth before he could stop it. He did have excellent self control, though, so he bit that back and said what he feared he needed to say. "I know where you need to go."

She looked at him searchingly. "Do you?"

He blew out his breath. "I fear I'm the one who needs to walk now, if you'll indulge me." He waited until they had reached the end of the lists where he was sure there were no cousins lurking, then sighed. "I have spent my share of time at

Ravensthorpe, of course, but I fear I first started to become acquainted with, ah—"

"Weird stuff?"

He smiled. "*Paranormal oddities* is what my father calls them. 'Tis a term I happily credited to his losing his wits. That was, as you might imagine, an occurrence I welcomed readily given that it meant I would take his seat that much sooner."

"You aren't serious."

He lifted his eyebrows briefly. "I love my sire, the irascible bastard, and nay, I'm not praying for his demise no matter how much I clamor for it. And of course I dismissed any mention of anything untoward as the fanciful imaginings of those too acquainted with the contents of their wine cellars." He had to take another breath or two, then he stopped and looked at her. "My uncle Montgomery's wife is from your time, as well."

She looked rather ill, all things considered. "Another one?"

"Doesn't that ease you?"

"I'm not sure anything would ease me right now." She pulled her hand away and wrapped her arms around her middle. "I think I might be sick."

He thought he might understand that all too well. For a man—or a maid, for that matter—to live his life secure in thinking the world behaved in a certain fashion, then to find out that nothing was as he'd believed it to be . . . Aye, it was unsettling indeed.

He nodded back toward the hall. "Let's go find something to drink, then. My uncle has an excellent cellar."

"Do you drink?"

"Not yet."

She smiled weakly, then took his arm when he offered it to her. He wasn't sure if she knew she was doing it or not. What he did know was that she looked fair to losing her supper and for that he couldn't blame her in the slightest.

He realized suddenly that he had a thousand questions for her. What did the Edinburgh of the future look like? Was Artane still standing? Had the world truly ended in the Year of Our Lord's Grace 1300?

What in the hell was why-fie and why did she continue to mutter about it?

There were other things as well, things that were less easy

for him to face. He couldn't quite decide if he was hurt because he'd been kept in the dark about details that others seemed to be terribly familiar with or because he thought Imogen might want to go back to the place where she'd come from.

He was tempted to take the hilt of his sword—the sword he'd had made to fit his hand, which apparently wasn't magical enough to transport anything through time—smash it into his own forehead and hopefully render himself senseless. By the saints, of course she was going to want to go home. Why would she want to stay in his current world with all its lack of wonders?

Why would she want to stay with him?

"Phillip."

He realized he was forcing her to trot to keep up with him. He stopped, took a deep breath, then looked at her. He hardly knew what to say. His entire world, everything that he thought he knew, had suddenly been ripped asunder. He realized, after indulging in a fair bit of self-pity, that she was in exactly the same place.

"Forgive me," he said. "Too much thinking. I'll stop running."

"I think I understand why you're doing it."

"I imagine you do." He started across the field with her again, keeping his pace to something he thought was reasonable. He glanced at her. "How did it happen? If I can ask."

"I put my hand on your sword and I fell through something," she said. "A gate? A doorway I didn't see? At first, I thought I'd just opened a trapdoor in the floor behind the lord's chair." She shrugged. "All I know is I wound up here."

"You must have been terrified."

"You caught me when I fell."

"Off the end of the drawbridge," he said wryly, "and given that I'm the one who told you to drop, I'm not sure that counts as a proper rescue."

"You still caught me." She let out a shuddering breath. "I'm starting to wonder if maybe it was just a quirk of fate that never should have happened." She looked at him bleakly. "You don't have your castle and I don't have my world."

"Aye, but we have my uncle's cellars," he managed, because he feared he might become maudlin if he spoke of anything more serious. "If those fail to impress, we might mount an assault on his kitchens. If nothing else, the man is very concerned with the state of his belly."

She smiled and he realized how far he was toward being lost in the eyes of a woman who didn't belong to his castle, his time, or his heart.

Damn them all three for being what he wanted.

Chapter 21

I mogen stood in the damp cellar of Ravensthorpe and thought she might like to be somewhere else.

At least it was where the wine and ale were apparently kept, not where prisoners were kept. She hadn't asked if Phillip's uncle Jake had a dungeon because she just didn't want to know. She couldn't imagine being a miscreant in medieval times and honestly didn't want to try, though she supposed she really should at least make mental notes about her surroundings for use when she got back to the future and actually had to do her job.

Assuming she could get back to the future.

She was starting to feel like she was in a movie complete with Juilliard-trained actors who would have sooner burned SAG cards than break character. She knew where she was and she knew *when* she was, but there was still a part of her that wanted to cling to the thought that she was in a sibling-created reality show or a drug-induced hallucination. She could have, with hardly any effort, believed that everyone around her at least thought they were living in the Middle Ages.

The upside to their commitment to craft was that she was living the dream of getting to see history firsthand, which she had to admit she had secretly wished for several times over the course of her life. She supposed it was a little on the ungrateful side to wish that experience had come with slightly more comfortable shoes and better food. She had the feeling Jake and Lady Amanda were pretty progressive when it came to dinnertime, so it could have been much worse.

She watched Phillip take the torch he'd been using to investigate corners and jam it into a sconce as if he'd been doing the same thing his entire life. Which she supposed he had.

Talk about surreal.

Apparently they weren't the first ones to choose the cellar as a place for a private chat. There was a handy semicircle of half casks set there for just that sort of thing. She took a seat and waited for Phillip to do the same. He rubbed his hands together and looked at her.

"Well," he said.

She paused to appreciate the strangeness of her current situation—talking to a man eight hundred years older than she was about things that would probably blow his mind—then attempted a smile.

"Well," she agreed.

He took a deep breath, then pushed himself to his feet. Imogen watched him fuss with a couple of mugs, filling them with what she hoped was drinkable stuff, then come and sit back down.

"I don't want to pry," he said slowly, "but I am curious about a few things, if you can stomach the thought of enlightening me."

She bought herself some time by tasting what was in the heavy silver mug Phillip gave her. It wasn't awful, but then again, she downed wheatgrass on a regular basis, so the bar was set pretty low. She had another sip, then looked at him.

"What do you want to know?"

"How it all began," he said. "Or perhaps even further back than that. How old are you? What were you doing when you . . . ah . . . when you . . . ?"

"I'm twenty-six," she said, because she thought if he wound himself any tighter, he just might come unraveled. "Pretty old for these days, isn't it?"

"My grandmère was well into her eightieth year when she

died, so nothing seems very old to me." He looked at her steadily. "It seems a bit unimportant compared to everything else."

"When you look at it that way, it does," she agreed. She had another swig of wine that at second blush wasn't at all nasty, then mentally girded her loins. "Are you sure you want to talk about any of this? Knowing too much about the future can be a dangerous thing." She paused and had to have another drink just to remind herself that she was really sitting in the basement of a medieval castle not on a movie set where the script called for lots of time traveling. "I can't believe I just said that."

He looked about as green as she felt. "I understand, believe me. And there is wisdom in what you say." He had a strengthening sip of his own drink. "Perhaps if you simply tell me about yourself and leave off with anything else."

"I'm not very interesting," she protested.

"I disagree," he said, looking at her seriously, "but we can argue that point later perhaps." He made himself more comfortable on his cask. "Tell me what you will. I'll believe it all, I guarantee it."

He had an amazing tolerance for crazy, she would say that much for him. She nodded. "As far as how I got here, that's pretty straightforward. I had flown over to the UK—"

"The . . . UK?"

"United Kingdom," she said. She realized immediately that she was really going to have to watch herself about even simple details. All she needed was to say the wrong thing and change the course of history. At least she wasn't going to have to keep up that watching of her words for as long as Jake had. "It's what they call England, Scotland, and Wales. Oh, and Ireland. Well, the north part at least."

"Scotland," he repeated, sounding stunned. "Wales as well? When did this unifying happen?"

"I'm not sure. Quite a while before the Revolutionary War in America, but I can't give you exact dates." Actually, she could give him exact dates but it seemed like an extraordinarily bad idea. He was trying to secure a keep right on England's border with Scotland. The last thing he needed was to have any idea what was coming down the pike toward him.

She could have made a mint as a medieval fortune teller, that much was certain.

"America?" he asked.

She started to answer, then shook her head. "I'm probably telling you things you don't need to know. Let's talk about something else."

He took a substantial swig of his wine. "Very well, What were you doing in the . . . United Kingdom?" he asked faintly. "Were you born here or is that also something we shouldn't talk about?"

"Probably the latter," she said. "I wasn't born in the UK. I was born in, ah, Jake's country, actually. I had gotten a job here and flown over—"

"Job? Flown?"

He was looking for wings. She knew he was trying to be discreet and it wasn't at all funny, but she almost laughed. She took a deep breath. "There are these, well they're sort of these long wine-cask things that have wings." She shrugged helplessly. "They go up in the sky and carry you long distances."

"What powers them?"

She smiled in spite of herself. "I've just told you that man will eventually fly like birds and you're more curious about how fast he goes than whether or not he actually gets off the ground?"

"I like fast horses." He smiled. "Familial failing, I'm afraid. I'm always interested in power."

She could have sworn she heard a snort, but it was just the two of them. She looked over her shoulder and also could have sworn that she saw the hint of blond hair, but maybe that was just her imagination. She opened her mouth to relate that interesting story about how she was just sure she'd seen someone who had to have been either Sam and Theo's older relative in the future, but thought better of it. She wasn't entirely sure they weren't being eavesdropped on by those two, so it was probably better not to give them any ideas.

Phillip obviously shared her suspicions given that he was looking into the shadows with a frown. He considered, then leaned closer. "We'll have to whisper. Tell me more about these wings and how they're powered."

Well, if there was one thing she could definitely talk about with the authority granted by experience, it was how many varieties of airplanes one evil sister could book for her younger, trusting sibling. She told Phillip everything she knew about every plane she had flown on during that endless fifty-three-hour trip to London. He set his wine aside about the time she flew into Chicago and the cup was all but forgotten by the time she'd reached Heathrow.

She was actually very sorry he would never get to at least drive a car. The man was, as he had admitted, obsessed with horsepower.

He finally sat back, fumbled for his cup, and drained it. He took a deep breath, then shook his head. "Almost beyond belief, but I suppose in the Future, the fantastical is common. So you had . . . flown . . . here from Chicago, then what?"

He was speaking in French, his version of French, which made the modern terms he attempted to sprinkle in here and there almost more charming than she could stand. She only wished she had a better grasp of the rest of what he was saying. It wasn't exactly eighteenth century poetic French, but he was trying and she thought it was possible that with enough time she would have gotten the hang of it. She almost wished she could be there long enough for that to happen.

Almost.

"So, I had landed in London," she said, "and then taken the train—no, never mind about that. Not nearly as interesting as flying. Let's just say that I was in Edinburgh for my job."

"A task to do," he said slowly. He smiled. "I've heard Jake use that word a time or two."

"He's going to land himself in hot water if he's not careful," she said easily. "But yes, a task to do. It happens that in my time, we have these plays." She stopped, then looked at him. "I suppose you do, too."

"We do," he agreed, "and isn't that an odd thing to have in common?"

"People need the occasional escape from too much reality," she said with a smile, "so maybe not as strange as we think. Anyway, my job was to find things for the actors to use in our plays."

"Here in England?"

"And Scotland, too, though I was starting in Edinburgh. I

was looking in this shop on the Royal Mile and this woman just sort of showed up behind me and asked me if I wanted to see a castle—and she wasn't talking about the one up the road."

"Which hall, then?" he asked. "Artane?"

She shook her head. "No, Haemesburgh."

He went very still. "And why did she have any right to show it to you?"

"Because she said it was her castle." She paused. "She said her name was Heather."

"Damn her." He started to say something else, then just shook his head. "I'm somehow not surprised. I'm guessing it is our missing Heather, but I imagine we'll have to determine later how she escaped my time. Very well, what happened then?"

"I traveled to Haemesburgh the next morning and Heather showed me around the place."

"It still stands in your day?" he asked in surprise.

"If you can believe it, and looking actually quite a bit better than it does at the moment." She smiled. "Maybe you clean it up in the future."

"The saints preserve me," he said uneasily, "what a terrible thought." He poured himself more wine. "The more I think about it, the more I'm not sure I want to know anything about the future."

Imogen wasn't sure he would want to, either. The Black Death, Henry's razing of the monasteries, good grief, Led Zeppelin. She took a deep breath and looked at him.

"If it makes you feel any better, the Magna Carta turns out to be a very good thing," she said. "You'll be glad you have that. It changes history."

He stared at her so long, she was almost afraid she'd said too much. Then he blinked rapidly once or twice. If she hadn't known better, she would have suspected he was growing misty-eyed. For all she knew, he was.

"My head pains me."

"Your mind is being blown. Don't worry. It'll pass."

"Mind-blowing," he murmured, in English, no less. "My uncle Nicholas is wont to mutter that from time to time, damn him to hell." He set his wine on the floor and rubbed his hands over his face. "All the things that have been right in front of me that I couldn't bring myself to look at."

"If it makes you feel better, I think we all do it."

He sighed. "You have that aright, I'm sure. And I continue to interrupt you. So, you had gone to Haemesburgh and Heather, damn her, had welcomed you inside. I almost hesitate to ask you what happened then."

"She showed me around for a bit, then we ended up in the great hall. There was a sword stuck in the floor behind the lord's table. It looked medieval but in surprisingly good condition, which at the time I thought was a bit strange. I admit I was surprised she let me anywhere near it, but that didn't seem to bother her. She invited me to put my hand on the hilt. I did, fainted, then when I woke up I was looking up not at her, but at the guys who were at the castle. In your day."

"A sword," he said slowly.

"Your sword."

He caught his breath. "That much is almost unbelievable."

"It is," she agreed. "I think there might be something magical about that sword." She paused, then looked at him with a smile. "I can't believe I'm saying that."

"I understand, believe me," he said fervently. He shook his head. "'Tis obvious Heather has found a way to your time. One wonders how she managed it."

Imogen started to agree that it was indeed something to wonder about and then it occurred to her that maybe she didn't need to spend all that much energy at it. If she herself had used the sword to come to the past, who was to say that Heather hadn't used it to get to the future?

She looked at Phillip. "How long ago did she swipe it from you?"

"Five years ago," he said. "I suppose I could bring the exact date to mind, if necessary."

"How did it happen?"

He shifted uncomfortably. "Whilst I was cursing over the condition of my clothing that had just become saturated with cesspit leavings, some whoreson came up behind me and clouted me over the head. When I woke, my sword was gone. 'Tis nothing more than I deserve, I daresay, for concentrating on the wrong things."

"And you didn't have any of your men with you?"

"Well, of course—" He stopped and frowned. "Just

Cederic, my captain. I hadn't wanted to frighten either Heather or her father by bringing along a small army."

"When did you get the rest of your motley crew?" she asked. Good grief, not even Mötley Crüe was around. Really, she was in primitive times.

"Immediately after," he said. "My father insisted, though I didn't argue." He lifted his eyebrows briefly. "I was a fool to go with only one man, but there you have it. The hubris of youth."

She wanted to ask him a dozen things, beginning and ending with how bizarre it must be to know you were in line for that gigantic castle on the edge of the sea and that your life was worth as much for that lineage as it was for just your own self. She could see where being a medieval guy might have had its downsides.

"Well, you seem to have a loyal group around you now," she said, realizing she was complimenting him on having a security detail who would kill first and ask questions later, then shook her head and tried to latch onto what they'd been discussing. "Well, however your sword got to her, I'm guessing that's how she traveled to the future. I'm not sure how she would have known to stick your sword in the floor, though."

"I think it was nothing but a happy coincidence," he said grimly. "Her brother had mocked me by telling me they had driven my blade into the floor and were using it to hang cloaks on. I would suspect that Heather had tossed her brother's gear on the floor, put hers there instead, then found herself where she hadn't intended to go."

"That must have been something."

He smiled faintly. "You would know."

"I would," she agreed.

She wondered very briefly what Heather had thought when she'd wound up in the future, if she had had any idea beforehand what was going to happen to her, how in the world she had managed to land herself in the position of lady of Haemesburgh. She wondered what Heather had thought the first time she'd used a phone, or watched TV, or ridden in a car. The entire world must have seemed either magical or like something from a very bad dream.

"Perhaps we should go make use of that fire in my uncle's solar," Phillip suggested. "You looked chilled."

She suspected the he was shivering more than she was, but she'd already had her freak-out. It was his turn. She agreed, then climbed with him back up to the kitchens, happy to leave the basement with its dank chill behind. She could have sworn she heard a muffled sneeze, but she supposed that catching a cold was the least that should happen to potential eavesdroppers.

She considered Phillip's sword as they walked. There was the sentimental value, true, but she hated to admit that she was slightly more interested in it for its reputedly magical properties. She could hardly believe she was taking that seriously, but experience was hard to deny.

She wasn't sure where that left her, but she was starting to suspect that his sword was the key to getting back to where she needed to go. The only problem was, she had no idea how to even begin to look for it. If it had come with her when she'd come to the past, it was probably hiding under Hamish's bed. If Heather still had it, it was probably hiding under *her* bed in modern-day Haemesburgh.

She wasn't sure how she was going to do it, but she had to get her hands on that sword.

Chapter 22

Phillip walked through the kitchens of Ravensthorpe, trying to maintain some semblance of looking as though he weren't three breaths from falling to the floor in a dead faint.

He supposed he had moved past the point of being utterly shocked by what he was hearing to perhaps simply being numb to any more surprise. The only thing he could say for certain was that his entire world had been turned upside-down and he wasn't sure if he would ever look at anything the same way again.

Knocking on his uncle's solar was a good example of how odd his life had become. He'd done the same thing hundreds of times over the course of his life, yet at the moment it felt utterly foreign simply because he now knew that he wasn't knocking on the door of a man of his father's time, he was knocking on the door of a man from the Future.

The door opened. Phillip wouldn't have been surprised at what he found there, anything from a faery to a monster. Instead, it was simply Jake, the man he had squired for briefly, the man he had parried with endlessly, the man who had sired two of his favorite relatives. The man who had concealed his past for reasons that Phillip thought he might actually be able to forgive with enough time.

He sighed to himself. Damnation, he'd forgiven the man already and was actually feeling more respect for him than he perhaps deserved. After all, Jake had walked onto the stage of the current day, wrested a title and a bride from extremely powerful men, and set himself up as a lord to be reckoned with.

Phillip admired him. There was nothing more to be said.

"You look chilled," Jake said to Imogen. "And your friend there looks less likely to chop off my head than he did a couple of hours ago. Why don't you both come inside? I'll leave you in peace for a bit."

Jake stood aside and allowed Imogen to come inside his solar. Phillip followed her, then paused next to his uncle. He held out his hand and waited until Jake had taken it.

"Forgive me," he said simply.

Jake clapped him on the shoulder with his free hand. "Nothing to forgive, Phillip."

"If you kiss me, I'll slay you."

Jake laughed, kissed him loudly on both cheeks just the same, then left his solar, pulling the door shut behind him. Phillip rolled his eyes, cursed a bit to make himself feel more himself, then went to stand with his backside to the fire. He'd done that more times than he could count as well, though he had to admit he'd never been entertaining the sort of mind-blowing thoughts he was examining at present.

He looked at Imogen. She was sitting in the chair she'd been sitting in before, the one next to the fire. She looked exhausted, which he could understand. Exhausted and a bit frightened. He cast about for something benign to discuss but feared he was not at his best at the moment. He would have asked her more about her family, but talking about them obviously wearied her.

He could understand that to some extent. He had endured his own moments of wishing his parents had stopped having children after his birth, but those moments had been fairly rare. He was remarkably fond of his brothers and younger sister and he couldn't think of a cousin he didn't love almost as much as his own siblings. Even those damned twin demons,

Theopholis and Samuel of Wyckham, who he was fairly sure had somehow recently managed to stuff themselves in ale kegs for more successful eavesdropping below, weren't intolerable. He didn't think Imogen wanted pity for her lot in life, but he couldn't help but wish for something different for her. Perhaps for as long as she remained in his time.

He forced himself not to find that as odd a thought as he likely should have. The truth was, she would need to return to her own world, assuming she *could* return.

"The countryside around Haemesburgh is lovely," she said without warning. "And someone did restore the castle quite nicely."

"Perhaps Heather hired souls to see to it. Or pressed them into service without pay," he added, half under his breath.

She smiled. "She is very pretty, but a little frightening."

"I wouldn't know. I've only ever had her fling untoward things at me. And I'm suspecting that wasn't even her engaging in that dastardly work. You would think someone from her keep would have found me to be an acceptable mate. After all, I have all my teeth and I have enough gold to purchase my future bride the odd bolt of material now and then."

"And let's not forget all that chivalry."

"For all the good it does me," he agreed, "but aye, there is that." He chewed on other words he desperately wanted to voice for several minutes before he dared spew them out. "I don't suppose you know what happens to Haemesburgh," he said gingerly. "Throughout the years, that is."

She looked at him steadily. "I know more than I should," she said, "but I'm not sure you should know that much. And to be perfectly honest, I'm not as up on my British history as I should be."

"British?"

"That's what we call you. You know." She shrugged. "Then."

"And you're not British? Or Scots?"

"Maybe back in the past somewhere," she said, then she frowned. "Which might be the now, if I look at it the right way." She shrugged helplessly that time. "I'm lost without the Internet."

"Why-fie?" he asked gravely.

She smiled. "Yes, that." She paused. "Want to see?"

He wondered if a hefty tankard of ale might be in order first, but he was a knight of the realm and heir to his father's vast estates. Surely he should be equal to some bit of magic from the future. "Very well."

"It's not the rack, Phillip."

He smiled. It was the height of foolishness and Kendrick would have laughed himself sick over it, but the sound of his name from her lips was . . . enchanting.

There was the word again. The saints pity him, he was in trouble.

She pulled something out of some pocket or other. It was that little box fashioned of that appalling color of whitish red. He'd already encountered it once against his jaw and wasn't exactly sure he wanted another go, but she didn't look intimidated. If she could bear up under the strain, so could he.

He pulled up a stool and sat down in front of her, leaning in so he might have a better look at what she wanted to show him. It was a tiny thing, about the size of her hand, but rectangular. He would have called it a bit of carved stone, but it was metal, with some sort of magically clear surface. She pushed on it and the damned thing sprang to life with colors that he had never before imagined.

Or that might have been the stars swirling around his head and the attendant agony of having clunked his head against something sharp. The edge of a chair perhaps.

He looked up to find Imogen peering down at him. Actually, if he were to be completely accurate, it was Imogen, Jake, and Amanda all peering down at him. When had his aunt and uncle entered the chamber? And why when he wiped his cheek did his hand come away damp? It wasn't blood. He decided it had to be drool, damn it anyway.

"I am well," he croaked. "Never better."

Jake hauled him back up first to his arse, then all the way to his feet. He felt his way down into his chair as if he'd been every day of four score. He put his hand over his eyes until his head stopped pounding as if the rubbish between his ears was determined to exit through his eyes. He pried his eyes open in time to see his uncle Jake sitting down next to Imogen, looking with great interest at her little box.

"How much battery do you have left?" he was asking.

"Enough for a game or two, if you want."

Apparently that was repayment enough for his hospitality. Phillip watched his uncle frown thoughtfully and poke at Imogen's box—whatever the hell an android was—and then periodically laugh.

The man was nothing short of daft.

"Let me see," Phillip said, "lest Jake lose his soul in some untoward fashion."

Jake handed him the beast. "Don't drop it."

"I've already dropped myself."

"You have and see where that got you. Those are zombies. They're not real."

"What's a zombie?" Phillip asked, peering at the creatures limping across the face of the box.

"The undead," Jake said, "and I changed my mind. Hand that back over, my lad. I'm losing plants right and left. Imogen, this is a great game. I don't think I had this on my phone."

"It's addicting," Imogen admitted.

Phillip listened to them babble for a few minutes in their almost incomprehensible modern English and realized that if he listened closely enough, he could make out most of the words. It gave him a rather decent appreciation of just how difficult the first few days in the past must have been for Imogen. And what pains in the head she must have suffered, though he supposed his own could have come from falling out of his own chair.

"So," Jake said finally, returning Imogen's box to her, "what do you want to do?"

"Well, I can't stay, obviously," she said, shifting uncomfortably. "I just am not sure how to get back. It's not like I have any experience with this whole thing, but I'm afraid I don't have very many options." She looked at him. "Any suggestions?"

Jake sighed deeply. "Time traveling is never a safe or reliable thing." He paused, then looked at her and laughed. "If you can believe those words even came out of my mouth to start with."

"At this point, I think I can believe almost anything."

Phillip had to admit, he understood. He was sitting in his uncle's solar, looking at two souls who had been born hundreds of years of out of his time, and he could scarce believe the words he was listening to. He listened to Imogen relate to Jake the same tale she'd told him, that of encountering Heather of Haemesburgh in Edinburgh, traveling to visit her the next day at the keep, then encountering his own sword in the Future. It sounded less fantastical the second time than it had the first, which left room in what was left of his poor head to consider things he hadn't before.

Heather had obviously taken his sword to the Future, but how had she gotten to the future in the first place and why had she taken his sword with her? So he couldn't follow her and retrieve it? But if she had no intention of ever coming back to the past, why hadn't she simply shoved the damned thing through some sort of gate or portal or whatever those travelers through time used and been done with it? Had she not had any idea where any of that sort of thing lay?

He paused, then allowed himself to think on other things. What of those trunks his uncle Montgomery had brought in occasionally for his wife? Those had come from somewhere, hadn't they? Perhaps there was a portal there at Sedgwick. And obviously Jake had managed to come to the past through some sort of doorway, hadn't he? He himself had always considered his grandfather's sword to be a spectacular piece of business, but he had never once considered that it might possess magical properties past what, as his sire would have said, his own swordplay embued it with. Perhaps the magic of the sword needed to connect with the proper location inside Haemesburgh at the perfect time—

Or perhaps he simply needed to excuse himself, go back to bed, and sleep until good sense returned.

"Well, you could consult with our local witch," Jake was saying with a smile. "She and her helpers have already gotten themselves settled for the night in the finest guest room, but I can introduce you to them in the morning. Phillip knows Berengaria quite well."

He nodded to himself over that. First magical swords, then witches. What next?

"She arrived this morning," Jake continued. "She visits now and again to take the sea air."

Considering that Berengaria could just as easily take the same sea air at Artane, Phillip imagined that wasn't her reason for visiting. But he wasn't going to argue. He looked at Imogen. "Mistress Berengaria is not a witch, nor are her helpers." He shot his uncle a look. "No witch could possibly brew things as vile as do Nemain and Magda both. They would be shamed out of their profession by their fellows."

Jake smiled. "You have a point there. All I know is that over the years, I've learned to trust that Mistress Berengaria has seen her share of very odd things. Wouldn't you agree, Phillip?"

Phillip sighed. "I will admit that she recently told me my sword was enspelled. I, of course, snorted heartily enough to put out their cooking fire."

"And there you have it," Jake said to Imogen pleasantly. "Karma, coming around to bite him in the arse."

"Karma?" Phillip asked.

"I'll explain it to you later," Jake promised. "For now, why don't you see your lady to her chamber and we'll discuss our plans in the morning. I have a gaming headache that is going to require something slightly stronger than watered-down wine."

Phillip didn't think he dared find out anything more about what sort of pains his uncle might be suffering. It was enough that the man would pay a price for the silence he'd indulged in over the years.

He collected Imogen and walked her to the chamber she was sharing with Rose. He stopped in front of the door and looked at her.

"Interesting day," he offered.

"I'm sorry," she said quietly. "I think this had to have been a bit of a shock."

"The shock is what an idiot I've been not to see what was going on under my nose," he said with a sigh, "which is hardly your doing." He paused. "Will you show me how to slay zombies in the morning?"

She smiled. "Of course. Better rest up. It can get pretty ugly."

He watched her go inside, then turned and looked down the passageway. There was no one there, but he had the feeling he wasn't alone. It wasn't the same feeling of being stalked he'd had on the way to the coast—that was something he was going to have to think about on the morrow as well—this was more a feeling of being heartily eavesdropped upon by cousins who should have known better.

Perhaps seeking his own rest could wait for a few more minutes until he had located and contained the problems, which he had the feeling were named Theo and Sam.

The saints only knew what sort of mischief those two would combine if they weren't limited to making their mischief in the Middle Ages.

Chapter 23

Imogen tiptoed through a darkened great hall, grateful for the pair of torches that were still burning, giving her enough light that she didn't trip over anyone who happened to be sleeping in front of the fires. Cinderella types or guardsmen, she couldn't say. She just knew they were all snoring to put lumberjacks to shame.

She managed to get to the front door before she turned around and looked back over the great hall. It was full of half-visible shapes on the floor and fires that burned low in their hearths. It was absolutely medieval in a lush, simple way that left her catching her breath. She would miss it. But she had a task to accomplish, and the sooner she got to it, the better.

She was going to find Phillip's sword.

She'd decided that about halfway through a night where she hadn't slept any at all. She'd been alone in Rose's room, which had led her to believe that maybe Amanda and Jake had requested a bit of privacy for her. It had also come in handy for rummaging through Rose's trunk for her backpack. It was gone as were her clothes. She supposed she should have been alarmed by that, but she wasn't. The most likely scenario was that Jake or Amanda had tossed everything in the kitchen fire the night before. It didn't really matter. She had her phone and her mission. Everything else was incidental.

Of course, figuring out where to go had been a bit of a question. Going all the way to Edinburgh, getting there in one piece was going to be something of a trick, but she'd already worked that out as well. She was going to borrow a horse and ride like hell. Well, in her case, she would be limping along like a tortoise, but she would get there eventually. She had deep suspicions that that shop on the Royal Mile hadn't been just full of things that looked as if they belonged in the bookcase of a coven of witches. That place was beyond spooky. Not only that, it was where she'd encountered Heather that fateful afternoon. There had to be some sort of gate there.

And while the exact route was in doubt, the end goal certainly wasn't. She was going to find Phillip's sword in the future and shove it back into the past. He would have what belonged to him and she would have indoor plumbing and Lemon Chicken. Everyone would be happy.

She opened the door, slipped outside, then pulled the door shut behind her. She hadn't managed to get down half the stairs before the bark of a very awake guardsman almost sent her stumbling down the rest.

"And where're you off to—oh, Lady Imogen."

"Ah—" Imogen looked frantically for something say, but came up with absolutely nothing.

"She's here to meet me."

A wizened old woman stepped out of the shadows and into the guard's torchlight. She smiled a gentle smile at him.

"A late night for you, Sir Robert."

The guardsman put his shoulders back. "A privilege it is, Mistress Berengaria, to guard my lord and his family. And see to his guests, of course."

Mistress Berengaria—she of the witchly fame, Imogen hoped—put her hand on his arm, patted him, then smiled again. "You are a good lad and valued by your master. I think, though, that the lady Imogen and I might better wear ourselves out if we could indulge shamelessly in the talk of women. If you know what I'm alluding to."

Apparently Sir Robert did and the thought terrified him. He made them both a quick bow, then trotted off. He paused several feet away, then turned toward them.

"I'll keep watch over you from a distance," he called.

"Very wise," Berengaria agreed. She looked at Imogen and smiled. "Now, my dear, let us take a turn about the courtyard ourselves."

Imogen found herself doing just that, trying to make out the features of a woman who had white hair but didn't move like a granny. If their turn seemed to lead them closer to the front gates, so much the better. She wasn't going to argue.

The woman, who again was reputedly less a witch than something tamer, stopped and turned to look at her. "I am Berengaria," she said with a smile, "and you're Imogen."

"Yes," Imogen said, because she wasn't sure exactly where the encounter was going.

"I think if you head to Edinburgh, you will find what you seek," Berengaria said. "Begin at the beginning."

Imogen frowned. "That's it?"

"'Tis all you need, my dear. The rest will follow."

And with that, she turned and melted into the shadows. Imogen would have been slightly flipped out by that, but she decided that her quota of weirdness had been already filled that month. She was impervious to any more.

She didn't say that out loud, of course. No sense in alerting Karma to any potential needers of cosmic lessons.

She made it to the front gate before she realized she had a problem. The portcullis was down and the drawbridge was up. She'd already had a ride on the end of the latter at Haemesburgh—twice—and decided that was probably enough for one lifetime. Raising the portcullis looked to be even more impossible. She put her hand on the heavy wood and supposed there was no point in even thinking about trying to heave that up. She imagined not even a couple of burly extras could have managed it, even if the whole thing had been made of painted Styrofoam.

She realized, when the hair on the back of her neck stood up, that not only did she have problems in front of her, she had some behind her, because she was most definitely not alone. Well, of course she wasn't alone, but this was a more substantial feeling than just the average there-are-frowning-guardsmen-behind-you preparing to tell you to-go-back-to-your-room feeling. She steeled herself for the worst, then turned slowly to see what that worst might be.

To her surprise, she found herself face-to-face with Rose Kilchurn, dressed for success.

Imogen had a hard time latching on to just the right thing to say, never mind trying to decide in which language to say it. Rose seemed unfazed.

"Off to do foul deeds?" she asked.

Imogen stared at her for a moment or two, trying to figure out what was wrong with that, then she realized what it was.

Rose was speaking in English. Modern English.

Imogen knew she shouldn't have been surprised, but she was. She waved a finger at her. "I *knew* you spoke English," she said. "You're bad."

"I'm discreet. Now, what are you doing?"

Imogen looked around to make sure they were as alone as possible. She supposed the likelihood of too many people speaking modern English wasn't all that great, so she forged ahead, quietly.

"I need to go home."

"Let my father help you."

"I have to get Phillip his sword back and straighten things out with Heather," she said. "I don't think your father can help me with either."

Rose nodded. "I thought as much, actually. I'll come along and help."

"You can't," Imogen said, not sure if she should be grateful or horrified. "What if something happened to you?"

Rose shrugged. "I have guardsmen."

"But—"

Rose pointed back over her shoulder. Five of the most terrifying men Imogen had ever seen stepped out of the shadows, though Imogen was fairly sure there hadn't been any shadows there before and there definitely wasn't a huge amount of torchlight to step into. If she'd been sitting in a theater, she would have been mentally handing props to the cinematographer for a job very well done. She felt a shiver go down her spine. The two who shadowed Phillip seemed tough. These guys were another level of that entirely.

"We like adventures," Rose said mildly.

Imogen just bet they did. "They weren't with you at Haemesburgh."

"Weren't they?"

Imogen started to say they definitely weren't, but realized that she honestly couldn't say that with any certainty. She laughed and after the fact hoped she hadn't sounded completely unhinged. "I see."

"Loyal," Rose said with a faint smile. "To a fault."

"That's an interesting word to choose."

"I like to be able to count on things being the way I want them to be."

"And so does your father, I imagine."

"Which is why these lads are mine," Rose agreed, "though they might guard his back in a pinch if I asked nicely."

"I'm sure he appreciates that."

"I suspect he does." She held out a bundle. "I think you should change clothes."

Imogen realized that Rose wasn't wearing skirts. She looked at what she held in her hands. "Boys' clothes?"

"It seems prudent."

"I'm not in shape to be scaling any castle walls," she warned.

Rose smiled. "We'll take care of that part. I'll clear out the guard's chamber briefly and you can change, then we'll be on our way."

"How are we going to get the gate up without anyone knowing?"

"We'll take care of that as well."

Imogen walked with her toward the guardroom, following after one of Rose's men who didn't seem like the sort who found himself argued with very often. She paused. "Why does Phillip only have two?"

Rose smiled. "He only needs two."

"He's that tough?"

"Much tougher."

"He seems so clean and tidy."

"He's a first-rate bastard when you cross him," Rose said dryly.

"Have you ever crossed him?"

"I should have put that differently," Rose said. "He's terrifying when you, as a lad, cross him, but the epitome of chivalry when you are a woman, no matter how you comport yourself. I've pushed him repeatedly far past where even my father would have tolerated my cheek and he's never done anything but return kindness for vexation."

"Never?"

"His jaw might have clenched once. I also might have clouted him on it when he refused me my way."

Imogen smiled. "You are very fond of him."

"Terribly," Rose admitted, "so I'll admit it is with mixed feelings that I aid you. I think he wouldn't argue if you wanted to stay. But I understand needing to go."

Imogen couldn't imagine that Phillip was interested in anything more than getting rid of her so he could get back to getting hold of his castle, but what did she know of medieval men?

She changed quickly, was faintly surprised that everything fit, wished futilely for underclothes, then went back outside to look for her escort. Rose was there with two of her men. Imogen didn't bother to ask where the others had gone. She simply walked without haste under the portcullis after it had risen silently, crossed the drawbridge with Rose when it came down silently, then turned to watch as it returned to its guardian position. All very normal and very medieval. There were horses waiting. She didn't ask how that was possible. She simply looked at her new friend.

"What will your father say?"

"Oh, what he always says," Rose said with a smile. "Many things he thinks I won't understand."

"You're his heir."

"Jackson is his heir," she said. "I'm the apple of his eye. And I have a keep of my own, actually, that belonged to my mother's grandmother, Joanna."

"Why aren't you there?"

"What man is going to take orders from a woman?"

"They did from Grandmère Joanna," a voice said from behind them.

Rose looked surprised for the first time so far that evening. She whirled around. "Thad," she whispered fiercely, "what by all the bloody saints do you think you're doing?"

"Coming along."

"Absolutely not," Rose said firmly. "I forbid it."

"Give me a good reason why not."

Imogen watched Rose list half a dozen reasons that seemed to make absolutely no difference to a boy who was as tall as she was, though obviously quite a bit younger. He was probably no more than sixteen, but there was something about him that left her thinking that he'd seen more than his share of things that had aged him. He stood there, his arms folded over his chest, listening with polite interest to what his sister was telling him. He also obviously wasn't buying a word of it.

Rose finally threw up her hands in frustration, then looked at Imogen. "Meet my younger brother, Thaddeus. I have been informed he's coming along."

"I was the one to arrange the horses," Thaddeus said mildly.

Rose stared at him for a moment or two in silence, then pursed her lips. "Very well. But we won't wait for you if you fall behind."

The look he shot her was priceless. Imogen would have laughed, but she had the distinct feeling that in the Kilchurn family, bravado ruled the day. She suspected they had the goods to back it up, which she appreciated greatly.

Rose rolled her eyes and looked at Imogen. "We'll ride hard. When Phillip discovers you're gone, he'll follow. If you don't want him to stop you and babble all manner of silliness at you, 'tis best we make haste."

"I've already thrown him off the scent," Thaddeus offered. "I pulled his squire aside and filled his ears full of all sorts of things."

"Little Bartholomew?" Rose said in disbelief.

"Who else was I going to talk to?" Thad asked. "Sir Myles? Sir Cederic? Of course I took Bartholomew aside. He's gullible enough to believe me and I promised him a year's supply of new quills if he didn't say anything to his master. Of course you know that's the first thing he'll do, then try to pry those implements of his trade from me after the fact."

"You have a point there," Rose said. "Where did you tell him we were going?"

"Back to Haemesburgh." Thaddeus shrugged. "I knew your destination, of course, but that seemed harmless enough."

"One could hope." Rose started to turn away, then looked at her brother. "Do you know where we're going?"

He tapped his forehead. "I guessed. I'm confident I guessed aright."

Rose flicked her brother companionably on the ear, nodded to her men, then looked at Imogen. "We'll still need to ride hard."

"I'm not good at it."

"Learn quickly."

Imogen supposed she could deal with the inability to walk later, when she was back in the future and had a hot tub at her disposal. Until then, she would ride with the collection of dark knights and their fearless leader, and hope she survived the journey.

She thought she could safely say her odds had just improved greatly.

Chapter 24

P*hillip* woke to torchlight in his face. He pushed away the hand that was holding the damned thing a foot from him and thought after the fact that he was very fortunate no stray spark had fallen on his face. He had enough trouble convincing women to wed him; he didn't need a scarred visage to add to his difficulties. He blinked for a moment or two, then managed to focus on the lad there. He swore.

"What?" he growled.

Jackson looked particularly unimpressed. "You'll want to hear these tidings."

That was the tone of voice that led him to believe those tidings were actually the last things he would want to hear. He threw his forearm over his eyes and tried to feign sleep. That resulted in a booted toe nudging him rather ungently in the side.

"Wake up, idiot," Jackson whispered.

Phillip sighed and looked up at his cousin. "All right. What is it?"

"Imogen's gone."

Phillip sat up so quickly, he almost hit his head against the end of Jackson's torch. His cousin leaped back, then scowled at him.

"I told you that you would want to know."

Phillip forced himself to wake fully. "How long ago?"

"I have no idea. None of your men saw her go."

"Then how do you know she left?"

"Thaddeus told Bartholomew that Imogen was off to do nefarious deeds and my sister was going along to aid her."

"Thad?" Phillip said incredulously. "Your brother, Thaddeus?" He wished he could do something besides gape at his cousin, but anything else was beyond him at the moment. "And Imogen went with Rose? No one bothered to stop them?"

"Aye, aye, and apparently not," Jackson said shortly. "The only good thing to note is that Rose took her lads with her. It will save her a thrashing at my father's hands to be sure. And she took Thad."

"Perfect." He knew his uncle never would have laid a hand on Rose, much less any of his other children, but there was a reason he had provided his eldest daughter with that handful of men who made even him uneasy. Rose and Imogen would be perfectly safe.

"Thad is always chafing for some sort of adventure," Jackson said with a shrug. "They'll keep him safe enough."

"One could hope." He rubbed his eyes. "Where were they going?"

"Haemesburgh, or so your squire says."

Phillip could only hope that was as far as they would manage to go. That was all the Future needed, to have Rose and her handful of demons rampaging about the countryside, terrorizing poor, hapless peasants.

"Did Bartholomew say why they were going there?" Phillip asked.

Jackson looked at him evenly. "I suspect you can lay your finger on a reason if you work at it long enough. And I understand part of the adventure is simply to return to you what is rightfully yours."

Phillip yawned, then shut his mouth abruptly as what Jackson was saying penetrated the fog that not enough sleep had cast over his mind.

She was going to try to get back to the Future. If that wasn't enough, she was going to attempt it by way of a hellhole where she would likely get herself killed.

He rolled out of bed, washed, and dressed, all without comment for there was nothing to be said. Either she intended to attempt one more jump on the spot she'd used to come to the past or she was off to look for his sword. It didn't matter which one it was, it was an errand that would put her in peril she couldn't possibly conceive of. It had absolutely nothing to do with her intelligence or canniness; it had to do with the fact that she was operating in a world where annoying men routinely disappeared in forests and the local authorities were too terrified of ghosts and bogles to lead a party to search for their remains.

He couldn't imagine Rose didn't know that perfectly well, which was no doubt why his cousin had insisted on being Imogen's escort. If he'd been a more callous soul, he would have left them to their adventure and gone to put his feet up in front of his uncle's fire.

But he was who he was, his chivalry demanded that he protect the women in his care no matter the cost to himself, and he thought he just might be having a few fond feelings for that remarkable woman from the Future who had gone to look for a part of his birthright.

He looked at his cousin. "I think secrecy is paramount. I'll go arrange—"

"No need," Jackson said. "I've thrown your lads off the scene. The party will consist of just you and me."

Phillip hesitated and had a curse as his reward. He looked heavenward, for aid or something to fall upon him, he couldn't decide which at the moment. He supposed there was no point in trying to be anything but honest with the man standing in front of him. After all, Jackson had eavesdropped more than he had. He sighed. "Very well. We'll go by ourselves."

Jackson hesitated. "In the interest of honesty, I don't think you'll manage to leave without at least Myles and Wiscard. I've already tried to slip past them. They were not impressed."

Phillip rubbed his hands over his face. The saints preserve him from men sworn to keep him alive. "And what do you suggest I tell them?"

"Make up a tale," Jackson said, shrugging. "Use your imagination."

"I don't have any."

"Make a last visit to Berengaria, then tell them you're

trotting off into the woods to look for herbs for her. The lads will leave you to that, I'm sure."

Phillip would have smiled, but he just couldn't bring himself to. "Nemain is always on the hunt for a spare wizard's thumb bone."

"And there you have it," Jackson said. "The beginnings of a legend."

Phillip could only hope that was the only legend he might be at the start of.

He nodded, then followed his cousin out of the keep as silently as possible. He parted company with Jackson in the middle of the courtyard, sending his cousin to find their pair of companions and secure horses whilst he pitted himself against the task of getting the portcullis raised without fuss.

That was accomplished in far less secrecy than he would have wished. He realized abruptly he was being observed by his uncle, who was leaning against the stone of the barbican gate. Jake lifted his eyebrows briefly, then nodded to one of his guardsmen. That lad walked off, presumably to see to the task of raising the portcullis.

Jake studied him dispassionately. He started at his boots, seemingly took note of the rest of his gear, then finished with a careful look at his face.

"Off on an adventure, are you?" he asked.

Phillip regarded him coolly. "And you would be in the lofty position of telling me to stay home?"

Jake smiled. "Oh no, nephew, not that. I just came to see you off after I offered you aid."

"Guilt has obviously led you to such a pass."

Jake sighed. "I won't tell you that someday you'll understand, but someday you'll understand."

Phillip realized that the question he hardly dared ask was suddenly clamoring to get out of his mouth. He chewed on it a good long time before he dared spit it out.

"Do you regret it?" he asked quietly.

Jake smiled gravely. "How can you ask?"

"I'm annoying."

"You're thorough," Jake corrected. "You're annoying as well, but I love you in spite of it. And to answer your question, no, I have not a one."

Phillip shook his head slowly. "I'm not sure I can begin to imagine what you've given up."

"I have the feeling you might soon find out," Jake said cheerfully. "If I'm reading you aright."

"I'm off to find a thumb bone for Mistress Nemain, not traipse into realms not my own."

"Sure you are, sport."

"Very well, your son suggested the quest. That would be your son Jackson who is coming with me, not your son Thaddeus who has gone with your daughter and my . . ." He had to take a deep breath. "With Imogen."

"Those boys of mine will be the death of me," Jake said, sighing deeply. "Especially Jackson. He worries me."

"I think he should, and here he comes with horses."

"And your two terrifying shadows," Jake agreed. "I didn't think you'd manage to get away without them following. I imagine you'll make up a tale suitable for their constitutions." He started to walk away, then paused and looked at Phillip. "Is there anything else you would like to ask me?"

Phillip forced himself to breathe normally. He had a score of questions that clamored for answers, but he supposed there was just one that couldn't be answered later.

"How does it all work?" he asked, feeling a little daft to utter the words.

Jake smiled. "You stand on the right spot and think about where you want to go, then voilà, you're there."

"I need my sword, though."

"You might," Jake agreed. "Hard to tell, actually. I suppose all you can do is the best you can do." He clapped Phillip on the shoulder. "Good hunting, Phillip."

Phillip nodded his thanks, then watched his uncle have a quiet word with his son. He imagined Jake wasn't going to avoid a more pointed conversation in the future, which the good lord of Ravensthorpe had likely been dreading for some time. It was difficult, generally always, to avoid one's doom.

Think about where he wanted to go and then he would arrive? Ridiculous.

But perhaps vital to the success of his venture. He turned away—and walked into something that squeaked and stumbled backward. He reached out and pulled the body into a bit of torchlight. He shook his head.

"Nay," he said firmly. "Absolutely not."

Hamish smoothed down the front of his tunic. "A squire's duty is to protect his lord at all times. You'll rob me of that opportunity if you leave me behind here."

Phillip studied him for a moment or two. "Did my lord uncle find you at the ale kegs?"

"He might have."

"In company with Theo and Sam?"

"I thought it best to make certain they didn't run afoul of trouble."

"And he threatened to have the three of you cleaning the cesspit on the morrow?"

"'Tis possible that was mentioned."

Phillip considered the possibilities he was now facing. If he left Hamish behind, the lad would have Ravensthorpe in an uproar within a se'nnight. If he took the lad with him, the saints only knew what mischief he would combine.

Then again, Hamish had answers.

Phillip looked at him sternly. "I'm on a quest."

Hamish patted his sword. "I am at your disposal, my lord, for all questing activities."

"I'm off to look for the thumb bone of a wizard."

Hamish blinked a time or two, then for the first time since Phillip had known him, he looked to be a lad of approximately ten summers. "By the saints," he squeaked. "The hell you say."

Phillip smiled. "Still want to come along?"

Hamish put his shoulders back. "Of course, my lord!"

"Go pack your gear then."

"Already done, my lord."

"Have you told Jackson you're coming along?"

Hamish swallowed, hard. "Didn't have the courage, my lord. He frightens me."

"He frightens everyone, my lad," Phillip said with a sigh. The whole affair was madness, but he supposed it could have been nothing else. He nodded toward the gates. "Let's be off, then."

Hamish fell in behind him and was absolutely silent, which Phillip supposed boded well for the future.

He felt suddenly as if he were walking over his own grave, a sensation he didn't care for in the least. It was enough to leave him standing just under the portcullis for a bit longer than he might have been comfortable with normally. He took a deep breath and carried on, because that was what he did.

Thumb bone, indeed.

Three days, three miserable, soggy, cursed days later, he stood behind the lord's table in Haemesburgh and looked at his cousin, who stood next to him. The price of getting them inside the keep had been steep, though perhaps not quite as steep as it might have been if Neill had actually managed to hold on to any of his garrison lads. There was something afoot that he couldn't see, someone moving men and events about like chess pieces, but in ways he couldn't predict. It was profoundly unnerving.

What was more unnerving still was that he couldn't find Imogen. He had assumed she would come to Haemesburgh, indeed he had been told as much by his squire, and he had further assumed she would be on the hunt for his sword. He hadn't seen her inside the keep and it wasn't possible that he'd missed her along the way. Sir Neill had looked puzzled when queried about her possibly having been there before they arrived.

Had she gone to Edinburgh instead?

Think about where you want to go . . .

He suspected that *after Imogen* wasn't exactly the direction Jake had been suggesting, but he wasn't sure what else to wish for.

And there was no more time to spend dithering over particulars he likely couldn't control. He had already sent Hamish off to see to the priest, which he hoped would leave him time to get where he was going without more of an audience than he was going to have.

He looked at Jackson. "You can't come with me."

Jackson looked grimmer than Phillip had ever seen him. "I will come, someday."

"If it is to be so."

"Stop quoting Berengaria."

"I believe that was your father."

Jackson nodded to Phillip's sword. "Use that and begone. I'll find an excuse for your absence."

Phillip refused to consider how difficult it was to breathe all of the sudden. "Think you it will work?"

"How would I know?" Jackson asked hoarsely. "Use the damned sword and hope you don't find yourself carried off to Hell. I definitely won't attempt to follow you there."

Phillip supposed there was nothing else to say. He drew his sword, not his knighting sword but the sword he'd had made for himself, to suit himself, for no other reason than to keep himself alive.

He jammed it into the floor with all his strength, exchanged a last look with his cousin, then put his hands over the hilt and thought of Imogen.

Something hit him over the head and he knew no more.

Chapter 25

Imogen couldn't begin to find the words to describe how exhausted she was. Rose and her cadre of keepers looked daisy-fresh and lethal; she knew she looked like a wrung-out, dingy dishrag. She was covered with the grime of travel and she wasn't sure she would ever, ever again walk as she was meant to. She would probably be accused of being bowlegged for the rest of her life. That was okay. She would just wear skirts.

Rose looked at her gravely. "This is the spot we've determined is the most haunted. I'm not sure I can aid you past that."

Imogen looked down the little alleyway and had to agree it looked pretty damned spooky. In fact, all of Edinburgh looked pretty damned spooky. It was slathered in a layer of medieval-ness far past what it wore draped about itself in the future. It was particularly bizarre to walk up a street with a handful of lethal men behind her and realize she'd walked down that same street not two weeks earlier with other men trailing her, only those men had only been interested in what had been plastered across her backside. She wished she'd had Rose's men within shouting distance then. She imagined she would have had far fewer comments about her availability.

She looked at the close that stood a dozen feet away, that gaping hole between two buildings. If she were going to choose a place to put a time-travel portal, she definitely would have been satisfied with what she was looking at. It screamed *here lies the path of no return*, but with a funky, medieval sort of accent that she thought she might suggest to the set designer for use on the movie she was just sure she was going to be back to doing pre-production work on in a few hours.

"Of course, I'm not an expert," Rose said slowly, "but if these things are gates, I have it on good authority that there is a gate there. Perhaps that's enough."

Imogen looked at her quickly. "Good authority?"

"Don't ask."

Imogen thought she wouldn't. "Any other suggestions?"

"Keep your fingers crossed?"

Imogen smiled in spite of the fact that her face felt as if it might be frozen forever in an expression that said *please let me off this horse before I never walk again*. "You know, this could be a very brief and humiliating experiment."

"Or it could be farewell for now," Rose said. "Safe journey to you."

Imogen embraced her briefly, then watched Rose herd her lads off around the corner. She could only hope her friend had taken her younger brother with her. Thad was too curious by half. Put him together with those little twins and no one stood a hope of any crannies remaining uninvestigated.

She took a deep breath . . . and immediately regretted it. If modern Edinburgh had a city sort of smell, medieval Edinburgh had another thing going entirely. She wasn't altogether certain that she wouldn't walk into that close, turn a little left, open that gate, and find herself in the middle of some sort of pigsty, but there was no sense in not at least attempting the trip.

No time like the present to get back to the, er, well, present. She refused to think about what she was potentially leaving behind. Phillip might be engaged in name only to Heather, but she had the feeling that he would move on quite quickly to some medieval miss with buckets of money and a big fancy title. What she needed to do was get herself back to her proper place in time, get his sword back from Heather and see it returned to him somehow, then get on with her own life. It had been great to be treated like a maiden in distress by a real live medieval knight, but she was just going to have to consign the whole experience to the past where it belonged. It might make a great movie some day. Too bad she wouldn't have Phillip de Piaget around to star in it.

She forced herself to walk forward, turned a little to the left, then opened the gate. The pigsty was disgusting and smelled horrendous, but she was nothing if not determined. She closed her eyes briefly, then stepped forward . . .

Into the middle of a coffee shop.

She dropped to her knees and almost wept.

"Are you unwell, miss?"

She looked up at the barista and wondered why it was she had never thought to get that sort of job. Free food, nice people, steady pay. Really, she might have to rethink her life plan now that she was back where she was supposed to be.

Or so she hoped.

"Brilliant costume, by the way," the girl added.

Imogen didn't want to point out that it wasn't a costume, so she didn't. She simply accepted help up to her feet, then swayed right down onto the nearest stool. Her new friend looked at her with obvious worry.

"What can I get you?"

"A mocha," Imogen managed. "Biggest one you've got."

The girl looked startled, but not unwilling to do what was necessary. Imogen would have burst into tears, but she was just too damned tired to. So she sat on her little stool and simply breathed in and out for a few minutes. When she thought she could manage it and not look as shell-shocked as she felt, she looked around the shop.

It was full of Future stuff. There were mirrors on the walls, trendy artwork, sayings about things that involved food and love. There were fairly clean millenials bent over phones and computers, taking advantage of what had to be free Wi-Fi. There was the smell of food that hadn't been caught and cooked earlier in the day.

She loved the Future.

"Here you go, miss. Enjoy."

Imogen patted herself for her wallet, then realized it was in Rose's trunk—or, rather, most likely in the kitchen fireplace at

Ravensthorpe. She fumbled for her phone, but the barista waved her off.

"My treat. If you don't mind my saying so, you look as if you could use it."

"You have no idea."

The girl smiled. "You might be surprised. We get all kinds in here."

Imogen didn't want to think about what that might mean, but she didn't doubt what the girl had said. Never mind the delicious coffee smell, it was obvious that there was something about the place that was odd. If it were some sort of gate between times . . . well, what a place to land for travelers from the past. Food, drink, and baristas who didn't seem to mind doling it out freely. She suspected Rose might have found the employees and patrons terribly hip—heaven only knew what her cadre of keepers would have thought—but she thought Phillip might have stared too long and blinded himself.

She sipped, closed her eyes, and tried to stop the tears from slipping down her cheeks. She knew she was on the verge of a really serious meltdown, something she just didn't want to have in public. It was almost impossible to believe that ten minutes ago, she had been walking though medieval Edinburgh with a couple of English noblepeople and their guards. Now, she was back to being all by herself in a crowd.

She knocked back the rest of her drink in record time, thanked her new java-dispensing friend for the sustenance, then pushed herself to her feet and stumbled out the front of the shop instead of the back.

No sense in tempting Fate.

She walked out into rain, which shouldn't have surprised her. What did surprise her was how nicely a medieval cloak kept that rain from leaving her shivering. She pulled it more tightly around her, then tried to get her bearings. After a few minutes, she gave up and just started walking. It was dark, so she hoped she wouldn't stand out all that much. It occurred to her that it was entirely possible that while she had come back to the future, she hadn't come to the right time in the future, but she supposed that was something she could put off figuring out until later.

She had to walk halfway up to Edinburgh Castle before she

realized really where she was. It took her half an hour to find where she'd been staying and by then she was so desperate for a shower and something real to eat, she was almost past reason.

She walked into the lobby of her little hotel only because she was afraid if she crawled in, people might talk. She saw the concierge and was vastly relieved to find it was the same guy she'd met before. When he gasped, she almost burst into tears on the spot. Right time, right place. She was back.

"Miss Maxwell?"

"Yes," she whispered. "I have a room—"

"But your family has taken a suite across town."

"My family?"

He looked profoundly unsettled. "When you went missing, Miss Jones called them and they immediately flew over to aid in the search."

She could just imagine. She put her hands on the desk and looked at the guy, trying to make sense of what he was saying. "Search?"

"For you, Miss Maxwell. There was a search made for you." He spoke slowly and distinctly, as if he feared she wasn't going to catch half of what he said. "They have a suite across town. They have your things there."

"That's great," she slurred. "I'm sure they'll enjoy it, but I don't want to enjoy it with them. I don't even need my clothes. I just need my key."

"But your family has taken a room somewhere else," the man said helplessly.

She frowned at the desk clerk. "But I paid for my room for three weeks, in advance—"

"You did, but we thought . . ." He considered, then shrugged. "'Tis empty, that room. The police have been all over it. Your family was insistent."

"Ah, I . . . I got lost," Imogen said, because it was the best she could come up with on short notice.

"Miss Jones has been working with them extensively, of course, but since you hadn't told her your plans . . ." He trailed off, then looked at her meaningfully.

"Yeah, I'm a flake," Imogen said with a careless laugh. "I'm working on a movie, see, and it's all sort of hush-hush. I was off doing research. My bad for not having at least let Tilly know, right? I'll do better next time."

"Would you like me to call your family?"

"Oh, why don't you give me their hotel name if you have it. I'll get in touch with them after I get upstairs and charge my phone." And she had to charge her phone because Jake Kilchurn, modern guy lost in the past, had run out her battery playing games—

"Imogen!"

Imogen looked around to find Tilly standing by the stairs, looking at her in shock. She attempted a smile. "Oh, Tilly," she said feebly. "Hi."

Tilly burst into tears.

Imogen left the security of the front desk and walked over to give Tilly a hug and a brisk pat on the back. "I'm all right. Just got lost."

"I don't believe you," Tilly said in a low voice, pulling back and looking at her with an expression that wasn't immediately identifiable. "What sort of crazy stuff are you into? Who are you doing crazy stuff with? Are you doing drugs?"

"Of course not," Imogen said in surprise. "I just got lost. I was off looking for stuff for the set and I took a wrong turn."

Tilly sniffed. "You couldn't have called? And you smell terrible, by the way."

"No, I couldn't. And I know. I went off to see a castle and got involved in a . . . in a reenactment sort of thing." She nodded vigorously. A little too vigorously, actually, because it made her want to sit down very soon. "It was a golden opportunity, you know, and I didn't have any signal that far out in the boonies and then I had to give up my cell phone for authenticity's sake." She smiled. "It was amazing. I'll tell you all about it later, after I've had a shower. And charged my phone. I ran out of battery in spite of not having it to use. You know how that goes."

Tilly still looked stricken. Imogen wasn't quite sure how to take that, but she was beginning to think that her disappearance had caused a bit more of a stir than she would have expected it to. She considered trying to reason with Tilly but decided that that conversation would go quite a bit better if she didn't look so much the part of someone who'd been out of cell phone reach for several days.

"I'll shower, then I'll fill you in," she said confidently, then she went back over to the desk to throw herself on the mercy of the court. She managed to wrangle a key out of the poor desk clerk—maybe time in medieval Scotland hadn't been without its benefits—then wondered how best to make a break for her room without having to offer more unsatisfying explanations for her whereabouts.

Tilly was putting her phone back in her pocket. "I just called your parents. They are only a couple of blocks away at supper. They'll be here soon."

Damn, caught. Imogen suppressed a gusty sigh. "Thank you."

"They were very worried. So was Marcus."

Imogen frowned. "Marcus Davis?"

"He was extremely worried." Tilly continued to look at her in that stricken way that wasn't at all reassuring. "I had no idea you two were engaged."

Imogen shut her mouth when she realized it had fallen open. "Um—"

"How long ago?" Tilly asked. "If I might ask that."

"It feels like just yesterday," Imogen said honestly.

"I'm sure that's not why you have this job," Tilly said, obviously trying to convince herself of that.

Imogen wanted to respond, but she was just too tired to. Tired and overwhelmed and, to her very great surprise, actually missing the peace and quiet of medieval times. No cell phones, no crazy family, no coworker looking at her as if Imogen were responsible for stabbing her in the heart.

"I'm sorry," Imogen said frankly. "That whole reenactment thing was so sudden and I had to jump on the chance to be a part of it before they left without me."

"But your clothes," Tilly said, gesturing at her. "Your shoes. Your hair!"

Imogen would have laughed, but it wasn't at all funny. "Again, it's a long story. But about Marcus, I'll tell you exactly what's going on—"

Or she would have if her family hadn't chosen that moment to assault the hotel's lobby. She had to admit there was no other way to describe her family's entrance into any space, enclosed or not. It was a little shocking just how quickly they'd managed to get there, but she had the feeling they'd been circling the place like vultures, just waiting for the proper moment to land.

She felt herself doing what she usually did when faced with that onslaught: she tried to sneak out of the middle of the action.

Her parents were having none of it. Her mother took her by the arm in a grip that felt less like a hold and more like a pinch.

"What is this?" her mother asked in astonishment. A look of horror descended on her face. "You've lost your mind and joined one of those nature cults, haven't you?"

"Well—"

"And your hair! It's horrible, Imogen, but I've been telling you for years that there's nothing you can do about it besides cut it very short and hope for the best."

Imogen's father assessed her with his usual disinterest, then looked around for the nearest useful sibling. The selection, Imogen was happy to see, wasn't as robust as it could have been. Only Prissy and Howard had apparently made the trip. She could guess why: Prissy had come to help her parents use their frequent flier miles and Howard had no doubt come along to assess any medical issues that might have cropped up. Either that, or their mother had brought him along for his ready access to an endless supply of Valium. At the moment, Imogen wasn't sure she wouldn't value him for the same thing.

"Prissy," Donald Maxwell said in a tone that brooked no argument, "go buy Imogen some decent clothes."

"I don't think anything is still open," Prissy said with a gusty sigh, "but I'll go look. It'll be a miracle if they have anything in her size."

Imogen could hardly wait to see what would come back in those shopping bags. She would have shot her sister a pleading look, but she knew there was no point in it. What she needed to do was get back upstairs and get her own stuff.

Which wasn't there any longer. Hadn't the desk guy said as much? Her room was empty because her parents had arrived or the police had been upstairs or something had happened and she was once again without anything to wear. She hoped that wasn't a harbinger of things to come in her life.

She found herself hustled out of the hotel before she could

use the key to her room or explain anything to Tilly or make sure that she was perhaps going to have some sort of job by morning. She was tired enough that she didn't kick up a fuss.

She would figure it all out, though what that would look like, she didn't know. She'd had an unbelievable adventure, met an unparalleled guy, and seen medieval life up close and personal. Now she was back where she belonged, her future was apparently laid out in front of her by people who wanted her to do things to suit them, and the guy she thought she might really want was hundreds of years in the past.

Maybe she was loving the future a bit less than she thought.

"Come along, Imogen," Donald said briskly. "I have a conference call in fifteen minutes. We might need a police escort to get us to our hotel in time."

Of course. Imogen sighed, made motions to Tilly indicating that she would call her later. Day One back in the Future was just not going like she'd planned. She spared a wish for a guy with a sword to come to her defense, then sighed and followed her family out the door.

Chapter 26

Phillip woke to a blinding headache. He blinked several times, realizing only after the fact that perhaps he shouldn't have given any indication that he was awake. 'Twas too late for subterfuge. All he could do was hope he wouldn't soon be feeling a blade going into his heart.

Time passed and still he breathed. It took more time yet, but his head finally cleared enough for him to be able to open his eyes fully and make sense of what he was seeing.

He was in the great hall at Haemesburgh, but things didn't look as they should have. Who had put bloody windows in the keep? There were no windows there in the great hall that he remembered, something he had wished from the beginning that he could have changed. It wasn't as if Artane had all that many either, but the hall was so enormous that it hadn't seemed to matter. Here, the keep was so much smaller and so dank and close—

Only it wasn't. He sniffed. Perhaps even more startling than the lack of foul smell was the lack of any smell at all. Well, save some sort of flowery bit of business that he supposed any woman of his acquaintance would have been pleased to wear. Imogen had carried such a pleasant perfume about her—

He sat up. Was Imogen there?

Nay, not Imogen. Someone who looked truly like no one he recognized, but might have been related to Robert of Haemesburgh if the light had been shining on her in just the most unfortunate of ways.

He felt his mouth fall open. *"Heather?"*

The woman, who he had to admit was damned beautiful, lifted a perfectly arched eyebrow slightly. "How clever you are, my lord Phillip. My father underestimated your intelligence."

Phillip used the edge of the lord's table to pull himself up until he was sitting and then remained there until his head stopped spinning. He drew his hand over his eyes, then looked at the woman sitting so comfortably in a chair facing him.

Well, she was most certainly not dressed in medieval gear, which led him to believe that perhaps he wasn't where he thought he should have been. He hardly dared believe that he might have reached the Future, but perhaps there was no other conclusion to draw. He looked at Heather carefully.

"I have questions." He had to chew on his next words for a bit before he thought he could spew them out. "I'm not sure if I want answers to them."

"Come now, my lord Phillip," she said with a more mocking tone than he thought she should have been using, "Fear? Surely not."

"I never said I was afraid," he said. He hadn't said he wasn't either, but that was perhaps beside the point. "I'm steeling myself for the answers, nothing more."

She rolled her eyes. "Why don't you see if you can get yourself into the lord's chair and I'll find some refreshments for you. Then we'll come to an understanding."

Phillip felt as if he were approximately ten summers, looking up at someone besides his mother, who never would have intimidated the hell out of him as Heather was now. "Where am I?"

"Modern-day Scotland. I would give you the date, but you might swoon."

He took a deep breath. "The Future?"

Heather's smile was utterly devoid of humor. "You could call it that, I suppose."

"Is Imogen here?"

"We'll discuss that in a moment. Up in your chair, there's a good lad."

Phillip found it in him to glare at her, but she only laughed—a seemingly genuine sound that time—and walked away, her shoes making a sound against the stone of the floor that was oddly reminiscent of a blacksmith's hammer against an anvil. Perhaps things were not so strange in the Future after all.

Or perhaps they were.

He looked around the great hall and wasn't sure if he was surprised by the changes or not. The place was definitely cleaner, he would give Heather that much. The floors were missing any sort of covering, yet they seemed not to suffer from the lack. The walls were scrubbed and covered here and there with well-made tapestries, things he certainly didn't remember having seen in another time.

He also didn't remember a gallery running around the upper edge of the hall, a gallery such as his uncle Nicholas had built for his lady wife, but he had to admit it was a decent change to the place. It looked rather less like a tomb.

It was the smell that he couldn't get past—or, rather, the lack of smell. He wasn't sure if that were a good thing or not, but it was definitely something different. It made him wonder what Imogen had thought of his time. Perhaps he didn't want to know.

He watched Heather walk back across the hall, her shoes making the same unsettling noises as at first. She was trailed by servants bearing a pair of trays. He tried not to gasp as a meal fit for royalty was laid out on the lord's table in front of him. The cloth alone that was placed down first was of such fine work, he was quite certain it had cost a fortune. He wasn't sure he could even begin to identify what serving pieces were being used, never mind trying to determine what foodstuffs were being presented.

He looked at Heather to find her watching him with less calculation than pity. She put her finger under her chin and lifted her face slightly, which he took to mean he should shut his own gaping mouth. He did so, hoping he hadn't made a complete arse of himself in front of her maids.

The serving gels were dismissed and Heather took her seat again. She waved him on to the meal before him.

"Help yourself."

"I hardly know where to start."

"I would mock you for it—and likely should—but I understand," she said simply. "Try a bit of everything. None of it's poisoned, if that worries you."

He had to admit, half an hour later, that he wasn't sure he agreed with her assessment of a few of the items he'd tasted, but on the whole it had been delicious and without a doubt the most rock-and-bug-free meal he had ever eaten. He had a sip of something extremely tasty in a cup that was so light and delicate, it had to have been made of faery wings, then set that cup down and looked at Heather.

"Where is my sword?"

"What sword?"

He shot her what he hoped was a look stern enough to make her rethink any plans she had to toy with him. "The one with the bloody large stone in the crossbar."

"Oh, that one," she said negligently. "Haven't seen it."

"Lying is still a sin, even in the Future."

She regarded him coolly. "And why would I give you my only means of getting from time to time?"

"Because 'tis *my* sword," he said pointedly. "And since you seem to be so comfortable here, I don't see where you need it any longer."

She seemed to consider the wisdom of that—or so he thought.

"Let's make a bargain, you and I," she said pleasantly. "I'll keep your sword, and you thank me for sending you such a lovely smelling wench before you go back to where you came from."

Well, he had to admit she had done a goodly work there. He considered for a moment or two just how sweet-smelling Imogen was, then realized what else Heather had just said. He looked at her in surprise.

"You sent Imogen?"

"You didn't think she arrived there by accident, did you?"

"Honestly, I had no idea what to think," he said. "How did you find her, or choose her, or send her—?"

"So many questions for a lad who is only here for his sword."

"Well, I might be here for other things as well," he admitted. "I hadn't thought that far ahead, to be entirely truthful. I simply wanted to keep Imogen safe."

"Such a noble lord you are, Phillip."

"I am trying," he said honestly, "but it is made more difficult by my lack of sword."

She looked around herself in confusion, then back at him. "I don't see your sword here, do you?"

"I could search the keep for it," he said.

"I suppose you might try," she agreed, "and I suppose you might find yourself in gaol come nightfall as a result. And think on that, my lord. You, a medieval sort of lad, trying to explain yourself to modern guards who might find your tale so interesting that they would want to keep you in their clutches for quite some time lest they miss out on any important details." She shivered delicately. "Medieval torture devices might have been brutal, but I daresay modern ones are more effective."

"Medieval," he repeated. "Aye, that is what they call our time, isn't it?"

"Or the Middle Ages, if you rather. And aye, that is what they call *your* time."

"I could tell them of your origins as well," he said.

She laughed a little, but it wasn't a pleasant laugh. "Do you honestly think I am so stupid not to have thought of that possibility before now? Nay, my lord Phillip, you will not have the upper hand here. This is my world, not yours. I have safeguards in place, of course."

He had to admit he wasn't surprised. The woman was canny, to be sure. He sighed deeply. "Very well, what do you want?"

"I want a hearty expression of thanks for sending you such a delightful wench," Heather said, "a bit of sport at your expense, and my freedom."

"I appreciate the temporary gift of a lovely gel," he said evenly, "I believe you already have your freedom, and I'm not at all interested in providing you with any sport."

"And if I promised you your sword at the end of it?"

"Why should I believe you?"

"Because you have no alternative?"

He pursed his lips. "Very well, what idiocy do you want me to demonstrate for you until you're satisfied?"

"I want you to woo and win Imogen Maxwell."

His mouth had fallen open. He knew it and heartily wished

he could have avoided it. It took a moment before he felt a little less like the floor was shifting beneath him, but he was made of stern stuff indeed. He retrieved his jaw and tried not to splutter.

"She couldn't possibly want to live in my time."

"How do you know?"

He gestured inelegantly at the food on the table. "If this is simply a foretaste of marvels to come, how can I possibly convince her to leave it all behind?"

"Are you not inducement enough?"

He flushed in spite of himself. "I never claimed to be anything like it."

She nodded. "In that, you speak the truth I suppose. Your family name speaks very loudly for itself, but you do have a reputation as a fairly humble sort."

"Thank you," he said. "I think."

"Use your vast charms to win yourself a wife," she suggested. "You have a fortnight. Win Imogen's heart and you'll have your sword."

"Just like that?" he managed. "Just march off into the Future, tell a Future gel she would prefer to live in the past, then come and collect my blade?"

"I don't care how you do it," she said, "just that you do it."

He didn't like to feel at such a loss, but this was a situation far beyond the normal events of his life, he hardly knew how to comport himself. He was tempted to ask Heather why she had set him to such a task, but there was something in her eye that he thought might be best left undisturbed. He took a deep breath and set that question aside for another time. "And if I don't manage it?" he asked.

"I'll shove you through the gate in the floor and leave you in misery for the rest of your days. If you manage it, I'll give you back your sword."

"I could use it to come here and vex you."

"Do you think I would leave that to chance, either?"

"And how do you think you'll stop it?"

"We'll discuss that later."

He loathed being forced to admit defeat. He also wasn't sure how he felt about defeat including the rather tempting possibility of taking a fortnight to woo Imogen in her own time. The one thing he knew for certain was that Heather of Haemesburgh was a woman he was very happy he had never wed. He suspected she felt the same way about him.

"Very well," he said, looking at her with a frown. "I win Imogen, you give me my sword, and then what?"

"You go back to the past and I stay here and live out my life in bliss."

He rubbed his hands over his face. "Checkmate, is it, then?"

"It would appear so."

He reached for his cup of whatever it was—tea, he thought Heather had termed it—downed a liberal amount of it in spite of his shaking hand, then looked at her. "Where is your father?"

"I imagine he's long dead by now."

"I mean in 1254."

"He was dead then, too."

"And your brother?"

"I've no idea. Off making mischief and siring scores of bastards, no doubt. Or plotting your demise." She shrugged. "He's unpredictable."

He suppressed the urge to curse. "And the state of your keep? Do you have any idea of the condition of it, who is manning the walls, who is styling himself lord of the hall?"

"I don't know and I couldn't possibly care less," she said dismissively. "Five years have passed, my lord, five years that have been alternately terrifying and blissful but mostly full of not being forced to inhabit this hellhole in all its medieval glory, which has been the best thing of all. I don't know what happened to my brother, to my father's men, to my father's hall. I just know what I have now and that is something I will not relinquish."

He held up his hand. "Wait. Five years?"

She considered. "You have it aright. A bit longer than that. Almost six years of bliss."

He considered her. "And you don't live here?"

"Good heavens, nay. I have a flat in Edinburgh. I wouldn't live here if you paid me a million quid."

He had no idea what a quid was, much less a million of them, but the way she said it left him with no doubt of how little she cared for the stones around them. "How did you know to put my sword in the floor?"

She smiled. "A witch told me."

He knew he was gaping at her, but he couldn't help himself. "A witch?"

"Witch, midwife, herbalist." She shrugged. "All the same back in the past, wouldn't you agree?"

"Did she give you her name?"

"If she did, do you actually think I'll give it to you? So you can travel back through time to an earlier time and put her to the sword before she could help me?"

But then I wouldn't have Imogen was the first thing that crossed his mind, and the thought shocked him so badly, he flinched. He couldn't decide if he were more surprised by the sudden pain of the thought of never having had her or that such a thing had snuck up on him so unexpectedly and unmarked to have him in such a state. He looked at Heather.

"I wouldn't."

She studied him for so long in silence he supposed he would have become uneasy if he hadn't been so accustomed to the same from his father. Robin of Artane was, as anyone would volunteer without prompting, a bit of a bastard from time to time.

Phillip loved him for it.

"I'll think about giving it to you, then. I don't think you'll be surprised. She travels a great deal, you see, and has compassion on gels who are desperate for a different life."

Phillip could only bring Berengaria of Artane to mind as one who would possibly have aided Heather, but he supposed in the end it didn't matter. He had a task to accomplish and 'twas best he make haste being about it. "You've been extraordinarily helpful."

"You're welcome. And you're welcome for sending you off to ply your chivalry on a lovely woman."

"I do appreciate that." He studied her for a moment or two. "Are you going to tell me how you chose her?"

"Who says I chose her?" Heather asked with a shrug. "Perhaps she was simply in the right place at the right time."

"Any ideas where I might begin my search?" he asked politely. "Or do you simply have her held captive here in the keep?"

"Oh nay, your cousin Rose sent her through a gate in Edinburgh."

He felt his mouth fall open. "How do you know that?"

"I have a phone and a selection of spies. How else?"

"And I'm to find her *there*?"

"I'll get you that far, at least. The rest is up to you."

And that, he discovered, was the absolute truth. She put him in a car—a heart-stopping conveyance if ever there were one—and ferried him north to a city that at least retained a fair bit of its medieval charm, though he had to admit it looked a bit more weathered than when he'd last seen it. The castle had definitely increased in size and scope.

Heather slowed her beast down, then stopped where she seemed to be greeted by friends who made very loud and, it had to be said, irritated noises with their own cars. She pointed at the crowd of souls milling about.

"Off you go, laddie."

He blinked. "That's it? That's all you're going to do?"

She handed him a phone. He knew what it was and felt just the slightest bit proud of himself over that.

"Call me if you need me," Heather said, leaning over to open his door for him. "Your hotel is up the way. I've booked you a room for the fortnight. You'll find what you need there. If you can't woo Imogen in that amount of time, you don't deserve my keep."

"My what is up the way?"

"Your inn, you fool. The Jester's Court, I believe 'tis called. Fool's Errand might be more apt, but I won't judge."

Phillip would have commented on that, but she'd given him such a shove that he had no choice but to continue on out the door. He'd barely hit the cobblestones before her car was pulling away. He sat up, pulled himself out of the street, then looked about him. That not a soul paid him any heed past stepping around him told him perhaps all he needed to know about modern Edinburgh.

He crawled to his feet and tried to get his bearings. He was surprised by the merchants who had invaded the lower portions of the surrounding buildings, but perhaps that was how they did things. He was even more surprised by their painfully bright torchlight, but that was also something to investigate later.

"Och, and where have you been?"

Phillip turned around to see a grizzled, elderly man standing behind him, scowling at him. "I'm sorry—"

"Aye, no doubt, and bugger if you're not blootered! Go have some coffee and sober yerself up. You have a tour in two hours."

"Blootered," Phillip repeated in disbelief. "A tour?"

The man rolled his eyes. "Ghost walks are what they are and you should be damned grateful you've got the work. Here, I'll buy you a coffee, then that's positively the last thing I do for you."

Phillip considered. That sounded like a foodstuff and he had to admit the repast at Heather's table had been elegant but not very filling. Perhaps he might find heartier fare at that man's board, then feel a bit more himself as he tried to assault the Future.

He curled his fingers into fists. It hid their shaking better that way, he thought. Poor Imogen. No wonder she had looked so horrified.

"I say," he managed, trailing after the man, "I wonder if you might direct me to my . . . hotel." The word felt strange on his tongue. Indeed, the whole bloody Future accent felt strange on his tongue but it was amazing how his early, secret experiments with the same at his uncle Montgomery's keep were serving him now.

Experiments he'd made the decision to forget for so many years.

"After the show," the man said impatiently. "What, you're trying to leave me stranded?"

"Nay, of course not," Phillip said.

"Then follow me, drink up, then I'll tell you what you'll be doing. And ye'd best do it well, else I'll sack you."

Phillip supposed having a job was one way to accustom himself to the strangeness of the Future. He didn't have the heart to tell the man that he'd latched on to the wrong servant, so he tucked his phone into the purse hanging from his belt, then followed after his new liege. As he walked, it occurred to him what had been bothering him all day.

How had Heather known he was coming?

Chapter 27

Imogen walked through the darkened streets of Edinburgh, trailing after her family at a distance that hopefully said she was as embarrassed by their behavior as everyone else had to be, and wondered if ghost walks ever yielded any fresh members. At the moment, she was sorely tempted to add a few to the ranks.

Her mother had buttonholed some poor tourist and was currently criticizing everything from the guide's accent to his lack of knowledge about historical happenings in Edinburgh, never mind that she was hardly any expert on Scottish history. Her father was attempting to likewise monopolize the tour guide, which had the bonus of leaving the man less able than he might have been otherwise to toss out a few more facts for her mother to dispute. She wasn't sure how much the poor man was appreciating her father's prying into his finances and business model, but what could she do about it? Her father was an unstoppable force of entrepreneurial know-how. When he had sniffed out a victim, there was no keeping him from distilling his vast wisdom upon him.

Then there was her sister Prissy, who looked as if her fondest wish was to shove Imogen somewhere where she could be walled up until she starved to death. Her brother Howard was watching her as well, but he was obviously making furious mental notes about her physical condition. She had the feeling he would have happily run any number of medical experiments on her if she'd let him.

She had consoled herself—although it was small consolation—many times that day that at least her sister the shrink and her brother the lawyer were still stateside, leaving them unable to psychoanalyze her to find out why she wasn't trying to sue someone. Things could have been worse.

She'd spent dinnertime satisfying the local police that she had traveled south, wandered off the beaten path, and gotten involved with a crazy cult that she was just sure wasn't there anymore. No harm, no foul, no need to investigate further. The officers had seemed happy to put the thing to bed and she'd been happy to let them go.

Another bright spot in the gloom was she had yet to see Marcus. He'd been busy getting a mani-pedi or soaking his vocal chords in gold-infused water or something else she couldn't afford and didn't understand. All she knew was it meant he wasn't following her to make sure she wasn't wandering off unsupervised and for that she was very grateful.

She walked along a particularly spooky bit of subterranean floor behind her family, falling farther back with each footstep until she could no longer hear either her mother or her father yakking or Prissy contemplating sisterly mayhem not quite under her breath. It was peaceful down there in places where whole families had lived in the cold and dark, too poor to live anywhere else. She was starting to think that even with all Haemesburgh's flaws, its medieval incarnation was definitely a step up from what she was looking at.

She yawned. If jet lag was bad, time-travel lag was worse. She knew she really had no reason to be so wiped out, but in her defense, it had been an unusual couple of weeks. At least she'd had a decent night's sleep the night before. She had gone with her parents to their hotel because it was easier than fighting them, happily indulged in an endless shower, then tried to squeeze herself into the clothes Prissy had found for her. Even her mother had remarked that Prissy had done a terrible job judging Imogen's size.

Imogen had known Prissy had done a perfect job judging her size, then made a point of buying things a size too small. She'd promised herself a pair of new jeans in the morning.

She'd eaten, then gone to bed on a random sofa, happy to have managed to avoid any serious conversation about her escape from the reenactment cult. If she tried hard enough, she could presently bring to mind how many times someone had woken her up that morning to make sure she wasn't dead. Her miraculous rise from her bed and subsequent trip to get new clothes she couldn't afford but had afforded thanks to the cash her brother the doctor had slipped her with a rare, conspiratorial wink had left her where she was at present: fed, clothed, but wishing she could go back to bed and try to process what she'd been through.

She wondered where Phillip was. Well, she suspected she could say with a fair bit of certainty where she supposed he'd been for the past seven hundred and fifty years, but she wondered, if time carried on in some kind of parallel manner, what he was doing at the moment back in good old 1254. Probably being very glad he didn't have to deal with her. She tried to find some sort of stiff-upper-lip attitude to go with that dose of probability, but all she could do was wish she'd met him under different circumstances.

Say, at a ghost walk.

She knew she was leaning against a four-hundred-year-old doorway where the stone was cold under her fingers. She knew she was in the twenty-first century. She knew her family was in the cave to her right, listening—or not, as the case might have been—to a poor Scot who was just trying to make a living bringing history to life. Yet with all that, she was having a hard time believing she wasn't dreaming.

Phillip de Piaget was standing ten feet away from her.

It occurred to her with a rush of horror that he was—

No, he wasn't. He wasn't a ghost.

She felt relief begin at her toes and crawl all the way to the top of her head. She looked at him again, hardly able to believe her eyes. He was wearing medieval clothes, which didn't surprise her, but he was standing in the current day, which did. She stumbled toward him, then realized that maybe that was presuming things she perhaps shouldn't presume. So she stopped a couple of feet away from him and looked up at him.

She almost asked him what he was doing there, but she imagined she could answer her own question easily enough. He'd come for his sword of course. She nodded, because she honestly couldn't have expected anything else. After all, wasn't she on the hunt for the same thing? It wasn't as if he would have come for her. She was a nobody, still that timid brown bunny who was forever scampering out of the way to avoid conflict and sisterly ire. Then again, when Pristine Maxwell was at the tiller, even sharks got out of her way.

Phillip looked at her for a moment or two, then reached out and took her hand. "Imogen."

She couldn't even respond. All she could do was look at him breathlessly and suppress the urge to wonder if she'd somehow fallen through a different portal back to the Middle Ages. The only thing that kept her grounded was his fingers laced with hers.

"Playing the part of a modern bloke?" she managed.

"Corporeal ghost, if you can fathom that," he said with a shiver. "I believe the leader of our company mistook me for someone else, but it seemed as good a chance as any to learn Future ways, so I accepted his offer of a job. I decided I would engage in method acting to pass the time. Heather told me all about that on the way here."

She started to tell him he'd already broken character more than a purist might allow, but what he'd said sank in before she could. "Heather brought you here?" she asked incredulously. "Heather of *Haemesburgh*?"

"'Tis a bit of a tale," he admitted, "and I'll tell it to you in full the first chance we have." He smiled. "'Tis good to see you, Imogen."

"You, too," she managed, though that seemed like a bit of an understatement.

He looked over her head briefly, then smiled at her. "I must be about my labors, for my new liege calls. A fine man, though a bit of a crankypants."

She smiled, because his Norman French mixed with modern English with an accent she couldn't quite lay her finger on was maybe one of the most charming things she'd ever heard.

"He bought me a coffee to remove the drunkenness from me," he said. "I didn't have the heart to tell him it wasn't wine that had baffled me so but Heather shoving me out of her automobile onto the street."

"Awful," Imogen managed.

"The coffee?" he asked thoughtfully. "Aye, profoundly vile upon my first encountering the brew, but after another sip or two—" He looked at the tour guide, then at her. "I must see to my task. You'll be here for the duration, won't you?"

"Wouldn't miss it," she managed.

He smiled.

She should have been immune, really she should have. She'd seen him smile before, several times. She had him take her hand a time or two as well. There was no reason why either of those two things coming her way at the moment should have been anything noteworthy.

Except he was in her time and for some reason that made all the difference.

He squeezed her hand. "I'll return when my duty is done," he said quietly. He paused, then smiled again. "I'm happy to see you."

She could only stare at him, mute. He didn't seem to take that personally. He simply smiled again, then went to see what his boss wanted from him. Imogen put her hand into her pocket to keep it safe. If she'd been a little less jaded, she might have made a solemn promise right then and there never to wash it.

"And who is that?" a voice purred from beside her.

"Never saw him before in my life," Imogen said without hesitation. She looked at Prissy and blinked innocently. "Decent looking, though, isn't he?"

Prissy patted her tousled locks, adjusted her assets, then hiked her skirt up another pair of inches. Never a good sign, that sort of thing. She couldn't have looked more on the prowl if she'd been a lioness preparing to stalk . . . something. Dinner. A good-looking lion. A tasty-looking tourist. Imogen felt a little sick, but she didn't show it. Prissy was a master at noticing any hint of weakness and then she would indeed pounce, claws unsheathed.

Imogen supposed all she could do was sit back and watch the show. Phillip was an adult. If he wanted to keep Prissy at bay, he could do it on his own. For all she knew, he would find her sister the most interesting thing he'd ever encountered and want to date her, if that's what medieval guys did.

Damn it, but she hated it when her inner brown bunny came out to play.

The tour continued on through more tunnels and caves. Maybe she should have been creeped out by the ghosts who were supposedly in attendance, but she was having a hard enough time just managing her sister who she could see very well. Ghosts were nothing compared to that one.

Phillip's job seemed to entail bringing up the rear of the company and helping old ladies when they looked like they might swoon. Imogen watched several white-haired mavens assess Phillip, then suddenly show signs of impending faints.

She understood.

The night wore on. Imogen wore out right along with it. She wasn't sure how Phillip was managing to keep going, but maybe he was used to less sleep and more stress than she was. His chivalry was getting quite a workout, but he didn't seem to mind. He was kind and solicitous and uncomplaining. She wasn't sure if watching him be just himself, even eight centuries out of his time as he was, was a good thing or not. After she'd toyed not once but three times with the idea of pretending to sprain her ankle, she decided that she needed to get a grip on herself. He wasn't there for her, he was there for his sword. It was the only thing that made sense.

Unfortunately.

The tour ended basically where it had begun but only after visits from a handful of ghosts who left several of the older ladies clinging to Phillip for support. She didn't begrudge them that. Prissy pretending to swoon was another thing entirely. Unfortunately, she was too used to simply letting her sister have her way to do anything to stop her. All she could do was stand helplessly to one side as Prissy elbowed several senior citizens out of the way and threw herself into Phillip's arms.

"Oooh," she said. "Scary."

Well, that was a word that could have been applied to more things than just ghosts, but Imogen decided it was probably better to keep her mouth shut. She did, however, have a good look at Phillip while he was in middle of being swooned on. He caught Prissy because she would have landed on her shapely derriere otherwise, then set her back on her feet because he was a nice guy, but that was the extent of his interest.

"Careful on those cobblestones," he said with a French twinge to his speech that sent the women standing close to him into another dimension of admiration entirely.

Imogen understood. As she had noted before, the guy would have had casting directors crawling over one another to have him sign on to any sort of film. If there was perfection embodied physically, it was standing right there in the person of Phillip de Piaget.

And then he did the unthinkable.

He made the ladies a bow, collected his pay from the tour guide, who wanted his cell phone number—Phillip promised it in a few minutes—then turned and walked away.

Toward her.

He stopped in front of her and smiled. "Terrified?"

"Of what my sister will do to me when she gets me alone?" Imogen asked breathlessly. "Damn skippy I am."

"Was that your sister?"

"Unfortunately—and here come my parents." If she hadn't been so overcome by the fact that he had ditched his groupies to come inquire about her state of post-ghost-walkish . . . well, her state in general, she might have been able to quickly give him a warning about what sort of storm was blowing his way. As it was, she could only stand there and watch disaster unfolding. Her father didn't waste any time.

"Who are you?" he demanded. "And why are you talking to my daughter?"

"Another refugee from the cult," Imogen lied without hesitation. Donald Maxwell had never in his life been that concerned about her conversational partners. She honestly had no idea what to make of it, but she knew it couldn't be good. "Be gentle. He's had a hard time."

Her mother eyed Phillip critically. "I'm not overly impressed with his costume. Not exactly authentic, is it?"

Imogen felt herself beginning to wilt. The only thing that saved the moment was that the tour guide distracted the parental units by exchanging numbers and cards with them. Another business conquest made and on foreign soil no less. Her father would be so proud.

At least the thought that Phillip was another reenactment victim had seemed to throw Prissy off her game, however temporarily. Imogen didn't hold out any hope that her sister would let that stand in the way of future conquesting, but stranger things had happened.

"Business is done," Donald announced. "Irene, call the driver and tell him we're ready."

Imogen was torn between trooping along after her father and dawdling so she could have a bit more conversation with Phillip. Just to find out if he needed help, of course. No other reason.

He watched her family for a moment, then looked at her. "Powerful souls, those."

"That's one way to describe them," she agreed. She took a deep breath, then plunged ahead while she had the guts to. "What's your plan?"

"Food, sleep, then wresting you away from your family on the morrow," he said seriously. He pulled a phone out of the purse hanging at his belt. "Heather gave this to me. Damn me if I have any idea how to use it, but perhaps you can show me tomorrow." He looked at her. "She also secured a chamber for me at a hotel I haven't seen yet." He glanced at her parents, then leaned closer. "How shall I find you?"

She ignored the tingle that went down her spine. "You could call me. I'll program in my cell phone number, then show you—" She stopped speaking, realizing she had begun to attract the attention of her sister the thwarted jaguar. She quickly put herself in as his second contact, then handed it back to him. "Did Heather show you at least how to plug it in?"

"Plug?"

In his defense, she wouldn't have known what to do with a sword. "Do you know where your hotel is?"

"She said it was the Fool's Errand, or something akin to that. 'Tis by the castle, I believe."

"It is," she agreed. "I have a room there as well."

He looked at her in surprise. "You do?"

"Yes, not that I can use it." She shifted. "My parents are making me stay with them."

He studied her family for another moment in silence, then looked at her. "Tomorrow," he said. "I'll use the phone to find you."

It was amazing how she could get through an entire paranormal experience without a single chill, but have a random guy say a simple thing to her and suddenly she felt as if she had just come down with a raging fever.

"Sleep well, Imogen."

She nodded, then followed her family to the car, because she had no choice. She didn't dare look back over her shoulder on the off chance that Prissy would take that as a sign of interest. All she could do was continue to breathe normally, yawn a bit, and look as if she didn't give a damn that a medieval knight had her number loaded into his cell phone and he intended to use it.

"Nice guy."

She looked up at her brother, Howard. "I don't think you know him well enough to judge."

He lifted his eyebrows briefly. "I wasn't being critical, Imo. He seems like a nice guy." He reached in a jacket pocket and held out a woman's wallet. "Here. You might need this."

"What is it?"

"A long overdue makeup call," he said.

She opened it surreptitiously. She did lots of things surreptitiously. It alerted fewer siblings to her activities that way.

The wallet was stuffed with cash that was keeping company with a credit card.

"Unlimited balance, of course," he said quietly. "You could buy a Lamborghini with that, but please don't. I'm still paying off my student loans."

"Liar," she said faintly, feeling stunned. She didn't bother to count the cash. It would have taken her too long. She looked up at him again. "Why now?"

"I was worried when we couldn't find you," he said. He paused, glanced over his shoulder at Phillip, then shrugged. "I'm not sure I want the details. I'm just glad you're safe."

"He kept me safe."

"Like I said, nice guy."

She took a deep breath. "I'm not sure why he's here."

Howard smiled. "Aren't you?"

She decided it probably wasn't a conversation she wanted to have with anyone at the moment, least of all her brother. She thanked him for the funds, then took a chance and looked back to find Phillip standing on the sidewalk, listening to his employer but watching her. She waved, surreptitiously.

"Imogen, get in the car," her mother said sternly.

Imogen looked at her mother and decided that at the very least, it was time to get out of the familial nest. She had, after all, gotten herself to England all on her own, gotten herself to Edinburgh mostly on her own, and gotten herself to and from medieval Scotland without the help of anyone in her family. She suspected her mother, bless her heart, wouldn't have lasted five minutes at Haemesburgh without someone deciding the only way to avoid having to listen to her sharp tongue would be to toss her in the dungeon.

She would manage it the next day on the pretext of needing to go to work. Not even her parents could argue with the sensible nature of that.

And then she would find out why Phillip de Piaget had really come to the future.

Chapter 28

Phillip looked at himself in the mirror—a startling thing in and of itself—then regarded the drawing lying on the table near him. Heather had left him the same, presumably so he didn't make a complete arse of himself by putting things on in the wrong order.

He was wearing jeans, a plaid shirt, and a leather jacket. He'd had to consult the drawing several times until he'd become familiar with the terms he should apply to what he was wearing, but he was fairly sure he'd gotten them right. The boots were a bit dodgy to start with, but he'd managed to get them on his feet with an acceptable amount of cursing.

He also had learned that his phone was of a particular kind that allowed him to obtain more apps than an android— Heather had said so in her note—which he supposed could only be a good thing, though the lad downstairs at the front gates had had a differing opinion on the desirability of apple products. What an apple had to do with apps and why he cared about any of it, he surely didn't know.

By the saints, he felt as if he had dropped onto a different planet.

He knew about planets, he supposed, because he'd overheard Montgomery and Pippa talking about them. Or had it been Jake and Amanda? For all he knew it had been Nicholas and Jenner. No wonder their children were such terrors. He had no doubts that Theo and Sam had spent more than their share of time eavesdropping at their parents' doorway. He didn't want to speculate on what those lads might know.

He paused and looked carefully over his shoulder. He wouldn't have been at all surprised to have found they had followed him to the Future. The chamber was empty save his own poor self, so perhaps he had eluded them. He was certain that wouldn't last and pitied the soul who found those two lurking behind a modern tapestry.

He rubbed the spot between his eyes briefly because it pained him in a way he wasn't accustomed to. He'd passed far too much of the night before watching videos on the computer Heather had left for him. She had left him instructions to simply turn the beast on and it would see to itself, which he found to be the case. To be honest, the contents of the little movies marching across the screen had almost been less startling than pushing the button as directed and having the bloody screen spring to life.

He suspected he'd eaten at some point when someone had brought him food, though he genuinely didn't remember tasting any of it. He'd been fixated on that flat sheaf of computer, fashioned from the same material as his phone only quite a bit larger. He'd initially been almost as curious about it as he had been what it had been revealing to him, though that had changed very quickly as he'd focused on what he was being shown.

The history of the world.

He was fairly certain that he'd crossed himself many times until he realized that what he was seeing wasn't evil.

It was mind-blowing.

That had taken up half the night. He'd watched souls who had lived centuries after he had died but centuries before Imogen had been born march across the world's stage, having their turn for good or ill. He'd seen death, destruction, war with weapons he simply couldn't wrap his mind around, fear on a scale he honestly couldn't believe was possible.

He'd also seen the inventions that had revolutionized life

on earth, art that had left him dumbfounded, music that had left him weeping. He wasn't sure he would ever stop shaking his head.

As the sun had been rising, he'd finished with the initial offerings. Heather had put little boxes on his homescreen labeled intriguing things like *Top One Hundred Vacation Destinations for Men with Time on Their Hands* and *All the Cuisine You'll Regret Not Having Eaten*. It had been torture to turn away, but sleep had called him relentlessly. He could only hope he would have time later that day to explore those and the other things he hadn't been able to uncross his eyes to read.

But first, Imogen.

He hadn't had the opportunity to talk to her the night before as he would have wished. First, he'd owed it to the man who thought he was there to help to actually be of some use. Second, and much more unsettling, he hadn't dared interfere with what seemed to be happening between her and her parents. He understood how things went when souls were cooped up in the same keep for months at a time, so he wasn't entirely surprised to see the jostling going on in her family. Where she fit into the whole thing was something he would need to determine.

His phone sang at him. It was a pleasing tune with a man who at one point during it stated proudly, "I'm sending you back to the Future." Heather might have been an opportunist and, it had to be said, a thief of the first water, but she had spared no expense to see him kitted out properly.

He tapped the green circle on the face of the beast, then put it to his ear. "Aye?"

"You learned to use the phone."

The pleasing mix of his vintage French, modern English, and all of it spoken with a Lowland accent was surprisingly comforting. "It would seem so."

"And to think my father thought you were an idiot. You're a rather clever lad, all things considered."

"Careful, woman. I'm your elder."

Heather snorted. "Not by much and I'm the one with the keys to your keep, my lord. Show some respect."

She might have had the keys to his keep, but he realized at that moment, in an inn that found itself hundreds of years out of his time, that there was another who had the keys to his heart. And he had Heather of Haemesburgh to thank for bringing her into the path he'd been doggedly marching up, never stopping long enough to note if there might be souls he was about to march right over.

He could, as Kendrick reminded him with alarming regularity, be a bit of a bastard sometimes.

"I'm curious about something," he said without preamble.

"Unsurprising," she said, "and predictable. The YouTube videos weren't enough?"

"I want to know about Imogen," Phillip said. "How did you find her?"

"You already asked and I already told you, 'tis a tale better told at another time. I don't want to overtax your feeble wits."

"I'm a de Piaget. We don't have feeble wits. But if you won't answer that, then tell me where your brother is."

She sighed gustily. "Meet me at Haemesburgh in a se'nnight's time and we'll have speech together."

"Why then?"

"I'm giving neither answers nor a sword to a man who can't win a woman and discover a few things on his own."

"You are an evil wench."

She laughed. "Aye, most likely. But I have a very lovely car, a driver when it suits me, and modern food, which I suppose makes me less evil than clever. My driver is downstairs waiting for you, by the way. He has instructions to teach you how to drive, if you care to learn. A car, not a cart. Think on the possibilities of that, my lad."

"Wait—"

There was silence. He looked at his phone but she had left the parley.

A car?

He checked himself in the mirror to make certain he was covered where he should have been and not looking like a fool everywhere else, then put his phone in his pocket, the key to his room in his other pocket, and a wallet with all sorts of things he certainly hadn't provided for himself inside in the back pocket of his jeans.

He was beginning to suspect that in her own way, Heather was trying to be nice to him. It was for her own nefarious reasons, of that he had no doubt, but the results were at least the same.

He left his chamber, bid a good late morning to the inn-keeper, then left the hotel to find Heather's driver waiting for him. Phillip shook the man's hand.

"A fine day for a turn in a car," he said pleasantly.

The man looked unconcerned, but then again, that one had apparently been ferrying Heather around for several years. "My lady wishes that you be taught to drive." He looked as if he anticipated a day that merited no more than a yawn. "She claims you already have a license. Not sure how that came about if you can't already drive, but I've learned not to question her ladyship when it comes to these things."

"Wise," Phillip said.

"We'll need to take a bus to where we're going. The city isn't the place for this."

Phillip imagined it wasn't. He nodded, then went with Heather's man to a contraption that was the length of Haemes-burgh's stables, a fraction of their width, and had wheels. A bus. What an oddity. It would carry him where he wanted to go though, so he wasn't about to argue with its looks.

After a fair bit of a ride, then quite a bit of walking, he arrived with Heather's driver at a car park that backed onto a derelict structure that had him for not the first time in the past day reaching for his sword. If her man—Bruce, he discovered was the fellow's name—noticed, he was too jaded to say anything.

A door was opened to reveal several automobiles.

"I say," Phillip said, feeling a little breathless, "what is that?"

"Nothing you'll be driving, my lord."

Phillip looked at the man archly. "I'm a very fast learner."

"And that Porsche Spyder is always going to be faster than your learning, if I can be so bold. It is also her favorite car. If you ding it, she will make you wish you were dead."

"Did she say that?"

"In exactly those words. We'll start with that little gray Ford over there."

Phillip realized there were five cars there, all parked in a tidy row. He could only assume they were Heather's given that one of them was the beast that had belched him out onto the street—admittedly with help—the night before. Phillip looked at the tiny little car on the end of the row and wondered how he was going to fit himself into it, much less force it to go anywhere. He would likely have better luck pushing the damned thing.

"If you're a very good student—*if*—the lady Heather says you may choose one of these." Bruce looked as if he thought that might be a very bad idea indeed, but the man was nothing if not courageous apparently. "She has a nice Mercedes in here as well. That might suit you best."

"Which one is the most powerful?"

"That depends on how many things you hit today."

Phillip imagined it did and vowed to be very careful with the little car that he might try a more powerful one, just as he'd done with the first horse he'd had for his own.

Perhaps things were not so different in the Future after all.

He looked at Bruce. "I need to make a text."

"Feel free."

He pulled his phone from his pocket and looked for Imogen in his contacts. Given that he only had two of them—Imogen and Heather—his task was accomplished quickly, he wrote his message and sent it in French before he thought anything of it. He was tempted to translate it, but he was sure she would understand what he'd been getting at. If he could spend a single day learning her Future ways, that would surely make a better impression than presenting himself as a rustic who had no idea where the airplane mode switch was on his phone.

The saints preserve him that such a thought might be rattling around in his head for the rest of his life.

His phone chirped at him. She had sent him a single *K*. Not exactly verbose, but there you had it. Perhaps her parents were watching her too closely for her to say anything else.

He put his phone back in his pocket, made certain his wallet was where he'd put it, then looked at Bruce.

"What first?"

The man took a deep, steadying breath, then held out the most delicate set of keys Phillip had ever seen. "Take these."

Ah, but the Future was a marvelous place indeed.

It was very late that night when he finally stumbled into his temporary bedchamber, tossed keys to a Porsche Spyder on the table there, and shrugged out of his jacket.

The day had been a success.

He would be the first to admit it had initially been a dodgy business indeed, that business of driving a car instead of steering a horse. In his world, he had come to understandings with the most powerful beasts in the stables of various kin and certainly collected his own share of steeds that no one else dared ride. It had been profoundly disconcerting to try to make a connection with the mind of that damned Ford and have it completely ignore him. He didn't want to think about it overmuch, but the truth was, he'd almost plowed them into several shrubberies before he'd realized that his foot was going to have to do the speaking for him.

Once he'd mastered that, things had gone very quickly for him. The other drivers on the road were rather sensible, all things considered, and he wasn't unaccustomed to having a very clear picture of the lay of the battlefield, as it were.

Bruce had made him wait until after dark before he'd allowed him to take the Spyder out of its lair, but take it out he had.

"Don't speed," had been Bruce's only suggestion. "Germany's the place for that."

Phillip didn't suppose he would have the time for a journey to the Continent, so he assured Bruce that he would most definitely not speed, he would watch out for the local sheriff and his lads with flashing lights, and he wouldn't turn Heather's prized possession into a heap of scrap metal.

His phone rang. He picked it up immediately, hoping for Imogen. It was Heather.

"Aye?" he said.

"How goes the wooing?"

"I thought I might present myself more successfully with a Porsche wrapped around me."

"If you destroy my car, Phillip de Piaget, I will hunt you down in whatever century you hide and put you to the sword. Slowly."

"By the saints, woman," he said with an uneasy laugh, "priorities."

"If you knew how much it had cost, you'd agree."

"Master Bruce made that very clear." Phillip didn't want to add that he hadn't believed the man at first. So much money for such a small thing.

Then again, it went rather fast.

"I won't ruin your car," he promised. "And I appreciate the gear you left for me."

She was silent for a moment or two. "I'm willing to do quite a few things to secure my peace."

Considering he was willing to live out a goodly portion of his life in Haemesburgh for the same reason, he thought he could understand.

"Good e'en to you, Heather."

She snorted at him and hung up.

He had a wash, trying not to feel as stunned as he still did by the luxuries he was currently enjoying, then crawled into bed. He spared a wish for his other sword that he assumed was now in Jackson's tender care, made certain his knives were by his head, then reached for his phone. He was tempted to text Imogen again and ask her what she planned for the morrow, but perhaps it would be better to seek her out in person. He put his phone on the little table next to the bed and turned out the light.

Perhaps in sleep he would stop wearing what he was certain was an expression of absolute astonishment.

Chapter 29

Imogen smoothed her hand over her hair and felt rather satisfied that it was as straight as it should have been. It wasn't that her hair was particularly curly, it was just that she liked to have even the bends out of it. She was afraid it wouldn't last, but at least for the moment, she had complete control over something.

Her hair was the only thing she had control over. She didn't even have control over her schedule. Marcus had called her the day before and told her to meet him at the castle. He wanted a professional's opinion on what backdrop made him look the most like a leading man. She didn't bother to remind him that his father's current project was a musical and he couldn't carry a tune.

She didn't even have any control over her very strange social life that wasn't really a social life. Phillip had texted her the day before and told her he was busy with a project she sincerely hoped didn't include an interview with the head of the local paranormal investigation society. He was an adult. He was probably eating his way from one end of the city to the other, then visiting historical sites to see what might be in store for him down the road when he was back in his proper time.

She exchanged a knowing look with her reflection, then turned away and steeled herself for a very long day.

The truth was, she had to get back to work. She was trying to hold down her dream job so she could pursue her dream career. She had contacts to impress, tone-deaf sons of executive producers to keep at bay, and an assistant who shouldn't have been her assistant to placate. She was busy, busy, busy.

At least she'd gotten a decent night's sleep. She had her brother Howard to thank for that, surprisingly enough. He'd provided her with her own room down the hall from her parents' presidential-level suite of the swankiest hotel in Edinburgh. It beat the hell out of being forced to share a bed with Prissy. She was fairly sure she'd slept on the floor the first night only because no one would let her touch any furniture. She hadn't been looking forward to waking up with one-inch bangs because Pristine Maxwell had been sleepwalking with scissors. It wouldn't have been the first time, that was for certain.

Howard had extricated her from the family after they'd returned from the ghost walk, then handed her a card key. When she'd asked him why, he'd said simply *guilty conscience*, smiled, and distracted her parents long enough for her to get her stuff out of their room and get to her own.

Her brother was turning forty in a month. Obviously it was having a bigger impact on him than he wanted to admit.

She opened her door very quietly and peeked out into the hallway. It was empty, fortunately, so she pulled the door shut behind her and escaped while she still could. There was no way she was going to wait for an elevator when there were perfectly good stairs right there. And if she scampered through the lobby at a dead run, who could blame her? She had things to do and places to go.

She ran out of the lobby and straight into an older man in a suit before she realized he was in front of her.

"Oh," she said, slightly horrified, "I'm so sorry. And glad I didn't knock you over."

The man only smiled pleasantly. "Not to worry, miss." He gestured toward a car parked where she suspected cars weren't supposed to be parked. "I'm at your disposal today."

She looked at him in surprise. "Did my brother hire you?"

"Och, nay, miss. I'm the lady Heather's chauffeur."

"Oh," Imogen said, "of course."

She got into the back when he opened the door for her, hoping she wasn't about to have another very quick trip into another century, then looked at the hotel as the car started to pull away. Her sister was standing there at the front door, her mouth working furiously. Imogen considered, then blew her sister a kiss. She would pay for that later, of course, but hopefully Prissy wouldn't be able to get into her room and trash the place. It wouldn't have been the first time.

"Where to, Miss Imogen?"

"The castle, if it wouldn't be too much trouble," she said. "I can get there myself, really—"

"'Tis my pleasure to drive you there," he said. "If you're not in a hurry, we can take the long way."

She wasn't sure that would be a good thing. The last time she'd taken the long way anywhere, she'd wound up in 1254, but the car wasn't giving off any sort of paranormal vibe and neither was Heather's chauffeur, so maybe she was safe.

"Sure," she said. "That'd be great."

She watched the city scenery as they rolled past it and had to admit she was grateful for a comfortable seat from which to do so. The horse Rose had chosen for her had been very fast and seemingly interested in keeping her on his back, but it hadn't been a comfortable trip north. No wonder Heather was so attached to the twenty-first century.

"I'll need to let you out here, miss," Heather's driver said suddenly. "'Tis as close as I can come and still wait for you."

"Oh, you don't need to wait," Imogen said. "I could be here for quite a while."

He looked at her in his rearview mirror. "As you say, then, but I'll give you my mobile number. Ring me when you're ready to be picked up."

Imogen nodded, then looked at the buildings that were just slightly lower than the castle itself. Or she would have been looking at them if she hadn't been so distracted by the sight of an extremely expensive-looking car parked right where she supposed she might like to be dropped off.

"Wow," she said without thinking.

The chauffeur sighed heavily. "That boy."

"Do you know the owner?" she asked in surprise.

"Owner and, I imagine, the driver as well." He stopped next to that incredible sports car, then looked over his shoulder. "Ring me when you're finished, aye?"

She nodded as she took the card he handed her, then got herself out of the backseat and onto the sidewalk. She watched the Rolls drive off and took the opportunity to have another little look at that bright red Porsche. It looked like it was going eighty just sitting there. She couldn't say she had very many weaknesses when it came to material things, but there was something about a crushingly expensive sports car that really got her going.

The driver's door opened.

And out stepped Phillip de Piaget.

She gaped at him for as long as it took him to lock up the car and come stand in front of her on the sidewalk. Then she laughed.

"What are you doing in that thing?"

"Trying not to ding it," he said with an uneasy laugh of his own. "What do you think?"

"I think you're going to have nightmares when you get back home."

"If I thought I could get that beast through Heather's floor, believe me, I would be taking it back with me."

"No fuel," she said, "and it's been tried before as a plot device in a movie. You'd have to just park it in your courtyard and stave off the guys who'd want to burn you at the stake for it."

He smiled. "Quite probably." He put his keys in his pocket as unthinkingly as if he'd been doing it his whole life. "I was hoping I would see you here."

"How did you know?"

"I encountered your brother at your hotel," he said. "He was good enough to share your plans with me."

She hardly knew what to think of Howard at the moment, but she wasn't going to start looking a gift horse in the mouth. "I'm going to the castle," she said, gesturing weakly in that direction. "I'm supposed to work."

"Might I come along?" he asked. "I'll keep myself in the background."

She imagined the background was the last place Phillip de

Piaget would ever find himself, but if he wanted to try, she wasn't going to argue with him. He extended his elbow toward her and smiled.

"Let's be off. I'll keep you safe."

She took his arm because it was impossible to resist a gorgeous medieval knight in jeans who had left a sports car parked in a place that would likely get it towed.

All right, so she might have taken his arm because she thought she might have a few fond feelings for him, fool that she was, but who was quibbling? She walked with him up the way to the castle, watching her feet for the most part. Or, actually, the cobblestones beneath her feet. Who knew how old they were? They looked uncomfortably like the ones she'd walked over with Rose and her guys, so for all she knew she was walking over the same set.

"Odd, isn't it?"

She looked up at Phillip and smiled. "The street?"

"Aye," he said, shuddering delicately. "I would like to make a poor jest, but the truth is, I'm not entirely certain I haven't walked over these stones in a different pair of boots."

"Spooky."

"Very," he agreed.

She continued up the way with him, fought him over paying for their entrance and lost, then continued on past the gift shop.

"This wasn't here," he said, taking a deep breath. "Before."

"I imagine it wasn't."

"My father would have gone completely silent by this point."

"And yet you're so chatty."

He smiled. "A constitution to be envied, surely." He took another deep breath. "I would say that I'm much more adaptable than he is, but now knowing what I know about the secrets he's held all these years, I'm not sure of anything except that I think I would like to visit the chapel soon."

"It's on the map," she said, pulling her hand away.

He put his hand over hers and kept it there. "I can look. You keep holding me on my feet." He pulled the map out of his pocket with his free hand, studied it, then paused and looked up. "I'm hearing something."

She was too and it wasn't pretty. "Um, about that . . ."

"It sounds as though something is dying."

"I believe it's supposed to be singing."

He looked at her in disbelief. "How do you know?"

"It's why I'm here."

He muttered something in the native tongue. It could have been a curse, but she suspected it was a prayer. She understood.

He nodded up the way. "We'll press on if we must."

She didn't want to have to, but it was her job, and considering who Marcus called Daddy, it was her career.

"You know that, ah, singer?"

"His name is Marcus," she said reluctantly. "His father is the executive producer on the movie I'm here researching for." She looked to see if he was still listening. He was watching her intently. "Max Davis has buckets of money and is paying for this movie to be made."

"And this Marcus thinks to be in this movie?"

"Yes, but that's sort of the problem, because it's a musical. You know, a play with singing and dancing."

He listened for a minute or two then shook his head. "I'm concerned."

"His father is tone-deaf."

"So is his father's son."

She smiled. "I've been trying to tell him that very gently for some time, but he doesn't believe me. The truth is, he doesn't know when he's on key and when he isn't, so telling him he's off doesn't make any difference to him."

"I don't think I have the stomach to ruin his dreams," Phillip said with a heavy sigh. "Surely there is someone else on your movie who can do that goodly work."

"I'm not sure anyone dares," she said seriously. "Marcus is sort of a strong personality. He always has to be right." She paused. "And there's another thing. He's very into paranormal investigations."

Phillip snorted. "Ghosts?"

"That's just the beginning. If it's spooky, he's right there with all his gear to investigate it."

"He sounds daft," Phillip said with a smile. "Ghosts? Bogles? They don't exist. Anyone who believes in any sorts of paranormal . . . oddities, well, I think they likely have too much time and not enough things to do. Wouldn't you agree?"

"You know, I almost believed that speech."

He laughed a little. "I'll try harder next time," he promised.

And that was the last thing he was able to say for a bit because they had rounded the corner and come upon the source of the caterwauling. She gulped. Phillip merely paused in his stride, then looked at her. She shrugged and they continued on.

If there was one thing that could be said for Marcus Davis, it was that he was thorough about trying to obtain his desires. She had no idea where he'd gotten the camera crew, but he had a full set going. Lights, cameras, sound, catering: it was all there and being used. If the sound guys were flinching now and then, it was probably because of a chill, not anything that was screeching into their headphones. A large crowd had gathered, which she knew would thrill Marcus to the soles of his rubber-soled, ghost-hunting shoes.

"Imogen, you're here!"

Imogen pulled her hand away from Phillip's arm before she thought how he might take it, but he didn't look offended. He simply stood there, unobtrusive—if that were possible.

Tilly came to an awkward stop in front of her. "Thanks for coming," she said. "I wasn't sure you would make it."

"Well, of course I would make it," Imogen said. "You texted me, so here I am. Thanks for letting me know about this."

"Well, he's your fiancé," Tilly said, her eyes glued to Phillip. "I thought you should know. I don't believe we've met?"

Imogen watched Phillip take Tilly's hand and shake it like a good twenty-first-century bloke would have.

"Phillip," he said easily. "Charmed."

Tilly looked less charmed than on the verge of a faint. She looked between the two of them for several moments in surprise that gave way to faint suspicion. She settled for looking sternly at Imogen.

"You're engaged to Marcus," she said.

Imogen shifted uncomfortably. "That really isn't settled."

"Well, he thinks it's settled, and you know who his father is."

At the moment, she was wishing she had never heard of Max Davis or any of the movie people he generally associated with. She definitely wished she wasn't hearing his son bellowing out show tunes at the top of his lungs.

"Oh, it's Imogen," he sang out, his voice booming against the stone of the castle. "Come set-dress me, honey!"

Imogen would have cringed, but she didn't want to draw attention to herself. She also would have hurried over to keep Marcus from belting out any more off-key melodies, but he was too quick for her. It was a wonder any self-respecting ghost stood a chance of escaping him. As he would tell anyone who would listen, he was one fast guy.

He strode over with the aura of a man for whom the world was a stage and he the lead baritone. He stopped in front of her with his hands on his hips and gave Phillip the once-over. He began to frown about ten seconds into it, which she supposed wasn't a good sign.

"I don't have time to sign autographs," he announced.

Phillip only inclined his head. "Don't let me inconvenience you."

Marcus looked at him, then grunted. "And don't count on me for any good words with my dad. I'm too busy preparing myself for my audition."

"Of course," Phillip said. "I can hear that."

Marcus puffed up. "I only do Howard Keel songs. He is the only one who fits my range. It's almost as if he'd been born for just that reason."

Phillip made some polite, noncommittal noises, then took a step backward. Imogen started to take a step with him, then realized she was the one who was supposed to be doing some Marcus dressing.

Heaven help her.

She found herself cast in the role not of set dresser but director. The longer the morning wore on, the less she was enjoying anything to do with movies and the more backed into a corner she felt. She glanced around at one point to find Phillip leaning against a bit of stone foundation wall, watching her. She had no idea what his expression meant, but the first chance she had, she left Marcus to his bellowing and eased back to stand beside him.

Phillip leaned closer to her. "I'd like to go somewhere."

She looked into his stunning gray eyes. "Would it be a place that doesn't find itself inside Edinburgh castle's walls?"

He smiled. "I'd like to go home."

"Haemesburgh?" she asked in astonishment.

He shook his head. "Artane."

"Oh," she managed. "Now?"

"My phone says 'tis but a pair of hours on the A1 to reach it." He lifted an eyebrow. "Perhaps faster in my conveyance."

"How in the world did you get a license?"

"Magic," he said dryly. "And I'm under a curse if I don't deliver Heather's car back to her unscratched, so you needn't fear for your life." He nodded toward the castle entrance. "Shall we?"

"Do you want me to come along?" she asked, surprised.

"Aye, very much," he said seriously. "You needn't feel obligated, but I would like you to if you were so inclined."

"I'd need to pack."

"I know where your hotel is."

That was all she needed to hear. She told Tilly where she was going, ignored Tilly's look of irritation, and forced herself to go tell Marcus how good it would be to have Tilly's opinion on his audition tape. She ignored Tilly's murderous look, then looked at Phillip.

"Let's run."

He smiled. "That might alert them to our joy at having our peace and quiet back. But a swift walk is definitely in order."

She walked with him out of the castle and down to where Heather's car was miraculously still there. That could have been because Heather's driver was leaning against the door, talking to a skeptical-looking policeman. Maybe he would get the ticket instead of Phillip and his license Heather had probably drawn by hand.

"Did you plan this?" she asked. "This trip to Artane?"

He opened her door for her. "I thought you might enjoy the journey."

"I've been dying to get inside that place."

"I also thought, modest lad that I am, that you might like to see my home." He shrugged, looking slightly uncomfortable. "I feel as though I'm a bit of a braggart, but all you've seen is Haemesburgh at its worst."

"Ravensthorpe was nice."

"Ravensthorpe will not be mine if my father ever decides to, as they say, shuffle off his damned mortal coil."

She smiled. "I think you love him very much."

"I'll love him much more when he's dead and the contents of his very fine cellar are mine."

She laughed, because she could tell that was absolutely not the case. "All right, let's go then and you can show off."

He smiled. "My ultimate plan, of course."

She honestly didn't care what his plan was as long as it meant she didn't have to spend the day with Marcus or her family. Though she had to admit, the thought of spending a couple of days with Phillip de Piaget was almost too good to be true.

She was tempted to remind herself that it wouldn't last, but she decided, as that medieval knight cursed his way through city traffic, that maybe she could just take a day or two and let herself believe that all kinds of things were possible. A medieval woman finding happiness in modern Scotland. A medieval knight traveling to the future and driving a sports car.

A wannabe film maker surviving a trip to the Middle Ages, falling hard for a man who was completely out of her league, yet having that same man come find her hundreds of years out of his time.

Impossible things didn't just happen on the silver screen.

She didn't want to think about how badly she wanted to believe that.

Chapter 30

Phillip decided that of all the Future inventions he had encountered thus far, traffic was the one he liked the least.

Escaping Edinburgh's environs had never been pleasant, not even in his time, but it was made far worse currently by the addition of too many automobiles. He had gotten caught on some sort of damned ring road, made the trip about the city one more time than he'd intended to, then finally managed to get himself on the road that led south. He supposed it would have helped if he'd recognized anything, but he didn't. He knew he shouldn't have been surprised that things had changed a bit over the centuries, but he was.

It occurred to him after a pair of hours on the road that he had been concentrating so hard on not getting them killed that he hadn't even looked to see if Imogen was still breathing. He glanced at her to find her watching him.

"Do you want to drive?" he asked.

"This thing?" she asked in astonishment. She paused. "Well, maybe later if we can find a deserted road. I don't want to wreck it." She shivered. "Heather would kill me."

"And you think she won't kill me?"

"You have a sword. Besides, I'll have plenty of chances to drive in the future."

He nodded and continued on, though he wasn't quite sure he wanted to ignore her last statement. Obviously he had come to the Future to . . . well, at the moment, he supposed saying that he'd come merely for his sword was untrue.

He wanted Imogen Maxwell.

The oddest thing about the situation was his own reticence. He wasn't accustomed to standing back and having to consider more than once his next move. He generally had a strategy planned out well in advance and things marched along just as he'd intended them to. He should have realized the first time he'd seen Haemesburgh covered in cesspit leavings that anything to do with the damned place wasn't going to go according to plan.

"Are you all right?"

Ah, concern. That was a promising start. He decided he would think about that instead of what was left to overcome in order to win her because thinking about that sort of thing felt too hopeless at the moment. The truth was, now that he'd seen even part of what the Future had to offer a body, he wasn't sure he could bring himself to ask Imogen if she might be willing to leave it for a life in the past with him.

He was beginning to wonder if the whole thing hadn't been a terrible idea. She had her life, her work to do, apparently a betrothed to wed. Who was he to think she might want to have anything to do with him?

Well, that was part of why he wanted to show her Artane, wasn't it?

"Phillip?"

He smiled when he would have preferred to growl, because his mother had taught him good manners. "I am well."

"Are you sure?"

"Nay," he said honestly. He wasn't sure if he could even begin to tell her what he was thinking, so he settled for an untruth. "I think too much traffic has given me pains in my head."

"What can I do?"

"Hold me?"

She blinked, then she smiled. "Smooth."

"I am known for my chivalry even under the most dire of circumstances." He shot her a quick look. "You could reward me for that, if you liked, but I would likely have to pull over for those accolades to be heaped upon my head. That looks to be a likely spot up ahead."

"That looks to be a likely castle up ahead."

"And so it does."

"Recognize it?"

"I might." He took a deep breath. "Can we drive all the way there, do you suppose? Up to the gates, I mean."

"Ask my phone."

"I don't think it speaks Norman French." He shook his head. "My father would have soiled himself by now."

"That's why you're here, I imagine."

He smiled. "One reason, perhaps. I'm sure there are others." And with any luck, he would have the chance to list them for her.

He listened to her ask her phone where they should go, spared a moment to marvel that such a thing was possible, then left thinking behind whilst he pitted himself against the task of getting them not only to the village but through it.

It helped that he recognized the landscape, if not the structures.

He passed a very fine car that was almost distracting enough to leave him not heeding where he was going, then he pushed on the brakes too hard. He supposed it was simply good fortune that he didn't land them in someone's front garden.

"What's wrong?" Imogen gasped.

Phillip pulled over and parked the car. He looked at her. "Wait for me, if you will."

She didn't seem opposed to it, but perhaps he sounded as gobsmacked as he felt. He crawled out of the car and looked behind him to see if the other car had decided to stop as well. He watched it turn about and come his way, pulling in behind Heather's Porsche and coming to an abrupt stop. He waited, hardly daring to indulge in any thinking lest he find that he was indeed imagining things.

A man flung open the door and leaped out.

It was his father.

He gaped at the apparition that hastened toward him. He

could hardly believe 'twas Robin, but what else was he to think? The man could not have looked any more like his sire—

Nay, not Robin.

Kendrick.

His younger brother looked at him as if he'd seen a ghost, then stepped forward and threw his arms around him in an embrace that robbed Phillip of breath. That was likely just as well, for it saved him from unmanning himself by squeaking in surprise.

Kendrick slapped him on the back a time or two, then pulled back and took him by the shoulders. "Phillip," he said with a laugh. "What in the hell are you doing here?"

The medieval French coming out of his brother's mouth was equal parts comforting and unsettling. Phillip looked around him to make certain he was still in the Future, then looked at his brother.

"Ah," he began.

"And where did you get that car?" Kendrick asked with another laugh. "By the saints, brother, do you have any idea how much they cost?"

Phillip wondered if he would manage decent speech at any time. All he could do was stand there and stare stupidly at his younger brother. First, why was Kendrick in the Future? Second, why was he so old? He had to have been at least a score and five. Third, why was there never a chair about when a man had the greatest need for one?

"And who do you have with you?" Kendrick asked, abandoning him without hesitation to go open the passenger side of the car.

Phillip watched him do it, then watched his brother go very still. Well, that was something. He honestly wasn't sure he wanted to know what his brother knew or what he was thinking or what he was speculating about. He elbowed his brother out of the way, then held down his hand to help Imogen out of the car. He looked at Kendrick.

"This is Imogen Maxwell," he said. "Imogen, this is my brother, Kendrick."

She looked as surprised as he felt. "Your brother?" she repeated faintly.

"I know, 'tis hard to believe something as ugly as Phillip

could be related to me," Kendrick said promptly, "but there
you have it. Quirk of nature, obviously. I'm Kendrick, the
handsome and brilliant one."

Imogen smiled. Phillip thought he might have to sit down
for other reasons. He leaned against Heather's car because he
supposed she might deserve it if he scratched the beast, but he
didn't lean too hard.

"I'm assuming he's told you all about me," Kendrick went
on. "'Tis difficult not to bring me into all our adventures. I am
the one, of course, who always wins the lady's hand and col-
lects the most spoils."

"Please, let's not discuss your spoils or ladies won," Phillip
said with a snort. "Imogen, don't listen to him. He's a terrible
braggart."

Kendrick only smiled that sunny smile he'd used to get his
way from the time he'd first understood its effect on those
around him. Phillip wasn't entirely immune himself.

"There is a tale here," Kendrick said, "and one I want to
hear at length, but perhaps the details can wait. Where are you
headed?"

Phillip pointed back over his shoulder. "Thought I would
pop by the old pile of stones and see what's left of it."

"It's in remarkably fine shape," Kendrick said with as much
seriousness as he mustered, ever. "Introduce yourself to the
current lord, Stephen. I imagine he'll even feed you luncheon,
if you kiss his arse well enough."

"I'll do my best," Phillip said dryly.

"Then come to Seakirk. I might let you sleep on my floor."

Phillip felt his jaw go slack. "Seakirk? What in the hell are
you doing at Seakirk? And now that I've found my tongue, I'll
ask the rest of what troubles me. Why are you so old? What
the hell happened to you?"

Kendrick looked at Imogen and winked. "He's vexed. He's
rude when he's vexed. Keep that in mind if you intend to carry
on with him for any length of time. The way to force him to
stop is to remind him that he's being rude." Kendrick looked
at him. "You're being rude."

"I'm being gobsmacked."

Kendrick pursed his lips. "I can see you've picked up a
useful word or two recently. Go have your visit at home, then

come to my hall. I'll tell you whatever you want to know. And I'll provide your lady at least with a decent place to rest her head." He held open Imogen's door for her. "Here, allow me to tuck you back into this fine vehicle."

Phillip watched his brother ply his abundant chivalry on a woman he wished he could find a way to woo himself, then waited until the door was shut before he spoke.

"I'm very curious."

"Of course you are," Kendrick said with a smirk. "Where's your gate?"

The conversation had taken such a radical turn away from where he could have reasonably expected it to go, he found it rather easy, all things considered, to just discuss things that at another time he would have considered to be completely daft. He looked at his brother closely. "What do you know? Or, rather, what did you know in the past?"

"More than you'd care to hear," Kendrick said, "but I used my time ferreting out secrets whilst you were in the lists. I'm not surprised that you're utterly oblivious. What did your gate look like?"

"The gaping maw of hell and it languishes behind the lord's chair in Haemesburgh."

Kendrick blinked, then laughed. "Why am I not surprised? At least it will be fairly easy to get to again, then."

"In this century or that one?"

"This one," Kendrick said.

"I need my sword."

Kendrick looked around him. "I don't see it."

"That's because Heather of Haemesburgh has it, you fool."

Kendrick lifted an eyebrow. "Did you want my aid?"

"Money for petrol, more like."

His brother laughed. "Ah, how the tables are turned. You, needing me for a change."

"Brother, I've never not needed you," Phillip said seriously. "I've spent more time looking over my shoulder in the past month than I have in my entire life."

"You used to look over your shoulder to make sure I was there and hadn't gone missing," Kendrick said with a snort. "I know, because Mother asked you to do the same endlessly."

"And then you stopped cutting yourself on your sword and

I thought you might be equal to guarding my back." He dragged his hand through his hair. "I need a drink."

"If only you indulged, and perhaps I should remind you that this is a conversation we've been having the whole of our lives." Kendrick smiled. "Trot off home for a visit, then come stay with me. I'll go have a nap so I'm well rested for the telling of tales."

Phillip found himself surprisingly loath to watch his brother walk away. Kendrick looked at him, then stepped forward and embraced him again, strongly enough that Phillip lost his breath.

"Come see me at Seakirk," Kendrick said, slapping Phillip on the back. "I'll be there."

"I'm honestly not sure I can find it," Phillip said. "The roads are so different."

"Do you have a phone?"

"Aye."

"Then pull yourself into the twenty-first century and bloody use it," Kendrick said with a grin. "Here, give me your phone and I'll program my number in. Ring me when you're on your way and I'll be sure to have the gates open. How long are you staying?"

"I have no idea," Phillip said honestly.

"You may have three days before I put you to cleaning the stables," Kendrick said absently, fiddling with Phillip's phone. He handed it back, clapped him on the shoulder, then walked back over to his car. "Ring me."

Phillip found that he could do nothing but gape as his brother got back into his car, waved, then whipped around and drove off in the direction he'd been going at first. He watched his brother go and tried not to think about the absolute oddness of what he'd just experienced.

He watched the road until he could no longer see Kendrick's car, then turned and looked at his father's hall, sitting as it had apparently for centuries up on that bluff, overlooking the sea and village both. It was a spectacular place, he was the first to admit. He had loved it with all his heart from the moment he'd known he belonged to it. Even going off to squire for as brief a time as he'd done so had been something of an agony. If he left the past behind, he would never in the Future be anything more there than a guest.

He put his hand on Heather's car and considered. He had to go back and Haemesburgh was the price he would pay to secure Artane for himself and his heirs. To have even that, he would need—

He looked out over the countryside and realized that in all his discussions about wooing a certain woman and finding a certain sword, he was missing the most obvious thing of all.

He needed to find out who wanted him dead before they managed to accomplish the deed.

He couldn't help but think Heather's brother had something to do with the whole tangle, but that was also something he wouldn't know until he'd gone off to do what he needed to do. The one thing he did know for certain was that he couldn't ask Imogen to be a part of any of that. In truth, he wasn't sure he could ask her to be a part of anything.

He took a deep breath and made the deliberate decision to put all that behind him. He was on the verge of seeing his home in a way that neither his father nor his grandfather could have imagined. He could at least give Imogen some relief from her stifling family for a day or two.

That would have to be enough.

Chapter 31

I mogen wasn't sure she could be more on edge than she had been for the past, oh, twenty-six years, but she found there was even more of that edge out there for her to perch on. She had just met Phillip's medieval brother and now she was about to assault a major landmark with a guy who she suspected wasn't going to want to buy a ticket to get in.

"Do they know you're coming?" she asked.

Phillip, good driver that he was, didn't take his eyes off the road. "Kendrick said it would do the current lord good to have a past lord simply appear at the doorway to inspect the place. I think I should be relieved to learn that I was—or will be, rather—a lord of that pile of stones. I was fairly sure my father would live forever."

And she was fairly sure he wasn't serious about that. Her siblings might have been eyeing the familial assets with jaundiced eyes on a regular basis, but she suspected Phillip wasn't that sort of guy. He did look like the sort of guy, though, who looked like he needed either a nap or a stiff drink.

She couldn't blame him. Once she'd gotten a good look at Artane, she thought she might want something bracing as well.

"You grew up here?" she asked. Well, it was more of a

squeak than anything else, but maybe he would ignore that. He seemed to be having his own troubles with clearing his throat.

"I did," he said quietly. "I can hardly believe 'tis still standing."

"Your family must have loved it very much over the years."

"I imagine they did." He tapped his fingers on the wheel. "We'll stop at the gates. I can't imagine we'll be able to go farther except on foot." He was silent as he drove up a rather steep road to where there looked to be a place where he could stash Heather's car, then he smiled briefly. "Easier with a horse."

She imagined so. She watched a rather seasoned old fellow come out of a little booth to investigate their arrival. He took one look at Phillip, blinked, then sighed.

"Don't suppose you're going to pay, are you?"

"I will, if you like."

"I'll charge you ten pounds," the man said without hesitation.

"My phone says the fee is five."

"You gave me a start. That'll cost you an extra five quid."

Phillip sighed, pulled out the required funds, then handed them over. The man took them, then winked at him.

"I would have let you park for free. You look like Lord Stephen."

"Distant relative."

"Aye, we get those often here. Off you go, lad. Park wherever you like."

Phillip laughed a little, then pulled the car as far away from the rest of the cars parked there as possible. Imogen waited for him to come get her door because he told her it would damage his chivalry if she didn't. She couldn't let that happen, so she waited, let him help her out of the car, then took a deep breath of the sea air.

"Spectacular."

"The shore hasn't changed," he said, sounding rather pleased by that. He locked the car, then looked at her. "Shall we?"

"Are you going to be okay?"

"That depends on what's left of the inside. We should have looked up the current lord on your phone to see what he's done to the place."

"I imagine his bio will be in the guide book. We can buy one when we get our tickets."

He blew out his breath. "I cannot believe I'm paying to gain access to my own home."

"Life's weird."

"Damn skippy, 'tis."

She laughed, because there was nothing like modern mixed with really, really vintage. If she'd been interested in starting a new career, she would have made a business out of that.

They made it to the outer gates before Phillip simply came to a stop. Imogen watched him and realized he was looking at the castle as if he'd never seen it before. She stopped with him and waited to see what he would do. It had to have been disconcerting to be looking at his home in a time period so far removed from his own. It was almost more than she could wrap her mind around merely to think she was looking at the place with someone who'd lived in it eight hundred years earlier.

He reached for her hand absently, as if he'd done it so many times in the past, he didn't think about it any longer.

"Thank you for coming with me," he said quietly.

"I'm hoping for the tour," she said, trying to inject a little lightness into things.

"We'll see if they'll let us in," he said. He squeezed her hand gently, then tucked it under his arm. "Paying to enter my own home," he said, shaking his head. "What next?"

She didn't want to speculate. She simply walked with him, ignoring a great deal of muttering that she assumed included medieval curses she didn't understand.

She stopped by the ticket window and looked at the woman inside. She was old, she was knitting, and she was looking at Phillip with the jaded expression of one who had just seen too much.

"Lord Stephen is in residence," she said briskly. "He'll be happy to see you, I'm sure."

"Do you know me?" Phillip asked in surprise.

"Cousin?"

"Something like that."

"I'm not surprised." She slid a guidebook toward him. "Ten pound fifty a piece or twenty-five for the two of you." She smiled. "You'll want to support the castle preservation efforts, of course."

"Of course," Phillip said, pulling money out of his wallet. "Thank you."

"You're welcome." She paused, looked both ways, then leaned forward. "Which one are you, if you don't mind my asking?"

"Phillip."

The woman looked at him, gave the quintessential, delicate, elderly woman snort. "Lord Robin's eldest?"

"I might be."

"I'm Mrs. Gladstone."

"*Enchanté,*" Phillip said, taking her hand and making a small bow over it.

Mrs. Gladstone smiled, looking very pleased. "Lovely manners you do Piaget lads have, to be sure. Enjoy the keep."

Imogen thought Phillip might have said something to the effect that he hoped he would, but she was too busy taking the brochure from him and scanning it for details about the current lord. She smiled at Mrs. Gladstone, then left the little guard tower.

"It says," she said, when they were clear of eager ears, "that the current lord, Stephen, was a full professor at Cambridge before he took over his duties as Earl of Artane. I'm guessing that means he must either be very smart or they're humoring him." She looked further and smiled. "He taught medieval studies."

Phillip snorted. "Unsurprising."

She showed him Stephen's picture. "Uncanny."

"Unoriginal. We'll see if he has any swordplay before I put any more labels on him. How long has he been warming my father's chair, does it say?"

"Only a few months."

"Good," Phillip said. "I can still intimidate him. Let's go get right to that."

Imogen nodded and walked up a cobblestone road with him. She tried not to be rude about gaping as she did so, but she could hardly believe her eyes. So she'd seen Artane from the train and thought it was enormous. She'd seen it from the village and realized it was bigger than she'd thought. It was another thing entirely to see it up close and in person.

Well, and with the man who would be lord over it someday.

He was walking next to her, that medieval lord dressed in jeans, jacket, and boots, with his hands clasped behind his back, simply looking at his surroundings. She could hardly believe it hadn't occurred to her at some point who she was actually dealing with. He wasn't just some random guy wandering around with a sword and an attitude, he was a nobleman from a powerful medieval family and he would be—had been, rather—the owner of the cobblestones she was walking over.

He glanced at her, then stopped. "What is it?"

She waved her hand around her helplessly. "This is yours."

"Not anymore."

"You know what I mean," she said, surprised by the wave of something that washed over her. Frustration that she hadn't made more of her life. Irritation that he hadn't made his own position in the world clearer before she started to care for him.

He blinked. "You're angry."

"This is *yours*," she accused. "And you didn't tell me."

"I was being humble."

She glared at him. He looked genuinely surprised, but he was a man, so perhaps that shouldn't have come as a shock.

"Does it matter?" he asked, looking far less baffled than perhaps he should have.

"Well, yes, it does matter," she said shortly. "You're not just a random medieval guy, you're . . . you're *this*."

"And you are your father's daughter, which means, according to something I read on the Internets yesterday, that you stand to inherit an obscene amount of your father's soul-sucking profits." He lifted an eyebrow. "How are we any different?"

"Where did you get that posh British accent?" she demanded.

"I learnt it from watching the Beeb," he said. "Which isn't the point. You're related to a man so rich, he could likely buy my keep even today. I'm related to the man who built my keep eight hundred years ago. What does either matter?"

"I think it matters," she muttered, "though I'm finding it difficult to decide how at the moment. I think I'm mad that I wish I'd known."

"And if you had known?"

"I would have been more deferential."

"The saints preserve us both if you tried," he said with a half laugh. "And if you want to look at the essence of it, our place in the world is something of an accident of birth. In that respect, we're no different, are we?"

"Powerful fathers?"

"Rich, powerful fathers who continually add to their empires?" he asked with a smile. "Aye."

She sighed. "I don't consider my father an asset."

"Well, in that we might differ, but our situations aren't dissimilar. You're on the cusp of domination of moviemaking, and I'm marching off to secure a strategic holding for my future." He shrugged. "We're the same."

"I don't have a house."

"And neither, at the moment, do I."

She had to concede that point. She didn't want to, but the truth was, they were both just trying to make their mark in the world. It was a little odd that Phillip had already done so centuries ago and she still had no idea if she would succeed or not, but at the moment, the future was still the future for both of them.

"Let's go torture my grandson," he suggested, "however far removed he is from me. My sire will approve. It might help him forget that I ignored women who have no doubt spent the past month eating through his larder."

She smiled. "Was that how it was?"

"Unfortunately," he agreed. "The last time I saw my home, I was escaping a keep full of the most eligible ladies the realm could produce, all come to examine my purse and see if it was heavy enough for them. I can guarantee not a damned one looked farther north than that."

"And yet you have such a nice face."

He seemed to be trying not to laugh. "Thank you."

"I'll admit," she said, "now that we're admitting a few things, that the first time I saw you, I thought you were a movie star."

"Did you?" he said, looking pleased.

"You have stunning cheekbones."

"Did you get no farther than my stunning cheekbones?"

"They're pretty arresting," she said. "I might have noticed your eyes as well. Maybe other things, but I'll never admit it."

"But you didn't notice my purse."

"I didn't know you had a purse."

He jammed his hands into his pockets. She wondered how he would possibly survive in the past when he didn't have pockets anymore. "This is all rubbish," he said nodding toward the castle. "It makes me eye-wateringly wealthy, of course, but gold does not make a man less of an arse."

She smiled. "How eye-wateringly wealthy?"

"Henry eyes my purse; he covets my father's. Imagine both combined and there you have what I have to look forward to."

She had the feeling he was perfectly serious. "And yet you're such a nice guy."

He looked at her for a moment or two, then pulled one of his hands out of his pockets and held it out. "What if you could give me a day or two to demonstrate how nice I can be?"

She looked at his hand, then quickly at his face. "Why?"

He took a deep breath. "The usual reasons, I suppose."

She had to think about that for a moment. "Do you want to date me?" she asked slowly. "Do disgustingly wealthy medieval lords in fancy sports cars date, do you think?"

He smiled. "I've no idea. Perhaps we can try it and see how it goes."

"But I'm the brown bunny," she protested. "You know, in a family of white bunnies. Why would you want to date me?"

He continued to hold out his hand. "I don't think, Imogen, that you have begun to realize your worth. And I can see how that might be possible given your, er, ah . . ." He seemed to be groping for the right word.

The man was a born diplomat.

"My family?" she supplied. "My parents are terrifying and my siblings brutal. I'm surprised one of them hasn't smothered me in my sleep long before now."

He smiled. "'Tis difficult to discover what one can be when he can never see the sun or stars for the shade of the mighty trees around him."

She considered what that meant, then understood things she hadn't understood before. "I see." She nodded. "Haemesburgh."

"I tell myself 'tis for its location, but—" He shrugged. "Aye."

"Is your father really that big?"

"Enormous. He gives the king pause." He continued to hold

out his hand. "What if we walk this path together for a bit and see what the sun feels like. Who knows, we might even manage to see a few stars."

She put her hand in his. He smiled, then tilted his head toward the top of the road.

"Let's go see who might be manning the front door."

"All right."

He was silent as they walked. She was wheezing and some of that definitely came from the incline. The rest of it came from having Phillip de Piaget rubbing his thumb over the back of her hand. It wasn't that she hadn't dated, as she had to keep reminding herself, or that she hadn't been in the occasional relationship. There was just something about the man walking next to her that left her feeling breathless. He seemed to be less breathless than overcome. He shook his head a lot.

It was profoundly weird to walk up a cobblestone street in present-day England with a guy who was lord of those cobblestones eight centuries in the past.

"I think you must have been a good ruler," she offered. "You know, in the past."

"Future."

"That," she agreed.

"What is that word you keep using?"

"Weird."

"That's the one," he said. He shook his head. "Weird."

"Where do we go from here?"

"I'll show you."

She supposed if anyone was qualified to do that, it was the man walking next to her, still holding her hand. She walked with him across the courtyard, thinking that perhaps it was best to ignore his muttering and the occasional flinch, then paused with him at the top of the steps leading up to the hall door. She looked at him.

"Are you okay?"

He smiled faintly. "If I take any more deep breaths, I will become senseless, I fear." He shook his head instead. "This is profoundly weird."

"I can't imagine."

He looked at the door for quite some time, reached out and touched it at one point, then sighed and knocked. The door opened almost instantly and someone who looked remarkably like Phillip stood there, phone in hand. He put that in his pocket, then smiled.

"You must be it."

Phillip looked at him. "What?"

"The surprise Kendrick rang and told me to expect."

"My brother is an obnoxious arse."

The man laughed and held out his hand. "Stephen de Piaget. And you are either Jason or Phillip, though I somehow have the feeling you're Phillip."

"Why do you think that?"

"There's a portrait of you in the upstairs hall."

Imogen caught Phillip as he swayed. He put his arm around her and looked at his grandson however many generations it had to have been.

"Interesting."

"Let me get you a drink before you look at it," Stephen suggested. He looked at Imogen and smiled. "I'm Stephen."

"I'm Imogen."

"Welcome to Artane. Is this your first visit, or have you seen it another time?" He smiled. "No pun intended."

"No, first time," she assured him.

"I hope you'll find it acceptable," he said. He looked at Phillip. "Come along, Granddaddy, and let's see you settled with something strengthening."

Phillip cursed him. "You've obviously spent too much time with my brother."

"As well as your uncle John and a pair of your cousins— oh, steady on your feet, lad. Miss Imogen, here, let me take his other side. One never knows what to say in these situations and one fears to say too much."

"One might refrain from announcing shocking tidings until one's guests are seated," Phillip wheezed. "No need to thank me for the advice. My uncle *John*?"

"Earl of Segrave and the husband of the current countess of Sedgwick—oh, I say, my lord Phillip, you *are* excitable, aren't you?"

Imogen looked at Stephen de Piaget and realized he was enjoying himself too thoroughly. She shot him a warning look, but he only winked at her.

"Let's find him somewhere comfortable to sit," Stephen said, still smiling. "The lord's solar. I'll fetch wine. Trust me, the cellar is exceptional."

"You likely have bottles my father hoarded," Phillip said darkly.

"That, my lord, is entirely possible," Stephen said. "Can you walk or must I carry you?"

"I'll lean on Imogen." He took a deep breath. "All part of my master plan."

Imogen couldn't believe that was anything more than just polite conversation, though she had to admit that there was something very nice about Phillip's arm around her and his holding her hand that he'd pulled around his back. He seemed quite a bit more steady than he claimed to be, but maybe that was part of his master plan as well. She would have loved to have known what that plan was, but if there was one thing she could say for herself it was that she never read the last five pages of a book until she got there.

She would wait.

Chapter 32

Phillip was beginning to wonder just how familiar his sire was with paranormal oddities.

He'd heard that spoken in hushed tones over the course of his life, but his father had said it with such reluctance that he'd determined early on that whatever those might be, they were things he definitely didn't want to become entangled in. That he should presently find himself in such straits shouldn't have surprised him.

He sat in the lord's solar in front of a roaring fire and tried to focus on what was happening around him. It was difficult. He had to continually look at the glass in his hand and the clothing on his person to remember when he was. The where was not as difficult, but the when . . . that gave him pause.

He was listening to his, er, grandson, Stephen, and Stephen's wife, Peaches, discuss events of the current day with Imogen, allowing the modern English with its lovely lilt wash over him. He could bring to mind innumerable such afternoons spent in his father's solar with his family, discussing the events of the day, wondering about the events of the future, enjoying the company of people he loved. It was powerfully odd to sit there with three souls he didn't know quite so well and do what was in essence the same thing yet have it be so different.

He looked back over his life and examined his time at Sedgwick with a new and jaundiced eye. He had been there when his aunt Persephone had arrived in the past. At the moment, he honestly couldn't remember what excuse his uncle had given for her oddities and he wasn't sure if with all the time that had passed he could remember them properly. The truth was, she had had a plethora of things he'd dismissed: words, ideas, habits.

He wondered if it was worth it to her presently.

If the rumors were true, his aunt Jenner was from the Future as well. 'Twas no wonder those little terrors Samuel and Theopholis were always on the prowl for things to investigate. Their mother was the biggest mystery of all and he couldn't imagine she was surrendering any of her secrets without a fight. Those two demons were likely simply honing their skills in other places for use at home.

He sipped on his wine, then had to set it aside because his hand was trembling more than he cared for anyone to see. It wasn't that he was unnerved. He was weary, that was it. The Future was loud and busy and seemingly endlessly awake.

"Would you like a tour?"

Phillip realized Stephen was asking that of Imogen. She started to answer, then looked at him.

"What do you think?"

"I think I might survive it," he managed.

"Then let's go," Stephen said. "Do you mind, love?"

Peaches de Piaget, who looked as if she might give birth any moment, smiled and waved them on. "Let me know how it goes and if Phillip has any secret hiding places he wants to tell us about."

"I'll be sure and ask," Stephen said with a laugh. He kissed his wife, then led them out of the solar.

Phillip followed, having made a less personal but no less heartfelt farewell to the lady of the house. He found it rather more natural than not to take Imogen's hand as they walked, which he hoped wouldn't annoy her beyond reason. She didn't seem averse, which he appreciated.

He wasn't completely surprised by the improvements he saw and 'twas fascinating, he had to admit, to listen to Stephen describe when those various additions had been made. He wasn't sure he would ever be comfortable with the vast amounts of happenings that lay ahead for him, but there was nothing to be done about it.

"Let's start in the portrait gallery," Stephen said. He smiled at Phillip. "You may want to see yourself, I believe. Your uncle Jackson painted you."

Phillip had to take a steadying breath. "I'm not sure I want to see that."

Stephen looked at him in surprise, then closed his eyes briefly. "Of course. I hadn't thought about it, actually. Why don't I just tell you that you looked very dashing and leave it at that?"

"Coward that I am," Phillip said, "I think that might be best." He looked at the current lord of Artane. "'Tis a bit like walking over my own grave, you see."

"I do see," Stephen said seriously. He stopped. "We needn't see anything, if it's too much. Or you can just wander as you care to on your own. It is, after all, your hall."

Phillip shook his head. "'Tis yours now. The thought that it was mine for any length of time at all—" He looked at Stephen. "I'm almost afraid to ask for any details about that."

"Oh, you were lord here," Stephen said with a smile, "but I won't tell you anything of it. Don't want to jinx you. I can show you the hall of weapons, if you like. We keep things behind glass for the tourists, but I'll admit to having picked the odd lock in my youth. Kendrick's lads are notorious for it now."

"He has lads?"

"A set of triplets and two others, plus a wee gel."

Phillip paused, then he laughed. It was, he had to admit, the first time he'd actually felt anything akin to true amusement, he hardly knew what to do with himself. "Tell me they're terrors."

"All six," Stephen said. "Delightful, of course, but if your brother has any gray hair, he can thank his children for it."

"It serves him right," Phillip said with a snort, "considering all the same he gave our sire." He looked at Imogen. "Would you call that a just recompense?"

"I'd call it Karma," she said dryly. "Be afraid of her."

He thought he just might be. He followed Stephen through the great hall and into a wing that hadn't been there in his time. He had to take a deep breath before he could cross the threshold where it had simply been cut into the stone of his home.

"New," Stephen supplied. "In the sixteenth century. It was originally a passage built to hide things. It originally cut through the foundation and led to something that looked remarkably like an aboveground cistern."

"To hide what?"

"Treasures from a greedy king and his rampaging henchmen," Stephen said.

"What did we hide?"

"Religious relics and a few important humans," Stephen said. "A dodgy time, but worth the sacrifice. We'll follow this passageway just for a bit, then you'll see the new wing. *New*, of course, is relative."

Phillip imagined it was. He looked at Imogen to find she was watching him. He smiled. "Paranormal oddities."

"I'll just bet."

He found himself rather glad, all things considered, that Heather had provided him with access to so much history. It made him feel far less overwhelmed to at least have some idea of what had gone on in the world after he'd had his turn tilting at it. He had to admit there was no small amount of satisfaction over the care his posterity had taken of his father's hall.

"And here we have weapons," Stephen said. "Lots of lovely things in surprisingly good condition."

Phillip had to stop himself from grunting simply because he supposed Stephen was thinking the same thing. Who knew what inhabitants of Artane had contributed things at what point? Given what he himself had already experienced over the past pair of days, he didn't suppose he would be surprised by much.

The collection was extensive, unfolding a thorough history before him as he walked past the glass cases. He found himself eventually back where he'd started, looking at a tall case that was empty. He frowned, then looked at Stephen.

"Something is missing."

"Unfortunately," Stephen said. "A sword, as it happens. Legend has it that the sword belonged to, well, your grandfather,

Rhys. It was used for knighting ceremonies by each of the lords of Artane until the dispensing of those honors was taken over by the crown. I understand the sword was actually used by the first lords in battle."

Phillip looked around. Damnation, didn't people need to *sit* in the Future? He didn't protest the offer of Imogen to lean on, though he supposed that was a less disinterested choice than it might have been otherwise. He looked at Stephen.

"Let me guess," he managed. "Tall sword, some inscriptions, large blue stone in the hilt."

Stephen didn't look surprised. "Yours?"

"My grandfather's, then my father's, then mine."

"It went missing—"

"Five years ago?" Phillip asked sourly.

For the first time since opening the front door, Stephen looked startled. "How did you know?"

"I know who has it."

"Wait," Imogen said, looking at him. "If Heather took it in the past, how did it disappear in the future? It was obviously here for at least some period of time and apparently used for centuries before that."

"She changed history," Phillip said, wondering if that was actually as daft a thought as it sounded. "I can think of nothing else."

Unless . . . unless the sword had gone missing in the past and he'd been too dead to recover it.

"Any thoughts on where to find it?" Stephen asked. "Sentimental value, and all that."

Phillip found it rather difficult to breathe, all of the sudden. It was difficult enough to think in terms of a single lifetime and all the plotting and scheming that such a thing required. Add to that multiple lifetimes, several centuries, and Heather of Haemesburgh's vile sense of jest, and he was truly in dire straits.

"I need to think," he said.

"Where?" Stephen asked.

"The great hall, perhaps."

Stephen nodded, then gestured toward a different doorway. "Private access."

"Another hiding place?"

"We're not sure," Stephen said honestly. "I suspect 'tis a

pair of lads simply burrowing behind the walls at some point during the castle's history, but that's just me."

Phillip looked at him sharply. "Do these suspects have names?"

"I hate to say," Stephen said with a shiver. "It's tantamount to summoning them, I've found, and I've seen more of that pair of Nicholas's sons than I care to."

"In the Future?" Imogen gasped.

He looked at her. "Perhaps."

"Why?" Phillip asked.

"Because I think one of them helped me with a suitcase that had come open in London," she said with a shiver. "I'm not sure I would have made my train north without him."

"Penance," Stephen said dryly. "They have a lifetime of it to make up for the havoc they've wreaked and the mischief they've made. It wouldn't surprise me in the least to find it was one of them." He looked at Phillip. "This way, my lord. I'll see to some wine."

Phillip followed him, but remembered very little of the journey save that Imogen's hand in his was very cold. He sat down finally with her in front of one of the massive hearths in the great hall and sighed. He stared into the flames for quite some time before he looked at her.

"'Tis baffling," he said. "If Heather took my sword in 1249, why did it just go missing five years ago now? In the Future, rather?"

"I have no idea," she said, shrugging helplessly. "She obviously had it a couple of weeks ago when I used it, which means she has to still have it now."

"But how can she have it now if the lords of Artane had it in the past?" he asked. He rubbed the space between his eyes. "The traveling back and forth gives me a pain right here."

"I understand, believe me."

Phillip closed his eyes. "Forgive me if I sit here and suffer stoically for a moment or two."

She laughed. "Suffer away. I'll keep watch."

He wasn't sure how long he suffered, but it was apparently long enough to lead to his falling asleep. He woke to a touch on his shoulder and sat up, reaching for his sword. He sighed, shot Imogen a smile, then looked at Stephen.

Something was wrong.

Stephen was smiling, though, in a way that a man was wont to smile when he didn't want to unsettle anyone in the vicinity who didn't need to be unsettled.

"If I could have your ear, old bean," Stephen said, "just for a moment." He smiled at Imogen. "If you don't mind?"

Imogen waved him on. "Please."

Phillip walked with Stephen across the great hall and toward the lord's solar. He frowned at his, ah, whatever he was.

"What is it?"

"Something you'll want to see. She arrived just a moment ago."

Phillip walked into the solar behind Stephen, then pulled up short at the sight of Heather of Haemesburgh sitting in a chair in front of the fire.

Phillip cursed and walked around the chairs to squat down in front of her. "What in the hell happened to you?" he demanded.

"I was attacked," she said, holding something to the eye that was going to be swollen shut by morning. "Trust me, he got worse than he gave."

"Attacked where?" Stephen asked.

"In your car park, my lord," Heather said. "Let me tell this once, then you two decide what you want to do." She pulled the cloth away from her eye. "I was following you, Phillip, to make certain you didn't ding my car. I thought to take a bit of sea air, when my foe assaulted me. I was taken by surprise, which is the only reason he made off with my automobile."

"The Ford?" Phillip asked in surprise.

"Range Rover," she said with a snort. "I wouldn't be caught dead driving that runabout and you're missing the issue here. My car is *gone*."

"Buy another," Phillip said.

"It has your sword in it, you fool!"

Phillip felt his way back into a chair. "My sword?"

She rolled her eyes. "Am I destined to be surrounded by men so thick I must repeat everything I say? Aye, you idiot, your sword! Worse still, 'twas someone who knows what to do with it and I'm talking about impaling you with it."

"Who?" Phillip asked, though he supposed he didn't need to ask.

"Robert, of course. My brother, Robert. And he vowed to destroy you."

"But I'm here in the Future."

"He doesn't know that."

Phillip sat back in his chair, then looked at Stephen. "What do you think?"

Stephen looked a little green. "I'm not sure what to think. I like my comfortable existence here, something I may be without if you find yourself dead." He sat with a gusty sigh. "I could dig up a history book."

"Don't," Phillip said, only to realize that Heather had said the same thing. He shot her a dark look. "In agreement at last."

She didn't look any better than Stephen. "Think this through, my lord Phillip. What if you find in some book that my brother slays you, then slays your family, what would you do?"

"Stop him."

"And if you found out that your family was safe because you acted," she said. "What would you do then?"

"Stop him."

"Exactly," she said. "There is no point in knowing the future, Phillip, because you're going to do your knightly duty just the same. I suggest you do what you need to do and leave events to proceed as they will."

He could see the sense in it, though he had to admit he didn't care for the not knowing. "I've no idea how to get to the past save through Haemesburgh, though I have to believe there are other means."

"Edinburgh has a gate or two," Heather said. "I can show you."

He imagined she could. He looked at Stephen. "Can you take care of Imogen? Get her back to Edinburgh tomorrow?"

"And just what are you going to do?"

"Take Heather back, then do what I must." He stood up and looked at Heather. "We'll leave in half an hour if you can travel."

"I can't drive, but I can travel."

"I'll drive."

She winced, then nodded. "As you will."

"I'll meet you in the courtyard in a quarter hour."

He clapped his grandson—and one day he would have to decide just how many generations separated them, if there were generations separating them and he had actually managed to become lord of Artane in the past—on the shoulder, then left the lord's solar. He walked out into the great hall, finding that it was a much less enjoyable experience than it had been but an hour before.

Imogen was standing in front of the fire, watching him. He walked over to her, then stopped in front of her.

"Heather is here."

She looked at him in surprise. "Why?"

"She followed us to make sure I didn't destroy her car. She was attacked in the car park by someone. I fear it was her brother."

She studied him. "You fear, or you know?"

He dragged his hands through his hair. "I know. He's vowed to go back to the past and slay my family. I have to go back and stop him."

"Without your sword."

"I don't have a choice."

She took a deep breath, then put her shoulders back. "I'll come along. I am extremely good at spotting trouble and avoiding it, you know, with the siblings and all. That might be useful for you."

He thought he just might love her. He reached out and pulled her into his arms. He closed his eyes and held her close for not nearly as long as he wanted to. He sighed finally and stepped back.

"I can't take you with me," he said seriously. "'Tis a difficult time, full of terrible dangers."

She took a deep breath. "Of course. I understand."

He wanted to tell her that she couldn't understand because he wasn't telling her the truth. He wanted to take her with him, wanted to drop to one knee and ask her to wed with him, wanted to damn Fate and all her incarnations and simply do what he wanted. But he couldn't, because he had seen the Future and knew what he would be asking her to give up to come with him.

Worse still, he had seen the past and knew how very likely it was he wouldn't survive what he intended to do.

"Stephen will get you back to Edinburgh," he said quietly. "Tomorrow, of course. He has a guest chamber you can stay in tonight. I've had your gear fetched from the car."

She nodded, then took another step back. "Good luck."

Her eyes were swimming with tears. He looked at her far longer than he should have, then made her a brief bow and walked away before he unmanned himself in front of her by shedding tears himself.

*I*t was late when he stood in the back of a coffee shop and contemplated his immediate future. Heather had assured him there was a gate there and he had every reason to suppose she wanted him to succeed as badly as he needed to. He took a deep breath and dialed his brother.

"Where are you?" Kendrick asked. "Still at home?"

"Nay," Phillip managed. "Edinburgh."

"Why the hell for?"

"I've got to go back. There's trouble that I must see to."

Kendrick sighed. "I would say you had all the time in the world, but having had all that time myself, I understand your concern."

"What in the bloody hell are you talking about?"

"Ask Jake when you get back home."

Phillip paused. "I want to come see you, but I'm not sure how I can manage that now."

Kendrick, to his credit and likely because he was so damned old, only cleared his throat roughly. "That's why there are so many bloody time gates. Again, ask Jake. Come for a holiday, you and Imogen."

Phillip frowned. "What do you know?"

"Nothing," Kendrick said. "Just that she might be amenable to a bit of a visit. Eventually."

Phillip supposed they had a bit more conversation, but he couldn't remember it. He was fairly certain he'd told his brother he loved him and that he would see him soon. Past, present, he had no idea which one it would be. All he knew was that he soon found himself looking at the phone in his hand and wondering how he might manage without one in the past. He looked at Heather.

"I'll do what I can."

"I know," she said. "Thank you."

"Why Imogen?" he asked, because he apparently had absolutely no self-control.

"Her brother did me a good turn five years ago," she said simply. "The particulars aren't important. Suffice it to say, he saved my life. I thought to repay him by making his sister happy."

"And you're rewarding them both with me?" Phillip asked in astonishment.

"I'm daft, I know," Heather said tartly. "You also haven't wooed and won anyone. If you don't do something other than stand there and blather on, you never will. Give me your phone. You won't be needing it."

He supposed she had a point there. He handed her his phone, then walked into the shop and into one of the serving wenches there. She was wearing all kinds of bits of metal on her face and had decorated herself in various ways that he genuinely wished he'd had the time to admire. She handed him a cup.

"A mocha. You look like you need it."

He accepted the cup, then turned around and walked out into the alley.

Chapter 33

I mogen stood on the outer walls of Artane and looked over the sea. It roared endlessly, timelessly, reminding her more painfully than she cared to admit that she was where she was and there was probably no way to get anywhere else.

In a timely fashion, as it were.

"Imogen?"

She jumped a little, then flinched at the sight of the current lord of Artane standing there. Stephen looked far too much like Phillip for her taste, but she forced herself to smile just the same.

"My lord."

"Stephen, if you don't mind. I'm not used to the title yet." He leaned against the wall next to her. "How are you?"

"Fine," she said automatically.

"No, how are you?" he asked. He smiled. "I'm prying, I know. It honestly isn't in my nature. Stiff upper lip and all that."

She sighed. "I feel like I'm dreaming, like this whole thing is a dream. Past, present, future. I can't tell the difference."

"Without sounding daft, I'll say that some of it is Artane," he said carefully. "There's something about the place that feels timeless."

"Phillip says his father calls them paranormal oddities."

"So I understand."

She turned and looked at him. "What should I do?"

"Do?" he echoed. "What are you choices?"

"Go back and save him or go forward and lose myself."

He seemed to consider. "I think going back is too dangerous. I've had my own very brief brush with the past and I can say with absolute honesty that when a man comes at you with a sword, he means it. If Phillip didn't tell you to stay safely here, I'm sure that was an oversight."

"He said just that."

"I'm not surprised," Stephen said seriously. "I'm quite sure he meant it."

She studied Phillip's descendant, if that's how it had all played out, and wondered why he looked to be so . . . purposeful. "So," she said, "did you come to tell me that?"

He smiled. "You know, in the Middle Ages, being able to read people was an important skill. Life or death in some cases, I imagine."

"I have no other skills."

"Have you had the chance to find that out?"

She opened her mouth to tell him she most certainly had, then realized that maybe that wasn't exactly the case. "I thought my sister was the only shrink I had to worry about."

Stephen smiled. "Just an observation. And to answer your question, no, I had another purpose besides trying to arrange your life for you."

"I can't wait to hear it."

"The sword is still gone."

She frowned. "And why should that mean anything?"

Stephen looked hesitant. "What that means to me is that it isn't yet in Phillip's hands. Considering he went back to accomplish that . . ."

"Oh," she said, feeling something settle in the pit of her stomach. Then she took a deep breath. "Heather has it."

He shook his head. "She rang me this morning. Don't know why, professional courtesy I suppose. I'm not sure if Stephen told you that she'd been assaulted in my car park and the sword stolen. By her brother, Robert."

The hole in her stomach grew bigger. "I knew, but I didn't

particularly want to think about the ramifications. What do you think Robert is going to do with that sword?"

"Use it as a key to get from place to place, I imagine." He shrugged. "Or perhaps from time period to time period. I'm a little surprised he didn't simply stab his sister and have done, but I'm guessing he thinks to go back in time and rearrange things to suit himself. I would do the same, in his shoes."

"Rewrite the script of his life?"

"Precisely."

"With himself in the starring role," she said faintly. "I know the type." She looked at him. "Then what am I to do about it?"

"Heather believes you are the only one who can put your hands on that sword and send it where it needs to go."

Imogen looked at him in surprise. "But what of her?"

Stephen shrugged. "She used it to come to the Future, but even though she brought it with her, it's never again worked for her. Apparently, she's tried several times. But it worked for you."

Imogen realized that what felt like a block of ice in her stomach was actually fear. She found that along with that fear came a serious inability to breathe.

"Me?" she managed. "Why me?"

Stephen smiled faintly. "I can't answer that, I'm afraid. Perhaps we're here on this rock with a list of things to accomplish and this is an item on your list. Perhaps you were fated to meet Phillip and rescue him. Perhaps you have magical powers we don't dare examine."

She smiled in spite of herself. "Well, I think we can discount the last."

"I suppose so," he agreed. He glanced at the ocean to his right. "All I know is that England is a magical place. Scotland is more so, I daresay. I'm fortunate to have spent so much time so near the crossroads of both. We are the caretakers of this place for the moment and I almost believe, looking back on it now, that perhaps I was prepared—for lack of a better word—for the roles I've taken on." He smiled at her. "Sorry. The walls tend to leave me more philosophical than I should be."

"And you think I have any part in any of this?" she asked

"It would seem that way, wouldn't it?"

She had to take a deep breath. "What should I do?"

"Go save your love."

"I have no idea how."

He smiled faintly. "Don't you?"

"I'm just supposed to go hang out at Haemesburgh, wait until Heather's brother shows up with Phillip's sword, then take it away from him?"

"You're a moviemaker," Stephen said with a shrug. "Arrange the scene to suit yourself."

She put her hand over her stomach. "I'll need a ride."

"I have one waiting for you downstairs. I'm not sure you'll need an introduction."

She took a deep breath, then followed him downstairs, trying simply to keep herself from falling on her face. She was used to sneaking past danger, not confronting it, but maybe it was time that changed.

She did indeed recognize the man in the great hall, slouching negligently against the lord's table with his hands in his pockets. He saw her, then straightened. He made her a slight bow.

"Miss Maxwell."

She was somehow utterly unsurprised. She looked at the blond demigod who had stuffed her underwear back in her suitcase, then decided she might make more of an impression if she glared at him.

"Sam or Theo?"

"Aye."

She scowled. "You aren't going to tell me, are you?"

"Where would be the sport in that?"

"You're not too big to punch in the nose, you know."

The twin, whichever one he was, only smiled and made her another bow before he looked at Stephen. "My lord Artane."

"I'm feeding you again tonight, aren't I?" Stephen asked with a sigh.

"After I've delivered Miss Maxwell safely to her destination, aye, that would be lovely."

Stephen shook his head. "My life . . ." He shook his head again, then reached out his hand. "Imogen, it's been a pleasure. I don't know what your plans are, but my hall is always open to you. Please take advantage of that any time you like.

I'll ask Mrs. Gladstone not to pick your pockets on the way in next time." He looked at the twin, sighed, then walked off.

Imogen looked at her ride. "I need to get to Haemesburgh."

"Of course."

"You know things."

"I might."

"But you're not going to tell me about them."

"Where would be the sport in that? Do you have your wee rucksack to replace the old one?"

"I'll go get it."

An hour later, she was watching one of Phillip's younger cousins—she still couldn't decide which—go off to park his obscenely expensive sports car she was sure he hadn't stolen. He seemed unconcerned about her safety, which she supposed could have been a good thing or a bad thing. He promised he would be wandering about the courtyard should she feel the need to scream for aid, but he thought she might want to be about her business on her own.

She looked at Haemesburgh's great hall and wondered if she might be about to get herself killed.

Well, if there was one thing she had, it was a nose for danger, and she didn't smell any at the moment. She walked into the great hall, let her eyes adjust, then paused to still her own racing heart so she could see if there might be anyone else in the place. She didn't hear any heavy breathing or the telltale cursing of a sibling or thug with mayhem on his or her mind.

There was, however, a sword behind the lord's table.

The feeling of déjà vu that washed over her was overwhelming. For a moment, she wasn't sure she hadn't gone back in time to relive the day when she'd first seen Phillip's sword.

But she hadn't. She knew too much, she'd seen too much. She walked across the floor silently, watching for any movement and feeling far too much like she was trapped on a set where the writers hadn't been able to decide between a horror movie or a spy flick.

She made it to the lord's table, then walked around it. She

looked at the sword for a moment or two, wrestling with herself, then reached out and put her hand on it.

The hall exploded around her.

She had seen battle scenes in movies, of course, and even been on the distant periphery of one being shot. But she'd never been *in* one, so to speak, until that moment.

She realized that while she was not only in the present, as long as she kept her hand on the sword, she was in the past as well. She could see the battle raging in the great hall; she could hear the shouts of the men. She realized with horror—and yes, it was apparently a horror film she was doing—that even though a pair of Phillip's men were there, they weren't going to be enough.

Phillip was fighting. She wasn't sure where the men he was fighting had come from or whom they served, but it apparently wasn't Phillip. It was so shocking to see him, bloodied, filthy, exhausted, she almost couldn't find her voice to speak.

And then he caught sight of her.

She knew at that moment that whatever happened, she would never, ever again find anyone like him.

He vaulted over the table and put his hand on his sword, over hers. "Thank you," he managed. "But how—?"

"My lord, behind you!"

Phillip pulled his sword away from her and spun around. Instantly, the connection was lost.

The sounds of battle faded. She stood there behind the lord's table and shook. Silence descended, accompanied by a stillness that she wasn't sure she cared for. She could almost hear her heartbeat.

It was all so anticlimactic. She looked around the hall and found it just as empty as it had been ten minutes earlier. If she hadn't known better, she might have supposed she'd just imagined everything she'd just seen.

But the sword was gone.

She supposed she could have picked up a history book and figured out what happened to him, but the thought of that was about as appealing as the thought of ripping out her heart with her bare hands.

She could have used her phone, she supposed. She could have simply asked for a bio of Phillip de Piaget, Lord of

Artane, Possessor of Stunning Cheekbones, and Keeper of Her Heart.

She supposed no search engine would have come up with anything for that last part.

She sat there until the hall began to grow dark. Heather didn't come to kick her out, staff didn't intrude to suggest tourist hours were over, thugs didn't come to make her life difficult. Not even the twin who refused to identify himself ventured inside the hall.

Phillip didn't come to get her, either.

She got up finally and pulled her coat around her. It wasn't the raincoat with the advertisement on the backside. This was a proper Mac with a plaid liner and an impervious shell. It was actually warm. She thought she might be able to blend in to a crowd without trouble at the moment. Lucky her.

She walked across the hall and opened the doors, both of them at once. It was raining outside, which didn't surprise her in the least. Lights had been turned on inside the courtyard, giving it an almost medieval sort of look. Well apart from the lack of smell, sound, and guys walking around with swords.

Her phone rang, startling her. She looked at it, hoping beyond hope for a number she thought she might want to see . . .

It was Prissy.

She sighed and answered. "Yes?"

"Get back to Edinburgh now."

She felt her heart leap and not in a good way. "Is something wrong?"

"Of course there's something wrong! You have family pouring in from all over the world and you're heaven knows where doing heaven knows what."

"What does it matter?" Imogen asked numbly.

"It matters, stupid, because you're getting married tomorrow! Father and Mr. Davis have arranged it all."

"I'm what?" Imogen said, her ears perking up. "They arranged what?"

"Your marriage! You didn't think Marcus was going to waste this place as a backdrop, did you? He's been singing 'Bless Your Beautiful Hide' all day. It's spectacular, really."

"Then why don't *you* marry him—?"

"Don't be ridiculous," Prissy said, then she tittered. "I mean, really."

"And I mean really," Imogen said. "Why not?"

Prissy was silent for so long, Imogen thought she might have lost her phone signal. But no, her sister was there on the other end, sniffing.

"He wants you. I have no idea why, but there you go. Congratulations. You win."

Imogen didn't want to win. She sighed and hung up the phone without saying anything else. What she wanted to do was be somewhere else, some*when* else. But since that didn't seem like it was going to happen, why not? Marriages had been arranged for centuries. Phillip would have agreed that was the case. She didn't loathe Marcus Davis. If she could get him to stop singing, he was manageable. Difficult, but manageable. Her father was difficult and they'd learned to manage him. She could make a decent life with him. At least he would understand her obsession with movies. With enough time, maybe they would develop a relationship that included both family and work. It could happen.

She looked back over her shoulder at the empty hall, sighed, then pulled the hall doors shut behind her.

Sam or Theo, whichever it was, was waiting for her. He got out of the car and opened the passenger door for her. She walked around the car, then looked at him.

"Sam or Theo?"

"We're interchangeable."

"You're killing me."

"'Tis all part of our mystique," he said.

She sighed and got into the car. She leaned back against the seat and closed her eyes.

If she hadn't been so tired, she would have wept.

Chapter 34

P*hillip* knew he was going to die.

Worse still, he was going to lose. He was going to lose everything because he was trying to have it all and Imogen as well.

The battle had been quick and brutal. He'd arrived in Haemesburgh to find it deserted. Or, rather, it had been until he'd walked into the hall. It was as if Hell had then suddenly unleashed its full fury against him. He had no idea who the men were or where they'd come from, but he had the feeling Robert of Haemesburgh was behind it.

Only he hadn't found Robert near the lord's table, directing the assault.

He'd found his own captain, Cederic.

It had surprised him so, he'd lowered his borrowed sword and almost lost his head as a result. If it hadn't been for Jackson having apparently decided it would be well to wait for him outside Haemesburgh's gates, he would have arrived in the keep alone and likely died there alone as well.

"Look who has come to help me," Cederic said. "A friendly face."

Phillip didn't bother to turn around. He simply looked at his captain. "Traitor," he said flatly.

"At least I'll have earned what I take," Cederic spat.

"My lord," said a voice from behind Phillip.

He turned around to find Hamish there. A sword was coming out of him where it shouldn't have been. Phillip looked over him to see none other than Robert of Haemesburgh, the son, standing there, gloating.

"I'll have your sword," Robert said triumphantly, "and be happy to tell anyone who'll listen where I came by it—"

"Robert, be silent!" Cederic exclaimed. "You and your ever-running mouth."

"You and your misplaced ambition," Robert shot back. "As if I ever would have ceded anything to . . . you . . ."

Phillip realized Cederic had thrown his sword at Robert only because it grazed him on the way by. He would have to have a word with his sire about having saddled him with that one. Cederic was so unskilled that Phillip hadn't even suffered a wound to his flesh. Nothing more than a slicing of the cloth of his tunic. He turned around to point that out in time to watch Cederic flinch. A look of surprise descended on his features.

Cederic looked over his shoulder. There was, unsurprisingly, a blade sticking out of his back.

He fell, taking the lord's chair with him as he did so. Phillip looked behind him to find Sir Myles standing there, his face betraying no emotion. Sir Wiscard, on the other hand, was leaning against the back of the wall, yawning. Phillip looked at the two of them, then choked out a curse.

"Thank you," he wheezed. "I think."

"Our pleasure," Sir Myles said. "Our pleasure, indeed."

Phillip looked at the two of them. "Is it possible, do you suppose, to have dual captains of my guard?"

Wiscard shook his head. "Too confining. We like to be free to move about and look under rocks for vermin such as that one there."

"The dead one," Myles added.

Phillip was, again, extremely happy those two weren't turning their sights on him. "I'll consider another for the post, then."

"As you will, my lord," Myles said, inclining his head. "I

believe we might want to see to the lad, my lord. He looks terribly pale."

Phillip nodded, then turned and knelt down by Hamish. The lad was looking up at him, but not truly seeing him.

"I believe," he said faintly, "that your captain is betraying you."

"Thank you," Phillip said dryly. "Anything else I should know?"

"I wasn't sure Lord Robert . . . was . . . alive." He groped for Phillip's hand. "I wanted to . . . serve . . . you. I lied to . . . have . . . that—"

"Let's call it something less dire," Phillip said. He looked at Hamish, watched his breathing grow more shallow, then looked over his shoulder at Myles. "Clear the hall of the living."

It had to be said that if nothing else, Myles and Wiscard had seen too many things to be surprised by much. They nodded as one, then did as Phillip had bidden.

Phillip waited until the hall was silent before he looked at Hamish. The lad was watching him with more trust than perhaps he deserved. He squeezed the lad's hand.

"Can you trust me?" he asked.

"Aye."

Phillip looked around himself one more time, then back at Hamish. "I'm still on a quest," he said, casting about for the first thing that came to mind. "To find the thumb bone of a wizard, as you know. Very important, that."

Hamish closed his eyes. "Indeed."

"You'll need to regain your strength if you're to aid me," Phillip continued. "I'm going to send you to the lady Heather. She'll take care of you until you're stronger, then I'll call for you."

Hamish only wheezed.

Phillip stood up, jammed his sword into the appropriate place in the floor behind the lord's chair, then carefully lifted Hamish to his feet. He put the lad's hand on the hilt of his sword, the put his hand over Hamish's.

Hamish took a deep breath, then disappeared.

Phillip let out his breath slowly, then pulled his sword free of the floor and resheathed it. He had no idea if it would ever work again and he couldn't bring himself to try it. He would leave it at Artane, safely tucked behind a handful of guardsmen, and let the future take care of it. But before he went to Artane, there was someone else he needed to see.

Someone who might have an idea where he could find a way to peer into the Future.

F_{our} days later, he walked into his father's hall. He'd gone first to Ravensthorpe to see his uncle for answers, but found the man had decided a journey somewhere else suited him at the moment. Phillip suspected Jake was simply avoiding him, but he had no way to prove that. He had turned for home, because he suspected the questions he had were the last ones his father would expect him to ask.

His father was standing on the top step of the stairs leading up to the hall door, surveying his domain when Phillip arrived. Phillip dismounted and climbed a pair of stairs, then stopped.

"My lord," he said.

Robin studied him in silence for a moment or two, then lifted an eyebrow. "You're early for supper."

Phillip scowled at him. "I'm not here for supper, though I won't refuse it, of course. I'm here for aid. I prefer to have that aid from my uncle Jackson, but he doesn't seem to be here unless he's ridden something besides his usual steed."

"You just missed him. He's off to Wyckham. We didn't have enough food left to suit him."

Phillip folded his arms over his chest. "I imagine you can help me."

"Can or will?"

"I think you might want to once you know why I need help."

"A woman?" Robin asked brightly.

"Surprisingly enough. And not Heather, though for all either of us know, she *is* Heather. Or she could be Robert of Haemesburgh's foster daughter."

"Or?"

Phillip ground his teeth. "Or she could be from the Future."

That his father didn't look shocked surprised him.

"Wondered when you'd find out."

"I imagine you did."

Robin studied him. "Can I assume you've made a visit?"

"I might have."

"Did you drive a car?"

"A Porsche."

"How many horsepower?"

Phillip looked at his father in astonishment. "Am I dreaming or am I actually having this conversation with you?"

"I may have a bit of a holiday in the Future someday," Robin said archly. "I need to know how to ferry myself and my lady about in style."

Phillip drew his hand over his eyes. "I need a drink of something very strong."

Robin elbowed his front doors open. "I have just the thing in my solar. We can talk there in privacy. I'm curious about your adventures."

He imagined his sire was, damn him to hell.

It took another day before he managed to pry out of his sire the details he needed. It was another day after that before Robin deigned to show him a spot in the grass near Artane where things had been rumored to have happened.

"This is weird," Phillip muttered under his breath.

"No kidding."

Phillip tried not to shudder at the sound of modern English coming from his sire's mouth.

He looked at his father, the man who had challenged him, corrected him, and loved him perhaps more than any son deserved to be loved.

"I admire you," he said simply.

"Is that better than love?" Robin asked, his eyes suspiciously moist.

"There's a bit of that in there as well."

Robin clapped him on the shoulder. "Off with ye, ye wee fiend. I'll keep the lord's chair warm for your return."

"Aye for a score more years whilst I cool my heels at Haemesburgh."

Robin grinned. "Can you expect anything else?"

He couldn't, though he wasn't going to give his father the satisfaction of saying as much. He studied the ground in front of him for a moment or two, then looked at the current lord of Artane. "Where will this take me?"

"Damned if I know," Robin said with a shrug. "I think 'tis easier than going all the way to Edinburgh, if that was your alternative. Though you're leaving me with Jackson and those two terrors of yours." He paused and shivered. "Not sure why I ever allowed either Myles or Wiscard in my front gates."

"They saved my life."

Robin shrugged. "As good a reason as any then, aye?"

Phillip thought it prudent to ignore his sire. No sense in encouraging the man to be even more vexing than he was naturally.

"I hope I'll return," Phillip began.

"Didn't you read that big book of de Piaget genealogy in the Future?" Robin asked incredulously. "You, who had to know the end of every jongleur's tale before you would toddle on off to bed and leave the adults to their wine? You didn't discover what happens to you?"

"I was afraid to know," Phillip said honestly, "lest I read something I didn't care for."

Robin shifted. "Can't say I wouldn't have avoided that knowledge as well, so I can't criticize." He nodded toward the shimmer. "Off with ye, lad, and fetch your bride."

"I don't know if she'll come." He paused. "I don't like not knowing the end from the beginning."

Robin smiled. "And isn't that exciting? The future is what you'll make of it, all on your own."

Phillip smiled in return, mostly in spite of himself. "I believe, my lord, that you should become a philosopher after you've hung up your spurs."

"Which I'll do approximately a quarter hour before I die," Robin said with a snort. "Not much time for philosophizing. I'll leave that to you, little lad." He kissed Phillip loudly on both cheeks, then walked away. "I'll see you in a bit, I imagine. Or not. Who knows?"

Phillip shook his head, then smiled to himself. Some things never changed.

But others did, which was why he was trying to do something that he wouldn't have believed possible before.

He took a deep breath, then stepped forward.

Chapter 35

I*mogen* Honoria Maxwell stood in the aisle of a very pretty church in Edinburgh, Scotland, in a white dress, with a bouquet in her hand, and wondered just how in the hell she'd wound up where she was.

She was getting married. She wasn't quite sure how it had happened or how it had happened so quickly, but there she was. The place was surprisingly packed, but Maximillian Davis was a powerful guy and apparently the relief of pawning his tone-deaf son off on someone was valuable enough to him to inspire him to rent a few Learjets to get guests across the Pond in record time.

Her father, not to be outdone by a mere movie funder, had imported his own collection of jetsetters. If she didn't know a damn person in the audience, what did that matter? She knew the groomsmen—her brothers—and her bridesmaids—her sisters. She supposed if she managed to get through the ceremony without Prissy suddenly getting a case of uncontrollable flu and barfing all over the very long train of her bridal gown, she would be fortunate.

Though at the moment, that sounded like a pretty good excuse to have to put things off a bit longer.

The truth was, she didn't want to get married. She especially didn't want to marry Marcus Davis. Unfortunately, the problem was, she wasn't going to be rescued by any knights in shining armor. Marrying that egotistical caterwauler might be her best chance at happiness.

Only the closer to the altar she got, the worse she felt until she realized she just couldn't go a single step farther.

She paused, ignoring her father's sound of impatience. Turning around and leaving would spell the end of her career in film, that much was certain. She would be working fast food for the rest of her life.

Somehow, that sounded blissful compared to what she was sure would be a miserable marriage to a man who was eyeing her sister. Pristine was blushing, a truly horrifying sight. She half suspected no one would notice if she pulled Prissy into the aisle, gave her a push in the right direction, and took herself back down the aisle and out the doors to freedom.

She ran through the rest of her family, quickly deciding what their reactions would be. Her mother wouldn't understand, her father would be busy destroying things and selling off the pieces, and her siblings would talk about her at Thanksgiving and shake their heads.

Well, all her siblings except perhaps her brother, Howard. He was only watching her with a faint smile, as if he almost approved of what she was thinking. How he could have known, she couldn't have said.

She thought about what she wanted to do for all of another thirty seconds before she made a decision. She looked at her father, then leaned up and kissed him on the cheek.

"Thanks, Dad, for coming, but I'm making a course correction."

Her father's jaw slipped downward. "You're doing what?"

"I'm allowing Prissy to marry the love of her life. Oh, look over there. She and Marcus are having a conversation and I think I'm hearing a few legal terms being bandied about. You might want to go supervise the prenup."

Those were fighting words, to be sure. Her father dropped her like a hot potato and trotted up the aisle without delay. She smiled at her brother, tossed her squawking mother her bouquet, then turned around and started back down the aisle the wrong way.

She came to an abrupt halt.

She had never teetered in her life, but she teetered then.

Phillip de Piaget was standing at the entrance to the chapel, leaning against the doorframe, watching her with a look she couldn't quite identify. If she hadn't known better, she might have suspected he was proud of her. What she did know, however, was that he was waiting for her.

She continued on her way down the aisle, then stopped in front of him.

"Hi."

He lifted an eyebrow. "A Futurism, obviously."

"It means *hello, my lord, what in the world are you doing here?*"

He smiled. "I imagine it can mean a great many things. And I'm here for you."

"Are you?" she asked breathlessly.

"I am."

She considered. "Do you need me to help you find your sword?"

"I believe you already did."

"Well, that's true, but I don't like to assume. Need me for something else, then?"

He smiled. "I believe I do."

She didn't want to presume anything, but it was hard to deny that just seeing him there was enough to lead her to thinking several impossible things. "What would you have done if I'd continued down that aisle?"

"I would have trotted after you and rendered that obnoxious slayer of tuneful melodies senseless with whatever I could have laid my hands on before you reached the priest." He considered. "A psalter would have served quite well, perhaps."

"I think you could have whispered *boo* in his ear and that would have done the trick."

"I considered that as well."

She considered him. "Were you waiting for me to make a decision before you acted?"

"It seemed prudent."

"And now?"

He reached for her hand. "I was thinking a mocha, then perhaps a journey."

"Do you have a destination in mind?" she asked.

"Home." He paused. "We might want to go there by way of a priest, or we can marry at Artane." He looked at her quickly. "If you're interested in that sort of thing."

"Is that a proposal?"

He smiled. "I'm terrible at chivalry."

"You said you were very good at it."

"I said it was desirable," he said. "I never said I was adept at it. But I will try, for you."

"I don't think you can marry a commoner."

"You're Robert the elder of Haemesburgh's foster daughter for anyone who cares. You're the light of my heart for the rest of the rabble." He nodded toward the door. "Let's be off, if that suits."

She found that suddenly she couldn't quite move. She looked at him seriously. "I appreciate the rescue, really I do, but I just don't see how this is really going to work. Regardless of how rich my father might be, I'm just a regular gal and you're medieval nobility. Our genealogy would be weird. I'll come out of nowhere."

"A fortuitous event I'm blessed by, to be sure."

She shook her head. "Your parents might not like me."

"My parents will adore you."

"Kendrick didn't know me," she said. "I think that might be checkmate there."

"I had breakfast with my brother earlier this morning," he said, "and he gave me a note he said would clear things up for me. He made me swear on my sword I wouldn't read the missive until we were in the past."

"And?"

"I read it on the way here, of course," Phillip said without the slightest hint of remorse. "It says, *I thought all this time she was Robert of Haemesburgh's foster daughter, a noblewoman from the wilds of Scotland. Who knew?*"

She let out a shaky breath. "I see."

He smiled. "Heather says we can take her car for one more journey. Let's go to Artane. There's a gate there, you know."

She didn't know, but she was somehow not surprised. She suspected she would be even less surprised if Phillip planted something over that gate eventually, like nettles.

She took his hand and walked with him out of the chapel and into their future.

Epilogue

Phillip stood on the parapet at Haemesburgh and looked out over the countryside. He'd seen it in another incarnation, true, but found he liked the one he was looking at presently. No traffic honking, no mobile phones ringing, no wires carrying power.

Well, he had to admit that last bit would have been useful, but he would survive.

"I love the hills."

He reached for his lady wife's hand, then smiled at her. "My father will never die, so we'll probably be looking at this forever."

She smiled. "We won't."

He turned to look at her. "Did you peek at that very large book of genealogy kept in the most secure and secluded chamber Artane can boast?"

"No, but I had a look at a quickly scribbled list I was given by a certain blond guy who somehow managed to get himself alive all the way to adulthood." She smiled. "That list only provided me with the names of the lords of Artane."

"That's useful enough," he said. "What shall we name our first son?"

"Heather."

His mouth fell open and she laughed.

"Just kidding. You come up with something appropriately masculine."

He considered that for quite some time before he looked again at his bride. "Perhaps we should have brought a history book with us. So I don't make a mistake."

"Too dangerous. Besides, you won't make any mistakes. You'll do what you do, I'll do what I do, and we'll hope that we do the right things. And if something really veers off course, you have me."

"I do, indeed."

She smiled at him wistfully. "Is that enough?"

"How can you ask?"

"I just like to hear you make that list you make when I ask."

He smiled, pulled her close, and whispered his list in her ear. It was a long list, all those reasons that he loved her and couldn't live without her, but he made it gladly. She teased him that he did it out of a sense of chivalric duty. He countered that he did it out of love. He imagined they would still be discussing the precise reasons for it far into their future.

He kept his arm around her and leaned on the wall, watching the sun set and the stars come out. He watched them appear until he thought it might be time to seek out the warmth of the fire in the hall. He looked at Imogen, light of his life and love of his heart, and smiled.

She had stars in her eyes.

He imagined he did, too.

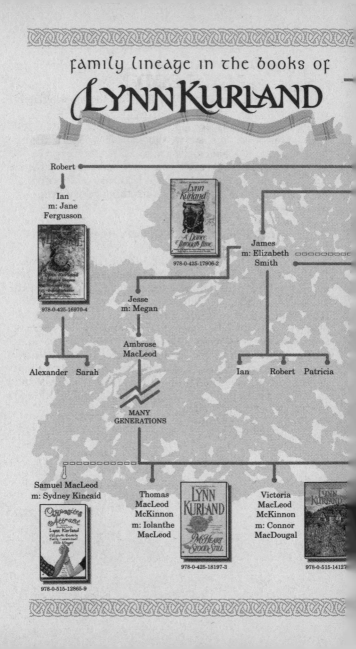

family lineage in the books of
Lynn Kurland

Robert

Ian
m: Jane
Fergusson

978-0-425-16970-4

A Dance Through Time
978-0-425-17906-2

James
m: Elizabeth
Smith

Jesse
m: Megan

Ambrose
MacLeod

Alexander **Sarah**

Ian **Robert** **Patricia**

MANY
GENERATIONS

Samuel MacLeod
m: Sydney Kincaid

978-0-515-12865-9

Thomas
MacLeod
McKinnon
m: Iolanthe
MacLeod

My Heart Stood Still
978-0-425-18197-3

Victoria
MacLeod
McKinnon
m: Connor
MacDougal

978-0-515-14127

MACLEOD

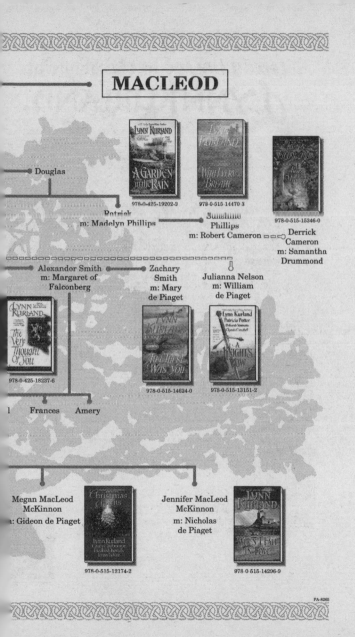

Douglas

Patrick
m: Madelyn Phillips

Sunshine
Phillips
m: Robert Cameron ⎯⎯⎯ Derrick
Cameron
m: Samantha
Drummond

978-0-425-19202-3   978-0-515-14470-3

978-0-515-15346-0

Alexander Smith ⎯⎯⎯⎯ Zachary
m: Margaret of   Smith
Falconberg   m: Mary
de Piaget

Julianna Nelson
m: William
de Piaget

978-0-425-18237-6

l   Frances   Amery

978-0-515-14624-0   978-0-515-13151-2

Megan MacLeod
McKinnon
m: Gideon de Piaget

Jennifer MacLeod
McKinnon
m: Nicholas
de Piaget

978-0-515-12174-2   978-0-515-14296-9

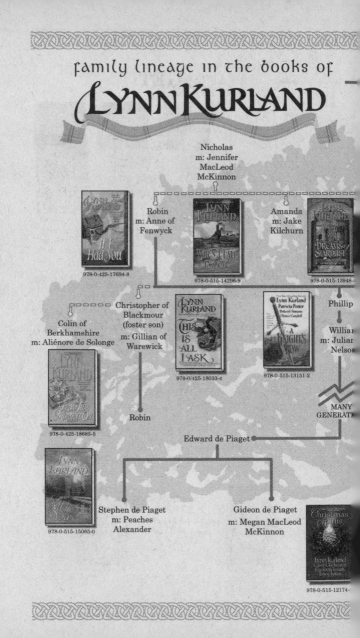

family lineage in the books of
Lynn Kurland

Nicholas
m: Jennifer MacLeod McKinnon

Robin
m: Anne of Fenwyck

978-0-425-17694-8

978-0-515-14296-9

Amanda
m: Jake Kilchurn

978-0-515-13948-

Colin of Berkhamshire
m: Aliénore de Solonge

Christopher of Blackmour (foster son)
m: Gillian of Warewick

978-0-425-18033-4

978-0-515-13151-2

Phillip

Willian
m: Julian Nelso

978-0-425-18685-5

Robin

MANY
GENERAT

978-0-515-15065-0

Edward de Piaget

Stephen de Piaget
m: Peaches Alexander

Gideon de Piaget
m: Megan MacLeod McKinnon

978-0-515-12174-

DE PIAGET

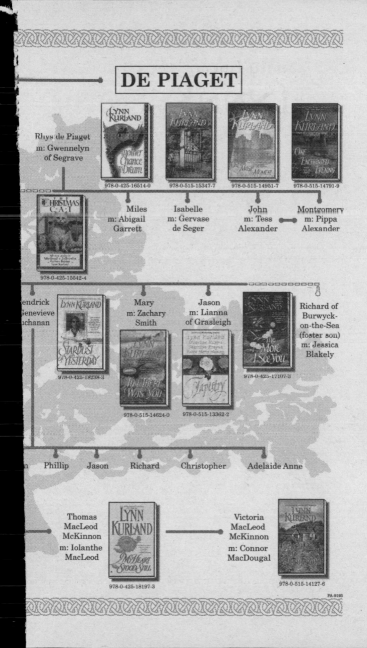

Rhys de Piaget
m: Gwennelyn
of Segrave

978-0-425-16514-0 978-0-515-15347-7 978-0-515-14951-7 978-0-515-14791-9

978-0-425-15542-4

Miles
m: Abigail
Garrett

Isabelle
m: Gervase
de Seger

John
m: Tess
Alexander

Montgomery
m: Pippa
Alexander

endrick
enevieve
uchanan

Mary
m: Zachary
Smith

Jason
m: Lianna
of Grasleigh

Richard of
Burwyck-
on-the-Sea
(foster son)
m: Jessica
Blakely

978-0-425-18238-4

978-0-515-14624-0 978-0-515-13362-2

978-0-425-17107-3

n   Phillip   Jason   Richard   Christopher   Adelaide Anne

Thomas
MacLeod
McKinnon
m: Iolanthe
MacLeod

Victoria
MacLeod
McKinnon
m: Connor
MacDougal

978-0-425-18197-3

978-0-515-14127-6

FROM *NEW YORK TIMES* BESTSELLING AUTHOR

LYNN KURLAND

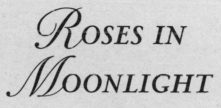

ROSES IN MOONLIGHT

Trapped first in Elizabethan England, then caught in a web of modern-day intrigues, a beautiful textile historian and an adventurous antiquities dealer are forced into an unlikely alliance by peril, never imagining that what they're forging is a timeless love...

PRAISE FOR THE NOVELS OF LYNN KURLAND

"Stepping into one of Lynn Kurland's time-travel novels is definitely one magic moment in itself."
—*All About Romance*

"Kurland is a skilled enchantress."
—*Night Owl Romance*

"One of romance's finest writers."
—*The Oakland Press*

lynnkurland.com
facebook.com/LoveAlwaysBooks
penguin.com

M1407T1113